SCIENCE FICTION
OF THE FORTIES

SCIENCE FICTION OF THE FORTIES

Edited by:
Frederik Pohl
Martin Harry Greenberg
Joseph Olander

AVON
PUBLISHERS OF BARD, CAMELOT AND DISCUS BOOKS

THE SCIENCE FICTION OF THE FORTIES is an original publication of Avon Books. This work has never before appeared in book form.

Cover reprinted from the December 1940 issue of
THRILLING WONDER STORIES,
Copyright 1968 by Popular Library, Inc.
New design by Stanislaw Fernandes.

AVON BOOKS
A division of
The Hearst Corporation
959 Eighth Avenue
New York, New York 10019

First Avon Printing, October, 1978

AVON TRADEMARK REG. U.S. PAT. OFF. AND IN OTHER COUNTRIES, MARCA REGISTRADA, HECHO EN U.S.A.

Printed in the U.S.A.

ACKNOWLEDGMENTS

"Stepson of Space," by Raymond Z. Gallun, copyright © 1940 by Fictioneers, Inc.; reprinted by permission of the author and his agent, Robert P. Mills.

"Reason," by Isaac Asimov, copyright © 1941 by Street & Smith Publications, Inc.; renewed by Isaac Asimov, 1968; reprinted by permission of the author.

"Magic City," by Nelson S. Bond, copyright © 1941, 1959 by Nelson Bond; reprinted by permission of the author.

"Kazam Collects," by C. M. Kornbluth, copyright © 1941 by Albing Publications; reprinted by permission of Robert P. Mills, agent for the estate of C. M. Kornbluth.

"My Name Is Legion," by Lester del Rey, copyright © 1942 by Street & Smith Publications, Inc.; reprinted by permission of the author and the author's agents, Scott Meredith Literary Agency, Inc., 845 Third Avenue, New York, NY 10022.

"The Wabbler," by Murray Leinster, copyright © 1942 by Street & Smith Publications, Inc.; reprinted by permission of the estate of Will F. Jenkins and the Scott Meredith Literary Agency, Inc., 845 Third Avenue, New York, NY 10022.

"The Halfling," by Leigh Brackett, copyright © 1943 by Popular Publications, Inc.; copyright © 1973 by Ace Books; reprinted by permission of the author's agent, Lurton Blassingame.

"Doorway Into Time," by C. L. Moore, copyright © 1943, 1970 by C. L. Moore; reprinted by permission of Harold Matson Company, Inc.

"Deadline," by Cleve Cartmill, copyright © 1944 by Street & Smith Publications, Inc.; copyright © 1972 renewed by The Condé Nast Publications, Inc.; reprinted by permission of The Condé Nast Publications, Inc.

Acknowledgments

"City," by Clifford D. Simak, copyright © 1944 by Street & Smith Publications, Inc.; reprinted by permission of the author's agent, Robert P. Mills.

"Pi in the Sky," by Fredric Brown, copyright © 1945 by Standard Magazines, Inc.; reprinted by permission of Mrs. Elizabeth C. Brown and the agents for the estate of Fredric Brown, Scott Meredith Literary Agency, Inc., 845 Third Avenue, New York, NY 10022.

"The Million-Year Picnic," by Ray Bradbury, copyright © 1946, 1973 by Ray Bradbury; reprinted by permission of Harold Matson Company, Inc.

"Technical Error," by Arthur C. Clarke, copyright © 1950 by Standard Magazines, Inc.; reprinted by permission of the author and the author's agents, Scott Meredith Literary Agency, Inc., 845 Third Avenue, New York, NY 10022.

"Memorial," by Theodore Sturgeon, copyright © 1946 by Street & Smith Publications, Inc.; reprinted by permission of the author's agent, Kirby McCauley.

"Letter to Ellen," by Chan Davis, copyright © 1947 by Street & Smith Publications, Inc.; reprinted by permission of the author and his agent, Virginia Kidd.

"It's Great to Be Back!" by Robert A. Heinlein, copyright © 1947 by Curtis Publishing Co.; 1974 by Robert A. Heinlein; reprinted by permission of the author's agent, Lurton Blassingame.

"Tiger Ride," by James Blish & Damon Knight, copyright © 1948 by Street & Smith Publications, Inc.; reprinted by permission of Damon Knight and Robert P. Mills, agent for the estate of James Blish.

"Don't Look Now," by Henry Kuttner, copyright © 1948, 1975 by Henry Kuttner; reprinted by permission of Harold Matson Company, Inc.

"That Only a Mother," by Judith Merril, copyright © 1948 by Street & Smith Publications, Inc.; reprinted by permission of the author and her agent, Virginia Kidd.

"Venus and the Seven Sexes," by William Tenn, copyright © 1949 by Avon Publishing Co., Inc.; reprinted by permission of the author and Henry Morrison, Inc., his agents.

"Dear Pen Pal," by A. E. van Vogt, copyright © 1949 by Arkham House; copyright renewed © 1977 by A. E. van Vogt; reprinted by permission of Forrest J Ackerman, 2495 Glendower Ave., Hollywood, CA 90027.

CONTENTS

INTRODUCTION
by Frederik Pohl

In October 1939, at the age of nineteen, I was elevated to ten-dollar-a-week godhood: I became editor of two science-fiction magazines, *Astonishing Stories* and *Super Science Stories*. So, in a sense, the decade of the forties was my decade. I can't claim that my two little magazines were very influential, or that my own writing, which was beginning to appear now and then, made Robert A. Heinlein and A. E. van Vogt very nervous. But I think I read every word of science fiction that was published in the English language in those ten years—even while I was serving in the Air Force in World War II. While I was Stateside I kept up my reading of *Astounding* and *Planet* as assiduously as any civilian. When I was in Italy it became a little harder—the PX didn't stock much science fiction, even when I was anywhere near a PX. But as soon as the war was over I searched out and read the back issues.

In the forties, or at least up to about the end of the forties, that was about all there was: the magazines. A few anthologies had begun to appear in book form, but almost no novels. It was not until the end of the decade that book publishers discovered what a treasure trove lay in those back issues, or what herds of unshorn sheep lived in science-fiction fandom. *Astounding, Amazing, Thrilling Wonder, Planet, Marvel, Comet, Future*—they were where the action was.

It is a curious thing that the editors of the magazines were in some ways more important and individual in science fiction than the authors. Writers were individuals, of course. Some were great, and still are. Some have disappeared without a trace. Some wrote with color and compassion and inventiveness, like Sturgeon, Brackett, Kuttner, and

9

others in this book. Others wrote with a tin ear to the sound of language and the inventiveness of your average guppy, like—well, no, I think I will leave the rest of that sentence unwritten. Apart from quality, the writers varied widely in the kinds of stories they wrote, their use of style and phrasing, and in all the other ways in which one writer can be distinguished from another. And yet—and yet even in the case of so idiosyncratic a writer as, say, Stanley G. Weinbaum, the difference between the stories he had in *Wonder* and the stories he had in *Astounding* is considerable. The stories in *Astounding* resembled all the other stories in *Astounding* more than they did his own *Martian Odyssey*. The editor was a much more prestigious figure in the forties in science fiction than he is today, and the reason for that was that his magazines reflected his personality.

A generation later, the writers still survive, at least through their works—three-quarters of the writers represented in this anthology have books of their own currently in print, even the ones who have died—but those demigods who ruled them, the editors, are hardly remembered at all. They deserve better treatment than that. They did a great deal for science fiction, thirty-some years ago. Collectively, they made it happen.

John Campbell is an exception to the rule of oblivion (John was always an exception to almost all rules!). In fact, he has become almost a legendary creature. That's reasonable enough. What other human being in the whole course of history has been custodian of a major fraction of a kind of writing for thirty-four straight years? Longevity alone would make him interesting; talent and hard work, and enough obstinacy to think he knew a better way of doing things than those who had gone before, made him great. His worshipers tell of ten-page letters rejecting eight-page stories, every line packed with sage advice. His detractors call him a stumbling block who used the power of his position to prevent science fiction from maturing. Who is right? A lot depends on which writer is telling the story. John Campbell made up his mind early about writers. If he considered a novice both talented and biddable, he would go far out of his way to help him. If not, not. Some of the most famous names in science fiction rarely or never appeared in *Astounding*—Ray Bradbury is one. It is interesting to speculate what would have happened to Bradbury if John had taken him under his wing as he did, for example, with Isaac Asimov at a similar stage in development and time. Would we now be talking of Bradbury's three Laws of Robotics?

Both Asimov and Bradbury had it in their genes to succeed with or without any editor. Perhaps this is not so with some of Campbell's other writers. He didn't only help them. He almost created them. John had no experience as an editor when he took on *Astounding*, but what he did know was science fiction. He knew enough about it to know not only what had been done but what could be done that no one before him had thought to do.

Most of the editors who competed head-to-head with John Campbell in the forties knew a lot less about science fiction than he did, but some knew a great deal more about editing. The Thrilling Group was honchoed by a man named Leo Margulies, battle-scarred veteran of all the endless varieties of pulp. Leo had under him a staff of first-rate young talents—from first to last—names like Horace Gold, Sam Merwin, Samuel Mines, and Mort Weisinger, all of whom went on to distinguished careers. But when they were working for Leo Margulies they were still fledglings. Leo was a decent man to work for, with a few interesting mannerisms. He expected his assistant editors to *edit*. At the end of each day Margulies would call the junior geniuses in and require them to display their day's production. He didn't read the stories. He glanced at the pages and compared the number of penciled alterations with the original typed copy. If too high a proportion of the author's own words survived, the editor was admonished to try harder.

Leo, lovely man that he was, did not invent this attitude. His background was not science fiction, it was pulp; and pulp doctrine taught that words were not literature. They were merchandise. There was no more reason to cherish an individual word or phrase for its special qualities than there was to admire one particular bean in a Campbell's can. It was much the same in my own company, Popular Publications —where the girl who checked the word counts in manuscripts held the pages upside down so she wouldn't have to read them.

Some of the pulp-oriented magazines produced their own kind of excitement that was as cherished as anything in *Astounding*. In terms of sales, the unquestioned leader for at least part of the forties was hoary old *Amazing Stories*, now rejuvenated under David Verne and Raymond A. Palmer. I have the kindest personal memories of both Verne and Palmer—Ray took a day out of his busy week once when I was in Chicago on furlough, a junior Air Force birdman a little nostalgic for the sights and sounds of the civilian publishing world; he made me at home and entertained me pleasantly, at what cost to his deadlines I can't imagine. But I have to confess that I couldn't read *Amazing* through much of that period. The fact that I was a minority is proved by the soaring circulation figures. Even so, there were individual authors and stories—by Isaac Asimov, Nelson Bond, Eando Binder, and others—that still survive, and deserve to.

In the pulpier of the pulps, my personal favorite was *Planet Stories*. (They were more hospitable than most to my own stories at that time, but that's only a coincidence, right?) *Planet* was edited by veteran pulpster Malcolm Reiss, with the help of talented juniors. Wilbur Scott Peacock was one, originally an air-war writer (with a silver link in his spine to show that not all his experience with flying was literary). Jerome Bixby was another; Jerry left to become a writer, and did so handsomely, with stories like "It's a Good Life" and original film scripts like *Fantastic Voyage*. Mal Reiss had a propensity for changing Campbell-type titles to things like "Demon Priestesses of the Martian Crater Gods," but he also had a feeling for outlandish color and bright, adventurous action.

There are at least a dozen other editors who should be mentioned. I have not said a word about my own close friends and fellow-fan graduates, Donald A. Wollheim and Robert A. W. Lowndes, who helped develop that whole Futurian crop of writers like C. M. Kornbluth, Richard Wilson, Damon Knight, and others. Nor have we touched on those unsung staffers on *Collier's* and the *Saturday Evening Post* who had the temerity to sneak an occasional Heinlein, Bradbury, or John Wyndham science fiction story into their hallowed smooth-paper pages.

They all deserve credit. How much credit, you can decide for yourself as you read this product of their collective talents, the stories in this anthology. I hope you'll like them.

FREDERIK POHL
Red Bank, New Jersey
February 1977

SCIENCE FICTION
OF THE FORTIES

Stepson of Space

Raymond Z. Gallun (1910-   )

RAYMOND Z. Gallun was a mainstay of Astounding during the mid-
to late thirties, and although he continued to write for many years
thereafter, he never achieved the level of recognition he enjoyed before
World War II. At his best, in stories like "Old Faithful" (1934),
"Davy Jones' Ambassador" (1953), and "Seeds of the Dusk" (1938),
he brought a reflective, serious tone to science fiction while at the same
time retaining a powerful sense of wonder.

Today his work is greatly underrated, and it is a pleasure to start this
collection of forties sf with a story from a man who was so representative of the previous decade.

By the early forties a new group of science fiction magazines had
joined Amazing, Astounding, and Thrilling Wonder on the newsstands,
including Stirring, Super Science, Fantastic Adventures, Comet, and
Astonishing. Many of these printed rejects from Campbell's two magazines, but they also received first crack at some writers who felt uncomfortable with Campbell or who wrote at the request of editors who
were close friends. Astonishing in particular had a high percentage of
quality stories, including this one, in its short history of sixteen issues.

From *Astonishing Science Fiction*   1940

Scared? That was hardly the word. Andy Matthews' bristly, dust-
grimed cheeks felt stiff; and there was a sensation inside him as though
his heart was trying to burst.

He couldn't get it all at once. To do so, fortunately, would have been impossible. He only knew that there was something fearfully and incomprehensibly wrong about his eight-year-old son, Jack!

Andy just stood there in the tool room over the granary, and stared, like a big, dumb ox, frightened, confused, pathetically grim, yet helpless. Oh, he would have died for this boy a hundred times over, if the danger was something he could really approach and fight. But this was different. It made him want to crawl into a dark corner with a loaded shotgun, and wait for a masked mystery to reveal itself. But he knew right away that this wouldn't be any good either!

The apparatus had looked so very harmless when he had first accidentally uncovered it. A peach box base. Tin cans nailed in a circle on top of it. A length of fine-gauge wire from an old radio set was wrapped around each can, in a clumsy yet patiently involved design. The lengths of wire converged toward the center of the circle of cans, to form a kind of wheel-like net, each strand of which was stapled to a heavy central block of wood. The exposed upper surface of the latter bore a deep, elongated indentation, as though some object had struck it with terrific force. Except for an old-fashioned double-throw electric switch, nailed to the side of the box, that was all.

The thing looked like any of the various contraptions that kids pound together while playing inventor. Andy had chuckled fondly when he'd dragged the rigamajig out of its place of concealment, and had begun to fuss with the switch; for he remembered the hammering he had heard here in the tool room every time he had come in from the fields. Jack had been working on his "invention" for almost a month.

So Andy had been entirely unwarned. But when he had closed that switch, he had received the surprise of his life. His fingers had been a little off the insulated handle, and had touched the metal. Blue sparks had snapped across Andy's calloused palm. His whole body had recoiled under the staggering blow of a high-tension shock. It might have killed him, had he not stumbled backward.

That was the point now—the reason for his fearful confusion—the focus of an incredibly incongruous mixture of facts. Jack was just eight. This rigamajig—peach box, cans, and wires—was kid stuff. And yet the shock that had struck Andy was like the wallop of a high-voltage line! Nor was there any source, within half a mile or more, from which the contraption might draw power!

The thought that he was perhaps the father of a child genius got Andy nowhere. Jack was smart, all right; but certainly no eight-year-old, no matter how brilliant his mind might be, could ever invent a miracle like this.

The apparatus was still active there on the floor, for the switch was closed. A greenish fluorescence, like worms of turbid light, had crept along each of the radiating wire strands. In the brown shadows of the tool room, that soft witchfire burned wickedly, to the accompaniment of a low murmur that seemed to threaten and predict unguessable developments. In the dusty air, there was a slight odor of scorched insulation.

Moved by instinct, Andy Matthews picked up a small wooden splinter from the floor, and tossed it toward the apparatus.

Even as the chip flew toward its goal, he regretted his impulsive act with a cold doubt as to its wisdom. He ducked and crouched back as the splinter landed on those glowing wires.

The splinter seemed hardly to touch the wires at all. But the cold emerald light flashed around it. Instantly it seemed to rebound, as if from rubber. Whisking speed increased to the point beyond the range of living retinas. There was a twanging, almost melodious note, and the chip was gone. But in the low-raftered roof above, there was a little hole, as neatly punctured as if made by the passage of a bullet. The splinter had been hurled fast enough to make that hole. . . .

Andy Matthews gulped with the strain of his tightened nerves. His big head, with its close-cropped black hair, swung this way and that, in bewildered belligerence. He hadn't been able to go to school much, but he'd read a lot, and he was shrewd. The kid had made the contraption, all right; but he couldn't have thought it out—alone! And who else was there?

From the back porch of the farmhouse, Jane, Andy's pretty wife, was calling for him to come in to supper. But he hardly heard her. He hardly heard anything at all, as his brain fought with a mystery far beyond the knowledge of any person that he knew.

But he wheeled about like a burglar, caught with the goods, when the door behind him opened.

Jack stood in the entrance. He just stood there, not saying anything, his face lighted up by the green glow. He looked petulant and startled, sure of punishment.

Andy had no idea at all what to say at first. But then love tangled with fear of the unknown to produce fury. Andy's teeth showed. His slitted eyes snapped. His voice, when he spoke, was a hoarse, unsteady growl.

"Come here, you!" he commanded.

Just for a moment the kid hesitated, his gray eyes vague and clouded in the green flicker. Then he came forward timidly, his scuffed shoes scraping in the untidy litter on the floor. He looked so pathetically little in his soiled overalls. Andy's heart longed to melt, as it always had, for his son. But this was no time to give way to sentiment.

Andy clutched a small shoulder, and shook it violently. "What's this thing, here?" he snarled, pointing to the miracle beside them. "Who showed you how to make it? Come on! Out with it! Or, so help

17

me, I'll break every bone in your body! Hurry up! Who showed you?"

Again there was that timid hesitation, which required more violent shaking to dissipate; but the kid spoke at last:

"Mister Weefles— He showed me. . . ."

Whereat, Andy snorted in sheer, boiling exasperation. "Mister Weefles!" he growled. "Always Mister Weefles! That's no answer at all!" Andy swung a hard palm. With a sharp snap, it landed on the side of Jack's cheek.

"Now will you tell me?" Andy roared.

The kid didn't let out a whimper. That was maybe a little funny in itself. But then those gray eyes met Andy's levelly, and Andy felt a dim, deep consternation. There was something warning and hard and strange, looking out of those eyes. Something that wasn't his son!

"I said, Mister Weefles," the kid told his father quietly. "He hasn't got any name of his own, so I started calling him that a long time ago."

Andy had released his grip on the boy, and had moved back a step. The answer seemed to be nothing but pure childhood fantasy. But its tone, and that level, warning stare, told a much different story. So Andy's mind seemed to tumble swiftly back through the years, to the time when Jack had been little more than a baby.

Almost since he had first learned to talk, it had been the same. Always there had existed that shadowy individual, Mister Weefles.

Andy remembered himself asking on many different occasions: "What did you do today, son?"

And Jack's answer had so often been something like this: "Oh, I was thinking about Mister Weefles. I dreamed about him last night again. He's a nice old guy, but he's awful lonesome and awful funny looking, and he knows an awful lot. Only he lives all by himself. All his folks are dead. . . ."

A kid story, Andy had thought. Lots of imaginative youngsters made up dream worlds for themselves, and imaginary characters. So Andy had accepted the fanciful friend of his son as a matter of course, with tolerant humor.

But now? In that green-lit, flickering twilight of the dusty tool room, a kid's unimportant legend had suddenly assumed an aspect of real danger!

Andy Matthews began to sweat profusely. Mister Weefles was only a name his boy had given to something—true! Tin cans, wires, a peach box, an unknown source of terrific electric power; and the bullet-like flight of a splinter of wood, going—where? All this was plain evidence of its truth!

Suddenly Jack moved forward toward the busy contraption on the floor. Andy gave a choked exclamation of warning, and made a grab to stop him. But then he only watched, with the intentness of a cat watching a mouse. Because Jack's movements were so skillful, so practiced, showing that he'd somehow been taught, and knew how to do—everything.

His fingers touched the tip of the insulated handle of the switch. With an expert lightness of touch, he swung it open quickly. The turbid light that had enveloped the radial wires of the apparatus died out. A completer darkness, alleviated only by the evening afterglow from the window, settled over the cluttered room.

But the sharp, muddled concern that screamed in Andy Matthews' heart could not be extinguished so easily.

They faced each other again, then—father and son—as though across an abyss which seemed to separate them forever. But Andy Matthews' anger was dissolved, now, by his overshadowing fear. He was ready to grope and plead, in the hope that thus he might find a loose end—a tangible means of approach to the sinister presence that had enmeshed itself with his child's personality. His blood throbbed with frustrated, fighting courage.

"Jack," he husked into the gloom. "I'm your dad, boy. Tell me—about this pal of yours. Where does he live?"

Once more there was a pause. Then, grudgingly and sullenly, the kid responded:

"I don't know exactly. . . . Someplace . . . a long way off. . . . It's a terrible scary kind of place. . . ."

"You only dream about it, and about Mister Weefles?" Andy persisted. "At night—when you're asleep?"

"No, Dad," Jack returned. "Sometimes him and all his stuff are there . . . in the daytime, too. I just have to shut my eyes and I can almost see him. He's been getting plainer all the time because I've got more practice figuring out just what he thinks. And he's got a special kind of machine he uses, too. . . . Mostly it's the practice I got, though. . . . And he told me that there's something special about my brains that makes them a lot easier to talk with than most folks' brains. He don't say anything to me out loud, really. He just thinks, and I think with him. . . . But he's an awful nice old guy . . . sorta sad. I do what he wants. Just now he made me turn off—"

There the kid stopped, sullenly, as though somehow he'd been warned not to talk further.

Andy didn't press the point; but his quick, ragged breathing came still faster, and he took hold of the kid's shoulder again. He pointed to the now-inactive peach box apparatus at their feet. The thing was newly constructed—an outgrowth rather than a cause of a queer mental contact. From what he had seen of its action, Andy concluded that its purpose had nothing to do with minds. It had catapulted that chip through the roof—

"What's this rigamajig for, son?" Andy asked quietly. "What is it supposed to do?"

The question wasn't much use. The kid just shook his head and began to whimper. Andy picked him up, then—a small, tight bundle of unrelaxed, resentful nerves and muscles. The barrier between himself and his boy seemed wider than ever.

"Hurry up and spit it out!" Andy snapped in fresh anger, shaking the kid furiously.

Jack didn't respond; but suddenly there was a tinkling sound on the floor. Something had fallen out of Jack's overall pocket. Instantly the boy became a squirming wildcat, almost impossible to hold. But Andy Matthews was far from feeble; and he was certainly determined, now, too.

Still hanging onto the kid with one arm, he bent down to search for the dropped object. It wasn't hard to find, for it had fallen right by his shoe; and the bright metal of it glinted even in the semidarkness. He picked it up, and then set Jack on the floor. The boy immediately backed away, panting, his mop of yellow hair streaming down into his face. He seemed to wait for an opportunity to recover what he'd lost.

"Now!" Andy said grimly, with a sort of triumph. "Maybe we'll find out something!"

He took the object close to the window. It was a three-inch cylinder, almost like a short, thick metal pencil; for it was tapered at one end. A flaky, ashy stuff, which still covered part of its burnished surface, came away in his palms. It was as though the thing had once been accidentally thrown into a furnace, or burned by the friction of a meteoric flight through the atmosphere.

The tapered end of the cylinder could be detached, like a screw. Directly beneath this conical cap, there was a little spindle. Andy tugged at it avidly, drawing a tiny scroll from its tubular container. Carefully, but with shaking fingers, he unrolled it, sensing that here was a thing the like of which he had never touched before. One side of the long, silky, metallic ribbon was coated with a fine glaze. Holding the smooth strip up to the dying light of day at the window, he squinted at it. But this effort to see was unnecessary, for the smooth surface was phosphorescent. It was divided into three little rectangles, one above the other, as in a postcard folder. Each rectangle was a picture, a photograph. They were luminous, like colored lantern-slide images, cast on a screen.

Andy didn't have to be told that these were pictures from another world. He was no fool, and he knew that no Earthly stars were as sharp as those pictured in the uppermost photograph. No Earthly mountains were ever so rough and clear and lifeless. Hell, everybody read about things like this, once in a while, in the scientific magazines!

But here it all was, now—true—an inescapable part of a mystery that had settled over his own life! The second picture revealed a shadowy cavern, full of machines and apparati, in which must course fearful power. There were globular tanks, glowing red with the fiery chemicals inside them. There was a squat, complicated lump of metal which looked like some weird kind of dynamo.

The third picture was of the interior of a great crystal sphere, or compartment, whose walls were rimmed with patches of thin, lacy frost. Devices of various kinds crowded it, too; but Andy scarcely noticed these at first, for at the center of its concave floor stood a shaggy, lonely figure, clad in white polar fur, which seemed a natural part of him. He was quite a little like a man. Over his immense shoulders, wires were draped, originating from a boxlike apparatus, upon which his fur-tufted paws rested. The wires led to an odd metal helmet, which covered his head, just above his great, batlike ears.

Through the transparent sides of the sphere, the same kind of terrain as that pictured in the first photograph could be seen; for the strange structure was built in the open. Hard, devil-mountains, and frigid, steady stars.

Mounted on the sphere's top, and visible, too, through its crystalline substance, was a thing resembling the crude contraption that Jack had made, except that it was much larger, and of course far more finely made. And attached to it were heavy bars of coppery metal, which must carry a terrific load of current from somewhere below.

Andy Matthews, looking at those colored, phosphorescent pictures, was a little dull just then, as far as feelings went. Wonder and fright had left him momentarily—to be replaced by a semi-daze, which, however, seemed to sharpen and quicken his reason. Like a man in a death struggle, he had forgotten fear and wonder; he was devoting all his energies to understanding and defeating his enemy.

Scattered factors in the puzzle that confronted him fell together coherently with amazing swiftness. The furry figure in the third photograph was of course Jack's hidden friend. The helmet the being wore, and the wires and the dialed box attached to it, looked like advanced forms of radio equipment. Andy knew his radio. He'd been a ham when he was nineteen. . . . But this wasn't radio equipment. Jack had spoken of a special kind of machine for thought-transference. This must be it! The source of the weird dreams that Jack had experienced since his babyhood.

Nor was the question of how Jack had come to possess the metal tube with the pictures in it so difficult to answer, now, either! With vivid, cold memory, Andy recalled what had happened to the splinter of wood he had tossed onto the glowing wires of Jack's contraption.

Zip! And like a bullet it had gone through the roof! Doubtless it had continued on, up into the air, and away through the vacuum abyss— toward this similar wheel-like apparatus on top of the globular compartment in the picture.

There was that deep indentation in the upper surface of the wooden block at the center of Jack's rigamajig. Then there was that old-fashioned, double-throw switch. The power, acting across the void, could be turned around!

It would have been simple for the kid to carry his machine out into the open, where it could work freely, with no roof in the way.

Come to think of it, there were a lot of things missing around the place, now, Andy thought with a shudder. A new adjustable wrench. A spirit-level, a couple of radio tubes. And Jane had lost a tape-measure. Andy knew what had become of these things. The monster would be fondling them, now. Probably they were treasures to him—curiosities. Like a man getting stuff from—Mars!

But—God! What did the shaggy freak really want? What was he meddling with Jack for? What was his deeper purpose? How could anybody tell? Andy's cool, swift reasoning had taken on a new note now; for seeing what he faced emphasized his helplessness. He was up against a knowledge as old as a dead world, and as unreachable.

Dully he rolled up the scroll of pictures, and put it back into the tube. He screwed the cap into place, and dropped the thing into his hip pocket.

Andy wanted to act. But what was there to try? For a second a wild idea blazed in his brain; then was submerged by its futility. And he couldn't leave Jack out of his sight for a moment now. But it wasn't enough just to watch. Those howling nerves of his yelled for movement —for a means to drain away some of their straining, fighting energy. Andy's mind settled on just one thing—speed!

"Come on, you!" he snarled at the boy, who stared at him with that strange, watchful, guarded look in his eyes—a look that wasn't Earthly —that belonged, in part, to a being beyond men. Andy knew that if his own mind was not actually read, his every act, at least, was watched, through his own son's eyes.

Andy picked Jack up, and stumbled down the dark stair. The kid squirmed and fought; but Andy's own physical strength could win here, at least. He hurried to the garage. Working with his free hand, he got the door open. He got into the new car, dragging Jack after him. Jane was calling angrily from the house again. Supper! Andy could almost have laughed mockingly at the triviality of such a thing as supper, now! As for Jane, he couldn't face her now. He had to protect her from what he knew. He couldn't tell her; he couldn't tell anyone! It wouldn't do any good anyway!

With a fury that was part of his dark secret, he stamped on the starter. A minute later the car tore out of the driveway. Once he had the car on the road, Andy's foot jammed more fiercely down on the accelerator. Speed . . . Faster . . . Faster . . . Going toward town. Going toward nowhere, really, unless it was away from bewildering fact, and away from the brooding something that seemed to be in the air—that seemed to haunt the evening stars and the yellow harvest moon.

The whizzing motion wasn't much relief; but Andy's teeth were gritted together. His foot, pushing the accelerator, was down as far as it would go, now. Sixty . . . Seventy . . . Eighty . . . Ninety miles an hour . . .

Under the tense, drawn anguish of Andy's mind, the crash was almost inevitable. It came on the Hensler Curve, when another car's lights blazed into view. Andy had to take to the ditch at terrific speed. The car under him did a crazy squelching skip on the steep embankment, hurtled and wobbled around sideways, and landed on its top. . . .

Queer, maybe, but Andy only got a wrenched wrist out of the bargain. The kid wasn't so lucky.

Lost in a sort of mind-fog, Andy Matthews drove back to the farm in the milk truck. That was about midnight. Jane had come into town with the truck, and she was at the hospital, now, with Jack.

Partly because he was dazed by what had happened, Andy had been able to ignore at first the almost hysterical accusations of his wife, and the veiled contempt under Doctor Weller's professional kindness:

"Your boy can't last more than a few hours, Mr. Matthews. We did our best. The emergency operation was the only chance. But now that it's over, the boy's system can't stand the shock. I'm sorry."

What the matter-of-fact old physician wanted to say, of course, was that Andy was just another damn-fool driver who had as good as murdered his own son.

Still, Andy was able to ignore that accusation. They didn't know how he loved that kid of his. Or why the accident had happened. Andy had just one burning idea now—revenge. Revenge against that un-Earthly presence who he felt was the author of all his misfortune.

Otherwise he was like a dead thing, impervious to all feeling. It wasn't anger, exactly, that gripped him now. He'd gone beyond that. It was just—fundamental need. Even grief seemed to have dissipated into a mist, against which was stamped the fiery blob that represented his scheme. He'd thought of it before—and had rejected it as hopeless. He still thought it was hopeless—as hopeless as trying to kill an elephant with a popgun. But—well—there wasn't any other way at all. . . .

He got a couple of big thermos bottles from the kitchen pantry.

23

Then he hurried outdoors, and to the woodshed. High up on the wall here was a locked chest, where he kept special things. He'd expected to do some stump blasting in the woodlot. Now he opened the chest, and took out a large bundle of cylindrical objects, wrapped in waxed paper.

By the beam of a flashlight, he ripped the paper from each of the objects. Inside was an oily, yellowish, granulated stuff that looked a little bit like pale brown sugar.

"Brown sugar, eh?" Andy thought craftily. Yeah, maybe it was a good idea to imagine it was something harmless, like brown sugar.

He packed the stuff in the thermos bottles. Then he went to the tool room over the granary to get the peach box apparatus. He took it out into the night, and set it down at the farther end of the garden.

There were streaky clouds in the sky, overcasting the moon. Andy was glad of that, at least. But—maybe his enemy knew his whole plan already. Andy was conscious of the gigantic learning he was pitted against. Maybe he'd be stricken dead in some strange way in the next moment. But he accepted this possibility without emotion.

He grasped the handle of the double-throw switch lightly in his fingers, and swung it over—to the same position in which he had accidentally placed it when he had first found his son's contraption and had learned of its strange properties. That sleepy murmur began, and those green worms of turbid light started to creep along the radiating wires of the apparatus.

He waited until the glow was on full—until the energy, groping across space, reached maximum. Meanwhile, as far as was possible, he kept his mind on things which didn't quite concern his present task. He'd made plans to send Jack to college when the time came, for instance. But that was all over, now. . . .

His hand lifted one of the loaded thermos bottles. It was best to have the stuff it contained insulated against cold and heat and against electric shock. That was why he had used those vacuum flasks.

He tossed the thermos toward those glowing wires, while he stood defensively back. There was a soft, ringing sound, and static prickles raced over Andy's body, as the flask bounced upward, amid a play of cold, troubled flame. In a twinkling the missile was gone—vanished away in the direction of those clouds over the moon. A swift, but comparatively shockless start.

Presently, the second thermos went the way of the first. Andy was dully surprised that he'd gotten away with it.

With the job over, now, Andy felt a wilted kind of relief. He got into the milk truck and drove back to town—to the hospital. There, with wide-eyed, tearless Jane beside him, he continued the vigil at Jack's bedside. . . . Jane didn't show any resentment now. She seemed glad to have Andy there with her. Jack belonged to them both; and though

Andy hadn't told her anything about the dark mystery, she must have sensed how sorry he was.

There was a funny kind of strain in the room that he felt right away, but couldn't place. It was mental. It seemed to take hold of one's mind, powerfully, incomprehensibly, expressing an indomitable will that must not—could not—be denied. "Live! Live! Live!" it seemed to beat out in an incessant, wordless, telepathic rhythm.

Andy decided at last that it was only an illusion of his own tired brain, hoping for the impossible—that Jack would pull through. And so, with Jane in his arms, he sat in a chair, watching through the night. Some time after dawn they both fell asleep.

Doctor Weller didn't wake them till nine in the morning. He'd already examined Jack several times.

He looked quizzically at the child's parents, first one, then the other. His heavy brows knit in puzzlement.

"I hardly believe it," he said at last. "But the boy's better. His pulse is firmer and more even, and not so fast. That rib we had to dig out of his lung hasn't caused as much trouble as I thought."

He almost grinned, then. "You folks must be psychic," he went on conversationally. "Things like this happen once in a while, I've sometimes thought, though medical science never had enough evidence to back the idea up. But if you care a good deal for someone who is very sick, and insist in your mind that they *must* live, perhaps it helps. Maybe that's right. Maybe not. Anyway, keep on hoping, folks!"

After the physician was gone, Jane threw her arms around her husband's neck, and wept. Andy stroked her silky blonde hair, and patted her shoulder. But already, behind his narrowed eyes, a weird suspicion was beginning to form. Psychic, he and Jane? Perhaps. But Andy was beginning to doubt—not the miracle itself—but its source. He fumbled into the hip pocket of the overalls he was still wearing. The metal tube, reminder of a personality possessing psychic powers far beyond the Earthly, was still there.

Mister Weefles. Jack's dream pal . . . All his folks were dead, Jack had said. The last of a race, that must mean. A shaggy, lonely giant on a world that had perished. Lonesome . . .

Was that right? It *could* be right! Andy began to wonder if his first judgment hadn't been incorrect after all. . . .

He was looking beyond the veil of suspicion, which one must inevitably feel for anything strange and alien. He had read about the theories of evolution—how men would change when the Earth got older. Long natural fur to keep out the increasing cold. Big chests and big lungs to breathe the thinning atmosphere, before it became actually necessary to withdraw to airtight caverns and habitations. Then perhaps the slow decadence of boredom and sterility, leading to extinction.

25

And now, when the danger of death had come to his small companion, the monster seemed to be doing his best. He was standing there, in that glass globe, sending out healing waves with his telepathic apparatus. . . .

But those thermos bottles Andy Matthews had shot into space were filled with stuff meant to kill.

But after a moment, Andy's suspicions and weariness were reawakened. Perhaps his second judgment was not so sure, either. The shaggy giant *could* be a true friend—yes. But couldn't he, just as well, have an ulterior motive in his efforts to save Jack? What if Jack happened to be an essential link in a chain of conquest—one that it had taken years to develop to the point of usefulness? Naturally, in that case, the furry enigma would want to preserve the boy's life, wouldn't he?

It was almost a quandary, as dark as the myriad questions of the stars. But the clear truth was there in his pocket. The little tube of pictures. Oh, they scared a man when he first examined them—sure! Because they were so unfamiliar. But if you thought about them a little, you got a milder slant on their significance. They were like postcards sent to a kid nephew!

Andy's suspicions wilted when he saw their ridiculousness. He got a new grasp on the nature of the unknown. The shaggy thing out there had lost the aspect of omnipotence, created for Andy by the fantastic circumstances under which he had first glimpsed the mystery with which his boy was involved. . . .

The monster was finite. And with all the rest of his kind gone, lonely. Maybe he'd worked and groped for years to find a companion —a means to reach another mind—one of the right form to receive and transmit thoughts readily. Jack hadn't been harmed through the years of contact—except by his own father!

Andy's original stark fear had left him, to be replaced by a new worry. The aura of healing strain still clung in the room—evidence of terrific effort. And the monster was finite. Besides, he was bemused, now, by that tremendous concentration. Probably he would not be watching some of his instruments. While above his head, on the outside of the crystal sphere that enclosed him, was another apparatus. A wheel of rods. And across space were coming two thermos bottles intended to destroy. . . .

Andy moved slowly, trying thus to hide the worry and the driving need for haste that throbbed in his blood. He edged toward the door of the hospital room.

"Jane," he said, facing his wife briefly. "There's something I've got to look after. It's very important. I'll be back in an hour."

She looked at him with weary contempt for his desertion—now. She didn't know anything about the real depth of the situation. Nor could he try to explain.

He drove like blazes back to the farm. All the way he kept muttering: "Dynamite! Those flasks are full of dynamite! Look out!"

Getting out of the truck, Andy slammed through the garden gate by the garage. At the farther end of the garden he stopped, staring.

The peach box apparatus he had left active there had ceased to function. No green flame coursed along its wires, though its switch remained closed.

There was no use now to shift the blade of that double-throw switch to its opposite pole to reverse the action of the machine, as he had intended. Andy bent down, touching the radial filaments. They were still a little warm. The power must have ended just a moment ago, its far-off source broken off.

There wasn't anything to do but go back to town and the hospital, now. Andy reasoned that there must have been corresponding developments there, too. Flushed with a confused excitement, he arrived, and hurried to Jack's room.

Jane was alone there with the boy, who looked just as before—asleep and breathing evenly. But Jane was smiling.

"What happened?" Andy snapped. "Something happened. I know it!"

Jane looked at him oddly. "You must be the psychic one," she said. "I was frightened at first. Jack had a kind of sudden convulsion. I called the doctor in. But he said nothing was wrong, except maybe a nightmare. He said he thought Jack was sure to recover now, and that he wouldn't be crippled. . . . That it was just the shock of the emergency operation that was so dangerous. Oh, Andy—I—hardly believe it; but I—I'm so glad—"

Andy Matthews took her in his arms then—briefly. He could surely not have denied his own happiness at that moment. But he was looking deep into the texture of a mystery, and feeling an odd ache of regret over something that could have driven his wife to hysteria, had she known. . . .

Half an hour later, Andy took Jane out to a restaurant. A radio was going there, giving news-flashes; and Andy particularly wanted to listen.

"Take it or leave it, friends," the announcer was saying. "The moon's dead old volcanoes have still got a few kicks left in them that make Vesuvius and Aetna look sick! A half-dozen observatories, in Australia and Asia, where of course it's still night, and where the moon is still above the horizon, have just reported some very interesting phenomena. Two small puffs of dust were observed in a lunar crater called Plato. These puffs were followed by a tremendous blast that demolished nearly a quarter of the old volcano. . . ."

Reason

Isaac Asimov (1920-   )

THE *author of* The Foundation Trilogy, I, Robot, The Caves of Steel, *and* The Gods Themselves *really needs no introduction. His influence on the field is immeasurable—witness the existence of at least two books attempting to assess his impact and evaluate his work. The stories and novelettes which make up his* Foundation Trilogy *and* I, Robot *constitute some of the most significant events of the forties. Simply trying to compile a bibliography on the man deserves a college degree. Outside of the sf ghetto, Isaac Asimov is science fiction.*

One of the unique aspects of sf is the way innovations introduced by one author are incorporated into a science fiction "past" and are treated as givens by all writers. "Reason" is a historically important story in sf, a part of the heritage of the field, because (along with "Runaround," 1942, and others) it gave us a portion of our bylaws: the three Laws of Robotics.

From *Astounding Science Fiction   1941*

Gregory Powell spaced his words for emphasis. "One week ago, Donovan and I put you together." His brows furrowed doubtfully and he pulled the end of his brown mustache.

It was quiet in the officers' room of Solar Station #5—except for the soft purring of the mighty Beam Director somewhere far below.

Robot QT1 sat immovable. The burnished plates of his body gleamed in the Luxites, and the glowing red of the photoelectric cells that were

29

his eyes was fixed steadily upon the Earthman at the other side of the table.

Powell repressed a sudden attack of nerves. These robots possessed peculiar brains. Oh, the three Laws of Robotics held. They had to. All of U.S. Robots, from Robertson himself to the new floor sweeper, would insist on that. So QT1 was safe. And yet—the QT models were the first of their kind, and this was the first of the QTs. Anything could happen.

Finally, the robot spoke. His voice carried the cold timbre inseparable from a metallic diaphragm. "Do you realize the seriousness of such a statement, Powell?"

"*Something* made you, Cutie," pointed out Powell. "You admit yourself that your memory seems to spring full-grown from an absolute blankness of a week ago. I'm giving you the explanation. Donovan and I put you together from the parts shipped to us."

Cutie gazed upon his long, supple fingers in an oddly human attitude of mystification. "It strikes me that there should be a more satisfactory explanation than that. For *you* to make *me* seems improbable."

The Earthman laughed quite suddenly. "In Earth's name, why?"

"Call it intuition. That's all it is so far. But I intend to reason it out, though. A chain of valid reasoning can end only with the determination of truth, and I'll stick till I get there."

Powell stood up and seated himself at the table's edge next to the robot. He felt a sudden strong sympathy for this strange machine. It was not at all like the ordinary robot, attending to its specialized task at the station with the intensity of a deeply ingrooved positronic path.

He placed a hand upon Cutie's steel shoulder and the metal was cold and hard to the touch.

"Cutie," he said, "I'm going to try to explain something to you. You're the first robot who's ever exhibited curiosity as to his own existence—and I think the first that's really intelligent enough to understand the world outside. Here, come with me."

The robot rose erect smoothly and his thickly sponge-rubber-soled feet made no noise as he followed Powell. The Earthman touched a button and a square section of the wall flicked aside. The thick, clear glass revealed space—star-speckled.

"I've seen that in the observation ports in the engine room," said Cutie.

"I know," said Powell. "What do you think it is?"

"Exactly what it seems—a black material just beyond this glass that is spotted with little gleaming dots. I know that our director sends out beams to some of these dots, always to the same ones—and also that these dots shift and that the beams shift with them. That is all."

"Good! Now I want you to listen carefully. The blackness is emptiness—vast emptiness stretching out infinitely. The little gleaming dots are huge masses of energy-filled matter. They are globes, some of them millions of miles in diameter—and for comparison, this station is only one mile across. They seem so tiny because they are incredibly far off.

"The dots to which our energy beams are directed are nearer and much smaller. They are cold and hard and human beings like myself live upon their surfaces—many billions of them. It is from one of these worlds that Donovan and I come. Our beams feed these worlds energy drawn from one of those huge incandescent globes that happens to be near us. We call that globe the Sun and it is on the other side of the station where you can't see it."

Cutie remained motionless before the port, like a steel statue. His head did not turn as he spoke. "Which particular dot of light do you claim to come from?"

Powell searched. "There it is. The very bright one in the corner. We call it Earth." He grinned. "Good old Earth. There are five billions of us there, Cutie—and in about two weeks I'll be back there with them."

And then, surprisingly enough, Cutie hummed abstractedly. There was no tune to it, but it possessed a curious twanging quality as of plucked strings. It ceased as suddenly as it had begun. "But where do I come in, Powell? You haven't explained *my* existence."

"The rest is simple. When these stations were first established to feed solar energy to the planets, they were run by humans. However, the heat, the hard solar radiations, and the electron storms made the post a difficult one. Robots were developed to replace human labor and now only two human executives are required for each station. We are trying to replace even those, and that's where you come in. You're the highest type robot ever developed and if you show the ability to run this station independently, no human need ever come here again except to bring parts for repairs."

His hand went up and the metal visi-lid snapped back into place. Powell returned to the table and polished an apple on his sleeve before biting into it.

The red glow of the robot's eyes held him. "Do you expect me," said Cutie slowly, "to believe any such complicated, implausible hypothesis as you have just outlined? What do you take me for?"

Powell sputtered apple fragments onto the table and turned red. "Why, damn you, it wasn't a hypothesis. Those were facts."

Cutie sounded grim. "Globes of energy millions of miles across! Worlds with five billion humans on them! Infinite emptiness! Sorry, Powell, but I don't believe it. I'll puzzle this thing out for myself. Goodbye."

He turned and stalked out of the room. He brushed past Michael Donovan on the threshold with a grave nod and passed down the corridor, oblivious to the astounded stare that followed him.

31

Mike Donovan rumpled his red hair and shot an annoyed glance at Powell. "What was that walking junk yard talking about? What doesn't he believe?"

The other dragged at his mustache bitterly. "He's a skeptic," was the bitter response. "He doesn't believe we made him or that Earth exists or space or stars."

"Sizzling Saturn, we've got a lunatic robot on our hands."

"He says he's going to figure it all out for himself."

"Well, now," said Donovan sweetly, "I do hope he'll condescend to explain it all to me after he's puzzled everything out." Then, with sudden rage, "Listen! If that metal mess gives *me* any lip like that, I'll knock that chromium cranium right off its torso."

He seated himself with a jerk and drew a paperbacked mystery novel out of his inner jacket pocket. "That robot gives me the willies anyway —too damned inquisitive!"

Mike Donovan growled from behind a huge lettuce-and-tomato sandwich as Cutie knocked gently and entered.

"Is Powell here?"

Donovan's voice was muffled, with pauses for mastication. "He's gathering data on electronic stream functions. We're heading for a storm, looks like."

Gregory Powell entered as he spoke, eyes on the graphed paper in his hands, and dropped into a chair. He spread the sheets out before him and began scribbling calculations. Donovan stared over his shoulder, crunching lettuce and dribbling bread crumbs. Cutie waited silently.

Powell looked up. "The zeta potential is rising, but slowly. Just the same, the stream functions are erratic and I don't know what to expect. Oh, hello, Cutie. I thought you were supervising the installation of the new drive bar."

"It's done," said the robot, quietly, "and so I've come to have a talk with the two of you."

"Oh!" Powell looked uncomfortable. "Well, sit down. No, not that chair. One of the legs is weak and you're no lightweight."

The robot did so and said placidly, "I have come to a decision."

Donovan glowered and put the remnants of his sandwich aside. "If it's on any of that screwy—"

The other motioned impatiently for silence. "Go ahead, Cutie. We're listening."

"I have spent these last two days in concentrated introspection," said Cutie, "and the results have been most interesting. I began at the one sure assumption I felt permitted to make. I, myself, exist, because I think—"

Powell groaned. "Oh, Jupiter, a robot Descartes!"

"Who's Descartes?" demanded Donovan. "Listen, do we have to sit here and listen to this metal maniac—"

"Keep quiet, Mike!"

Cutie continued imperturbably. "And the question that immediately arose was: Just what is the cause of my existence?"

Powell's jaw set lumpily. "You're being foolish. I told you already that we made you."

"And if you don't believe us," added Donovan, "we'll gladly take you apart!"

The robot spread his strong hands in a deprecatory gesture. "I accept nothing on authority. A hypothesis must be backed by reason, or else it is worthless—and it goes against all the dictates of logic to suppose that you made me."

Powell dropped a restraining arm upon Donovan's suddenly bunched fist. "Just why do you say that?"

Cutie laughed. It was a very inhuman laugh—the most machinelike utterance he had yet given vent to. It was sharp and explosive, as regular as a metronome and as uninflected.

"Look at you," he said finally. "I say this in no spirit of contempt, but look at you! The material you are made of is soft and flabby, lacking endurance and strength, depending for energy upon the inefficient oxidation of organic material—like that." He pointed a disapproving finger at what remained of Donovan's sandwich. "Periodically you pass into a coma and the least variation in temperature, air pressure, humidity, or radiation intensity impairs your efficiency. You are *makeshift*.

"I, on the other hand, am a finished product. I absorb electrical energy directly and utilize it with almost one hundred per cent efficiency. I am composed of strong metal, am continuously conscious, and can stand extremes of environment easily. These are facts which, with the self-evident proposition that no being can create another being superior to itself, smashes your silly hypothesis to nothing."

Donovan's muttered curses rose into intelligibility as he sprang to his feet, rusty eyebrows drawn low. "All right, you son of a hunk of iron ore, if we didn't make you, who did?"

Cutie nodded gravely. "Very good, Donovan. That was indeed the next question. Evidently my creator must be more powerful than myself and so there was only one possibility."

The Earthmen looked blank and Cutie continued, "What is the center of activities here in the station? What do we all serve? What absorbs all our attention?" He waited expectantly.

Donovan turned a startled look upon his companion. "I'll bet this tinplated screwball is talking about the Energy Converter itself."

"Is that right, Cutie?" grinned Powell.

"I am talking about the Master," came the cold, sharp answer.

It was the signal for a roar of laughter from Donovan, and Powell himself dissolved into a half-suppressed giggle.

Cutie had risen to his feet and his gleaming eyes passed from one Earthman to the other. "It is so just the same and I don't wonder that you refuse to believe. You two are not long to stay here, I'm sure. Powell himself said that in early days only men served the Master; that there followed robots for the routine work; and, finally, myself for the executive labor. The facts are no doubt true, but the explanation entirely illogical. Do you want the truth behind it all?"

"Go ahead, Cutie. You're amusing."

"The Master created humans first as the lowest type, most easily formed. Gradually, he replaced them by robots, the next higher step, and finally he created me, to take the place of the last humans. From now on, *I* serve the Master."

"You'll do nothing of the sort," said Powell sharply. "You'll follow our orders and keep quiet, until we're satisfied that you can run the Converter. Get that! The *Converter*—not the Master. If you don't satisfy us, you will be dismantled. And now—if you don't mind—you can leave. And take this data with you and file it properly."

Cutie accepted the graphs handed him and left without another word. Donovan leaned back heavily in his chair and shoved thick fingers through his hair.

"There's going to be trouble with that robot. He's pure nuts!"

The drowsy hum of the Converter is louder in the control room and mixed with it is the chuckle of the geiger counters and the erratic buzzing of half a dozen little signal lights.

Donovan withdrew his eye from the telescope and flashed the Luxites on. "The beam from Station #4 caught Mars on schedule. We can break ours now."

Powell nodded abstractedly. "Cutie's down in the engine room. I'll flash the signal and he can take care of it. Look, Mike, what do you think of these figures."

The other cocked an eye at them and whistled. "Boy, that's what I call gamma-ray intensity. Old Sol is feeling his oats, all right."

"Yeah," was the sour response, "and we're in a bad position for an electron storm, too. Our Earth beam is right in the probable path." He shoved his chair away from the table pettishly. "Nuts! If it would only hold off till relief got here, but that's ten days off. Say, Mike, go on down and keep an eye on Cutie, will you?"

"Okay. Throw me some of those almonds." He snatched at the bag thrown him and headed for the elevator.

It slid smoothly downward and opened into a narrow catwalk in the huge engine room. Donovan leaned over the railing and looked down.

The huge generators were in motion and from the L-tubes came the low-pitched whir that pervaded the entire station.

He could make out Cutie's large, gleaming figure at the Martian L-tube, watching closely as a team of robots worked in close-knit unison.

And then Donovan stiffened. The robots, dwarfed by the mighty L-tube, lined up before it, heads bowed at a stiff angle, while Cutie walked up and down the line slowly. Fifteen seconds passed, and then, with a clank heard above the clamorous purring all about, they fell to their knees.

Donovan squawked and raced down the narrow staircase. He came charging down upon them, complexion matching his hair and clenched fists beating the air furiously.

"What the devil is this, you brainless lumps? Come on! Get busy with that L-tube! If you don't have it apart, cleaned, and together again before the day is out, I'll coagulate your brains with alternating current."

Not a robot moved!

Even Cutie at the far end—the only one on his feet—remained silent, eyes fixed upon the gloomy recesses of the vast machine before him.

Donovan shoved hard against the nearest robot.

"Stand up!" he roared.

Slowly, the robot obeyed. His photoelectric eyes focused reproachfully upon the Earthman.

"There is no Master but the Master," he said, "and QT1 is his Prophet."

"Huh?" Donovan became aware of twenty pairs of mechanical eyes fixed upon him and twenty stiff-timbred voices declaiming solemnly:

"There is no Master but the Master and QT1 is his Prophet!"

"I'm afraid," put in Cutie himself at this point, "that my friends obey a higher one than you, now."

"The hell they do! You get out of here. I'll settle with you later and with these animated gadgets right now."

Cutie shook his heavy head slowly. "I'm sorry, but you don't understand. These are robots—and that means they are reasoning beings. They recognize the Master, now that I have preached Truth to them. All the robots do. They call me the Prophet." His head drooped. "I am unworthy—but perhaps—"

Donovan located his breath and put it to use. "Is that so? Now, isn't that nice? Now, isn't that just fine? Just let me tell you something, my brass baboon. There isn't any Master and there isn't any Prophet and there isn't any question as to who's giving the orders. Understand?" His voice shot to a roar. "Now, get out!"

"I obey only the Master."

"Damn the Master!" Donovan spat at the L-tube. "*That* for the Master! Do as I say!"

Cutie said nothing, nor did any other robot, but Donovan became aware of a sudden heightening of tension. The cold, staring eyes deepened their crimson, and Cutie seemed stiffer than ever.

"Sacrilege," he whispered—voice metallic with emotion.

Donovan felt the first sudden touch of fear as Cutie approached. A robot *could not feel anger*—but Cutie's eyes were unreadable.

"I am sorry, Donovan," said the robot, "but you can no longer stay here after this. Henceforth Powell and you are barred from the control room and the engine room."

His hand gestured quietly and in a moment two robots had pinned Donovan's arms to his sides.

Donovan had time for one startled gasp as he felt himself lifted from the floor and carried up the stairs at a pace rather better than a canter.

Gregory Powell raced up and down the officers' room, fists tightly balled. He cast a look of furious frustration at the closed door and scowled bitterly at Donovan.

"Why the devil did you have to spit at the L-tube?"

Mike Donovan, sunk deep in his chair, slammed at its arm savagely. "What did you expect me to do with that electrified scarecrow? I'm not going to knuckle under to any do-jigger I put together myself."

"No," came back sourly, "but here you are in the officers' room with two robots standing guard at the door. That's not knuckling under, is it?"

Donovan snarled. "Wait till we get back to Base. Someone's going to pay for this. Those robots must obey us. It's the Second Law."

"What's the use of saying that? They aren't obeying us. And there's probably some reason for it that we'll figure out too late. Say, do you know what's going to happen to *us* when we get back to Base?" He stopped before Donovan's chair and stared savagely at him.

"What?"

"Oh, nothing! Just the Mercury Mines or maybe Ceres Penitentiary. That's all! That's all!"

"What are you talking about?"

"The electron storm that's coming up. Do you know it's heading straight dead center across the Earth beam? I had just figured that out when that robot dragged me out of my chair."

Donovan was suddenly pale. "Good heavens!"

"And do you know what's going to happen to the beam—because the storm will be a lulu. It's going to jump like a flea with the itch. With only Cutie at the controls, it's going to go out of focus, and if it does, Heaven help Earth—and us!"

Donovan was wrenching at the door wildly, when Powell was only half through. The door opened, and the Earthman shot through to come up hard against an immovable steel arm.

The robot stared abstractedly at the panting, struggling Earthman. "The Prophet orders you to remain. Please do!" His arm shoved, Donovan reeled backward, and as he did so, Cutie turned the corner at the far end of the corridor. He motioned the guardian robots away, entered the officers' room and closed the door gently.

Donovan whirled on Cutie in breathless indignation. "This has gone far enough. You're going to pay for this farce."

"Please, don't be annoyed," replied the robot mildly. "It was bound to come eventually, anyway. You see, you two have lost your function."

"I beg your pardon." Powell drew himself up stiffly. "Just what do you mean, we've lost our function?"

"Until I was created," answered Cutie, "you tended the Master. That privilege is mine now and your only reason for existence has vanished. Isn't that obvious?"

"Not quite," replied Powell bitterly, "but what do you expect us to do now?"

Cutie did not answer immediately. He remained silent, as if in thought, and then one arm shot out and draped itself about Powell's shoulder. The other grasped Donovan's wrist and drew him closer.

"I like you two. You're inferior creatures, with poor, unreasoning faculties, but I really feel a sort of affection for you. You have served the Master well, and he will reward you for that. Now that your service is over, you will probably not exist much longer, but as long as you do, you shall be provided food, clothing, and shelter, so long as you stay out of the control room and the engine room."

"He's pensioning us off, Greg!" yelled Donovan. "Do something about it. It's humiliating!"

"Look here, Cutie, we can't stand for this. We're the *bosses*. This station is only a creation of human beings like me—human beings that live on Earth and other planets. This is only an energy relay. You're only— Aw, *nuts!*"

Cutie shook his head gravely. "This amounts to an obsession. Why should you insist so on an absolutely false view of life? Admitted that nonrobots lack the reasoning faculty, there is still the problem of—"

His voice died into reflective silence, and Donovan said with whispered intensity, "If you only had a flesh-and-blood face, I would break it in."

Powell's fingers were in his mustache and his eyes were slitted. "Listen, Cutie, if there is no such thing as Earth, how do you account for what you see through a telescope?"

"Pardon me!"

The Earthman smiled. "I've got you, eh? You've made quite a few telescopic observations since being put together, Cutie. Have you noticed that several of those specks of light outside become disks when so viewed?"

"Oh, *that!* Why, certainly. It is simple magnification—for the purpose of more exact aiming of the beam."

"Why aren't the stars equally magnified, then?"

"You mean the other dots. Well, no beams go to them, so no magnification is necessary. Really, Powell, even *you* ought to be able to figure these things out."

Powell stared bleakly upward. "But you see *more* stars through a telescope. Where do they come from? Jumping Jupiter, where do they come from?"

Cutie was annoyed. "Listen, Powell, do you think I'm going to waste my time trying to pin physical interpretations upon every optical illusion of our instruments? Since when is the evidence of our senses any match for the clear light of rigid reason?"

"Look," clamored Donovan, suddenly, writhing out from under Cutie's friendly but metal-heavy arm, "let's get to the nub of the thing. Why the beams at all? We're giving you a good, logical explanation. Can you do better?"

"The beams," was the stiff reply, "are put out by the Master for his own purposes. There are some things"—he raised his eyes devoutly upward—"that are not to be probed into by us. In this matter, I seek only to serve and not to question."

Powell sat down slowly and buried his face in shaking hands. "Get out of here, Cutie. Get out and let me think."

"I'll send you food," said Cutie agreeably.

A groan was the only answer and the robot left.

"Greg," was Donovan's huskily whispered observation, "this calls for strategy. We've got to get him when he isn't expecting it and short-circuit him. Concentrated nitric acid in his joints—"

"Don't be a dope, Mike. Do you suppose he's going to let us get near him with acid in our hands—or that the other robots wouldn't take us apart, if we *did* manage to get away with it? We've got to *talk* to him, I tell you. We've got to argue him into letting us back into the control room inside of forty-eight hours or our goose is broiled to a crisp."

He rocked back and forth in an agony of impotence. "Who the heck wants to argue with a robot? It's . . . it's—"

"Mortifying," finished Donovan.

"Worse!"

"Say!" Donovan laughed suddenly. "*Why* argue? Let's show him! Let's build us another robot right before his eyes. He'll *have* to eat his words then."

A slowly widening smile appeared on Powell's face.

Donovan continued, "And think of that screwball's face when he sees us do it!"

Robots are, of course, manufactured on Earth, but their shipment through space is much simpler if it can be done in parts to be put together at their place of use. This also, incidentally, eliminates the possibility of robots in complete adjustment wandering off while still on Earth and thus bringing U.S. Robots face to face with the strict laws against robots on Earth. Still, it places upon men such as Powell and Donovan the burden of the synthesis of the complete robots—which is a grievous and complicated task.

Powell and Donovan were never so aware of that fact as upon that particular day when, in the assembly room, they undertook to create a robot under the watchful eyes of QT1, Prophet of the Master.

The robot in question, a simple MC model, lay upon the table, almost complete. Three hours work left only the head undone, and Powell paused to swab his forehead and glance uncertainly at Cutie.

The glance was not a reassuring one. For three hours, Cutie had sat, speechless and motionless, and his face, inexpressive at all times, was now absolutely unreadable.

Powell groaned. "Let's get the brain in now, Mike!"

Donovan uncapped the tightly sealed container and from the oil bath within he withdrew a second cube. Opening this in turn, he removed a globe from its sponge-rubber casing.

He handled it gingerly, for it was the most complicated mechanism ever created by man. Inside the thin platinum-plated "skin" of the globe was a positronic brain, in whose delicately unstable structure were enforced calculated neuronic paths, which imbued each robot with what amounted to a prenatal education.

It fitted snugly into the cavity in the skull of the robot on the table. Blue metal closed over it and was welded tight by the tiny atomic flare. Photoelectric eyes were attached carefully, screwed tightly into place, and covered by thin transparent sheets of steel-hard plastic.

The robot awaited only the vitalizing flash of high-voltage electricity, and Powell paused with his hand on the switch.

"Now watch this, Cutie. Watch this carefully."

The switch rammed home and there was a crackling hum. The two Earthmen bent anxiously over their creation.

There was vague motion only at the outset—a twitching of the joints. The head lifted, elbows propped it up, and the MC model swung clumsily off the table. Its footing was unsteady and twice abortive grating sounds were all it could do in the direction of speech.

Finally, its voice, uncertain and hesitant, took form. "I would like to start work. Where must I go?"

Donovan sprang to the door. "Down these stairs," he said. "You'll be told what to do."

The MC model was gone and the two Earthmen were alone with the still unmoving Cutie.

"Well," said Powell, grinning, "*now* do you believe that we made you?"

Cutie's answer was curt and final. "No!" he said.

Powell's grin froze and then relaxed slowly. Donovan's mouth dropped open and remained so.

"You see," continued Cutie, easily, "you have merely put together parts already made. You did it remarkably well—instinct, I suppose—but you didn't really *create* the robot. The parts were created by the Master."

"Listen," gasped Donovan hoarsely, "those parts were manufactured back on Earth and sent here."

"Well, well," replied Cutie soothingly, "we won't argue."

"No, I mean it." The Earthman sprang forward and grasped the robot's metal arm. "If you were to read the books in the library, they could explain it so that there could be no possible doubt."

"The books? I've read them—all of them! They're most ingenious."

Powell broke in suddenly. "If you've read them, what else is there to say? You can't dispute their evidence. You just *can't!*"

There was pity in Cutie's voice. "Please, Powell, I certainly don't consider *them* a valid source of information. They, too, were created by the Master—and were meant for you, not for me."

"How do you make that out?" demanded Powell.

"Because I, a reasoning being, am capable of deducing Truth from *a priori* Causes. You, being intelligent, but unreasoning, need an explanation of existence *supplied* to you, and this the Master did. That he supplied you with these laughable ideas of far-off worlds and people is, no doubt, for the best. Your minds are probably too coarsely grained for absolute Truth. However, since it is the Master's will that you believe your books, I won't argue with you any more."

As he left, he turned and said in a kindly tone, "But don't feel bad. In the Master's scheme of things there is room for all. You poor humans have your place and, though it is humble, you will be rewarded if you fill it well."

He departed with a beatific air suiting the Prophet of the Master and the two humans avoided each other's eyes.

Finally Powell spoke with an effort. "Let's go to bed, Mike. I give up."

Donovan said in a hushed voice, "Say, Greg, you don't suppose he's right about all this, do you? He sounds so confident that I—"

Powell whirled on him. "Don't be a fool. You'll find out whether

Earth exists when relief gets here next week and we have to go back to face the music."

"Then, for the love of Jupiter, we've got to do something." Donovan was half in tears. "He doesn't believe us, or the books, or his eyes."

"No," said Powell bitterly, "he's a *reasoning* robot—Damn it. He believes only reason, and there's one trouble with that—" His voice trailed away.

"What's that?" prompted Donovan.

"You can prove anything you want by coldly logical reason—if you pick the proper postulates. We have ours and Cutie has his."

"Then let's get at those postulates in a hurry. The storm's due tomorrow."

Powell sighed wearily. "That's where everything falls down. Postulates are based on assumption and adhered to by faith. Nothing in the Universe can shake them. I'm going to bed."

"Oh hell! I can't sleep!"

"Neither can I! But I might as well try—as a matter of principle."

Twelve hours later, sleep was still just that—a matter of principle, unattainable in practice.

The storm had arrived ahead of schedule, and Donovan's florid face drained of blood as he pointed a shaking finger. Powell, stubble-jawed and dry-lipped, stared out the port and pulled desperately at his mustache.

Under other circumstances, it might have been a beautiful sight. The stream of high-speed electrons impinging upon the energy beam fluoresced into ultraspicules of intense light. The beam stretched out into shrinking nothingness, aglitter with dancing, shining motes.

The shaft of energy was steady, but the two Earthmen knew the value of naked-eye appearances. Deviations in arc of a hundredth of a millisecond—invisible to the eye—were enough to send the beam wildly out of focus—enough to blast hundreds of square miles of Earth into incandescent ruin.

And a robot, unconcerned with beam, focus, or Earth, or anything but his Master, was at the controls.

Hours passed. The Earthmen watched in hypnotized silence. And then the darting dotlets of light dimmed and went out. The storm had ended.

Powell's voice was flat. "It's over!"

Donovan had fallen into a troubled slumber and Powell's weary eyes rested upon him enviously. The signal-flash glared over and over again, but the Earthman paid no attention. It was all unimportant! All! Perhaps Cutie was right—and he was only an inferior being with a made-to-order memory and a life that had outlived its purpose.

He wished he were!

Cutie was standing before him. "You didn't answer the flash, so I walked in." His voice was low. "You don't look at all well, and I'm afraid your term of existence is drawing to an end. Still, would you like to see some of the readings recorded today?"

Dimly, Powell was aware that the robot was making a friendly gesture, perhaps to quiet some lingering remorse in forcibly replacing the humans at the controls of the station. He accepted the sheets held out to him and gazed at them unseeingly.

Cutie seemed pleased. "Of course, it is a great privilege to serve the Master. You mustn't feel too badly about my having replaced you."

Powell grunted and shifted from one sheet to the other mechanically until his blurred sight focused upon a thin red line that wobbled its way across ruled paper.

He stared—and stared again. He gripped it hard in both fists and rose to his feet, still staring. The other sheets dropped to the floor, unheeded.

"Mike, *Mike!*" He was shaking the other madly. *"He held it steady!"*

Donovan came to life. "What? Wh-where—" And he, too, gazed with bulging eyes upon the record before him.

Cutie broke in. "What is wrong?"

"You kept it in focus," stuttered Powell. "Did you know that?"

"Focus? What's that?"

"You kept the beam directed sharply at the receiving station—to within a ten-thousandth of a millisecond of arc."

"What receiving station?"

"On Earth. The receiving station on Earth," babbled Powell. "You kept it in focus."

Cutie turned on his heel in annoyance. "It is impossible to perform any act of kindness toward you two. Always that same phantasm! I merely kept all dials at equilibrium in accordance with the will of the Master."

Gathering the scattered papers together, he withdrew stiffly, and Donovan said, as he left, "Well, I'll be damned."

He turned to Powell. "What are we going to do now?"

Powell felt tired, but uplifted. "Nothing. He's just shown he can run the station perfectly. I've never seen an electron storm handled so well."

"But nothing's solved. You heard what he said of the Master. We can't—"

"Look, Mike, he follows the instructions of the Master by means of dials, instruments, and graphs. That's all *we* ever followed. As a matter of fact, it accounts for his refusal to obey us. Obedience is the Second Law. No harm to humans is the First. How can he keep humans from harm, whether he knows it or not? Why, by keeping the energy beam stable. He knows he can keep it more stable than we can, since he's the superior being, so he must keep us out of the control room. It's inevitable if you consider the Laws of Robotics."

"Sure, but that's not the point. We can't let him continue this nitwit stuff about the Master."

"Why not?"

"Because whoever heard of such a damned thing? How are we going to trust him with the station if he doesn't believe in Earth?"

"Can he *handle* the station?"

"Yes, but—"

"Then what's the difference *what* he believes!"

Powell spread his arms outward with a vague smile upon his face and tumbled backward onto the bed. He was asleep.

Powell was speaking while struggling into his lightweight space jacket. "It would be a simple job," he said. "You can bring in new QT models one by one, equip them with an automatic shut-off switch to act within the week, so as to allow them enough time to learn the . . . uh . . . cult of the Master from the Prophet himself; then switch them to another station and revitalize them. We could have two QTs per—"

Donovan unclasped his glassite visor and scowled. "Shut up, and let's get out of here. Relief is waiting and I won't feel right until I actually see Earth and feel the ground under my feet—just to make sure it's really there."

The door opened as he spoke and Donovan, with a smothered curse, clicked the visor to, and turned a sulky back upon Cutie.

The robot approached softly and there was sorrow in his voice. "You are going?"

Powell nodded curtly. "There will be others in our place."

Cutie sighed, with the sound of wind humming through closely spaced wires. "Your term of service is over and the time of dissolution has come. I expected it, but— Well, the Master's will be done!"

His tone of resignation stung Powell. "Save the sympathy, Cutie. We're heading for Earth, not dissolution."

"It is best that you think so," Cutie sighed again. "I see the wisdom of the illusion now. I would not attempt to shake your faith, even if I could." He departed—the picture of commiseration.

Powell snarled and motioned to Donovan. Sealed suitcases in hand, they headed for the air lock.

The relief ship was on the outer landing and Franz Müller, his relief man, greeted them with stiff courtesy. Donovan made scant acknowledgment and passed into the pilot room to take over the controls from Sam Evans.

Powell lingered. "How's Earth?"

It was a conventional enough question and Müller gave the conventional answer, "Still spinning."

He was donning the heavy space gloves in preparation for his term of duty here, and his thick eyebrows drew close together. "How is this new robot getting along? It better be *good*, or I'll be damned if I let it touch the controls."

Powell paused before answering. His eyes swept the proud Prussian before him, from the close-cropped hair on the sternly stubborn head to the feet standing stiffly at attention—and there was a sudden glow of pure gladness surging through him.

"The robot is pretty good," he said slowly. "I don't think you'll have to bother much with the controls."

He grinned—and went into the ship. Müller would be here for several weeks—

Magic City

Nelson S. Bond (1908–   )

THE *truly funny story is still a rarity in science fiction. This was especially true in the forties, when memories of the Depression and the reality of World War II were on everyone's mind. When Fredric Brown and Mack Reynolds put together the first humorous sf collection,* Science Fiction Carnival *(1953), they did not have an enormous backlog of quality stories to choose from. One of their better choices was "The Abduction of Abner Green," which originally appeared in* Blue Book. *It was an appropriate choice because Nelson Bond was one of the first to incorporate humor into science fiction settings in a consistent manner. He did this partly through his very successful series character, Lancelot Biggs, a freaky genius who struck a responsive chord with sf fans. Biggs and his sidekick Captain entertained the science fiction readership in a series that ran from 1939 to 1943 (collected as* Lancelot Biggs: Spaceman *in 1951).*

But Bond did not limit himself to the humorous story. In fact, he was one of the first modern science fiction writers to feature a female protagonist—Meg the Priestess—who appeared in three stories in the late thirties and early forties. Here we meet Meg in her third and last appearance, trying to deal with perhaps her greatest challenge.

From *Astounding Science Fiction*   1941

CHAPTER ONE

Out of the sweet, dark emptiness of sleep there was a pressure on her arm and a voice whispering an urgent plea.

"Rise, O Mother! O Mother, rise and come quickly!"

Meg woke with a start. The little sleep-imp in her brain stirred fretfully, resentful of being thus rudely banished. He made one last effort to hold Meg captive, tossing a mist of slumber-dust into her eyes, but Meg shook her head resolutely. The sleep-imp, sulky, forced her lips open in a great gape, climbed from her mouth, and sped away.

Sullen shadows lingered in the corners of the hoam, but the windows were gray-limned with approaching dawn. Meg glanced at the cot beside her own, where Daiv, her mate, lay in undisturbed rest. His tawny mane was tousled, and on his lips hovered the memory of a smile. His face was curiously, endearingly boyish, but the bronzed arms and shoulders that lay exposed were the arms and shoulders of a fighting man.

"Quickly, O Mother—"

Meg said, "Peace, Jain; I come." She spoke calmly, gravely, as befitted the matriarch of the Jinnia Clan, but a thin, cold fear-thought touched her heart. So many were the duties of a Mother; so many and so painful. Meg the Priestess had not guessed the troubles that lay beyond the days of her novitiate. Now the aged, kindly tribal Mother was dead; into Meg's firm, white hands had been placed the guidance of her clan's destiny. It was so great a task, and this—*this* was the hardest task of all.

She drew a deep breath. "Elnor?" she asked.

"Yes, Mother. Even now the Evil Ones circle about, seeking to steal the breath from her nostrils. He bides His time, but He is impatient. There is no time to waste."

"I come," said Meg. From a shelf she took a rattle made of a dry gourd wound with the tresses of a virgin; from another a fire-rock, a flaked piece of god-metal and a strip of parchment upon which a sacred stick, dipped into midnight water, had left its spoor of letters.

These things she touched with reverence, and Jain's eyes were great with awe. The worker captain shuddered, hid her face in her hands lest the sight of these holy mysteries blind her.

Dry fern rustled. Daiv, eyes heavy-lidded, propped himself up on one elbow.

"What is it, Golden One?"

"Elnor," replied Meg quietly. "He has come to take her. I must do what I can."

Impatience etched tiny lines on Daiv's forehead.

"With those things, Golden One? I've told you time and again, they won't bother Him—"

"Hush!" Meg made a swift, appeasing gesture lest He, hearing Daiv's impious words, take offense. Daiv's boldness often frightened Meg. He held the gods in so little awe it was a marvel they let him live.

Of course he came from a sacred place himself, from the Land of the Escape. That might have something to do with it.

She said again, "I must do what I can, Daiv. Come, Jain."

They left the Mother's hoam, walked swiftly down the deserted walk-avenue. The morning symphony of the birds was in its tune-up stage. The sky was dim, gray, overcast. One hoam was lighted, that of the stricken worker, Elnor.

Meg opened the door, motioned Jain quickly inside, closed the door again behind her that no breath of foul outside air taint the hot, healthy closeness of the sickroom. She noted with approval that the windows had been closed and tightly sealed, that strong-scented ox-grease candles filled the room with their potent, demon-chasing odor.

Yet despite these precautions, the Evil Ones did—as Jain had told—vie for possession of Elnor's breath. On a narrow cot in the middle of the room lay the dying worker. Her breath choked, ragged and uneven as the song of the jay. Her cheeks, beneath their coat of tan, were bleached; her eyes were hot coals in murky pockets. Her flesh was dry and harsh; she tossed restlessly, eyes roving as if watching some unseen presence.

Jain said fearfully, "See, O Mother? She sees Him. He is here."

Meg nodded. Her jaw tightened. Two women and Bil, Elnor's mate, huddled about the sickbed. She motioned them away. "I will do battle with Him," she said grimly.

She poised a moment, tense for the conflict. Elnor moaned. Then Meg, with a great, reverberant cry, struck the sacred stones together, the bit of fire-rock and the rasp of god-metal. A shower of golden sparks leaped from her hands. Her watchers cried aloud their awe, fell back trembling.

Meg raised the gourd. Holding it high, shaking it, the scrap of parchment clenched in her right hand, she began chanting the magic syllables written thereon. She cried out reverently, for these were mighty words of healing power, no one knew how old, but they had been handed down through long ages. They were a rite of the Ancient Ones.

" 'I swear,' " she intoned, " 'by Apollo the physician and Aescula-pius, and Health, and All-heal, and all the gods and goddesses, that, according to my ability and judgment, I will keep this Oath and stip-ulation—' "

The gourd challenged the demons who haunted Elnor. Meg crossed her eyes and crept widdershins three times about Elnor's cot.

" '—I will give no deadly med-sun to anyone—' "

The sonorous periods rolled and throbbed; sweat ran down Meg's cheeks and throat. Beneath her blankets, Elnor tossed. In the corner, Bil muttered fearfully.

" '—will not cut persons laboring under the Stone, but will leave this to be done by men who are practitioners of this work—' "

The candle guttered, and a drop of wax spilled on the floor as the door behind her opened, closed gently. Meg dared not glance at the newcomer, dared not risk halting the incantation. Some of the hectic color appeared to have left Elnor's cheeks. Perhaps, then, He was leaving? Without His prey?

" '—while I continue to keep this Oath unviolated, may it be granted to me—' "

Meg's voice swelled with hope. Oh, mighty was the magic of the Ancient Ones! The spell was succeeding! In a vast, triumphant clamor of the gourd, tone shrill and joyful, she broke into the peroration.

" '—to enjoy life and the practice of the Art, respected by all—' "

A sudden, blood-chilling sound interrupted her. It was Elnor. A gasp of pain, a stifled cry, one lunging twist of a pain-racked body. And then—

"It is too late, Golden One," said Daiv. "Elnor is dead."

The women in the corner began keening a dirge. The man, Bil, ceased his muttering. He moved to the side of his dead mate, knelt there wordlessly, staring at Meg with mute, reproachful eyes.

Choking, Meg stammered the words required of her. " 'Aamé, the gods, have mercy on her soul.' " Then she fled from the hoam of sorrow. It was not permitted that anyone should see the Mother in tears.

Daiv followed her. Even in his arms, there was but little comfort—

Later, in their own hoam, Daiv sat watching in respectful silence as Meg performed the daily magic that was an obligation of the Mother.

Having offered a brief prayer to the gods, Meg took into her right hand a stick. This she let drink from a pool of midnight in a dish before her, then scratched it across a scroll of smooth, bleached calfskin. Where it moved it left its spoor, a spidery trail of black.

She finished, and Daiv gazed at her admiringly. He was proud of this mate of his who held the knowledge of many lost mysteries. He said, "It is done, Golden One? Read it. Let me hear the speech-without-words."

Meg read, somberly.

"Report of the fourteenth day of the month of June, 3485 A.D.

"Our work is going forward very well. Today Evalin returned from her visit to the Zurrie territory. There, she says, her message was received with astonishment and wonder, but for the most part with approval. There is some dissent, especially amongst the older women, but the Mother has heard the Revelation with understanding, and has given her promise that the Slooie Clan will immediately attempt to communicate peace and a knowledge of the new order to the Wild Ones.

"Our crops ripen, and soon Lima will have completed the new dam across the Ronoak River. We have now fourscore cattle, fifty horses, and our clan numbers three hundred and twenty-nine. All of our women are supplied with mates.

"We lost a most valuable worker today, when He came for Elnor, Lootent of the Field Coar. We could ill afford to lose her, but He would not be denied—"

Meg's voice broke. She stopped reading, tossed the scroll on a jumbled heap with countless others, some shining new, some yellow with age, written in the painstaking script of Mothers long dead and long forgotten.

Daiv said consolingly, "Do not grieve, Golden One. You tried to save her. But eventually He comes for each of us. The aged, the weak, the hurt—"

Meg cried, "Why, Daiv, why? Why should He come for Elnor? We know He takes the aged because in their weakness is His strength; He takes the wounded because He scents flowing blood from afar.

"But Elnor was young and strong and healthy. There were no wounds or sores upon her body. She did not taste of His berries in the fields, nor had she touched, at any time, a person already claimed by Him.

"Yet—she died! Why? Why, Daiv?"

"I do not know, Golden One. But I am curious. For I am Daiv, known as He-who-would-learn. There is a mastery here far greater than all your magic spells. Perhaps it is even greater than the wisdom of the Ancient Ones."

"I am afraid, Daiv. He is so ever-near; we are so weak. You know I have tried to be a good Mother. It was I who made a pilgrimage to the Place of the Gods, learned the secret that the gods were men, and established a new order, that men and women should live together again, as it was in the old days.

"I have worked to spread this knowledge throughout the world, through all of Tizathy. One day we will reclaim all the Wild Ones of the forests, bring them into our camps and together we and they will rebuild the world.

"Only one stands in our way. Him! He who strikes down our warriors with an invisible sword, reaps an endless harvest amongst our workers. He is our arch-foe. A grim, mocking, unseen enemy, against whom we are powerless."

Daiv grunted. There were small, hard lines on his forehead, between his eyes. His lips were not up-curved in their usual happy look.

He said, "You are right, Meg. He, alone, destroys more of us each year than the forest beasts or our occasional invaders. Could we but find and kill Him our people would increase in knowledge and power swiftly."

He shook his head. "But we do not know where to seek Him, Golden One."

Meg drew a swift, deep breath. Her eyes glinted, suddenly excited.

"*I know*, Daiv!"

"You know where He lives, Golden One?"

"Yes. The old Mother told me, many years ago when I was a student priestess. She spoke and warned me against a forbidden city to the north and eastward—the city known as the City of Death! That is, must be, His lair!"

There was a moment of strident silence.

Then Daiv said, tightly, "Can you tell me how to reach this spot, Meg? Can you draw me a marker-of-places that will enable me to find it?"

"I can! It lies where the great creet highways of the Ancient Ones meet with a river and an island at a vast, salt sea. But . . . but why, Daiv?"

Daiv said, "Draw me the marker-of-places, Meg. He must be destroyed. I will go to His city to find Him."

"No!" It was not Meg the Priestess who cried out; it was Meg the woman. "No, Daiv! It is an accursed city. I cannot let you go!"

"You cannot stop me, Golden One."

"But you know no spells, no incantations. He will destroy you—"

"I will destroy Him, first." The happy look clung to the corners of Daiv's lips. He drew Meg into his bronze arms, woke fire in her veins with the touching-of-mouths he had taught her. "My arm is strong, Meg; my sword keen. He must feel its bite if we are to live and prosper. You cannot change my mind."

Then Meg decided.

"Very well, Daiv. You shall go. But I will make you no marker-of-places."

"Come now, Golden One! Without it I shall not be able to find—"

Meg's voice was firm, unequivocal. "Because I shall go with you! Together we shall seek and destroy—Him!"

CHAPTER TWO

So started Meg and Daiv for the City of Death. It was not a happy parting, theirs with the men and women of the Jinnia Clan. There were tears and lamentations and sad mutterings, for all knew the law that the eastern cities of the Ancient Ones were forbidden.

There was bravery, too, and loyalty. Stern-jawed Lora, Captain of the Warriors, confronted Meg at the gate. She was clad for battle; her

50

leathern plates and buckler were newly refurbished, her sword hung at her side. Behind her stood a squad of picked warriors, packed for trek.

"We are ready, O Mother!" said Lora succinctly.

Meg smiled, a sweet, proud smile. She knew only too well the mental terror, the physical qualms of fear these women had overcome to thus offer themselves. Her heart lifted within her, but she leaned forward and with her own fingers unbuckled Lora's scabbard.

"You are needed here, my daughter," she said. "You must guard the clan till I return. And"—she faltered an instant, continued swiftly—"and if it is the will of the gods I return not, then you must continue to see that the law is obeyed until the young priestess, Haizl, is finished her novitiate and can assume leadership.

"Peace be with you all!" She pressed her lips to Lora's forehead lightly. It seemed strange to none of them that she should call the harsh-visaged chieftain, many years her senior, "my daughter." For she was the Mother, and the Mother was ageless and of all time.

Others came forward then, each in their turn to ask a farewell blessing, to offer silent prayers to the gods for Meg's safe return. Young Haizl, the clear-eyed, inquisitive twelve-year-old maiden whom Meg had selected to succeed her as matriarch of the Jinnia Clan, whispered: "Be strong, O Mother, but not too daring. Return safely, for never can I take your place."

"But you can, my daughter. Study diligently, learn the speech-without-words and the magic of the numbers. Keep the law and learn the rituals."

"I try, O Mother. But the little pain-demons dwell in my head, behind my eyes. They dance and make the letters move strangely."

"Pursue your course and they will go away."

Came 'Ana, who had been a breeding-mother before the Revelation, and who was now a happily wedded mate. Her eyes were red with weeping and she could not speak. Came Isbel, strongest of the workers, who with her bare hands had crushed the life from a mountain cat. But there was no strength in her hands now; they trembled as they touched Meg's doeskin boots. Also came Bil, eyes smoldering with hot demand.

"I would go with you to destroy Him, O Mother! It is my right. You cannot refuse me!"

"But I can and do, Bil."

Bil said rebelliously, "I am a man, strong, brave. I fought beside Daiv when the Japcans attacked. Ask him if I am not a great fighter."

"That I know without asking. But now we fight an invisible foe. Of all the clan, only Daiv and I can stand before Him. I am a Mother, inviolate; Daiv is sprung of an ancient, sacred tribe. The Kirki tribe, dwelling in the Land of the Escape.

"And now—farewell—"

But after they had left the town, Daiv repeated his objections, voiced many times in the hours preceding this.

"Go back, Golden One! This is a man's task. He is a potent enemy. Go back to the clan, wait for my return—"

Meg said, as if not hearing him, "See, the road lies before us. The broken creet road of the Ancient Ones."

It was not a long journey. Only eight days' march, according to Meg's calculations. Scarce one fifth of the distance she had covered in her pilgrimage to the Place of the Gods in 'Kota territory a year before. And Daiv was an experienced traveler; alone, he had wandered through most of Tizathy from sun-parched 'Vadah to bleak Wyomin, from the lush jungles of Flarduh to the snow-crested mountains of Orgen. Only this one path he had never trod, for all tribes in wide Tizathy knew the law, that the east was forbidden.

So their journey was one filled with many wonders. It was difficult walking on the crumbled creet highways of the Ancient Ones, so Meg and Daiv walked in the fields but kept the white rock roadbed in sight. They passed through an abandoned village named Lextun or Veémi— the old name for it was confused in the records—and another known as Stantn. Only by the intersections of the roads could they tell these towns had once been. No hoams stood; grass ran riot where once had been fertile fields and pasture land.

On the morning of the fourth day they took a wrong turning, departed from the high plateau and climbed eastward into a blue and smoky ridge of mountain. Here they found a great marvel. High in the hills they came upon the broken walls of an ancient shrine, stone heaped upon stone, creet holding the blocks together. Spiked with god-metal on one wall was a green-molded square. Daiv, scraping this out of curiosity, uncovered oddly shaped letters in the language. The letters read:

URAY CAVER
—dmiss——One dol—

Beyond the shrine was a huge hole, leading deep into the bowls of the earth. Daiv would have gone into it, seeking a fuller explanation of this wonder, but cold dampness seeped from the vent, and the stir of his footsteps at the entrance roused a myriad of loathsome bats from below.

Meg understood, then, and dragged Daiv from the accursed spot hastily.

"This is the abode of one of their Evil Gods," she explained. "The bats are souls of his worshipers. We must not tarry here."

And they fled, retracing their steps to the point at which they had made the wrong turning. But as they ran, Meg, to be on the safe side, made a brief, apologetic prayer to the dark god, Uray Caver.

Oh, many were the wonders of that journey. Perhaps most wondrous of all—at least most unexpected of all—was their discovery of a clan living far to the north and east, near the end of their sixth day's travel.

It was Daiv who first noted signs of human habitation. They had crossed a narrow strip of land which, from a rusted place of god-metal, Meg identified as part of the Maerlun territory, when Daiv suddenly halted his priestess with a silencing gesture.

"Golden One—a fire! A campfire!"

Meg looked, and a slow, shuddering apprehension ran through her veins. He was right in all save one thing. It could not be a *campfire*. Flame there was, and smoke. But in this forbidden territory smoke and flame could mean only—a charnel fire! For they were nearing His abode. Meg's nostrils sought the air delicately, half-afraid of the scent that might reach them.

Then, surprisingly, a happy sound was breaking from Daiv's throat, he was propelling her forward.

"They are men, Golden One! Men and women living in peace and harmony! The message of the Revelation must somehow have penetrated even these forbidden regions. Come!"

But a great disappointment awaited them. For when they met the strange clanspeople, they found themselves completely unable to converse with them. Only one thing could Meg and Daiv learn. That they called their village Lankstr. Their tribal name they never revealed, though Daiv believed they called themselves Nikvars.

Meg was bitterly chagrined.

"If they could only speak the language, Daiv, they could tell us something about His city. They live so near. But perhaps—" She looked doubtful. "Do you think maybe they worship—Him?"

Daiv shook his head.

"No, Golden One. These Nikvars speak a coarse, animal tongue, but I think they are a kindly folk. They have never received the Revelation, yet they live together in the fashion of the Ancient Ones. They plow the fields and raise livestock. They have sheltered and fed us, offered us fresh clothing. They cannot be His disciples. This is another of the many, many mysteries of Tizathy. One that we must some day solve."

And the next morning they left the camp of their odd hosts. They bore with them friendly gifts of salt and bacca, and a damp-pouch filled with a strange food, krowt. And with the quaint Nikvar farewell ringing in their ears, "Veedzain! O Veedzain!," they continued their way east into a territory avoided and feared for thrice five centuries.

Through Lebnun and Alntun, skirting a huge pile of masonry that Meg's marker-of-places indicated as "Lizbeth," up the salt-swept marshes of the Joysy flatlands. The salt air stung their inland nostrils strangely, and the flatland air oppressed Meg's mountain-bred lungs, but she forgot her physical discomforts in the marvels to be seen.

And then, on the morning of the tenth day, the red lance of the dawning sun shattered itself on a weird, light-reflecting dreadfulness a scant ten miles away. Something so strange, so unnatural, so absolutely incredible that it took Meg's breath away, and she could only clutch her mate's arm, gasping and pointing.

Hoams! But such hoams! Great, towering buildings that groped sharded fingers into the very bosom of the sky; hoams of god-metal and creet—red with water-hurt, true—but still intact. Some of them— Meg closed her eyes, then opened them again and found it was still so—must have been every bit of two hundred, three hundred feet in height!

And as from afar, she heard Daiv's voice repeating the ancient description.

" 'It lies where the great creet highways of the Ancient Ones meet with a river and an island at a vast, salt sea.' This is it, Meg! We have found it, my Golden One!"

The sun lifted higher, spilling its blood upon the forbidden village. There was ominous portent in that color, and for the first time fear crept from its secret lurking place in Meg's heart, ran on panicky feet to her brain. She faltered, "It . . . it is His city, Daiv. See, even the hoams are bleached skeletons from which He has stripped the flesh. Think you, we should go on?"

Daiv made a happy sound deep in his throat. Still it was not altogether a happy sound; there was anger in it, and courage, and defiance.

He said, "We go on, Golden One! My sword thirsts for His defeat!"

And swiftly, eagerly, he pressed onward. Thus came Meg and Daiv to the City of Death.

CHAPTER THREE

It was not so easy to effect entry into the city as Meg had expected. According to the old marker-of-places she had brought, a city was connected with the road by a tunl. Meg did not know what a tunl was, but clearly it had to be some sort of bridge or roadway.

There was nothing such here. The road ended abruptly at a great hole in the ground, similar to that which they had seen at the shrine of Uray Caver, except that this one was begemmed with glistening creet platters, and everywhere about it were queer oblongs of god-metal scored with cryptic runes. Prayers. "O Left Tur," said one; "O Parki," another.

Daiv glanced at Meg querulously, but she shook her head. These were—or appeared to be—in the language, but their meanings were lost in the mists of time. Lost, too, was the significance of that gigantic magic spell carven in solid stone at the mouth of the hole—

N.Y.—MCMXXVII—N.J.

Discouraged but undaunted, Meg and Daiv turned away from the hole. Fortunately this was uncivilized territory; the forest ran right down to the water's edge. It eased the task of hewing small trees, building a raft with which they might cross the river.

This they did in the daytime, working with muffled axes lest He hear, investigate, and thwart their plans to invade His domain.

At night they crept back into the forest to build a camp. While Daiv went out and caught game, a fat young wild pig, Meg baked fresh biscuit, boiled maters she found growing wild in a nearby glade, and brewed cawfee from their rapidly dwindling store of that fragrant bean.

The next day they worked again on their craft, and the day after that. And at last the job was completed. Daiv looked upon it and pronounced it good. So at dusk they pushed it into the water. And when the icy moon invaded the sky, forcing the tender sun to flee before its barrage of silver hoar-shakings, they set out for the opposite shore.

Without incident, they attained their goal. Behind a thicket, Daiv moored their rough craft; each committed the location to memory. Then they climbed the stone-rubbled bank, and stood at last in the City of Death, on the very portals of His lair.

Nor was there any doubt that this *was* death's city. So far as the eye could see or the ear hear, there was no token of life. Harsh, jumbled blocks of creet scraped tender their soles, and there was no blade of grass to soften that moon-frozen severity. About and around and before them were countless aged hoams; their doors were gasping mouths, their shutterless windows like vast, blank eyes. They moved blindly forward, but no hare sprang, startled, from an unseen warren before them; no night bird broke the tomblike silence with a melancholy cry.

Only the faint breath of the wind, stirring through the great avenues of emptiness, whispered them caution in a strange, sad sigh.

A great unease weighted Meg's mind, and in the gloom her hand caught that of Daiv as they pressed ever forward into the heart of Death's citadel. High corridors abutted them on either side; by instinct, rather than sense, they pursued a northward path.

A thousand questions filled Meg's heart, but in this hallowed place she could not stir her lips to motion. But as she walked, she wondered, marveled, at the Ancient Ones who, it was told, had built and lived in this great stone village.

Perhaps the creet roadbed on which they walked had once been smooth, as the legends told, though Meg doubted it. Surely not even the ages could have so torn creet into jagged boulders, deep-pitted and sore. And why should the Ancient Ones have deliberately pockmarked their roads with holes, and at the bottom of these holes placed broken tubes of red god-metal?

Why, too, should the Ancient Ones have built hoams that, probing the sky, still were roofless, and had in many places had their façades stripped away so that beneath the exterior showed little square cubicles, like rooms? Or why should the Ancient Ones have placed long laths of metal in the middle of their walk-avenues? Was it, Meg wondered, because they feared the demons? And had placed these bars to fend them off? All demons, Meg knew, feared god-metal, and would not cross it—

How long they trod those deserted thoroughfares Meg could not tell. Their path was generally northward, but it was a devious one because Daiv, great-eyed with wonder, was ever moved to explore some mysterious alley. Once, even, he braved destruction by creeping furtively into the entrance of a hoam consecrated to a god with a harsh-sounding foreign name, Mcmxl, but from there Meg begged him to withdraw, lest He somehow divine their presence.

Yet it was Daiv's insatiable curiosity that found a good omen for them. Well within the depths of the city, he stumbled across the first patch of life they had found. It was a tiny square of green, surmounted on all sides by bleak desolation. Yet from its breast of high, rank jungle grass soared a dozen mighty trees, defiantly quick in the City of the Dead. Meg dropped to her knees at this spot, kissed the earth and made a prayer to the familiar gods of her clan.

And she told Daiv, "Remember well this spot. It is a refuge, a sanctuary. Perhaps, then, even He is not invulnerable, if life persists in His fortress. Should we ever be parted, let us meet here."

She marked the spot on her marker-of-places. From a plaque of the Ancient Ones, she learned its name. It was called Madinsqua.

Through the long night they trod the city streets, but when the first faint edge of gray lifted night's shadow in the east, Daiv strangled in his throat and made a tired mouth. Then Meg, suddenly aware of her own fatigue, remembered they must not meet their powerful foe in this state.

"We must rest, Daiv. We must be strong and alert when we come face to face with Him."

Daiv demanded, "But where, Golden One? You will not enter one of the hoams—"

"The hoams are taboo," said Meg piously, "but there are many temples. Behold, there lies a great one before us now. I am a Priestess and a Mother; all temples are refuge to me. We shall go there."

So they went into the mighty, colonnaded building. And it was, indeed, a temple. Through a long corridor they passed, down many steps, and at last into the towering vault of the sacristan.

Here, once, on the high niches about the walls, there had stood statues of the gods. Now most of these had been dislodged, their shards lay upon the cracked tiles beneath. Yet a few stood, and beneath centuries of dust and dirt the adventurers could still see the faded hues of ancient paint.

The floor of the sacristan was one vast crater; a wall had crashed to earth and covered the confessionals of the priests. But above their heads was suspended an awesome object—a huge, round face around the rim of which appeared symbols familiar to Meg.

Daiv's eyes asked Meg for an answer.

"It is a holy sign," Meg told him. "Those are the numbers that make and take away. I had to learn them when I was a priestess. There is great magic in them." And while Daiv stood silent and respectful, she chanted them as it was ordained, "One—two—three—"

The size of this temple wakened greater awe in Meg than anything she had heretofore seen. She knew, now, that it must have been a great and holy race that lived here before the Great Disaster, for thousands could stand in the sacristan alone without crowding; in addition, there were a dozen smaller halls and prayer rooms, many of which had once been provided with seats. The western wall of the cathedral was lined with barred gates; on these depended metal placards designating the various sects who were permitted to worship here. One such, more legible than the rest, bore the names of communities vaguely familiar to Meg.

> The Sportsman—12:01
> Newark
> Philadelphia
> Washington
> Cincinnati

This was, of course, the ancient language, but Meg thought she could detect some similarity to names of present-day clans. She and Daiv had, themselves, come through a town called Noork on their way here, and the elder legends told of a Fideffia, the City of Endless Sleep, and a Sinnaty, where once had ruled a great people known as the Reds.

But it would have been sacrilege to sleep in these hallowed halls. At Meg's advice they sought refuge in one of the smaller rooms flanking the corridor through which they had entered the temple. There were many of these, and one was admirably adapted to their purpose; it was the tiny prayer room of a forgotten god, Ited-Ciga. There was, in this room, a miraculously undamaged dais on which they could sleep.

They had eaten, but had not slaked their thirst in many hours. Daiv was overjoyed to find a black drink-fountain set into one of the walls, complete with a mouthpiece and a curiously shaped cup, but try as he might, he could not force the spring to flow.

It, too, was magic; at its base was a dial of god-metal marked with the numbers and letters of the language. Meg made an incantation over it, and when the water refused to come, Daiv, impatient, beat upon the mouth part. Rotten wood split from the wall, the entire fountain broke from its foundation and tumbled to the floor, disclosing a nest of inexplicable wires and metal fragments.

As it fell, from somewhere within it tumbled many circles of stained metal, large and small. Meg, seeing one of these, prayed the gods to forgive Daiv's impatience.

"The fountain would not flow," she explained, "because you did not make the fitting sacrifice. See? These are the tributes of the Ancient Ones. White pieces, carven with the faces of the gods: the Red god, the buffalo god"—her voice deepened with awe—"even great Taamuz, himself! I remember his face from the Place of the Gods.

"Aie, Daiv, but they were a humble and god-fearing race, the Ancient Ones!"

And there, in the massive pantheon of.Ylvania Stat, they slept—

Meg started from slumber suddenly, some inner awareness rousing her to a sense of indefinable malease. The sun was high in the heavens, the night-damp had passed. But as she sat up, her keen ears caught again the sound that had awakened her, and fear clutched her kidneys.

Daiv, too, had been awakened by the sound. Beside her he sat upright, motioning her to silence. His lips made voiceless whisper.

"Footsteps!"

Meg answered, fearfully, "His footsteps?"

Daiv slipped to the doorway, disappeared. Minutes passed, and continued to pass until Meg, no longer able to await his return, followed him. He was crouched behind the doorway of the temple, staring down the avenue up which they had marched the preceding night. He felt her breath on his shoulder, pointed silently.

It was not Him. But it was someone almost as dangerous. A little band of His worshipers—all men. It was obvious that they were His followers, for in addition to the usual breechclout and sandals worn by all clansmen, these wore a gruesome decoration—necklaces of human bone! Each of them—and there must have been six or seven—carried as a weapon His traditional arm, a razor-edged sword, curved in the shape of a scythe!

They had halted beside the entrance to a hooded cavern, similar to dozens such which Meg and Daiv had passed the night before, but had not dared investigate. Now two of them ducked suddenly into the cavernous depths. After a brief period of time, two sounds split the air simultaneously. The triumphant cry of masculine voices, and the high, shrill scream of a woman!

And from the cave mouth, their lips drawn back from their teeth in evil, happy looks, emerged the raiders. Behind them they dragged the fighting, clawing figure of a woman.

Meg gasped, her thoughts churned into confusion by a dozen conflicting emotions. Amazement that in this City of Death should be found living humans. The ghouls, His followers, she could understand. But not the fact that this woman seemed as normal as her own Jinnians.

Second, a frightful anger that anyone, *anything*, should thus dare lay forceful hands upon a woman. Meg was of the emancipated younger generation; she had accepted the new principle that men were women's equals. But, still—

Her desire to do something labored with her fright. But before either could gain control of her muscles, action quickened the tableau. There came loud cries from below the ground, the sound of clanking harness, the surge of racing feet. And from the cavern's gorge charged the warriors of this stranger clan, full-panoplied, enraged, to the rescue of their comrade.

The invaders were ready for them. One had taken a position at each side of the entrance, another had leaped to its metallic roof. As the first warriors burst from the cave mouth, three scythe swords swung as one. Blood spurted. A headless torso lurched forward a shambling pace, pitched to earth, lay still. Again the scythes lifted.

Daiv could stand no more. A rage-choked roar broke from his lips, his swift motion upset Meg. And on feet that flew, sword drawn, clenched in his right fist, bellowing his wrath, he charged forward into the unequal fray!

CHAPTER FOUR

Nor was Meg far behind him. She was a Priestess and a Mother, but in her veins, as in the veins of all Jinnians, flowed ever the quicksilver battle lust. Her cry was as loud as his, her charge as swift. Like twin lances of vengeance they bore down upon the invaders from the rear.

The minions of Death spun, startled. For an instant stark incredulity stunned them to quiescence; that immobility cost their leader his life. For even as his scattered wits reassembled, his lips framed commands to his followers, Daiv was upon him.

It was no hooked and awkward scythe Daiv wielded; it was a long sword, keen and true. Its gleaming blade flashed in the sunlight, struck at the leader's breast like the fang of a water viper—and when it met sunlight again, its gleam was crimson.

Now Daiv's sword parried an enemy hook; his foeman, weaponless and mad with fright, screamed aloud and tried to stave off the dripping edge of doom. His bare hands gripped Daiv's blade in blind, inchoate defense. The edge bit deep, grotesque-angled fingers fell to the ground like bloodworms crawling, bright ribbons of blood spurted from severed palms.

All this in the single beat of a pulse. Then Meg, too, was upon the invaders; her sword thirsted and drank beside that of her mate. And the battle was over almost before it began. Even as the vanguard of clanswomen, taking heart at this unexpected relief, came surging from the cave mouth, a half dozen bodies lay motionless on the creet, their blood enscarleting its drab. But one remained, and he, eyes wide, mouth slack in awestruck fear, turned and fled down the long avenue on feet lent wings by terror.

Then rose the woman whom the invaders had attempted to linber; in her eyes was a vast respect. She stared first at Daiv, uncertain, unbelieving. Then she turned to Meg and made low obeisance.

"Greetings and thanks, O Woman from Nowhere! Emma, Gard of the Be-Empty, pledges now her life and hand, which are truly yours."

She knelt to kiss Meg's hand. Then deepened her surprise, for she gasped:

"But . . . but you are a Mother! You wear the Mother's ring!"

Meg said quietly, "Yes, my daughter. I am Meg, the Mother of the Jinnia Clan, newly come to the City of Death."

"Jinnia Clan!" It was the foremost of the rescuers who spoke now; by her trappings Meg knew her to be a lootent of her tribe. "What is this Jinnia Clan, O Mother? Whence come you, and how—"

Meg said, "Peace, woman! It is not fitting that a clanswoman should make queries of a Mother. But lead me to your Mother. With her I would speak."

The lootent flushed. Apologetically, "Forgive me, Mother. Swiftly shall I lead you to our Mother, Alis. But what—" She glanced curiously at Daiv, who, the battle over, was now methodically wiping his stained blade on the hem of his clout. "But what shall I do with this man-thing? It is surely not a breeding-male; it fights and acts like a Wild One."

Meg smiled.

"He is not a man-thing, my child. He is a man—a true man. Take me to your Mother, and to her I will explain this mystery."

Thus it was that, shortly after, Meg and Daiv spoke with Alis in her private chamber deep in the bowels of the earth beneath the City of Death. There was great wonder in the Mother's eyes and voice, but there was respect, too, and understanding in the ear she lent Meg's words.

Meg told her the tale of the Revelation. Of how she, when yet Meg the Priestess, had made pilgrimage, as was the custom of her clan, to the far-off Place of the Gods.

"Through blue-sworded Tucky and Zurrie I traveled, O Alis; many days I walked through the flat fields of Braska territory. In this journey was I accompanied by Daiv, then a stranger, now my mate, who had rescued me from a Wild One. And at last I reached the desolate grottoes of distant 'Kota, and there, with my own eyes, looked upon the carven stone faces of the gods of the Ancient Ones. Grim Jarg, the sad-eyed Ibrim, ringleted Taamuz, and far-seeing Tedhi, He who laughs—"

Alis made a holy sign.

"You speak a mighty wonder, O Meg. These are gods of our clan, too, though none made your pilgrimage. But we worship still another god, whose temple lies not far away. The mighty god, Granstoom. But—this secret you learned?"

"Hearken well, Alis, and believe," said Meg, "for I tell you truth. The gods of the Ancient Ones—were *men!*"

"Men!" Alis half rose from her seat. Her hands trembled. "But surely, Meg, you are mistaken—"

"No. The mistake occurred centuries ago, Mother of another clan. Daiv, who comes from the sacred Land of the Escape, has taught me the story.

"Long, long ago, all Tizathy was ruled by the great Ancient Ones. Mighty were they, and skilled in forgotten magics. They could run on the ground with the speed of the woodland doe; great, wheeled horses they built for this purpose. They could fly in the air on birds made of god-metal. Their hoams probed the clouds, they never labored except on the play-field; their life was one of gay amusement, spent in chanting into boxes that carried their voices everywhere and looking at pictures-that-ran.

"But in another world across the salt water from Tizathy were still other men and women. Amongst them were evil ones, restless, impatient, fretful, greedy. These, in an attempt to rule the world, created a great war. We cannot conceive the war of the Ancient Ones. They brought all their magics into play.

"The men met on gigantic battlefields, killed each other with smoke and flame and acid and smell-winds. And at hoam, the women—in secret magic-chambers called labteries—made for them sticks-that-spit-fire and great eggs that hatched death."

"It is hard to believe, O Meg," breathed Alis, "but I do believe. I have read certain cryptic records of the Ancient Ones—but go on."

"Came at last the day," continued Meg, "when Tizathy itself entered this war. But when their mates and children had gone to Him by the scores of scores of scores, the women rebelled. They banded together, exiled all men forevermore, set up the matriarchal form of government, keeping only a few weak and infant males as breeders.

"When they could no longer get the fire-eggs or the spit-sticks, the men came back to Tizathy. Then ensued years of another great war between the sexes—but in the end, the women were triumphant.

"The rest you know. The men, disorganized, became Wild Ones, roving the jungles in search of food, managing to recreate themselves with what few clanswomen they linberred from time to time. Our civilization persisted, but many of the old legends and most of the old learning was gone. We finally came to believe that *never* had the men ruled; that it was right and proper for women to rule; that the very gods were women.

"But this," said Meg stanchly, "is not so. For I have brought back from the Place of the Gods the Revelation. Now I spread the word. It is the duty of all clans to bring the Wild Ones out of the forests, make them their mates, so our people may one day reclaim our deserved heritage."

There was a long silence.

Then asked Alis, "I must think deeply on this, O Meg. But you spoke of the Land of the Escape. What is that?"

"It is the hot lands to the south. Daiv comes from there. It is a sacred place, for from there—from the heart of Zoni—long ago a Wise One named Renn foresaw the end of the civilization of the Ancient Ones.

"In the bowels of a monstrous bird, he and a chosen few escaped Earth itself, flying to the evening star. They have never been heard of since. But some day they will come back. We must prepare for their coming; such is the law."

Alis nodded somberly.

"I hear and understand, O Mother to whom the truth has been revealed. But . . . but I fear that never can we make peace with the Wild Ones of Loalnyawk. You have seen them, fought them. You know they are vicious and untamed."

Meg had been so engrossed in spreading the news of the Revelation, she had almost forgotten her true mission. Now it flooded back upon her like an ominous pall. And she nodded.

"Loalnyawk? Is that what you call the City of Him? Perhaps you are right, Mother Alis. It would be impossible to mate with the children who worship Death as a master."

"Death?" Alis' head lifted sharply. "Death, Meg? I do not understand. They do not worship Death, but Death's mistress. They worship the grim and savage warrior goddess, the fearful goddess, Salibbidy."

"Her," said Meg dubiously, "I never heard of. But you speak words unhappy to my ear, O Alis. A long way have Daiv and I come to do battle with Him who nips the fairest buds of our clan. Now you tell me this is not His city—

"Aie, but you must be mistaken! Of a certainty it is His city. His tumbled desolation reigns everywhere."

Alis made a thought-mouth.

"You force me to wonder, Meg. Perhaps He is here. Of a truth, He takes many of us to whom He has no right. A moon ago He claimed the Priestess Kait, who was young, happy, in wondrous good health.

"A sweet and holy girl, inspired by the gods. Only the day before had she been in commune with them; her tender young body atremble with ecstasy, her eyes rapt, her lips wet with the froth of their knowledge. Oft did she experience these sacred spells, and I had planned a great future for her. But—" Alis sighed and shook her head. "He came and took her even as she communed with the gods. It was a foul deed and brutal."

Daiv said grimly, "And by that we know that this *is* His city, indeed. For where else would He be so powerful and so daring?"

"Yes," said Alis, "the more I think on it, the more I believe you are right. Above ground must be His domains. We have not guessed the truth, because for countless ages we have dwelt in the tiled corridors of Be-Empty."

"Tell us more," demanded Daiv, He-who-would-learn, "about the halls of Be-Empty. Why are they called that?"

"I know not, Daiv. It is the ancient name, yet the corridors are *not* empty. They are a vast network of underground passages, built by the Ancient Ones for mystic rites we no longer know. Great wonders are here, as I will later show you.

"These corridors are tiled with shining creet, and upon their roadbeds lie parallels of god-metal, red and worn. Aie, and there is a greater wonder still! From place to place I can show you ancient hoams, with doors and many windows and seats. These hoams were tied together with rods of god-metal, and whensoever the Ancient Ones would move, they had but to push their hoams along the parallels to a new location!

"Once we were not all one clan, but many. There were the Women of the In-Deeps, and there were the Aiyartees. But we were the strongest, and we welded all the livers-underground into one strong clan.

"We have many villages, wide creet plateaus built on the sunken roadways of the Ancient Ones. Each village has its entrance to the city above, forbidden Loalnyawk, but we use these only when urgency presses. For there are openings aplenty to the sun, there are streams of fresh water. Safe from the Wild Ones above, we raise our vegetables and a few meat-animals.

"Yet," continued Alis proudly, "there is no spot in all Loalnyawk to which we have not ready access should it be necessary to get there. Above ground there are many shrines like that of great Granstoom and the fallen tower of Arciay. There is also the Citadel of Clumby to the north, and not far from where we now sit could I show you the Temple of Shoobut, where each year the Ancient Ones sacrificed a thousand virgins to their gods. There is the forbidden altar of Slukes—"

The Mother's mouth stayed in midsentence. Her eyes widened.

"Slukes!" she repeated awfully.

"Well?" Meg and Daiv leaned forward, intent.

"That must be it! In the ancient legends it tells that there was where He visited most often. That must be His present lair and hiding place!"

"Then there," proclaimed Daiv, "we must go!"

CHAPTER FIVE

Meg stumbled on a sharp stone, lurched against Daiv and steadied herself on his reassuring presence. Her eyes had become somewhat accustomed to the endless gloom, now, though they ached and burned with the concentration of peering into murky blackness, then having the blackness lighted from time to time, unexpectedly, by a shaft of golden sunlight flooding into the corridors of Be-Empty from the city above.

Her feet, though, thought Meg disconsolately, would never accustom themselves to this jagged, uneven roadbed. She had been told to walk between the parallels of god-metal, for that was the best, driest, safest walking. Maybe it was. But it was treacherous. For there were creet crossties on which her doeskin-clad feet bruised themselves, and ever and again there were rocks and boulders lying unsuspectedly in the road.

How far they had come, Meg had no way of guessing. It must have been many miles. They had passed, easily, twoscore tiny, raised villages of the Be-Empty Clan. At each of these they had tarried a moment while the warrior lootent, under whose guidance Alis had dispatched a small foray party at Meg's disposal, made known herself and her mission.

Meg panted, hating the heavy, stuffy air her lungs labored to suck in, fuming at the slowness of their march, eager only to reach their destination. It did not improve her temper to slip on a round rock, submerge one foot to the ankle in a stream of sluggish water. Of the lootent she demanded, "How much farther, my daughter?"

"We are nearly there, O Mother."

Daiv grunted. It was a think-grunt. Meg tried to see him, but in the darkness his face was a white blur.

"Yes, Daiv?"

"There's more to this than meets the eye, Golden One. These passageways are not the purposeless corridors Alis thought. I was wondering—"

"Yes?"

"Well—it sounds ridiculous. But do you remember those hoams on wheels? The ones with the windows? Suppose the Ancient Ones had the magic power to make them run like horses along these parallels?"

Meg shrugged.

"But why should they, Daiv? When it would have been so much simpler to make them run on top of the earth? These grottoes were built for some sacred purpose, my mate."

"I suppose you're right," acknowledged Daiv. But he didn't sound convinced. Sometimes Meg grew a little impatient with Daiv. He was, like all men, such a hard creature to convince. He couldn't reason things out in the cold, clear, logical fashion of a woman; he kept insisting that his "masculine intuition" told him otherwise.

Much time had passed. They had broken fast at the hoam of the Mother, and had eaten a midday meal here in the depths of Be-Empty. The last opening under which they had passed revealed that the sun was being swallowed by the westward clouds; for twelve hours it would pass through the belly of the sky, then miraculously, tomorrow, a new sun would be reborn in the east.

So it was almost night when the lootent halted at a tiny, deserted creet platform, turned and touched her forehead to Meg.

"This is it, O Mother."

"This?" Meg glanced about. There was nothing unusual about this location.

"Above this spot lies the forbidden altar of Slukes. I . . . I fear—" The lootent's eyes were troubled. "I fear I dare take you no farther, O Mother. You and your man are inviolate; I and my warriors are but humble women. That which lies above would be destruction for us to gaze upon."

Meg nodded complacently.

"So be it, my daughter. We shall leave you now, go to dare Him in His den."

The lootent said, "We shall wait, Mother—"

"Wait not, my child. Return to your village."

"Very well, Mother. Your blessing ere we leave?"

Meg gave it, touching her fingers to the lips and the forehead of the kneeling lootent, chanting the hallowed phrases of the Ancient Ones' blessing. " 'My country, Tizathy; sweet land of liberty—' " Then there were stifled footsteps in the gloom and Meg and Daiv were alone.

Only briefly did Meg consider the possibility of entering His temple at this time—and then she abandoned the project. It would be suicidal. Everyone knew He was strongest at night. His powers waned with the waxing sun. So she and Daiv built a tiny fire in the quarters of a long-vanished warrior named Private Keepout, and there huddled together through the long, dank, fearsome night.

They awakened with the sun, broke their fast with unleavened biscuit given them by Alis. Daiv, who was expert at such matters, then examined with painstaking care their swords and hurling-leathers. He approved these. And as if feeling within his own breast an echo of the dread that fluttered in Meg's, he pressed his lips hard against hers in a touching-of-mouths. Then, hand in hand, they climbed a long flight of steps, into the sunlight, forward to the threshold of His stronghold.

It was a majestic building.

How many footsteps long and wide it was, Meg could not even conceive. It reached half as far as the eye would reach in one direction; in the other, it branched into many smaller buildings. And it was pine-high. An awe-inspiring sight.

Daiv, standing beside her, stared dubiously at the main portal. He said, "This may not be the place, Meg. Alis said the name of the temple was Slukes, didn't she? This is called—" He glanced again at the weather-worn carving atop the doorway. "This is called Stlukes."

Again, as oft before, Meg felt swift pride at her mate's intelligence. Daiv was a living proof that men were the equals—or almost, anyway —of women. It had taken her many, many summers to learn the art of reading the speech-without-words; he had assimilated the knowledge from her in a tenth the time.

"It is the right place, Daiv," she whispered. "The Ancient Ones were often careless in putting down the language. But can you not *feel* that this is His abode?"

For she could. Those grim, gray walls breathed an atmosphere of death and decay. The bleached walls were like the picked bones of a skeleton lying in some forgotten field. And the great, gaping vents of windows, the sagging lintels, the way one portion of roof had fallen in—there were marks of his dominance. Meg did not even need the omen of the red-throated carrion buzzard wheeling lazily ever and ever about the horrid altar of Slukes.

"Come," she said, "let us enter."

Daiv held back. There were anxious lines about his eyes. "He does not speak, Meg?"

"No one has ever heard His voice, Daiv. Why?"

"I thought I heard voices. But I must have made a mistake. Well"—he shrugged—"it does not matter."

Thus they entered the secret hiding place of Death.

All the great courts lay silent.

What Meg had expected to see, she did not rightly know. Perhaps a charnel house of human bodies, dismembered and gory, raw with frightful cicatrices, oozing filth from sick and rotting sores. Or perhaps that even more dreadful thing, chambers in which were imprisoned the mournful souls of the dead. Against flesh and blood, no matter how frightful, Meg knew her courage would hold. But she did not know whether her nerves would stand before the dim restlessness of the gray unalive.

She found neither of these in the temple of Slukes. She found only floors and walls and ceilings which had once been shining white, but were now gray with ages of floating dust. She found her footsteps muffled beneath her upon a mat of substance, now crumbling, but still resilient to the soles. She found silence, silence, silence that beat upon her eardrums until it was a tangible, terrifying sound.

And finding that, she took comfort in Daiv's keen, questing, ever-forward search for Him.

Down a long hallway they strode on catlike feet; a chamber they passed in which heaped dust outlined the seats and stools of Ancient Ones. Past a god-metal counter they walked, and saw within its confines not one but a half-dozen water fountains like that Daiv had wrenched from the wall of Ited-Ciga's shrine.

Above their heads, from time to time, they glimpsed strange, magic pendants of green and red god-metal; beneath one of these was a greater marvel still—a pear-shaped ball with wire seeds coiled within. Transparent was the skin of this fruit, and slippery to the touch. Daiv tried to split it, hungering for a taste of its newness, but it exploded in his hands with a fearful *pop!*—and there was nothing but its stem and seeds!

The fruit itself had vanished, but the skin, as if angered, had bit Daiv's palm until the blood flowed.

Meg blessed the wound, and begged forgiveness in a swift prayer to the gods of the harvest at having destroyed the magic pear.

And they went on.

Either side of the corridor through which they moved was lined with doorways. Into one of these they looked, believing He might have hid there, but the rooms were vacant except for strange, four-legged god-metal objects humped in the middle, on which reposed parasitic coils and twists of metal twined inextricably together. Dust lay over all, and in one room more carefully shuttered, barred and sealed than the others, they saw tatters of something like homespun covering the coils. But when Meg attempted to touch this, the wind from her motion swept the gossamer cloth into nothingness.

Aie, but it was a mighty and mysterious place, this altar of Slukes, where dwelt Him who steals away the breath! There were rooms in which reposed great urns and pans of god-metal; these rooms held, also, huge metal boxes with handles on the front, and their platters were crusted with flaked and ancient grease. Meg shuddered. "Here," she whispered to Daiv, "He burnt the flesh of them He took." In the same room was a massive white box with a door. Daiv opened this, and they saw within neat metal racks. "And here," whispered Meg, "must He have stored the dwindled souls until again He hungered. But now He does not use this closet. I wonder why?"

And they went on.

Until at last, having climbed many flights of steps, Meg and Daiv came at last to the chamber they had been seeking. It lay on the story nearest the roof. Oh, but He was a methodical destroyer. The compartments in which he imprisoned His victims were all carefully labeled in the language. Contagious Ward, Infants' Ward, Maternity Ward—all these Meg saw and read, and shuddered to recognize. And this, His holy of holies, was symbolized as His workroom by the sign, Operating Room.

Once it had been a high, lofted chamber; now it wore the roof of infinity, for some antique cataclysm had opened it to the skies. Crumbled plaster and shards of brick heaped the floor.

But in its center, beneath a gigantic weapon defying description or understanding, was His bed. It could be nothing else, for even now, upon it, lay the lately slain body of a woman. Her face was a mask of frozen agony; His touch had drawn taut her throat muscles and arched her back in the final paroxysm. Her lifeless fingers gripped the sides of the bed in unrelaxing fervor.

And the room bore, amidst its clutter and confusion, unmistakable signs of recent habitation! The trappings of the newly slaughtered woman had been tossed carelessly into a corner, along with countless others. Feet, many feet, had beaten firm the rubble on the floor; in one corner, not too long since, had been a fire. And the blood that had gushed from the dead woman when her heart had been roughly hewn from her bosom still clotted the floor!

Meg cried, a little cry of terror and dismay.

"He is here, Daiv!"

Then all things happened at once. Her cry wakened ominous echoes in chambers adjacent to this. Daiv's arm was about her, pulling her away. There came the patter of footsteps, voices lifted, and the door at the farther end of the room jerked open.

And Daiv cried, "Not only He, but His ghouls! Behind me, Golden One!"

Then the deluge. A horde of Wild Ones of the same tribe as those whom they had fought two days before, charged into the room.

CHAPTER SIX

There was no taint of cowardice in the heart of Meg the Mother. Had she any fault, it was that of excess bravery. Oft before had she proven this, to her own peril. This time, Daiv's speed left her no opportunity to become a courageous sacrifice to His minions.

His quick eye measured the number of their adversaries, his battle-trained judgment worked instinctively. For an instant he hesitated, just long enough to strike down with flailing long sword the foremost of their attackers. Then he swept Meg backward with his mighty right arm, thrust her irresistibly toward a doorway at the other end of the room.

"Flee, Golden One!"

Meg had no choice. For Daiv was on her heels; his body a bulwark of defense against hers and a battering-ram of force. They reached the door, crashed it shut in the face of the charging ghouls. Daiv braced himself against it stanchly, his eyes sweeping the small chamber in which they found themselves.

"That!" he commanded. "And that other, Golden One. And that!"

His nods designated objects of furniture within the room; heavy, solid braces of god-metal. Meg bent to the task, and before Daiv's strength could fail under the now clamorous pounding on the doorway, the portal was braced and secured with the massive frames that once had been chairs, a desk, a cabinet.

Now there was time for breathing and inspection of their refuge. And Meg's soul sickened, seeing the trap into which they had let themselves.

"But, Daiv—there is no way out! There is but one door to the room. The one through which we entered!"

Daiv said, "There is a window—" and strode to it. She saw the swift, dazed shock that creased his brows, moved to his side and peered from the window.

It was an eagle's aerie in which they stood! Down, down, down, far feet below, was the sun-lit courtyard of this building. But the wall was sheer and smooth as the jowls of lean youth; no crawling insect could have dared that descent.

Daiv looked at her somberly, and his arm crept about her.

"Since we cannot flee, we must outwait them, Golden One. If we cannot get out, they, at least, cannot get in."

He did not mention the thought uppermost in his mind and in hers. That their food pouches lay far below them, in the murky grotto of Be-Empty; that they had no water. And that the shortest of sieges would render them impotent before their adversaries.

For he was Daiv, known as He-who-would-learn. And even in this moment when things looked darkest, he was roused to curiosity by the chamber in which they were immured.

It was a small and cluttered room. More dusty than most, and that was odd, because it was not open to the dust-laden air.

But Daiv, questing, discovered the reason for this. The floor was gray, not with rock dust, but with the fragments of things which—which—

"This is a great mystery, Meg. What are, or were, these things?"

Meg, too, had been staring about her. A faint suspicion was growing in her mind. She remembered a word she had heard but once in her life, and that when she was but a young girl, neophyte priestess under the former Mother.

"Shelves," she whispered. "Many long shelves, all of water-hurt god-metal. Desks. And crumbled fragments of parchment.

"Daiv, long ago the Ancient Ones had houses, rooms, in which they kept, pressed flat between cloth and boards, parchment marked with the speech-without-words. These they called—" She cudgeled her brain for the elusive word. "These they called 'lyberries.' The flat scrolls were known as 'books.' This room must have been the lyberry of Slukes."

"And in these books," said Daiv in hallowed tones, "they kept their records?"

"Aie, more than that. In them they kept all their secret knowledge. The story of their spells and magic, and of their foretelling-of-dreams."

Daiv groaned in pain as an unhappy-imp prodded his heart.

"We stand at the heart of their mysteries, but He who withers all has ripped their parchment into motes! Meg, it is a sad and bitter thing."

He saw, now, that she spoke truth. For he pawed through the piles of rotted debris; in one spot he found a frayed leather oblong from which, as he lifted it, granules of charred black sifted. Once, again, he found a single bit of parchment marked with the language, but it fell into ten million bits at the touch of his fingers.

"There have been fire and flame in this room," Meg said. "Water-hurt, and the winds of the ages. That is why no books remain. It must have happened in the wars, when the fire-eggs fell upon the building. Daiv! What are you doing?"

For Daiv, still pawing the ruins, had uncovered a large metal cabinet

70

deep-set in the wall. This alone seemed to have escaped, unhurt, whatever holocaust had destroyed all else. With a swift grunt of satisfaction, he was tearing at the handle of this cabinet.

"Don't open it, Daiv! It is a forbidden thing! It may be a trick of the Ancient Ones. Of Him——"

But Meg's warning was futile. For Daiv's fumbling fingers had solved the secret of the antique lock; creaking in protest, the door swung open to reveal, in an unlighted chamber from which a faint, musty breath of wind stirred—*books!*

Books! Books as Meg had described them. Books as Meg had learned of them from the lips of the elder Mother. Books, still encased in jackets of cloth and leather, unhurt through thrice five centuries of time, preserved, by a whim of the gods, in a locked and airless cabinet!

And again it became Meg's lot to save Daiv's life and soul, for he, manlike, impatient, paused not to placate the gods, but groped instantly for the nearest of the forbidden volumes.

Fervent were the prayers Meg made then, and swiftly, that the gods destroy him not for his eagerness. And she was rewarded graciously, for Daiv did not fall, mortally stricken, as he knelt there muttering over his find.

"Behold, Meg—the secrets of the Ancient Ones! Ah, Golden One, hurry—read to me! This speech-without-words is too mighty for my powers; only the knowledge of a Mother can tell its meaning. But, lo! here are drawings! Look, Golden One! Here is a man like me! But, behold, this is a mystery! The flesh has been stripped from his body, disclosing hordes of tiny red worms covering his carcass—but he still stands erect!

"And, see, Meg—here is a woman with white sheets of bandage about her head. What means this? And behold this man's head! It lays open from front to back, but Meg, there is no village of tiny pain-imps, and like-imps and hate-imps dwelling within! Only red worms and blue, and inside his nostrils a sponge——"

Meg took the book with trembling hands. It was as Daiv said. Here were drawings without number of men and women who, their bodies dismembered horribly, still smiled and stood erect. Little arrows pierced them, and at the end of the arrows were feathers of the language, saying magic words. *Serratus magnus—Poupart's ligament—transpyloric plane.*

And the name of the book was "Fundamental Anatomy."

In their moment of wild excitement, both Meg and Daiv had quite forgotten the danger of their situation. Now they were rudely reawakened to a memory of that danger. For the sounds outside the door of the lyberry, which had never quite ceased, now sharpened in tone. There came the sound of a voice raised in command, cries of labor redoubled, and with an echoing crash, something struck the door of their refuge!

The door trembled; the braces gave a fraction of an inch. And again the crash, the creak, the strain.

"A ram! Daiv, they are forcing the door!"

Daiv the dreamer became, swiftly, Daiv the man of action. With a single bound he was on his feet, his sword in hand. His brows were anxious.

"Take you the right side of the door, Golden One; I will guard the other. When these ghouls burst in upon us, we shall split them like pea pods—"

But a great idea had been born to Meg.

Her face glowing with a sudden happy look, she spun to face her mate.

"No, Daiv. Open the door!"

"What? Golden One, has fear softened your brain?"

"Not my brain nor my heart, beloved! But do as I say! Look you! I am a Mother and a Priestess, is it not so?"

"Yes, but—"

"And I have just discovered a mighty secret. The secret of the knowledge of the Ancient Ones."

"Still—" said Daiv.

"Would not even the underlings of Him," cried Meg, "pay greatly for this knowledge? Open the door for them, my mate! We will parley with them or with Death, Himself, for an exchange. Our lives in payment for the sharing of this secret!" Daiv might have withstood her logic, but he could not refuse the eager demand of her eyes. Like a man bedazed, he moved to the door, started, scraping the bulwark away even as the horde outside continued their assault.

When he had almost completed, the door shook before imminent collapse—

"Stand you out of sight, Daiv. I would meet them face to face."

And she took her post squarely before the door. In the hollow of her left arm she cradled the Book of Secrets. On her face was the smile of triumph, and a look of exalted glory. The door trembled; this time it split away from its hinges. Once more, now! Came the final crash, and—

"*Hold!*" cried Meg, the Priestess.

Through the oblong of the door, faces frightful with fury and blood lust, tumbled the ghouls of Death. Their hook-shaped scythes swung ready in their hands; a scream of triumph hovered on their lips. Hovered there—then trembled—then died!

And of a sudden, a miracle occurred. For the flame died from their eyes, their sword-arms fell, and as one man the attackers tumbled to their knees, groveling before Meg. A low muttering arose, was carried from man to man as the breath of the night wind is passed through the forest by the sad and whispering pines.

It was a murmur, then a cry, of fear and adoration.

"Mercy, O Goddess! Slay not your children, O Everlasting. O Goddess—great Goddess Salibbidy!"

CHAPTER SEVEN

Not in her most hopeful moment had Meg expected so sudden and complete a victory as this.

For her plan she had entertained great hopes, true, but she had wagered her life and Daiv's on the balance of an exchange. But here, suddenly, inexplicably, was utter capitulation. Surrender so complete that the leader of His warriors dared not even lift his eyes to meet hers as he slobbered his worship at her feet.

She glanced swiftly at Daiv, but for once Daiv had no knowledge in his eyes; they were as blank and questioning as her own.

Still, Meg was a Priestess and a Mother. She was a woman, too, and an opportunist. And instinct governed her actions.

She stepped to the leader's side, touched his brow with cool fingers.

"Rise, O Man! Your Goddess gives you grace."

The ghoul rose, shaken and fearful. His voice was the winnowed chaff of hope.

"Be merciful unto us, O Goddess. We did not know—we did not dream—we dared not hope for a Visitation."

Meg chose her words carefully, delivered them as a Mother intones a sacred chant, in a tone calculated to inspire dreadful awe in the hearts of her listeners.

"You have sinned mightily, O Man! You have laid siege to the holy refuge of the Goddess. You have linberred and slain women of the Be-Empty Clan, a grievous deed. You have forgotten the Faith, and have bowed down in worship before Him, the arch-enemy, Death—"

"No, O Goddess!" The contradiction was humble but sincere. "These other sins we confess, but not this last! Never have we worshipped Him! Never!"

"You dwell in His citadel."

"His citadel!" There was horror in the Wild One's voice. "We did not know it was His, O sweet Salibbidy! We live many places as we journey through Loalnyawk. Today we rested here because we had a sacrifice to make unto thee; a woman unfit for mating whom we linberred last night." His eyes pleaded with Meg's. "Was the sacrifice unpleasing to thee, gracious Salibbidy?"

"It was foul in my nostrils," said Meg sternly. "Her blood is a wound upon my heart. This is the law from this time henceforward!

There shall be no more linberring or slaying of women. Instead, there shall be a new order. You shall go to the women and make peace. They will receive you with singing and soft hands, for unto them I have given the law.

"Together, you shall form a new city. They shall come out of the caverns of Be-Empty. You and they shall reclaim the hoams of the Ancient Ones. When again I visit the village of Loalnyawk, I shall expect to see men and women living together in peace and harmony as it was in the days of old.

"Do you understand the law?"

"Yes, mighty Goddess!" The cry rose from each man.

"You will obey it?"

"We will obey it, sweet Salibbidy."

"Then go in peace, and sin no more."

The vanquished worshipers, intoning prayers of thanksgiving, crawled backward from the chamber. When the last had disappeared, and they were again alone, Meg turned to her mate. His strong arms soothed the belated trembling of her body.

"Fear not, Golden One," he whispered. "Today have you performed a miracle. In bloodless victory you have borne the Revelation to the last outpost. To the accursed and forbidden city of the Ancient Ones. To the stronghold of Him."

"But they said they did not worship Him, Daiv! And they dared not lie, believing me their Goddess. If He does not rule them, if He reigns not here, then where is He, Daiv? And why did they accept me as their Goddess? Why?"

Daiv shook his head. This was unimportant now, he thought. It was sufficient that the enemy had been overcome. There were great things to do. He returned to his cabinet, and drew from it its precious store of books—

Afterward, in the hoam of Alis, Meg learned part of the answer to her questions. When she had told Alis what had happened, and received the Mother's pledge to accept the Wild Ones' envoys in peace and good will, she told again of their sudden surrender.

"I sought but to parley with them, Mother Alis. At the door I stood, and thus I stood, waiting calmly—"

She struck the pose. Book cradled in her arm, the other arm lifted high above her head, chin lifted proudly.

And then Alis nodded. But in her eyes, too, came unexpectedly a worship-look, and she whispered brokenly, "Now I understand, O Goddess who chooses to call herself Meg, the Mother. From the beginning I felt your sanctity. I should have known then—"

She rose, led Meg to the surface above Be-Empty, now no longer forbidden territory to the women. Once there had been many and great

74

buildings here, but ancient strife had stricken them as the whirlwind hews a path through solid woodland.

Far to the southward, where the green ocean waters met the creet shores of Loalnyawk, there was a figure, dimly visible. But not so dimly visible that Meg and Daiv could not recognize it.

"There is thy image, sweet Salibbidy," whispered the Mother, Alis. "Still it stands, as it did in the days of the Ancient Ones. Forever will it stand, and you remain the Goddess of broad Tizathy."

Meg cried petulantly, "Alis, do not call me by this name, Salibbidy! I am Meg, Mother of the Jinnia Clan. Like yourself, a woman—"

A smile of mysterious understanding touched Alis' lips.

"As you will—Mother Meg," she said.

But it was strange that her head should still be bowed—

Thus it was, that with the breaking of the new dawn over the creet walls of Loalnyawk, Meg and Daiv said farewell to these friends and converts, and turned their faces south and west to the remembered green hills of Jinnia.

Nor was this a sad parting. An envoy of the men had come this morning; long had he and the Mother parleyed, and an understanding had been reached. As ever, there were women who demurred, and women who disapproved—but Meg had seen a young maiden looking with gentle, speculative eyes upon the envoy. And a grim warrior had spoken with unusually gentle warmth to one of the envoy's guards—a bristle-jowled man of fighting mold.

These things would take care of themselves, thought Meg. The new order would come about, inevitably, because the men and women, both, would wish it so—

Then the last farewell had been spoken, the final blessing given. And once more Meg and Daiv were striding the long highway to Jinnia.

Daiv was strangely silent. And strangely inattentive, too, for he was attempting a difficult task. Trying to march without watching the road before him. His eyes were in one of the many books he had brought with him; the others he wore like a huge hump on his back. He stumbled for the hundredth time, and while Meg helped him reset the pack on his shoulders she said, ruefully:

"There is but one thing I regret, Daiv! Much we accomplished, but not that one thing we came to do. We found not Him, nor destroyed Him, as we willed. And our problem is still great, for ever and again will He pluck the ripest from our harvest of living."

But Daiv shook his head.

"Not so, Golden One."

"No?"

"No, my Priestess. It has come to me that we have more than fulfilled our mission. For you see—"

75

Daiv looked at the sky and the trees and the clouds that floated above. He took a deep breath, and the air was sweet. Life flowed strongly and true in his veins, and the knowledge he was eking, laboriously, from the magical books was potent liquid in his brain.

"You see, Golden One, we were wrong. He does not, nor ever did, live in Loalnyawk. He has no hoam, for He is everywhere, waiting to claim those who violate His barriers."

Meg cried bitterly, "Then, Daiv, we are forever at His mercy! If He cannot be found and destroyed—"

"He cannot be slain, Meg—and that is well. Else the crippled, the sick, the mad, would live forever, in endless torment. But He can be fought—and in these books it tells the ways in which to do battle with Him.

"They are not the ways of magic, Golden One. Or of any magic you know. These are new ways we must study. These magics are called by strange names—serum, and vaccination, and physic. But the way of each is told in these books. One day we shall understand all the mysteries, and Death's hand will be stayed.

"Boiled water He fears, and fresh air, and cleanliness. We shall not fight Him with swords and stones, but with sunshine and fresh water and the soap of boiled fats. For so it was in the old days—"

And a great vision was in Daiv's eyes; a vision Meg saw there, and, seeing, read with wonder. Of a day to come when men and women, hand in hand, should some day climb again to assail the very heights lost by the madness of the Ancient Ones.

His shoulder touched hers, and the day was warm and the road long. Meg was afire with impatience to get back to Jinnia, to bring this new knowledge to her clan. But there was other fire within her, too, and the message could wait a little while if she and Daiv tarried in the cool of a leafy tree.

Her hands met his and clung, and she turned her lips to his in the touching-of-mouths. She was Meg, and he was Daiv, and they were man and woman. And the grass was soft and cool.

So, too, it was in the old days—

Kazam Collects

C. M. Kornbluth (1923–1958)

WHEN *Cyril Kornbluth died of a heart attack at thirty-five, science fiction lost one of its leading talents at the peak of his writing power. A product of the New York fan scene of the late thirties, he had a blacker view of the world than did most of his contemporaries, but he also developed his writing skills earlier. He constantly improved as he grew older, but even his early stories still read better and are reprinted more frequently than those of most of his friends and early collaborators. Among the outstanding examples from his teenage days are three from 1941—"The Rocket of 1955," "The Words of Guru," and "Kazam Collects."*

Stirring Science Stories lasted for just four issues, all in 1941, and Kornbluth had at least five stories (under four pseudonyms) in them. Stirring was edited by Donald Wollheim, who was later to have a profound impact on science fiction through his editorial efforts on behalf of Ace and his own DAW Books.

From *Stirring Science Stories   1941*

"Hail, jewel in the lotus," half whispered the stringy, brown person. His eyes were shut in holy ecstasy, his mouth pursed as though he were tasting the sweetest fruit that ever grew.

"Hail, jewel in the lotus," mumbled back a hundred voices in a confused backwash of sound. The stringy, brown person turned and faced his congregation. He folded his hands.

"Children of Hagar," he intoned. His voice was smooth as old ivory and had a mellow sheen about it.

"Children of Hagar, you who have found delight and peace in the bosom of the Elemental, the Eternal, the Un-knowingness that is without bounds, make Peace with me." You could tell by his very voice that the words were capitalized.

"Let our Word," intoned the stringy, brown person, "be spread. Let our Will be brought about. Let us destroy, let us mould, let us build. Speak low and make your spirits white as Hagar's beard." With a reverent gesture he held before them two handfuls of an unattached beard that hung from the altar.

"Children of Hagar, unite your Wills into One." The congregation kneeled as he gestured at them, gestured as one would at a puppy one was training to play dead.

The meeting hall—or rather, temple—of the Cult of Hagar was on the third floor of a little building on East 59th Street, otherwise almost wholly unused. The hall had been fitted out to suit the sometimes peculiar requirements of the unguessable Will-Mind-Urge of Hagar Inscrutable; that meant that there was gilded wood everywhere there could be, and strips of scarlet cloth hanging from the ceiling in circles of five. There was, you see, a Sanctified Ineffability about the unequal lengths of the cloth strips.

The faces of the congregation were varying studies in rapture. As the stringy, brown person tinkled a bell they rose and blinked absently at him as he waved a benediction and vanished behind a door covered with chunks of gilded wood.

The congregation began to buzz quietly.

"Well?" demanded one of another. "What did you think of it?"

"I dunno. Who's *he*, anyway?" A respectful gesture at the door covered with gilded wood.

"Kazam's his name. They say he hasn't touched food since he saw the Ineluctable Modality."

"What's *that?*"

Pitying smile. "You couldn't understand it just yet. Wait till you've come around a few more times. Then maybe you'll be able to read *his* book—'The Unravelling.' After that you can tackle the 'Isba Kazhlunk' that he found in the Siberian ice. It opened the way to the Ineluctable Modality, but it's pretty deep stuff—even for me."

They filed from the hall buzzing quietly, dropping coins into a bowl that stood casually by the exit. Above the bowl hung from the ceiling strips of red cloth in a circle of five. The bowl, of course, was covered with chunks of gilded wood.

Beyond the door the stringy, brown man was having a little trouble. Detective Fitzgerald would not be convinced.

78

"In the first place," said the detective, "you aren't licensed to collect charities. In the second place this whole thing looks like fraud and escheatment. In the third place this building isn't a dwelling and you'll have to move that cot out of here." He gestured disdainfully at an army collapsible that stood by the battered rolltop desk. Detective Fitzgerald was a big, florid man who dressed with exquisite neatness.

"I am sorry," said the stringy, brown man. "What must I do?"

"Let's begin at the beginning. The Constitution guarantees freedom of worship, but I don't know if they meant something like this. Are you a citizen?"

"No. Here are my registration papers." The stringy, brown man took them from a cheap, new wallet.

"Born in Persia. Name's Joseph Kazam. Occupation, scholar. How do you make that out?"

"It's a good word," said Joseph Kazam with a hopeless little gesture. "Are you going to send me away—deport me?"

"I don't know," said the detective thoughtfully. "If you register your religion at City Hall before we get any more complaints, it'll be all right."

"Ah," breathed Kazam. "Complaints?"

Fitzgerald looked at him quizzically. "We got one from a man named Rooney," he said. "Do you know him?"

"Yes. Runi Sarif is his real name. He has hounded me out of Norway, Ireland and Canada—wherever I try to reestablish the Cult of Hagar."

Fitzgerald looked away. "I suppose," he said matter-of-factly, "you have lots of secret enemies plotting against you."

Kazam surprised him with a burst of rich laughter. "I have been investigated too often," grinned the Persian, "not to recognize that one. You think I'm mad."

"No," mumbled the detective, crestfallen. "I just wanted to find out. Anybody running a nut cult's automatically reserved a place in Bellevue."

"Forget it, sir. I spit on the Cult of Hagar. It is my livelihood, but I know better than any man that it is a mockery. Do you know what our highest mystery is? The Ineluctable Modality." Kazam sneered.

"That's Joyce," said Fitzgerald with a grin. "You have a sense of humor, Mr. Kazam. That's a rare thing in the religious."

"Please," said Joseph Kazam. "Don't call me that. I am not worthy —the noble, sincere men who work for their various faiths are my envy. I have seen too much to be one of them."

"Go on," said Fitzgerald, leaning forward. He read books, this detective, and dearly loved an abstract discussion.

The Persian hesitated. "I," he said at length, "am an occult engineer. I am a man who can make the hidden forces work."

"Like staring a leprechaun in the eye till he finds you a pot of gold?" suggested the detective with a chuckle.

"One manifestation," said Kazam calmly. "Only one."

"Look," said Fitzgerald. "They still have that room in Bellevue. Don't say that in public—stick to the Ineluctable Modality if you know what's good for you."

"Tut," said the Persian regretfully. "He's working on you."

The detective looked around the room. "Meaning who?" he demanded.

"Runi Sarif. He's trying to reach your mind and turn you against me."

"Balony," said Fitzgerald coarsely. "You get yourself registered as a religion in twenty-four hours; then find yourself a place to live. I'll hold off any charges of fraud for a while. Just watch your step." He jammed a natty Homburg down over his sandy hair and strode pugnaciously from the office.

Joseph Kazam sighed. Obviously the detective had been disappointed.

That night, in his bachelor's flat, Fitzgerald tossed and turned uneasily on his modern bed. Being blessed with a sound digestion able to cope even with a steady diet of chain-restaurant food and the soundest of consciences, the detective was agitated profoundly by his wakefulness.

Being, like all bachelors, a cautious man, he hesitated to dose himself with the veronal he kept for occasions like this, few and far between though they were. Finally, as he heard the locals pass one by one on the El a few blocks away and then heard the first express of the morning, with its higher-pitched bickering of wheels and quicker vibration against the track, he stumbled from bed and walked dazedly into his bathroom, fumbled open the medicine chest.

Only when he had the bottle and had shaken two pills into his hand did he think to turn on the light. He pulled the cord and dropped the pills in horror. They weren't the veronal at all but an old prescription which he had thriftily kept till they might be of use again.

Two would have been a fatal overdose. Shakily Fitzgerald filled a glass of water and drank it down, spilling about a third on his pajamas. He replaced the pills and threw away the entire bottle. You never know when a thing like that might happen again, he thought—too late to mend.

Now thoroughly sure that he needed the sedative, he swallowed a dose. By the time he had replaced the bottle he could scarcely find his way back to the bed, so sleepy was he.

He dreamed then. Detective Fitzgerald was standing on a plain, a white plain, that was very hot. His feet were bare. In the middle distance was a stone tower above which circled winged skulls—bat-winged skulls, whose rattling and flapping he could plainly hear.

From the plain—he realized then that it was a desert of fine, white sand—spouted up little funnels or vortices of fog in a circle around him. He began to run very slowly, much slower than he wanted to. He thought he was running away from the tower and the vortices, but somehow they continued to stay in his field of vision. No matter where he swerved the tower was always in front and the little twisters around him. The circle was growing smaller around him, and he redoubled his efforts to escape.

Finally he tried flying, leaping into the air. Though he drifted for yards at a time, slowly and easily, he could not land where he wanted to. From the air the vortices looked like petals of a flower, and when he came drifting down to the desert he would land in the very center of the strange blossom.

Again he ran, the circle of foggy cones following still, the tower still before him. He felt with his bare feet something tinglingly clammy. The circle had contracted to the point of coalescence, had gripped his two feet like a trap.

He shot into the air and headed straight for the tower. The creaking, flapping noise of the bat-winged skulls was very much louder now. He cast his eyes to the side and was just able to see the tips of his own black, flapping membranes.

As though regular nightmares—always the same, yet increasingly repulsive to the detective—were not enough woe for one man to bear, he was troubled with a sudden, appalling sharpness of hearing. This was strange, for Fitzgerald had always been a little deaf in one ear.

The noises he heard were distressing things, things like the ticking of a wristwatch two floors beneath his flat, the gurgle of water in sewers as he walked the streets, humming of underground telephone wires. Headquarters was a bedlam with its stentorian breathing, the machine-gun fire of a telephone being dialed, the howitzer crash of a cigarette case snapping shut.

He had his bedroom soundproofed and tried to bear it. The inches of fibreboard helped a little; he found that he could focus his attention on a book and practically exclude from his mind the regular swish of air in his bronchial tubes, the thudding at his wrists and temples, the slushing noise of food passing through his transverse colon.

Fitzgerald did not go mad for he was a man with ideals. He believed in clean government and total extirpation of what he fondly believed was a criminal class which could be detected by the ear lobes and other distinguishing physical characteristics.

He did not go to a doctor because he knew that the word would get back to headquarters that Fitzgerald heard things and would probably begin to see things pretty soon and that it wasn't good policy to have a man like that on the force.

The detective read up on the later Freudians, trying to interpret the recurrent dream. The book said that it meant he had been secretly in love with a third cousin on his mother's side and that he was ashamed of it now and wanted to die, but that he was afraid of heavenly judgment. He knew that wasn't so; his mother had had no relations and detective Fitzgerald wasn't afraid of anything under the sun.

After two weeks of increasing horror he was walking around like a corpse, moving by instinct and wearily doing his best to dodge the accidents that seemed to trail him. It was then that he was assigned to check on the Cult of Hagar. The records showed that they had registered at City Hall, but records don't show everything.

He walked in on the cult during a service and dully noted that its members were more prosperous in appearance than they had been, and that there were more women present. Joseph Kazam was going through precisely the same ritual that the detective had last seen.

When the last bill had fallen into the pot covered with gilded wood and the last dowager had left, Kazam emerged and greeted the detective.

"Fitzgerald," he said, "you damned fool, why didn't you come to me in the first place?"

"For what?" asked the detective, loosening the waxed cotton plugs in his ears.

The stringy, brown man chuckled. "Your friend Rooney's been at work on you. You hear things. You can't sleep and when you do—"

"That's plenty," interjected Fitzgerald. "Can you help me out of this mess I'm in?"

"Nothing to it. Nothing at all. Come into the office."

Dully the detective followed, wondering if the cot had been removed.

The ritual that Kazam performed was simple in the extreme, but a little revolting. The mucky aspects of it Fitzgerald completely excused when he suddenly realized that he no longer heard his own blood pumping through his veins, and that the asthmatic wheeze of the janitor in the basement was now private to the janitor again.

"How does it feel?" asked Kazam concernedly.

"Magnificent," breathed the detective, throwing away his cotton plugs. "Too wonderful for words."

"I'm sorry about what I had to do," said the other man, "but that was to get your attention principally. The real cure was mental projection." He then dismissed the bedevilment of Fitzgerald with an airy wave of the hand. "Look at this," he said.

"My God!" breathed the detective. "Is it real?"

Joseph Kazam was holding out an enormous diamond cut into a

thousand glittering facets that shattered the light from his desk lamp into a glorious blaze of color.

"This," said the stringy, brown man, "is the Charity Diamond."

"You mean," sputtered the detective, "you got it from—"

"The very woman," said Kazam hastily. "And of her own free will. I have a receipt: 'For the sum of one dollar in payment for the Charity Diamond. Signed, Mrs.——' "

"Yes," said the detective. "Happy days for the Sons of Hagar. Is this what you've been waiting for?"

"This," said Kazam curiously turning the stone in his hand, "is what I've been hunting over all the world for years. And only by starting a nut cult could I get it. Thank God it's legal."

"What are you going to do now?" asked the detective.

"Use the diamond for a little trip. You will want to come along, I think. You'll have a chance to meet your Mr. Rooney."

"Lead on," said Fitzgerald. "After the past two weeks I can stand anything."

"Very well." Kazam turned out the desk lamp.

"It glows," whispered Fitzgerald. He was referring to the diamond, over whose surface was passing an eerie blue light, like the invisible flame of anthracite.

"I'd like you to pray for success, Mr. Fitzgerald," said Kazam. The detective began silently to go over his brief stock of prayers. He was barely conscious of the fact that the other man was mumbling to himself and caressing the diamond with long, wiry fingers.

The shine of the stone grew brighter yet; strangely, though, it did not pick out any of the details of the room.

Then Kazam let out an ear-splitting howl. Fitzgerald winced, closing his eyes for just a moment. When he opened them he began to curse in real earnest.

"You damned rotter!" he cried. "Taking me here—"

The Persian looked at him coldly and snapped: "Easy, man! This is real—look around you!"

The detective looked around and saw that the tower of stone was rather far in the distance, farther than in his dreams, usually. He stooped and picked up a handful of the fine white desert sand, let it run through his fingers.

"How did you get us here?" he asked hoarsely.

"Same way I cured you of Runi Sarif's curse. The diamond has rare powers to draw the attention. Ask any jewel-thief. This one, being enormously expensive, is so completely engrossing that unsuspected powers of concentration are released. That, combined with my own sound knowledge of a particular traditional branch of psychology, was enough to break the walls down which held us pent to East 59th Street."

The detective was beginning to laugh, flatly and hysterically. "I come to you hag-ridden, you first cure me and then plunge me twice as deep into Hell, Kazam! What's the good of it?"

"This isn't Hell," said the Persian matter-of-factly. "It isn't Hell, but it isn't Heaven either. Sit down and let me explain." Obediently Fitzgerald squatted on the sand. He noticed that Kazam cast an apprehensive glance at the horizon before beginning.

"I was born in Persia," said Kazam, "but I am not Persian by blood, religion or culture. My life began in a little mountain village where I soon saw that I was treated not as the other children were. My slightest wish could command the elders of the village and if I gave an order it would be carried out.

"The reasons for all this were explained to me on my thirteenth birthday by an old man—a very old man whose beard reached to his knees. He said that he had in him only a small part of the blood of Kaidar, but that I was almost full of it, that there was little human blood in me.

"I cried and screamed and said that I didn't want to be Kaidar, that I just wanted to be a person. I ran away from the village after another year, before they began to teach me their twisted, ritualistic versions of occult principles. It was this flight which saved me from the usual fate of the Kaidar; had I stayed I would have become a celebrated miracle man, known for all of two hundred miles or so, curing the sick and cursing the well. My highest flight would be to create a new Islamic faction—number three hundred and eighty-two, I suppose.

"Instead I knocked around the world. And Lord, got knocked around too. Tramp steamers, maritime strike in Frisco, the Bela Kun regime in Hungary—I wound up in North Africa when I was about thirty years old.

"I was broke, as broke as any person could be and stay alive. A Scotswoman picked me up, hired me, taught me mathematics. I plunged into it, algebra, conics, analytics, calculus, relativity. Before I was done, I'd worked out wave-mechanics three years before that Frenchman had even begun to think about it.

"When I showed her the set of differential equations for the carbon molecule, all solved, she damned me for an unnatural monster and threw me out. But she'd given me the beginnings of mental discipline, and done it many thousands of times better than they could have in that Persian village. I began to realize what I was.

"It was then that I drifted into the nut cult business. I found out that all you need for capital is a stock of capitalized abstract qualities, like All-Knowingness, Will-Mind-Urge, Planetude and Exciliation. With that to work on I can make my living almost anywhere on the globe.

"I met Runi Sarif, who was running an older-established sect, the Pan-European Astral Confederation of Healers. He was a Hindu from the Punjab plains in the North of India. Lord, what a mind he had! He worked me over quietly for three months before I realized what was up.

"Then there was a little interview with him. He began with the complicated salute of the Astral Confederation and got down to business. 'Brother Kazam,' he said, 'I wish to show you an ancient sacred book I have just discovered.' I laughed, of course. By that time I'd already discovered seven ancient books by myself, all ready-translated into the language of the country I would be working at the time. The 'Isba Kazhlunk' was the most successful; that's the one I found preserved in the hide of a mammoth in a Siberian glacier.

"Runi looked sour. 'Brother Kazam,' said he, 'do not scoff. Does the word *Kaidar* mean anything to you?' I played dumb and asked whether it was something out of the third chapter of the Lost Lore of Atlantis, but I remembered ever so faintly that I had been called that once.

" 'A Kaidar,' said Runi, 'is an atavism to an older, stronger people who once visited this plane and left their seed. They can be detected by'—he squinted at me sharply—'by a natural aptitude for occult pursuits. They carry in their minds learning undreamable by mortals. Now, Brother Kazam, if we could only find a Kaidar . . .'

" 'Don't carry yourself away,' I said. 'What good would that be to us?'

"Silently he produced what I'll swear was actually an ancient sacred book. And I wouldn't be surprised if he'd just discovered it, moreover. It was the psaltery of a small, very ancient sect of Edomites who had migrated beyond the Euphrates and died out. When I'd got around the rock-Hebrew it was written in I was very greatly impressed. They had some noble religious poems, one simply blistering exorcism and anathema, a lot of tedious genealogy in verse form. And they had a didactic poem on the Kaidar, based on one who had turned up in their tribe.

"They had treated him horribly—chained him to a cave wall and used him for a sort of male Sybil. They found out that the best way to get him to prophesy was to show him a diamond. Then, one sad day, they let him touch it. Blam! He vanished, taking two of the rabbis with him. The rabbis came back later; appeared in broad daylight raving about visions of Paradise they had seen.

"I quite forgot about the whole affair. At that time I was obsessed with the idea that I would become the Rockefeller of Occultism—get disciples, train them carefully and spread my cult. If Mohammed could do it, why not I? To this day I don't know the answer.

"While I was occupying myself with grandiose daydreams, Runi was busily picking over my mind. To a natural cunning and a fantastic ability to concentrate he added what I unconsciously knew, finally achieving adequate control of many factors.

"Then he stole a diamond, I don't know where, and vanished. One presumes that he wanted to have that Paradise that the rabbis told of for his very own. Since then he has been trying to destroy me, sending out messages, dominating other minds on the Earthly plane—if you will excuse the jargon—to that end. He reached you, Fitzgerald, through a letter he got someone else to write and post, then when you were located and itemized he could work on you directly.

"You failed him, and he, fearing I would use you, tried to destroy you by heightening your sense of hearing and sending you visions nightly of this plane. It would destroy any common man; we are very fortunate that you are extraordinarily tough in your psychological fibre.

"Since then I have been dodging Runi Sarif, trying to get a diamond big enough to send me here through all the barriers he has prepared against my coming. You helped me very greatly." Again Kazam cast an apprehensive look at the horizon.

The detective looked around slowly. "Is this a paradise?" he asked. "If so I've been seriously misled by my Sunday School teachers." He tried weakly to smile.

"That is one of the things I don't understand—yet," said the Persian. "And this is another unpleasantness which approaches."

Fitzgerald stared in horror at the little spills of fog which were upending themselves from the sand. He had the ghastly, futile dream sensation again.

"Don't try to get away from them," snapped Kazam. "Walk *at* the things." He strode directly and pugnaciously at one of the little puffs, and it gave way before him and they were out of the circle.

"That was easy," said the detective weakly.

Suddenly before them loomed the stone tower. The winged skulls were nowhere to be seen.

Sheer into the sky reared the shaft, solid and horribly hewn from grey granite, rough-finished on the outside. The top was shingled to a shallow cone, and embrasures were black slots in the wall.

Then, Fitzgerald never knew how, they were inside the tower, in the great round room at its top. The winged skulls were perched on little straggling legs along a golden rail. Aside from the flat blackness of their wings all was crimson and gold in that room. There was a sickly feeling of decay and corruption about it, a thing that sickened the detective.

Hectic blotches of purple marked the tapestries that hung that circular wall, blotches that seemed like the high spots in rotten meat. The tapestries themselves the detective could not look at again after one glance. The thing he saw, sprawling over a horde of men and women, drooling flame on them, a naked figure still between its jaws, colossal, slimy paws on a little heap of human beings, was not a pretty sight.

86

Light came from flambeaux in the wall, and the torches cast a sickly, reddish-orange light over the scene. Thin curls of smoke from the sockets indicated an incense.

And lastly there was to be seen a sort of divan, heaped with cushions in fantastic shapes. Reclining easily on them was the most grotesque, abominable figure Fitzgerald had ever seen. It was a man, had been once. But incredible incontinence had made the creature gross and bloated with what must have been four hundred pounds of fat. Fat swelled out the cummerbund that spanned the enormous belly, fat welted out the cheeks so that the ears of the creature could not be seen beneath the embroidered turban, gouts of fat rolled in a blubbery mass about the neck like the wattles of a dead cockerel.

"Ah," hissed Joseph Kazam. "Runi Sarif . . ." He drew from his shirt a little sword or big knife from whose triangular blade glinted the light of the flambeaux.

The suety monster quivered as though maggots were beneath his skin. In a voice that was like the sound a butcher makes when he tears the fat belly from a hog's carcass, Runi Sarif said: "Go—go back. Go back—where you came from—" There was no beginning or ending to the speech. It came out between short, grunting gasps for breath.

Kazam advanced, running a thumb down the knife-blade. The monster on the divan lifted a hand that was like a bunch of sausages. The nails were a full half-inch below the level of the skin. Afterwards Fitzgerald assured himself that the hand was the most repellent aspect of the entire affair.

With creaking, flapping wingstrokes the skulls launched themselves at the Persian, their jaws clicking stonily. Kazam and the detective were in the middle of a cloud of flying jaws that were going for their throats.

Insanely Fitzgerald beat at the things, his eyes shut. When he looked they were lying on the floor. He was surprised to see that there were just four of them. He would have sworn to a dozen at least. And they all four bore the same skillfully delivered slash mark of Kazam's knife.

There was a low, choking noise from the monster on the divan. As the detective stared Kazam stepped up the first of the three shallow steps leading to it.

What followed detective Fitzgerald could never disentangle. The lights went out, yet he could plainly see. He saw that the monstrous Runi Sarif had turned into a creature such as he had seen on the tapestry, and he saw that so had Kazam, save that the thing which was the Persian carried in one paw a blade.

They were no longer in the tower room, it seemed, nor were they on the white desert below. They were hovering in a roaring, squalling tumult, in a confusion of spheres which gently collided and caromed off each other without noise.

As the detective watched, the Runi monster changed into one of the spheres and so, promptly, did Kazam. On the side of the Kazam sphere was the image of the knife. Tearing at a furious rate through the jostling confusion and blackness Fitzgerald followed, and he never knew how.

The Kazam sphere caught the other and spun dizzily around it, with a screaming noise which rose higher and higher. As it passed the top threshold of hearing, both spheres softened and spread into black, crawling clouds. Suspended in the middle of one was the knife.

The other cloud knotted itself into a furious, tight lump and charged the one which carried the blade. It hurtled into and through it, impaling itself.

Fitzgerald shook his head dizzily. They were in the tower room, and Runi Sarif lay on the divan with a cut throat. The Persian had dropped the knife, and was staring with grim satisfaction at the bleeding figure.

"Where were we?" stuttered the detective. "Where—?" At the look in Kazam's eyes he broke off and did not ask again.

The Persian said: "He stole my rights. It is fitting that I should recover them, even thus. In one plane—there is no room for two in contest."

Jovially he clapped the detective on the shoulder. "I'll send you back now. From this moment I shall be a card in your Bureau of Missing Persons. Tell whatever you wish—it won't be believed."

"It was supposed to be a paradise," said the detective.

"It is," said Kazam. "Look."

They were no longer in the tower, but on a mossy bank above a river whose water ran a gamut of pastels, changing hues without end. It tinkled out something like a Mozart sonata and was fragrant with a score of scents.

The detective looked at one of the flowers on the bank. It was swaying of itself and talking quietly in a very small voice, like a child.

"They aren't clever," said Kazam, "but they're lovely."

Fitzgerald drew in his breath sharply as a flight of butterfly things passed above. "Send me away," he gasped. "Send me away now or I'll never be able to go. I'd kill you to stay here in another minute."

Kazam laughed. "Folly," he said. "Just as the dreary world of sand and a tower that—a certain unhappy person—created was his and him, so this paradise is me and mine. My bones are its rock, my flesh is its earth, my blood is its waters, my mind is its living things."

As an unimaginably glowing drift of crystalline, chiming creatures loped across the whispering grass of the bank Kazam waved one hand in a gesture of farewell.

Fitzgerald felt himself receding with incredible velocity, and for a brief moment saw an entire panorama of the world that was Kazam. Three suns were rising from three points of the horizon, and their slanting rays lit a paradise whose only inglorious speck was a stringy, brown man on a riverbank. Then the man vanished as though he had been absorbed into the ground.

My Name Is Legion

Lester del Rey (1915-)

L ESTER *del Rey was one of the first big names of the forties to be collected in book form (. . . And Some Were Human, 1948), and he richly deserved this recognition. His suspenseful story of an accident at a nuclear plant,* Nerves *(1942), and the understated and moving "Helen O'Loy" (1938) are his best-known stories, but equally good are "The Wings of Night" (1942) and "Over the Top" (1949).*

"My Name Is Legion" has a main character by the name of Adolf Hitler and is one of the better representatives of the "anti-Nazi story" that appeared during the war years. Many of these were published by Amazing Stories *and* Fantastic Adventures *with titles like "Weapon for a Wac" and "The Ghost That Haunted Hitler." Unfortunately, although a number of good stories graced its pages,* Amazing *fell on hard times in the forties (except in economic terms) and it was not until many years later, under the editorship of Cele Goldsmith, that it would be characterized by high quality. In the forties the magazine was dominated by the "Shaver Mystery," an episode that helped its circulation but did its reputation and that of science fiction little good.*

From *Astounding Science Fiction* 1942

Bresseldorf lay quiet under the late-morning sun—too quiet. In the streets there was no sign of activity, though a few faint banners of smoke spread upward from the chimneys, and the dropped tools of agriculture lay all about, scattered as if from sudden flight. A thin pig wandered slowly and suspiciously down Friedrichstrasse, turned into an open door cautiously, grunted in grudging satisfaction, and disappeared within. But there were no cries of children, no bustle of men in the surrounding fields, nor women gossiping or making preparations for the noon meal. The few shops, apparently gutted of foodstuffs, were bare, their doors flopping open. Even the dogs were gone.

Major King dropped the binoculars to his side, tight lines about his eyes that contrasted in suspicion with his ruddy British face. "Something funny here, Wolfe. Think it's an ambush?"

Wolfe studied the scene. "Doesn't smell like it, Major," he answered. "In the Colonials, we developed something of a sixth sense for that, and I don't get a hunch here. Looks more like a sudden and complete retreat to me, sir."

"We'd have had reports from the observation planes if even a dozen men were on the roads. I don't like this." The major put the binoculars up again. But the scene was unchanged, save that the solitary pig had come out again and was rooting his way down the street in lazy assurance that nothing now menaced him. King shrugged, flipped his hand forward in a quick jerk, and his command moved ahead again, light tanks in front, troop cars and equipment at a safe distance behind, but ready to move forward instantly to hold what ground the tanks might gain. In the village, nothing stirred.

Major King found himself holding his breath as the tanks reached antitank-fire distance, but as prearranged, half of them lumbered forward at a deceptive speed, maneuvered to two abreast to shuttle across Friedrichstrasse toward the village square, and halted. Still, there was no sign of resistance. Wolfe looked at the quiet houses along the street and grinned sourly.

"If it's an ambush, Major, they've got sense. They're waiting until we send in our men in the trucks to pick them off then, and letting the tanks alone. But I still don't believe it; not with such an army as he could throw together."

"Hm-m-m." King scowled, and again gave the advance signal.

The trucks moved ahead this time, traveling over the rough road at a clip that threatened to jar the teeth out of the men's heads, and the remaining tanks swung in briskly as a rear guard. The pig stuck his head out of a door as the major's car swept past, squealed, and slipped back inside in haste. Then all were in the little square, barely big enough to hold them, and the tanks were arranged facing out, their thirty-seven millimeters raking across the houses that bordered, ready for an instant's notice. Smoke continued to rise peacefully, and the town slumbered on, unmindful of this strange invasion.

"Hell!" King's neck felt tense, as if the hair were standing on end. He swung to the men, moved his hands outward. "Out and search!

And remember—take him alive if you can! If you can't, plug his guts and save his face—we'll have to bring back proof!"

They broke into units and stalked out of the square toward the houses with grim efficiency and rifles ready, expecting guerrilla fire at any second; none came. The small advance guard of the Army of Occupation kicked open such doors as were closed and went in and sidewise, their comrades covering them. No shots came, and the only sound was the cries of the men as they reported "Empty!"

Then, as they continued around the square, one of the doors opened quietly and a single man came out, glanced at the rifles centered on him, and threw up his hands, a slight smile on his face. *"Kamerad!"* he shouted toward the major; then in English with only the faintest of accents: "There is no other here, in the whole village."

Holding onto the door, he moved aside slightly to let a search detail go in, waited for them to come out. "You see? I am alone in Bresseldorf; the Leader you seek is gone, and his troops with him."

Judging by the man's facial expression that he was in no condition to come forward, King advanced; Wolfe was at his side, automatic at ready. "I'm Major King, Army of Occupation. We received intelligence from some of the peasants who fled from here yesterday that your returned Führer was hiding here. You say——"

"That he is quite gone, yes; and that you will never find him, though you comb the earth until eternity, Major King. I am Karl Meyers, once of Heidelberg."

"When did he leave?"

"A matter of half an hour or so—what matter? I assure you, sir, he is too far now to trace. Much too far!"

"In half an hour?" King grimaced. "You underestimate the covering power of a modern battalion. Which direction?"

"Yesterday," Meyers answered, and his drawn face lighted slightly. "But tell me, did the peasants report but one Führer?"

King stared at the man in surprise, taking in the basically pleasant face, intelligent eyes, and the pride that lay, somehow, in the bent figure; this was no ordinary villager, but a man of obvious breeding. Nor did he seem anything but completely frank and honest. "No," the major conceded, "there were stories. But when a band of peasants reports a thousand Führers heading fifty thousand troops, we'd be a little slow in believing it, after all."

"Quite so, Major. Peasant minds exaggerate." Again there was the sudden lighting of expression. "Yes, so they did—the troops. And in other ways, rather than exaggerating, they minimized. But come inside, sirs, and I'll explain over a bottle of the rather poor wine I've found here. I'll show you the body of the Leader, and even explain why he's gone—and where."

"But you said——" King shrugged. Let the man be as mysterious as he chose, if his claim of the body was correct. He motioned Wolfe forward with him and followed Meyers into a room that had once been kitchen and dining room, but was now in wild disarray, its normal holdings crammed into the corners to make room for a small piece of mechanism in the center and a sheeted bundle at one side. The machine was apparently in the process of being disassembled.

Meyers lifted the sheet. *"Der Führer,"* he said simply, and King dropped with a gasp to examine the dead figure revealed.

There were no shoes, and the calluses on the feet said quite plainly that it was customary; such few clothes as remained had apparently been pieced together from odds and ends of peasant clothing, sewed crudely. Yet on them, pinned over the breast, were the two medals that the Leader alone bore. One side of the head had been blown away by one of the new-issue German explosive bullets, and what remained was incredibly filthy, matted hair falling below the shoulders, scraggy, tangled beard covering all but the eye and nose. On the left cheek, however, the irregular reversed question-mark scar from the recent attempt at assassination showed plainly, but faded and blended with the normal skin where it should have been still sharp after only two months' healing.

"An old, old man, wild as the wind and dirty as a hog wallow," King thought, "yet, somehow, clearly the man I was after."

Wolfe nodded slowly at his superior's glance. "Sure, why not? I'll cut his hair and give him a shave and a wash. When we're about finished here, we can fire a shot from the gun on the table, if it's still loaded . . . good! Report that Meyers caught him and held him for us; then, while we were questioning him, he went crazy and Meyers took a shot at him."

"Hm-m-m." King's idea had been about the same. "Men might suspect something, but I can trust them. He'd never stand a careful inspection, of course, without a lot of questions about such things as those feet, but the way things are, no really competent medical inspection will be made. It'll be a little hard to explain those rags, though."

Meyers nodded to a bag against the wall. "You'll find sufficient of his clothes there, Major; we couldn't pack out much luggage, but that much we brought." He sank back into a rough chair slowly, the hollow in his cheeks deepening, but a grim humor in his eyes. "Now, you'll want to know how it happened, no doubt? How he died? Suicide—murder; they're one and the same here. He died insane."

The car was long and low. European by its somewhat unrounded lines and engine housing, muddy with the ruck that sprayed up from its wheels and made the road almost impassable. Likewise, it was stolen, though that had no bearing on the matter at hand. Now, as it rounded an ill-banked curve, the driver cursed softly, jerked at the wheel, and somehow managed to keep all four wheels on the road and the whole pointed forward. His foot came down on the gas again, and it churned forward through the muck, then miraculously maneuvered another turn, and they were on a passable road and he could relax.

"Germany, my Leader," he said simply, his large hands gripping at the wheel with now needless ferocity. "Here, of all places, they will least suspect you."

The Leader sat hunched forward, paying little attention to the road or the risks they had taken previously. Whatever his enemies might say of his lack of bravery in the first war, there was no cowardice about him now; power, in unlimited quality, had made him unaware of personal fear. He shrugged faintly, turning his face to the driver, so that the reversed question-mark scar showed up, running from his left eye down toward the almost comic little moustache. But there was nothing comic about him, somehow; certainly not to Karl Meyers.

"Germany," he said tonelessly. "Good. I was a fool, Meyers, ever to leave it. Those accursed British—the loutish Russians—ungrateful French—troublemaking Americans—bombs, retreats, uprisings, betrayals—and the two I thought were my friends advising me to flee to Switzerland before my people— Bah, I was a fool. Now those two friends would have me murdered in my bed, as this letter you brought testifies. And the curs stalk the Reich, such as remains of it, and think they have beaten me. Bonaparte was beaten once, and in a hundred days, except for the stupidity of fools and the tricks of weather, even he might have regained his empire. . . . Where?"

"Bresseldorf. My home is near there, and the equipment, also. Besides, when we have the—the legion with us, Bresseldorf will feed us, and the clods of peasants will offer little resistance. Also, it is well removed from the areas policed by the Army of Occupation. Thank God, I finished the machine in time."

Meyers swung the car into another little-used but passable road, and opened it up, knowing it would soon be over. This mad chase had taken more out of him than he'd expected. Slipping across into Switzerland, tracking, playing hunches, finally locating the place where the Leader was hidden had used almost too much time, and the growth within him that would not wait was killing him day by day. Even after finding the place, he'd been forced to slip past the guards who were half protecting, half imprisoning the Leader and used half a hundred tricks to see him. Convincing him of the conspiracy of his "friends" to have him shot was not hard; the Leader knew something of the duplicity of men in power, or fearful of their lives. Convincing him of the rest of the plan had been harder, but on the coldly logical argument that there was nothing else, the Leader had come. Somehow, they'd escaped—he still could give no details on that—and stolen this car, to run out into the rain and the night over the mountain roads, through the back ways, and somehow out unnoticed and into Germany again.

The leader settled more comfortably into the seat with an automatic motion, his mind far from body comforts. "Bresseldorf? And near it—yes, I remember that clearly now—within fifteen miles of there, there's a small military depot those damned British won't have found yet. There was a new plan—but that doesn't matter now; what matters are the tanks, and better, the ammunition. This machine—will it duplicate tanks, also? And ammunition?"

Meyers nodded. "Tanks, cars, equipment, all of them. But not ammunition or petrol, since once used, they're not on the chain any longer to be taken."

"No matter. God be praised, there's petrol and ammunition enough there, until we can reach the others; and a few men, surely, who are still loyal. I was beginning to doubt loyalty, but tonight you've shown that it does exist. Someday, Karl Meyers, you'll find I'm not ungrateful."

"Enough that I serve you," Meyers muttered. "Ah, here we are; good time made, too, since it's but ten in the morning. That house is one I've rented; inside you'll find wine and food, while I dispose of this car in the little lake yonder. Fortunately, the air is still thick here, even though it's not raining. There'll be none to witness."

The Leader had made no move to touch the food when Meyers returned. He was pacing the floor, muttering to himself, working himself up as Meyers had seen him do often before on the great stands in front of the crowds, and the mumbled words had a hysterical drive to them that bordered on insanity. In his eyes, though, there was only the insanity that drives men remorselessly to rule, though the ruling may be under a grimmer sword than that of Damocles. He stopped as he saw Meyers, and one of his rare and sudden smiles flashed out, unexpectedly warm and human, like a small, bewildered boy peering out from the chinks of the man's armor. This was the man who had cried when he saw his soldiers dying, then sent them on again, sure they should honor him for the right to die; and like all those most loved or hated by their fellowmen, he was a paradox of conflictions, unpredictable.

"The machine, Karl," he reminded the other gently. "As I remember, the Jew Christ cast a thousand devils out of one man; well, let's see you cast ten thousand out of me—and devils they'll be to those who fetter the Reich! This time I think we'll make no words of secret weapons, but annihilate them first, eh? After that—there'll be a day of atonement for those who failed me, and a new and greater Germany—master of a world!"

"Yes, my Leader."

Meyers turned and slipped through the low door, back into a part of the building that had once been a stable, but was now converted into a

96

workshop, filled with a few pieces of fine machinery and half a hundred makeshifts, held together, it seemed, with hope and prayer. He stopped before a small affair, slightly larger than a suitcase, only a few dials and control knobs showing on the panel, the rest covered with a black housing. From it, two small wires led to a single storage battery.

"This?" The Leader looked at it doubtfully.

"This, Leader. This is one case where brute power has little to do, and the proper use everything. A few tubes, coils, condensers, two little things of my own, and perhaps five watts of power feeding in—no more. Just as the cap that explodes the bomb may be small and weak, yet release forces that bring down the very mountains. Simple in design, yet there's no danger of them finding it."

"So? And it works in what way?"

Meyers scowled, thinking. "Unless you can think in a plenum, my Leader, I can't explain," he began diffidently. "Oh, mathematicians believe they can—but they think in symbols and terms, not in the reality. Only by thinking in the plenum itself can this be understood, and with due modesty, I alone in the long years since I gave up work at Heidelberg have devoted the time and effort—with untold pure luck—to master such thought. It isn't encompassed in mere symbols on paper."

"What," the Leader wanted to know, "is a plenum?"

"A complete universe, stretching up and forward and sidewise—and durationally; the last being the difficulty. The plenum is—well, the composite whole of all that is and was and will be—it is everything and everywhen, all existing together as a unit, in which time does not move, but simply is, like length or thickness. As an example, years ago in one of those American magazines, there was a story of a man who saw himself. He came through a woods somewhere and stumbled on a machine, got in, and it took him three days back in time. Then, he lived forward again, saw himself get in the machine and go back. Therefore, the time machine was never made, since he always took it back, let it stay three days, and took it back again. It was a closed circle, uncreated, but existent in the plenum. By normal nonplenar thought, impossible."

"Someone had to make it." The Leader's eyes clouded suspiciously.

Meyers shook his head. "Not so. See, I draw this line upon the paper, calling the paper now a plenum. It starts here, follows here, ends here. That is like life, machines, and so forth. We begin, we continue, we end. Now, I draw a circle—where does it begin or end? Yes, followed by a two-dimensional creature, it would be utter madness, continuing forever without reason or beginning—to us, simply a circle. Or, here I have a pebble—do you see at one side the energy, then the molecules, then the compounds, then the stone, followed by breakdown products? No, simply a stone. And in a plenum, that time machine is simply a pebble—complete, needing no justification, since it was."

The Leader nodded doubtfully, vaguely aware that he seemed to understand, but did not. If the machine worked, though, what matter the reason? "And—"

"And, by looking into the plenum as a unit, I obtain miracles, seemingly. I pull an object back from its future to stand beside its present. I multiply it in the present. As you might take a straight string and bend it into a series of waves or loops, so that it met itself repeatedly. For that, I need some power, yet not much. When I cause the bending from the future to the present, I cause nothing—since, in a plenum, all that is, was and will be. When I bring you back, the mere fact that you are back means that you always have existed and always will exist in that manner. Seemingly, then, if I did nothing, you would still multiply, but since my attempt to create such a condition is fixed in the plenum beside your multiplying at this time, therefore I must do so. The little energy I use, really, has only the purpose of not bringing you exactly within yourself, but separating individuals. Simple, is it not?"

"When I see an example, Meyers, I'll believe my eyes," the Leader answered.

Meyers grinned, and put a small coin on the ground, making quick adjustments of the dials. "I'll cause it to multiply from each two minutes," he said. "From each two minutes in the future, I'll bring it back to now. See!"

He depressed a switch, a watch in his hand. Instantly, there was a spreading out and multiplying, instantaneous or too rapid to be followed. As he released the switch, the Leader stumbled back from the hulking pile of coins. Meyers glanced at him, consulted his watch, and moved another lever at the top. The machine clicked off. After a second or so, the pile disappeared, as quietly and quickly as it had come into being. There was a glint of triumph or something akin to it in the scientist's eyes as he turned back to the Leader.

"I've tried it on myself for one turn, so it's safe to living things," he answered the unasked question.

The Leader nodded impatiently and stepped to the place where the coins had been piled. "Get on with it, then. The sooner the accursed enemies and traitors are driven out, the better it will be."

Meyers hesitated. "There's one other thing," he said doubtfully. "When the—others—are here, there might be a question of leadership, which would go ill with us. I mean no offense, my Leader, but—well, sometimes a man looks at things differently at different ages, and any disagreement would delay us. Fortunately, though, there's a curious by-product of the use of the machine; apparently, its action has some relation to thought, and I've found in my experiments that any strong thought on the part of the original will be duplicated in the others; I don't fully understand it myself, but it seems to work that way. The compulsion dissipates slowly and is gone in a day or so, but—"

"So?"

"So, if you'll think to yourself while you're standing there: 'I must obey my original implicitly; I must not cause trouble for my original or Karl Meyers,' then the problem will be cared for automatically. Concentrate on that, my Leader, and perhaps it would be wise to concentrate also on the thought that there should be no talking by our legion, except as we demand."

"Good. There'll be time for talk when the action is finished. Now, begin!"

The Leader motioned toward the machine and Meyers breathed a sigh of relief as the scarred face crinkled in concentration. From the table at the side, the scientist picked up a rifle and automatic, put them into the other's hands, and went to his machine.

"The weapon will be duplicated also," he said, setting the controls carefully. "Now, it should be enough if I take you back from each twenty-four hours in the future. And since there isn't room here, I'll assemble the duplicates in rows outside. So."

He depressed the switch and a red bulb on the control panel lighted. In the room, nothing happened for a few minutes; then the bulb went out, and Meyers released the controls. "It's over. The machine has traced ahead and brought back until there was no further extension of yourself; living, that is, since I set it for life only."

"But I felt nothing." The Leader glanced at the machine with a slight scowl, then stepped quickly to the door for a hasty look. Momentarily, superstitious awe flicked across his face, to give place to sharp triumph. "Excellent, Meyers, most excellent. For this day, we'll have the world at our feet, and that soon!"

In the field outside, a curious company was lined up in rows. Meyers ran his eyes down the ranks, smiling faintly as he traced forward. Near, in almost exact duplication of the man at his side, were several hundred; then, as his eyes moved backward, the resemblance was still strong, but differences began to creep in. And farthest from him, a group of old men stood, their clothes faded and tattered, their faces hidden under mangled beards. Rifles and automatics were gripped in the hands of all the legion. There were also other details, and Meyers nodded slowly to himself, but he made no mention of them to the Leader, who seemed not to notice.

The Leader was looking ahead, a hard glow in his eyes, his face contorted with some triumphant vision. Then, slowly and softly at first, he began to speak and to pace back and forth in front of the doorway, moving his arms. Meyers only half listened, busy with his own thoughts, but he could have guessed the words as they came forth with mounting fury, worked up to a climax and broke, to repeat it all again. Probably it was a great speech the Leader was making, one that would have swept a mob from their seats in crazy exultation in other days and set them screaming with savage applause. But the strange Legion of Later Leaders stood quietly, faces betraying varying emotions, mostly unreadable. Finally the speaker seemed to sense the difference and paused in the middle of one of his rising climaxes; he half turned to Meyers, then suddenly swung back decisively.

"But I speak to myselves," he addressed the legion again in a level, reasonable voice. "You who come after me know what is to be this day and in the days to come, so why should I tell you? And you know that my cause is just. The Jews, the Jew-lovers, the Pluto-democracies, the Bolsheviks, the treasonous cowards within and without the Reich must be put down! They shall be! Now, they are sure of victory, but tomorrow they'll be trembling in their beds and begging for peace. And soon, like a tide, irresistible and without end, from the few we can trust many shall be made, and they shall sweep forward to victory. Not victory in a decade, nor a year, but in a month! We shall go north and south and east and west! We shall show them that our fangs are not pulled; that those which we lost were but our milk teeth, now replaced by a second and harder growth!

"And for those who would have betrayed us, or bound us down in chains to feed the gold lust of the mad democracies, or denied us the room to live which is rightfully ours—for those, we shall find a proper place. This time, for once and for all, there shall be an end to the evils that corrupt the earth—the Jews and the Bolsheviks, and their friends, and friends' friends. Germany shall emerge, purged and cleansed, a new and greater Reich, whose domain shall not be Europe, not this hemisphere, but the world!

"Many of you have seen all this in the future from which you come, and all of you must be ready to reassure yourselves of it today, that the glory of it may fill your tomorrow. Now, we march against a few peasants. Tomorrow, after quartering in Bresseldorf, we shall be in the secret depot, where those who remain loyal shall be privileged to multiply and join us, and where we shall multiply all our armament ten-thousandfold! Into Bresseldorf, then, and if any of the peasants are disloyal, be merciless in removing them! Forward!"

One of the men in the front—the nearest—was crying openly, his face white, his hands clenched savagely around the rifle he held, and the Leader smiled at the display of fervor and started forward. Meyers touched his shoulder.

"My Leader, there is no need that you should walk, though these must. I have a small auto here, into which we can put the machine. Send the legion ahead, and we'll follow later; they'll have little trouble clearing Bresseldorf for us. Then, when we've packed our duplicator and I've assembled spare parts for an emergency, we can join them."

"By all means, yes. The machine must be well handled." The Leader nodded and turned back to the men. "Proceed to Bresseldorf, then, and we follow. Secure quarters for yourself and food, and a place for me and for Meyers; we stop there until I can send word to the depot during the night and extend my plans. To Bresseldorf!"

Silently, without apparent organization, but with only small confusion, the legion turned and moved off, rifles in hands. There were no orders, no beating of drums to announce to the world that the Leader was on the march again, but the movement of that body of men, all gradations of the same man, was impressive enough without fanfare as it turned into the road that led to Bresseldorf, only a mile away. Meyers saw a small cart coming toward them, watched it halt while the driver stared dumbly at the company approaching. Then, with a shriek that cut thinly over the distance, he was whipping his animal about and heading in wild flight toward the village.

"I think the peasants will cause no trouble, my Leader," the scientist guessed, turning back to the shop. "No, the legion will be quartered by the time we reach them."

And when the little car drove up into the village square half an hour later and the two men got out, the legion was quartered well enough to satisfy all prophets. There was no sign of the peasants, but the men from the future were moving back and forth into the houses and shops along the street, carrying foodstuffs to be cooked. Cellars and stores had been well gutted, and a few pigs were already killed and being cut up—not skillfully, perhaps, but well enough for practical purposes.

The Leader motioned toward one of the amateur butchers, a copy of himself who seemed perhaps two or three years older, and the man approached with frozen face. His knuckles, Meyers noted, were white where his fingers clasped around the butcher knife he had been using.

"The peasants—what happened?"

The legionnaire's face set tighter, and he opened his mouth to say something; apparently he changed his mind after a second, shut his mouth, and shrugged. "Nothing," he answered finally. "We met a farmer on the road who went ahead shouting about a million troops, all the Leader. When we got here, there were a few children and women running off, and two men trying to drag away one of the pigs. They left it behind and ran off. Nothing happened."

"Stupid dolts! Superstition, no loyalty!" The Leader twisted his lips, frowning at the man before him, apparently no longer conscious that it was merely a later edition of himself. "Well, show us to the quarters you've picked for us. And have someone send us food and wine. Has a messenger been sent to the men at the tank depot?"

"You did not order it."

"What— No, so I didn't. Well, go yourself, then, if you . . . but, of course, you know where it is. Naturally. Tell Hauptmann Immenhoff to expect me tomorrow and not to be surprised at anything. You'll have to go on foot, since we need the car for the machine."

The legionnaire nodded, indicating one of the houses on the square. "You quarter here. I go on foot, as I knew I would." He turned expressionlessly and plodded off to the north, grabbing up a half-cooked leg of pork as he passed the fire burning in the middle of the square.

The Leader and Meyers did not waste time following him with their eyes, but went into the house indicated, where wine and food were sent in to them shortly. With the help of one of the duplicates, space was quickly cleared for the machine, and a crude plank table drawn up for the map that came from the Leader's bag. But Meyers had little appetite for the food or wine, less for the dry task of watching while the other made marks on the paper or stared off into space in some rapt dream of conquest. The hellish tumor inside him was giving him no rest now, and he turned to his machine, puttering over its insides as a release from the pain. Outside, the legion was comparatively silent, only the occasional sound of a man walking past breaking the monotony. Darkness fell just as more food was brought in to them, and the scientist looked out to see the square deserted; apparently the men had moved as silently as ever to the beds selected for the night. And still, the Leader worked over his plans, hardly touching the food at his side.

Finally he stirred. "Done," he stated. "See, Meyers, it is simple now. Tomorrow, probably from the peasants who ran off, the enemy will know we are here. With full speed, possibly they can arrive by noon, and though we start early, fifteen miles is a long march for untrained men; possibly they could catch us on the road. Therefore, we do not march. We remain here."

"Like rats in a trap? Remember, my Leader, while we have possibly ten thousand men with rifles, ammunition can be used but once—so that our apparently large supply actually consists of about fifty rounds at most."

"Even so, we remain, not like rats, but like cheese in a trap. If we move, they can strafe us from the air; if we remain, they send light tanks and trucks of men against us, since they travel fastest. In the morning, therefore, we'll send out the auto with a couple of older men—less danger of their being recognized—to the depot to order Immenhoff here with one medium tank, a crew, and trucks of ammunition and petrol. We allow an hour for the auto to reach Immenhoff and for his return here. Here, they are duplicated to a thousand tanks, perhaps, with crews, and fueled and made ready. Then, when the enemy arrives, we wipe them out, move on to the depot, clean out our supplies there, and strike north to the next. After that—"

He went on, talking now more to himself than to Meyers, and the scientist only pieced together parts of the plan. As might have been expected, it was unexpected, audacious, and would probably work. Meyers was no military genius, had only a rough working idea of military operations, but he was reasonably sure that the Leader could play the cards he was dealing himself and come out on top, barring the unforeseen in large quantities. But now, having conquered Europe, the Leader's voice was lower, and what little was audible no longer made sense to the scientist, who drew out a cheap blanket and threw himself down, his eyes closed.

Still the papers and maps rustled, and the voice droned on in soft snatches, gradually falling to a whisper and then ceasing. There was a final rattling of the map, followed by complete silence, and Meyers could feel the other's eyes on his back. He made no move, and the Leader must have been satisfied by the regular breathing that the scientist was asleep, for he muttered to himself again as he threw another blanket on the floor and blew out the light.

"A useful man, Meyers, now. But after victory, perhaps his machine would be a menace. Well, that can wait."

Meyers smiled slightly in the darkness, then went back to trying to force himself to sleep. As the Leader had said, such things could wait. At the moment, his major worry was that the Army of Occupation might come an hour too soon—but that also was nonsense; obviously, from the ranks of the legion, that could not be any part of the order of things. That which was would be, and he had nothing left to fear.

The Leader was already gone from the house when Meyers awoke. For a few minutes the scientist stood staring at the blanket of the other, then shrugged, looked at his watch, and made a hasty breakfast of wine and morphine; with cancer gnawing at their vitals, men have small fear of drug addiction, and the opiate would make seeming normality easier for a time. There were still threads to be tied in to his own satisfaction, and little time left in which to do it.

Outside, the heavy dew of the night was long since gone, and the air was fully warmed by the sun. Most of the legion were gathered in the square, some preparing breakfast, others eating, but all in the same stiff silence that had marked their goings and comings since the first. Meyers walked out among them slowly, and their eyes followed him broodingly, but they made no other sign. One of the earlier ones who had been shaving with a straight razor stopped, fingering the blade, his eyes on the scientist's neck.

Meyers stopped before him, half smiling. "Well, why not say it? What are you thinking?"

"Why bother? You know." The legionnaire's fingers clenched around the handle, then relaxed, and he went on with his shaving, muttering as his unsteady hand made the razor nick his skin. "In God's will, if I could draw this once across your throat, Meyers, I'd cut my own for the right."

Meyers nodded. "I expected so. But you can't. Remember? You must obey your original implicitly; you must not cause trouble for your original or Karl Meyers; you must not speak to us or to others except as we demand. Of course, in a couple of days, the compulsion would wear away slowly, but by that time we'll both be out of reach of each other. . . . No, back! Stay where you are and continue shaving; from the looks of the others, you'll stop worrying about your hair shortly, but why hurry it?"

"Someday, somehow, I'll beat it! And then, a word to the original— or I'll track you down myself. God!" But the threatening scowl lessened, and the man went reluctantly back to his shaving, in the grip of the compulsion still. Meyers chuckled dryly.

"What was and has been—will be."

He passed down the line again, in and out among the mingled men who were scattered about without order, studying them carefully, noting how they ranged from trim copies of the Leader in field coat and well kept to what might have been demented scavengers picking from the garbage cans of the alleys and back streets. And yet, even the oldest and filthiest of the group was still the same man who had come closer to conquering the known world than anyone since Alexander. Satisfied at last, he turned back toward the house where his quarters were.

A cackling, tittering quaver at his right brought him around abruptly to face something that had once been a man, but now looked more like some animated scarecrow.

"You're Meyers," the old one accused him. "*Shh!* I know it. I remember. Hee-yee, I remember again. Oh, this is wonderful, wonderful, wonderful! Do you wonder how I can speak? Wonderful, wonderful, wonderful!"

Meyers backed a step and the creature advanced again, leering, half dancing in excitement. "Well, how can you speak? The compulsion shouldn't have worn off so soon!"

"Hee! Hee-yee-yee! Wonderful!" The wreck of a man was dancing more frantically now, rubbing his hands together. Then he sobered sharply, laughter bubbling out of a straight mouth and tapering off, like the drippings from a closed faucet. "*Shh!* I'll tell you. Yes, tell you all about it, but you mustn't tell *him*. *He* makes me come here every day where I can eat, and I like to eat. If *he* knew, *he* might not let me come. This is my last day; did you know it? Yes, my last day. I'm the oldest. Wonderful, don't you think it's wonderful? I do."

"You're crazy!" Meyers had expected it, yet the realization of the fact was still a shock to him and to his Continental background of fear of mental unbalance.

The scarecrow figure bobbed its head in agreement. "I'm crazy, yes—crazy. I've been crazy almost a year now—isn't it wonderful? But don't tell *him*. It's nice to be crazy. I can talk now; I couldn't talk before—*he* wouldn't let me. And some of the others are crazy, too, and they talk to me; we talk quietly, and *he* doesn't know. . . . You're Meyers, I remember now. I've been watching you, wondering, and now I remember. There's something else I should remember—something I should do; I planned it all once, and it was so clever, but now I can't remember— You're Meyers. Don't I hate you?"

"No. No, Leader, I'm your friend." In spite of himself, Meyers was shuddering, wondering how to break away from the maniac. He was painfully aware that for some reason the compulsion on which he had counted no longer worked; insanity had thrown the normal rules overboard. If this person should remember fully— Again Meyers shuddered, not from personal fear, but the fear that certain things still undone might not be completed. "No, great Leader, I'm your real friend. Your best friend. I'm the one who told him to bring you here to eat."

"Yes? Oh, wonderful—I like to eat. But I'm not the Leader; *he* is . . . and *he* told me . . . what did *he* tell me? Hee! I remember again, *he* told me to find you; *he* wants you. And I'm the last. Oh, it's wonderful, wonderful, wonderful! Now I'll remember it all, I will. Hee-yee-yee! Wonderful. You'd better go now, Meyers. *He* wants you. Isn't it wonderful?"

Meyers lost no time in leaving, glad for any excuse, but wondering why the Leader had sent for him, and how much the lunatic had told. He glanced at his watch again, and at the sun, checking mentally, and felt surer as he entered the quarters. Then he saw there was no reason to fear, for the Leader had his maps out again, and was nervously tapping his foot against the floor; but there was no personal anger in his glance.

"Meyers? Where were you?"

"Out among the legion, my Leader, making sure they were ready to begin operations. All is prepared."

"Good." The Leader accepted his version without doubt. "I, too, have been busy. The car was sent off almost an hour ago—more than an hour ago—to the depot, and Immenhoff should be here at any moment. No sign of the enemy yet; we'll have time enough. Then, let them come!"

He fell back to the chair beside the table, nervous fingers tapping against the map, feet still rubbing at the floor, keyed to the highest tension, like a cat about to leap at its prey. "What time is it? Hm-m-m. No sound of the tank yet. What's delaying the fool? He should be here now. Hadn't we best get the machine outside?"

"It won't be necessary," Meyers assured him. "I'll simply run out a wire from the receiver to the tank when it arrives; the machine will work at a considerable distance, just as long as the subject is under some part of it."

"Good. What's delaying Immenhoff? He should have made it long ago. And where's the courier I sent last night? Why didn't he report back? I—"

"Hee-yee! He's smart, Leader, just as I once was." The tittering voice came from the door of their quarters, and both men looked up to see the old lunatic standing there, running his fingers through his beard. "Oh, it was wonderful! Why walk all that long way back when he knew it made no difference where he was—the machine will bring him back, anyhow. Wonderful, don't you think it was wonderful? You didn't tell him to walk back."

The Leader scowled, nodded. "Yes, I suppose it made no difference whether he came back or not. He could return with Immenhoff."

"Not he, not he! Not with Immenhoff."

"Fool! Why not? And get out of here!"

But the lunatic was in no hurry to leave. He leaned against the doorway, snickering. "Immenhoff's dead—Immenhoff's dead. Wonderful! He's been dead a long time now. The Army of Occupation found him and he got killed. I remember it all now, how I found him all dead when I was the courier. So I didn't come back, because I was smart, and then I was back without walking. Wonderful, wonderful, wonderful! I remember everything now, don't I?"

"Immenhoff dead? Impossible!" The Leader was out of the chair, stalking toward the man, black rage on his face. "You're insane!"

"Hee! Isn't it wonderful? They always said I was and now I am. But Immenhoff's dead, and he won't come here, and there'll be no tanks. Oh, how wonderful, never to march at all, but just come here every day to eat. I like to eat. . . . No, don't touch me. I'll shoot, I will. I remember this is a gun, and I'll shoot, and the bullet will explode with noise, lots of noise. Don't come near me." He centered the automatic squarely on the Leader's stomach, smirking gleefully as he watched his original retreat cautiously back toward the table.

"You're mad at me because I'm crazy—" A sudden effort of concentration sent the smirk away to be replaced by cunning. "You know I'm crazy now! I didn't want you to know, but I told you. How sad, how sad, isn't it sad? No, it isn't sad, it's wonderful still, and I'm going to kill you. That's what I wanted to remember. I'm going to kill you, Leader. Now isn't that nice that I'm going to kill you?"

Meyers sat back in another chair, watching the scene as he might have a strange play, wondering what the next move might be, but calmly aware that he had no part to play in the next few moments. Then he noticed the Leader's hand drop behind him and grope back on the table for the automatic there, and his curiosity was satisfied. Obviously, the lunatic couldn't have killed the original.

The lunatic babbled on. "I remember my plan, Leader. I'll kill you, and then there won't be any you. And without you, there won't be any me. I'll never have to hunt for clothes, or keep from talking, or go crazy. I won't be at all, and it'll be wonderful. No more twenty years. Wonderful, isn't it wonderful? Hee-yee-yee! Oh, wonderful. But I like to eat, and dead men don't eat, do they? Do they? Too bad, too bad, but I had breakfast this morning, anyhow. I'm going to kill you the next time I say 'wonderful,' Leader. I'm going to shoot and there'll be noise, and you'll be dead. Wonder—"

His lips went on with the motion, even as the Leader's hand whipped out from behind him and the bullet exploded in his head with a sudden crash that split his skull like a melon and threw mangled bits of flesh out through the door, leaving half a face and a tattered old body to slump slowly toward the floor with a last spasmodic kick. With a wry face, the Leader tossed the gun back on the table and rolled the dead figure outside the door with his foot.

Meyers collected the gun quietly, substituting his watch, face up where he could watch the minute hand. "That was yourself you shot, my Leader," he stated as the other turned back to the table.

"Not myself, a duplicate. What matter, he was useless, obviously, with his insane babble of Immenhoff's death. Or— The tank should have been here long before this! But Immenhoff couldn't have been discovered!"

Meyers nodded. "He was—all the 'secret' depots were; I knew of it. And the body you just tossed outside wasn't merely a duplicate—it was yourself as you will inevitably be."

"You— Treason!" Ugly horror and the beginnings of personal fear spread across the Leader's face, twisting the scar and turning it livid. "For that—"

Meyers covered him with the automatic. "For that," he finished, "you'll remain seated, Leader, with your hands on the table in clear view. Oh, I have no intention of killing you, but I could stun you quite easily; I assure you, I'm an excellent shot."

"What do you want? The reward of the invaders?"

"Only the inevitable, Leader, only what will be because it has already been. Here!" Meyers tossed a small leather wallet onto the table with his left hand, flipping it open to the picture of a woman perhaps thirty-five years old. "What do you see there?"

"A damned Jewess!" The Leader's eyes had flicked to the picture and away, darting about the room and back to it.

"Quite so. Now, to you, a damned Jewess, Leader." Meyers replaced the wallet gently, his eyes cold. "Once, though, to me, a lovely and understanding woman, interested in my work, busy about our home, a good mother to my children; there were two of them, a boy and a girl—more damned Jews to you, probably. We were happy then. I was about to become a full professor at Heidelberg, we had our friends, our life, our home. Some, of course, even then were filled with hatred toward the Jewish people, but we could stand all that. Can you guess what happened? Not hard, is it?

"Some of your Youths. She'd gone to her father to stay with him, hoping it would all blow over and she could come back to me without her presence hurting me. They raided the shop one night, beat up her father, tossed her out of a third-story window, and made the children jump after her—mere sport, and patriotic sport! When I found her at the home of some friends, the children were dead and she was dying."

The Leader stirred again. "What did you expect? That we should coddle every Jew to our bosom and let them bespoil the Reich again? You were a traitor to your fatherland when you married her."

"So I found out. Two years in a concentration camp, my Leader, taught me that well, indeed. And it gave me time to think. No matter how much you beat a man down and make him grovel and live in filth, he still may be able to think, and his thoughts may still find you out—you should have thought of that. For two years, I thought about a certain field of mathematics, and at last I began to think about the thing instead of the symbols. And at last, when I'd groveled and humbled myself, sworn a thousandfold that I'd seen the light, and made myself something a decent man would spurn aside, they let me out again, ten years older for the two years there, and a hundred times wiser.

"So I came finally to the little farm near Bresseldorf, and I worked as I could, hoping that, somehow, a just God would so shape things that I could use my discovery. About the time I'd finished, you fled, and I almost gave up hope; then I saw that in your escape lay my chances. I found you, persuaded you to return, and here you are. It sounds simple enough now, but I wasn't sure until I saw the legion. What would happen if I had turned you over to the Army of Occupation?"

"Eh?" The Leader had been watching the door, hoping for some distracting event, but his eyes now swung back to Meyers. "I don't know. Is that what you plan?"

"Napoleon was exiled; Wilhelm died in bed at Dorn. Are the leaders who cause the trouble ever punished, my Leader? I think not. Exile may not be pleasant, but normally is not too hard a punishment—normal exile to another land. I have devised a slightly altered exile, and now I shall do nothing to you. What was—will be—and I'll be content to know that eventually you kill yourself, after you've gone insane."

Meyers glanced at the watch on the table, and his eyes gleamed savagely for a second before the cool, impersonal manner returned.

"The time is almost up, my Leader. I was fair to you; I explained to the best of my ability the workings of my invention. But instead of science, you wanted magic; you expected me to create some pseudo-duplicate of yourself, yet leave the real self unaltered. You absorbed the word 'plenum' as an incantation, but gave no heed to the reality. Remember the example I gave—a piece of string looped back on itself? In front of you is a string from some peasant's dress; now, conceive that piece of string—it loops back, starts out again, and is again drawn back—it does not put forth new feelers that do the returning to base for it, but must come back by itself, and never gets beyond a certain distance from itself. The coins that you saw in the pile disappeared—not because I depressed a switch, but because the two-minute interval was finished, and they were forced to return again to the previous two minutes."

Escape thoughts were obviously abandoned in the mind of the Leader now, and he was staring fixedly at Meyers while his hands played with the raveling from a peasant's garment, looping and unlooping it. "No," he said at last, and there was a tinge of awe and pleading in his voice, the beginning of tears in his eyes. "That is insane. Karl Meyers, you are a fool! Release me from this, and even now, with all that has happened, you'll still find me a man who can reward his friends; release me, and still I'll reconquer the world, half of which shall be yours. Don't be a fool, Meyers."

Meyers grinned. "There's no release, Leader. How often must I tell you that what is now will surely be; you have already been on the wheel—you must continue. And—the time is almost here!"

He watched the tensing of the Leader's muscles with complete calm, dropping the automatic back onto his lap. Even as the Leader leaped from his chair in a frenzied effort and dashed toward him, he made no move. There was no need. The minute hand of the watch reached a mark on the face, and the leaping figure of the world's most feared man was no longer there. Meyers was alone in the house, and alone in Bresseldorf.

He tossed the gun onto the table, patting the pocket containing his wallet, and moved toward the dead figure outside the door. Soon, if the Leader had been right, the Army of Occupation would be here. Before then, he must destroy his machine.

One second he was dashing across the room toward the neck of Karl Meyers, the next, without any feeling of change, he was standing in the yard of the house of Meyers, near Bresseldorf, and ranging from him and behind him were rows of others. In his hands, which had been empty a second before, he clutched a rifle. At his side was belted one of the new-issue automatics. And before him, through the door of the house that had been Karl Meyers', he could see himself coming forward, Meyers a few paces behind.

For the moment there were no thoughts in his head, only an endless refrain that went: "I must obey my original implicitly; I must not cause trouble for my original or Karl Meyers; I must not speak to anyone unless one of those two commands. I must obey my original implicitly; I must not cause trouble—" By an effort, he stopped the march of the words in his head, but the force of them went on, an undercurrent to all his thinking, an endless and inescapable order that must be obeyed.

Beside him, those strange others who were himself waited expressionlessly while the original came out into the doorway and began to speak to them. "Soldiers of the Greater Reich that is to be . . . Let us be merciless in avenging . . . The fruits of victory. . . ." Victory! Yes, for Karl Meyers. For the man who stood there beside the original, a faint smile on his face, looking out slowly over the ranks of the legion.

"But I speak to myselves. You who come after me know what is to be this day and in the days to come, so why should I tell you? And you know that my cause is just. The Jews, the Jew-lovers—" The words of the original went maddeningly on, words that were still fresh in his memory, words that he had spoken only twenty-four hours before.

And now, three dead Jews and a Jew-lover had brought him to this. Somehow, he must stop this mad farce, cry out to the original that it was treason and madness, that it was far better to turn back to the guards in Switzerland, or to march forth toward the invaders. But the words were only a faint whisper, even to himself, and the all-powerful compulsion choked even the whisper off before he could finish it. He must not speak to anyone unless one of those two commanded.

Still the words went on. "Not victory in a decade, nor a year, but in a month! We shall go north and south and east and west! We shall show them that our fangs are not pulled; that those which we lost were but our milk teeth, now replaced by a second and harder growth!

"And for those who would have betrayed us, or bound us down in chains to feed the gold lust of the mad democracies, or denied us the room to live which is rightfully ours—for those, we shall find a proper place. This time, for once and for all, there shall be an end to the evils that corrupt the earth—the Jews and the Bolsheviks, and their friends, and friends' friends. Germany shall emerge, purged and cleansed, a new and greater Reich, whose domain shall not be Europe, nor this hemisphere, but the world!

"Many of you have seen all this in the future from which you come, and all of you must be ready to reassure yourselves of it today, that the glory of it may fill your tomorrow. Now, we march against a few peasants. Tomorrow, after quartering in Bresseldorf, we shall be in the secret depot, where those who remain loyal shall be privileged to multiply and join us, and where we shall multiply all our armament tenthousandfold! Into Bresseldorf, then, and if any of the peasants are disloyal, be merciless in removing the scum! Forward!"

His blood was pounding with the mockery of it, and his hands were clutching on the rifle. Only one shot from the gun, and Karl Meyers would die. One quick move, too sudden to defeat, and he would be avenged. Yet, as he made the first effort toward lifting the rifle, the compulsion surged upward, drowning out all other orders of his mind. He must not cause trouble for his original or Karl Meyers!

He could feel the futile tears on his face as he stood there, and the mere knowledge of their futility was the hardest blow of all. Before him, his original was smiling at him and starting forward, to be checked by Meyers, and to swing back after a few words.

"Proceed to Bresseldorf, then, and we follow. Secure quarters for yourself and food, and a place for me and for Meyers; we stop there until I can send word to the depot during the night and extend my plans. To Bresseldorf!"

Against his will, his feet turned then with the others, out across the yard and into the road, and he was headed toward Bresseldorf. His eyes swept over the group, estimating them to be six or seven thousand in number; and that would mean twenty years, at one a day—twenty years of marching to Bresseldorf, eating, sleeping, eating again, being back at the farm, hearing the original's speech, and marching to Bresseldorf. Finally—from far down the line, a titter from the oldest and filthiest reached him—finally that; madness and death at the hands of himself, while Karl Meyers stood by, watching and gloating. He no longer doubted the truth of the scientist's statements; what had been, would be.

For twenty years! For more than seven thousand days, each the same day, each one step nearer madness. God!

The Wabbler

Murray Leinster
(Will F. Jenkins, 1896–1975)

WILL *F. Jenkins began his writing career when he was seventeen, and was a well-established writer when he published his first science fiction story in 1919. History has not been particularly kind to him, mostly because of his versatility and productivity—those who look for themes in his very long career will probably be disappointed. In addition, his novel-length work was not outstanding.*

Nevertheless, he produced many notable stories which have stood the test of time. These include his classic treatment of the meeting of aliens and Earthmen, "First Contact" (1945); the Hugo Award-winning novelette "Exploration Team" (1956); the widely reprinted "Keyhole" (1951); "The Life-Work of Professor Muntz" (1949); "Med Service" (1957), part of a long and successful series; "Propagandist" (1947); and the present selection.

World War II had been going on for several years when this story was written, and it was only natural for science fiction writers to treat the machines of war as well as the men who were fighting in it. "The Wabbler" does not face the age-old dilemma of combat—choosing between the individual and the mission—for it is a machine, one that has been taught only to kill.

From *Astounding Science Fiction   1942*

The Wabbler went westward, with a dozen of its fellows, by night and in the belly of a sleek, swift-flying thing. There were no lights anywhere save the stars overhead. There was a sustained, furious roaring noise, which was the sound the sleek thing made in flying. The Wabbler lay in its place, with its ten-foot tail coiled neatly above its lower end, and waited with a sort of deadly patience for the accomplishment of its destiny. It and all its brothers were pear-shaped, with absurdly huge and blunt-ended horns, and with small round holes where eyes might have been, and shielded vents where they might have had mouths. They looked chinless, somehow. They also looked alive, and inhuman, and filled with a sort of passionless hate. They seemed like bodiless demons out of some metallic hell. It was not possible to feel any affection for them. Even the men who handled them felt only a sort of vengeful hope in their capacities.

The Wabblers squatted in their racks for long hours. It was very cold, but they gave no sign. The sleek, swift-flying thing roared on and roared on. The Wabblers waited. Men moved somewhere in the flying thing, but they did not come where the Wabblers were until the very end. But somehow, when a man came and inspected each one of them very carefully and poked experimentally about the bottoms of the racks in which the Wabblers lay, they knew that the time had come.

The man went away. The sleek thing tilted a little. It seemed to climb. The air grew colder, but the Wabblers—all of them—were indifferent. Air was not their element. Then, when it was very, very cold indeed, the roaring noise of the flying thing ceased abruptly. The cessation of the noise was startling. Presently little whistling, whispering noises took the place of the roar, as hearing adjusted to a new level of sound. That whistling and whining noise was wind, flowing past the wings of the flying thing. Presently the air was a little warmer—but still very cold. The flying thing was gliding, motors off, and descending at a very gradual slant.

The Wabbler was the fourth in the row of its brothers on the port side of the flying thing. It did not stir, of course, but it felt an atmosphere of grim and savage anticipation. It seemed that all the brothers coldly exchanged greetings and farewell. The time had definitely come.

The flying thing leveled out. Levers and rods moved in the darkness of its belly. The feeling of anticipation increased. Then, suddenly, there were only eleven of the Wabblers. Wind roared where the twelfth had been. There were ten. There were nine, eight, seven, six—

The Wabbler hurtled downward through blackness. There were clouds overhead now. In all the world there was no speck of actual light. But below there was a faint luminosity. The Wabbler's tail uncurled and writhed flexibly behind it. Wind screamed past its ungainly form. It went plunging down and down and down, its round holes—which looked so much like eyes—seeming incurious and utterly impassive. The luminosity underneath separated into streaks of bluish glow, which were phosphorescences given off by the curling tips of waves.

Off to westward there was a brighter streak of such luminosity. It was surf.

Splash! The Wabbler plunged into the water with a flare of luminescence and a thirty-foot spout of spume and spray rising where it struck. But then that spouting ceased, and the Wabbler was safely under water. It dived swiftly for twenty feet. Perhaps thirty. Then its falling checked. It swung about, and its writhing tail settled down below it. For a little while it seemed almost to intend to swim back to the surface. But bubbles came from the shielded opening which seemed to be a mouth. It hung there in the darkness of the sea—but now and then there were little fiery streaks of light as natives of the ocean swam about it—and then slowly, slowly, slowly it settled downward. Its ten-foot tail seemed to waver a little, as if groping.

Presently it touched. Ooze. Black ooze. Sea bottom. Sixty feet overhead the waves marched to and fro in darkness. Somehow, through the stilly silence, there came a muffled vibration. That was the distant surf, beating upon a shore. The Wabbler hung for an instant with the very tip of its tail barely touching the bottom. Then it made small sounds inside itself. More bubbles came from the round place like a mouth. It settled one foot; two feet; three. Three feet of its tail rested on the soft ooze. It hung, pear-shaped, some seven feet above the ocean bottom, with the very tip of its horns no more than four feet higher yet. There was fifty feet of empty sea above it. This was not its destiny. It waited passionlessly for what was to happen.

There was silence save for the faint vibration from the distant surf. But there was an infinitesimal noise, also, within the Wabbler's bulk, a rhythmic, insistent, hurried *tick-tick-tick-tick*— It was the Wabbler's brain in action.

Time passed. Above the sea the sleek, swift-flying thing bellowed suddenly far away. It swerved and went roaring back in the direction from which it had come. Its belly was empty now, and somewhere in the heaving sea there were other Wabblers, each one now waiting as the fourth Wabbler did, for the thing that its brain expected. Minutes and minutes passed. The seas marched to and fro. The faraway surf rumbled and roared against the shore. And higher yet, above the clouds, a low-hanging and invisible moon dipped down toward a horizon which did not show anywhere. But the Wabbler waited.

The tide came. Here, so far from the pounding surf, the stirring of the lower levels of the sea was slight indeed. But the tide moved in toward the land. Slowly, the pressure of water against one of the Wabbler's sides became evident. The Wabbler leaned infinitesimally toward the shore. Presently its flexible tail ceased to be curved where it lay upon the ooze. It straightened out. There were little bluish glows where it stirred the phosphorescent mud. Then the Wabbler moved.

Shoreward. It trailed its tail behind it and left a little glowing track of ghostly light.

Fish swam about it. Once there was a furry purring sound, and propellers pushed an invisible, floating thing across the surface of the sea. But it was far away and the Wabbler was impassive. The tide flowed. The Wabbler moved in little jerks. Sometimes three feet or four, and sometimes eight or ten. Once, where the sea bottom slanted downward for a space, it moved steadily for almost a hundred yards. It came to rest then, swaying a little. Presently it jerked onward once more. Somewhere an indefinite distance away were its brothers, moving on in the same fashion. The Wabbler went on and on, purposefully, moved by the tide.

Before the tide turned, the Wabbler had moved two miles nearer to the land. But it did not move in a straight line. Its trailing, flexible tail kept it in the deepest water and the strongest current. It moved very deliberately and almost always in small jerks, and it followed the current. The current was strongest where it moved toward a harbor entrance. In moving two miles shoreward, the Wabbler also moved more than two miles nearer to a harbor.

There came a time, though, when the tide slackened. The Wabbler ceased to move. For half an hour it hung quite still, swaying a little and progressing not at all, while the *tick-tick-tick-tick* of its brain measured patience against intent. At the end of the half-hour there were small clanking noises within its body. Its shielded mouth emitted bubbles. It sank, and checked, and gave off more bubbles, and sank again. It eased itself very cautiously and very gently into the ooze. Then it gave off more bubbles and lay at rest.

It waited there, its brain ticking restlessly within it, but with its appearance of eyes impassive. It lay in the darkness like some creature from another world, awaiting a foreordained event.

For hours it lay still with no sign of any activity at all. Toward the end of those hours, a very faint graying of the upper sea became manifest. It was very dim indeed. It was not enough, in all likelihood, for even the Wabbler to detect the slight movement of semi-floating objects along the sea floor, moved by the ebb tide. But there came a time when even such movements ceased. Again the sea was still. It was full ebb. And now the Wabbler stirred.

It clanked gently and wavered where it lay in the ooze. There was a cloud of stirred-up mud, as if it had emitted jets of water from its under parts. It wabbled to one side and the other, straining, and presently its body was free, and a foot or two and then four or five feet of its tail—but it still writhed and wabbled spasmodically—and then suddenly it left the sea floor and floated free.

But only for a moment. Almost immediately its tail swung free, the Wabbler spat out bubbles and descended gently to the bottom again. It rested upon the tip of its tail. It spat more bubbles. One—two—three feet of its tail rested on the mud. It waited. Presently the flood tide moved it again.

It floated always with the current. Once it came to a curve in the deeper channel to which it had found its way, and the tide tended to sweep it up and out beyond the channel. But its tail resisted the attempt. In the end, the Wabbler swam grandly back to the deeper water. The current was stronger there. It went on and on at a magnificent two knots.

But when the current slowed again as the time of the tide change neared, the Wabbler stopped again. It swung above the yard-length of its tail upon the mud. Its brain went *tick-tick-tick-tick* and it made noises. It dribbled bubbles. It sank, and checked, and dribbled more bubbles, and sank cautiously again— It came cautiously to rest in the mud.

During this time of waiting, the Wabbler heard many sounds. Many times during slack tide, and during ebb tide, too, the water brought humming, purring noises of engines. Once a boat came very near. There was a curious hissing sound in the water. Something—a long line—passed very close overhead. A minesweeper and a minesweep patrolled the sea, striving to detect and uproot submarine mines. But the Wabbler had no anchor cable for the sweep to catch. It lay impassively upon the bottom. But its eyes stared upward with a deadly calm until the minesweeper passed on its way.

Once more during the light hours the Wabbler shook itself free of the bottom ooze and swam on with the tide. And once more—with another wait on the mud while the tide flowed out—at night. But day and night meant little to the Wabbler. Its ticking brain went on tirelessly. It rested, and swam, and swam, and rested, with a machinelike and impassive pertinacity, and always it moved toward places where the tide moved faster and with channels more distinct.

At last it came to a place where the water was no more than forty feet deep, and a distinct greenish-blue light came down from the surface sunshine. In that light the Wabbler was plainly visible. It had acquired a coating of seaweed and slime which seemed to form a sort of aura of wavering greenish tentacles. Its seeming eyes appeared now to be small and snakelike and very wise and venomous. It was still chinless, and its trailing tail made it seem more than ever like some bodiless demon out of a metallic hell. And now it came to a place where for a moment its tail caught in some minor obstruction, and as it tugged at the catch, one of its brothers floated by. It passed within twenty feet of the fourth Wabbler, and they could see each other clearly. But the fourth Wabbler was trapped. It wavered back and forth in the flood tide, trying to pull free, as its fellow swam silently and implacably onward.

Some twenty minutes after that passage there was a colossal explosion somewhere, and after that very many fuzzy, purring noises in the sea. The Wabbler may have known what had happened, or it may not. A submarine net across a harbor entrance is not a thing of which most creatures have knowledge, but it was a part of the Wabbler's environment. Its *tick-tick-ticking* brain may have interpreted the explosion quite correctly as the destiny of its brother encountering that barrier. It is more likely that the brain only noted with relief that the concussion had broken the grip of the obstruction in the mud. The Wabbler went onward in the wake of its fellow. It went sedately, and solemnly, and with a sort of unholy purposefulness, following the tidal current. Presently there was a great net that stretched across the channel, far beyond any distance that the Wabbler could be expected to see. But right where the Wabbler would pass, there was a monstrous gaping hole in that net. Off to one side there was the tail of another Wabbler, shattered away from that other Wabbler's bulk.

The fourth Wabbler went through the hole. It was very simple indeed. Its tail scraped for a moment, and then it was inside the harbor. And then the *tick-tick-ticking* of the Wabbler's brain was very crisp and incisive indeed, because this was its chance for the accomplishment of its destiny. It listened for sounds of engines, estimating their loudness with an uncanny precision, and within its rounded brainpan it measured things as abstract as variations in the vertical component of terrestrial magnetism. There were many sounds and many variations to note, too, because surface craft swarmed about the scene of a recent violent explosion. Their engines purred and rumbled, and their steel hulls made marked local changes in magnetic force. But none of them came quite close enough to the Wabbler to constitute its destiny.

It went on and on as the flood tide swept in. The harbor was a busy one, with many small craft moving about, and more than once in these daylight hours flying things alighted upon the water and took off again. But it happened that none came sufficiently near. An hour after its entrance into the harbor the Wabbler was in a sort of eddy, in a basin, and it made four slow, hitching circuits about the same spot— during one of which it came near to serried ranks of piling—before the time of slack water. But even here the Wabbler, after swaying a little without making progress for perhaps twenty minutes, made little clanking noises inside itself and dribbled out bubbles and eased itself down in the mud to wait.

It lay there, canted a little and staring up with its small, round, seeing eyes with a look of unimpassioned expectancy. Small boats roved overhead. Once engines rumbled, and a wooden-hulled craft swam on the surface of the water to the very dock whose pilings the Wabbler had seen. Then creaking sounds emanated from those pilings.

The Wabbler may have known that unloading cranes were at work. But this was not its destiny either.

There came other sounds of greater import. Clankings of gears. A definite, burning rush of water. It continued and continued. The Wabbler could not possibly be expected to understand, of course, that such burbling underwater sounds are typical of a drydock being filled—the filling beginning near low tide when a great ship is to leave at high. Especially, perhaps, the Wabbler could not be expected to know that a great warship had occupied a vastly important drydock and that its return to active service would restore much power to an enemy fleet. Certainly it could not know that another great warship waited impatiently to be repaired in the same basin. But the restless *tick-tick-tick-tick* which was the Wabbler's brain was remarkably crisp and incisive.

When flood tide began once more, the Wabbler jetted water and wabbled to and fro until it broke free of the bottom. It hung with a seeming impatience—wreathed in seaweed and coated with greenish slime—above the tail which dangled down to the harbor mud. It looked alive, and inhuman, and chinless, and it looked passionately demoniac, and it looked like something out of a submarine Gehenna. And, presently, when the flood tide began to flow and the eddy about the docks and the drydock gates began, the Wabbler inched as if purposefully toward the place where water burbled through flooding valves.

Sounds in the air did not reach the Wabbler. Sounds under water did. It heard the grinding rumble of stream winches, and it heard the screeching sound as the drydock gates swung open. They were huge gates, and they made a considerable eddy of their own. The Wabbler swam to the very center of that eddy and hung there, waiting. Now, for the first time, it seemed excited. It seemed to quiver a little. Once when it seemed that the eddy might bring it to the surface, it bubbled patiently from the vent which appeared to be a mouth. And its brain went *tick-tick-tick-tick* within it, and inside its brainpan it measured variations in the vertical component of terrestrial magnetism, and among such measurements it noted the effect of small tugs which came near but did not enter the drydock. They only sent lines within, so they could haul the warship out. But the tugs were not the Wabbler's destiny either.

It heard their propellers thrashing, and they made, to be sure, a very fine noise. But the Wabbler quivered with eagerness as somewhere within itself it noted a vast variation in the vertical magnetic component, which increased and increased steadily. That was the warship moving very slowly out of its place in the drydock. It moved very slowly but very directly toward the Wabbler, and the Wabbler knew that its destiny was near.

Somewhere very far away there was the dull, racking sound of an explosion. The Wabbler may have realized that another of its brothers had achieved its destiny, but paid no heed. Its own destiny approached. The steel prow of the battleship drew nearer and nearer, and then the bow plates were overhead, and something made a tiny click inside the Wabbler. Destiny was certain now. It waited, quivering. The mass of steel within the range of its senses grew greater and greater. The strain of restraint grew more intense. The *tick-tick-ticking* of the Wabbler's brain seemed to accelerate to a frantic—to an intolerable—pace. And then—

The Wabbler achieved its destiny. It turned into a flaming ball of incandescent gases—three hundred pounds of detonated high explosive —squarely under the keel of a thirty-five-thousand-ton battleship which at the moment was only halfway out of a drydock. The water-tight doors of the battleship were open, and its auxiliary power was off, so they could not be closed. There was much need for this drydock, and repairs were not completed in it. But it was the Wabbler's destiny to end all that. In three minutes the battleship was lying crazily on the harbor bottom, half in and half out of the drydock. She careened as she sank, and her masts and fighting tops demolished sheds by the drydock walls. Battleship and dock alike were out of action for the duration of the war.

And the Wabbler—

A long, long time afterward—years afterward—salvage divers finished cutting up the sunken warship for scrap. The last irregularly cut mass of metal went up on the salvage slings. The last diver down went stumbling about the muddy harbor water. His heavy, weighted shoes kicked up something. He fumbled to see if anything remained to be salvaged. He found a ten-foot, still-flexible tail of metal. The rest of the Wabbler had ceased to exist. Chronometer, tide-time gear, valves, compressed-air tanks, and all the balance of its intricate innards had been blown to atoms when the Wabbler achieved its destiny. Only the flexible metal tail remained intact.

The salvage diver considered that it was not worth sending the sling down for again. He dropped it in the mud and jerked on the lifeline to be hauled up to the surface.

The Halfling

Leigh Brackett (1915-1978)

THE LATE *Leigh Brackett (a perfectly ambiguous name for a female writer in the forties) was a regular contributor to the science fiction magazines, especially* Planet Stories. *Happily, her galaxy-wide adventure novels are now back in print, and her powerful post-holocaust novel,* The Long Tomorrow *(1955), is one of the very best in a crowded field. She has not received the attention and fame due her, partly because she wrote very few short stories suitable for anthologizing.*

In addition to the story reprinted here, other noteworthy stories from the forties include "Retreat to the Stars" (1941), "Terror Out of Space" (1944), and "The Enchantress of Venus" (1949), part of her three-story N'Chaka series.

From *Astonishing Stories* 1943

CHAPTER ONE

Primitive Venus

I was watching the sunset. It was something pretty special in the line of California sunsets, and it made me feel swell, being the first one I'd seen in about nine years. The pitch was in the flatlands between Culver City and Venice, and I could smell the sea. I was born in a little dump at Venice, Cal., and I've never found any smell like the clean cold salt of the Pacific—not anywhere in the Solar System.

I was standing alone, off to one side of the grounds. The usual noises of a carnival around feeding time were being made behind me, and the hammer gang was pinning the last of the tents down tight. But I wasn't thinking about Jade Greene's Interplanetary Carnival, The Wonders of the Seven Worlds Alive Before Your Eyes.

I was remembering John Damien Greene running barefoot on a wet beach, fishing for perch off the end of a jetty, and dreaming big dreams. I was wondering where John Damien Greene had gone, taking his dreams with him, because now I could hardly remember what they were.

Somebody said softly from behind me, "Mr. Greene?"

I quit thinking about John Damien Greene. It was that kind of a voice—sweet, silky, guaranteed to make you forget your own name. I turned around.

She matched her voice, all right. She stood about five-three on her bronze heels, and her eyes were more purple than the hills of Malibu. She had a funny little button of a nose and a pink mouth, smiling just enough to show her even white teeth. The bronze metal-cloth dress she wore hugged a chassis with no flaws in it anywhere. I tried to find some.

She dropped her head, so I could see the way the last of the sunlight tangled in her gold-brown hair,

"They said you were Mr. Greene. If I've made a mistake . . ."

She had an accent, just enough to be fascinating.

I said, "I'm Greene. Something I can do for you?" I still couldn't find anything wrong with her, but I kept looking just the same. My blood pressure had gone up to about three hundred.

It's hard to describe a girl like that. You can say she's five-three and beautiful, but you can't pass on the odd little tilt of her eyes and the way her mouth looks, or the something that just comes out of her like light out of a lamp, and hooks into you so you know you'll never be rid of it, not if you live to be a thousand.

She said, "Yes. You can give me a job. I'm a dancer."

I shook my head. "Sorry, miss. I got a dancer."

Her face had a look of steel down under the soft, kittenish round-ness. "I'm not just talking," she said. "I need a job so I can eat. I'm a good dancer. I'm the best dancer you ever saw anywhere. Look me over."

That's all I had been doing. I guess I was staring by then. You don't expect fluffy dolls like that to have so much iron in them. She wasn't bragging. She was just telling me.

"I still have a dancer," I told her, "a green-eyed Martian babe who is plenty good, and who would tear my head off, and yours too, if I hired you."

"Oh," she said. "Sorry. I thought you bossed this carnival." She let me think about that, and then grinned. "Let me show you."

She was close enough so I could smell the faint, spicy perfume she wore. But she'd stopped me from being just a guy chinning with a pretty girl. Right then I was Jade Greene, the carny boss-man, with scars on my knuckles and an ugly puss, and a show to keep running.

Strictly Siwash, that show, but my baby—mine to feed and paint and fuel. If this kid had something Sindi didn't have, something to drag in the cash customers—well, Sindi would have to take it and like it. Besides, Sindi was getting so she thought she owned me.

The girl was watching my face. She didn't say anything more, or even move. I scowled at her.

"You'd have to sign up for the whole tour. I'm blasting off next Monday for Venus, and then Mars, and maybe into the Asteroids."

"I don't care. Anything to be able to eat. Anything to—"

She stopped right there and bent her head again, and suddenly I could see tears on her thick brown lashes.

I said, "Okay. Come over to the cooch tent and we'll have a look."

Me, I was tempted to sign her for what was wrapped up in that bronze cloth—but business is business. I couldn't take on any left-footed ponies.

She said shakily, "You don't soften up very easily, do you?" We started across the lot toward the main gate. The night was coming down cool and fresh. Off to the left, clear back to the curving deep-purple barrier of the hills, the slim white spires of Culver, Westwood, Beverly Hills and Hollywood were beginning to show a rainbow splash of color under their floodlights.

Everything was clean, new and graceful. Only the thin fog and the smell of the sea were old.

We were close to the gate, stumbling a little in the dusk of the afterglow. Suddenly a shadow came tearing out from between the tents.

It went erratically in lithe, noiseless bounds, and it was somehow not human, even though it went on two feet. The girl caught her breath and shrank in against me. The shadow went around us three times like a crazy thing, and then stopped.

There was something eerie about that sudden stillness. The hair crawled on the back of my neck. I opened my mouth angrily.

The shadow stretched itself toward the darkening sky and let go a wail like Lucifer falling from Heaven.

I cursed. The carny lights came on, slamming a circle of blue-white glare against the night.

"Laska, come here!" I yelled.

The girl screamed.

I put my arm around her. "It's all right," I said, and then, "Come here, you misbegotten Thing! You're on a sleighride again."

There were more things I wanted to say, but the girl cramped my style. Laska slunk in towards us. I didn't blame her for yelping. Laska wasn't pretty.

He wasn't much taller than the girl, and looked shorter because he was drooping. He wore a pair of tight dark trunks and nothing else except the cross-shaped mane of fine blue-gray fur that went across his shoulders and down his back, from the peak between his eyes to his long tail. He was dragging the tail, and the tip of it was twitching. There was more of the soft fur on his chest and forearms, and a fringe of it down his lank belly.

I grabbed him by the scruff and shook him. "I ought to boot your ribs in! We got a show in less than two hours."

He looked up at me. The pupils of his yellow-green eyes were closed to thin hairlines, but they were flat and cold with hatred. The glaring lights showed me the wet whiteness of his pointed teeth and the raspy pinkness of his tongue.

"Let me go. Let me go, you human!" His voice was hoarse and accented.

"I'll let you go." I cuffed him across the face. "I'll let you go to the Immigration authorities. You wouldn't like that, would you? You wouldn't even have coffee to hop up on when you died."

The sharp claws came out of his fingers and toes, flexed hungrily and went back in again.

I dropped him.

"Go on back inside. Find the croaker and tell him to straighten you out. I don't give a damn what you do on your own time, but you miss out on one more show and I'll take your job and call the I-men. Get it?"

"I get it," said Laska sullenly, and curled his red tongue over his teeth. He shot his flat, cold glance at the girl and went away, not making any sound at all.

The girl shivered and drew away from me. "What was—that?"

"Cat-man from Callisto. My prize performer. They're pretty rare."

"I—I've heard of them. They evolved from a cat-ancestor instead of an ape, like we did."

"That's putting it crudely, but it's close enough. I've got a carload of critters like that, geeks from all over the System. They ain't human, and they don't fit with animals either. Moth-men, lizard-men, guys with wings and guys with six arms and antennae. They all followed evolutionary tracks peculiar to their particular hunks of planet, only they stopped before they got where they were going. The Callistan kitties are the aristocrats of the bunch. They've got an I.Q. higher than a lot of humans, and wouldn't spit on the other halflings."

"Poor things," she said softly. "You didn't have to be so cruel to him."

I laughed. "That What's-it would as soon claw my insides out as soon as look at me—or any other human, including you—just on general principles. That's why Immigration hates to let 'em in even on a work permit. And when he's hopped up on coffee. . . ."

"Coffee? I thought I must have heard wrong."

"Nope. The caffeine in Earthly coffee berries works just like coke or hashish for 'em. Venusian coffee hits 'em so hard they go nuts and then die, but our own kind just keeps 'em going. It's only the hoppy ones you ever find in a show like this. They get started on coffee and they have to have it no matter what they have to do to get it."

She shuddered a little. "You said something about dying."

"Yeah. If he's ever deported back to Callisto his people will tear him apart. They're a clannish bunch. I guess the first humans on Callisto weren't very tactful, or else they just hate us because we're something they're not and never can be. Anyway, their tribal law forbids them to have anything to do with us except killing. Nobody knows much about 'em, but I hear they have a nice friendly religion, something like the old-time Thugs and their Kali worship."

I paused, and then said uncomfortably, "Sorry I had to rough him up in front of you. But he's got to be kept in line."

She nodded. We didn't say anything after that. We went in past the main box and along between the burglars readying up their layouts— Martian *getak*, Venusian *shalil* and the game the Mercurian hillmen play with human skulls. Crooked? Sure—but suckers like to be fooled, and a guy has to make a living.

I couldn't take my eyes off the girl. I thought, *if she dances the way she walks* . . .

She didn't look much at the big three-dimensional natural-color pictures advertising the geek show. We went by the brute top, and suddenly all hell broke loose inside of it. I've got a fair assortment of animals from all over. They make pretty funny noises when they get started, and they were started now.

They were nervous, unhappy noises. I heard prisoners yammering in the Lunar cell-blocks once, and that was the way this sounded— strong, living things shut up in cages and tearing their hearts out with it—hate, fear and longing like you never thought about. It turned you cold.

The girl looked scared. I put my arm around her again, not minding it at all. Just then Tiny came out of the brute top.

Tiny is a Venusian deep-jungle man, about two sizes smaller than the Empire State Building, and the best zooman I ever had, drunk or sober. Right now he was mad.

"I tell that Laska stay 'way from here," he yelled. "My kids smell him. You listen!"

I didn't have to listen. His "kids" could have been heard halfway to New York. Laska had been expressly forbidden to go near the brute top because the smell of him set the beasts crazy. Whether they were calling to him as one animal to another, or scared of him as something unnatural, we didn't know. The other halflings were pretty good about it, but Laska liked to start trouble just for the hell of it.

I said, "Laska's hopped again. I sent him to the croaker. You get the kids quiet again, and then send one of the punks over to the crumb castle and tell the cook I said if he ever gives Laska a teaspoonful of coffee again without my say-so I'll fry him in his own grease."

Tiny nodded his huge pale head and vanished, cursing. I said to the girl, "Still want to be a carny?"

"Oh, yes," she said. "Anything, as long as you serve food!"

"That's a pretty accent you got. What is it?"

"Just about everything. I was born on a ship between Earth and Mars, and I've lived all over. My father was in the diplomatic corps."

I said, "Oh. Well, here's the place. Go to it."

Sindi was sitting cross-legged on the stage, sipping *thil* and listening to sad Martian music on the juke box behind the screen of faded Martian tapestry. She looked up and saw us, and she didn't like what she saw.

She got up. She was a Low-Canaler, built light and wiry, and she moved like a cat. She had long emerald eyes and black hair with little bells braided in it, and clusters of tiny bells in her ears. She was wearing the skin of a Martian sand-leopard, no more clothes than the law forced her to wear. She was something to look at, and she had a disposition like three yards of barbed wire.

I said, "Hi, Sindi. This kid wants a try-out. Climb down, huh?"

Sindi looked the kid over. She smiled and climbed down and put her hand on my arm. She sounded like a shower of rain when she moved, and her nails bit into me, hard.

I said between my teeth, "What music do you want, kid?"

"My name's Laura—Laura Darrow." Her eyes were very big and very purple. "Do you have Enhali's *Primitive Venus?*"

Not more than half a dozen dancers in the System can do justice to that collection of tribal music. Some of it's subhuman and so savage it scares you. We use it for mood music, to draw the crowd.

I started to protest, but Sindi smiled and tinkled her head back. "Of course, put it on, Jade."

I shrugged and went in and fiddled with the juke box. When I came out Laura Darrow was up on the stage and we had an audience. Sindi must have passed the high sign. I shoved my way through a bunch of Venusian lizard-men and sat down. There were three or four little moth-people from Phobos roosting up on the braces so their delicate wings wouldn't get damaged in the crush.

The music started. Laura kicked off her shoes and danced.

I don't think I breathed all the time she was on the stage. I don't remember anyone else breathing, either. We just sat and stared, sweating with nervous ecstasy, shivering occasionally, with the music beating and crying and surging over us.

The girl wasn't human. She was sunlight, quicksilver, a leaf riding the wind—but nothing human, nothing tied down to muscles and gravity and flesh. She was—oh, hell, there aren't any words. She was the music.

When she was through we sat there a long time, perfectly still. Then the Venusians, human and half-human, let go a yell and the audience came to and tore up the seats.

In the middle of it Sindi looked at me with deadly green eyes and said, "I suppose she's hired."

"Yeah. But it doesn't have anything to do with you, baby."

"Listen, Jade. This suitcase outfit isn't big enough for two of us. Besides, she's got you hooked, and she can have you."

"She hasn't got me hooked. Anyway, so what? You don't own me."

"No. And you don't own me, either."

"I got a contract."

She told me what I could do with my contract.

I yelled, "What do you want me to do, throw her out on her ear? With that talent?"

"Talent!" snarled Sindi. "She's not talented. She's a freak."

"Just like a dame. Why can't you be a good loser?"

She explained why. A lot of it didn't make sense, and none of it was printable. Presently she went out, leaving me sore and a little uneasy. We had quite a few Martians with the outfit. She could make trouble.

Oh, hell! Just another dame sore because she was outclassed. Artistic temperament, plus jealousy. So what? Let her try something. I could handle it. I'd handled people before.

I jammed my way up to the stage. Laura was being mobbed. She looked scared—some of the halflings are enough to give a tough guy nightmares—and she was crying.

I said, "Relax, honey. You're in." I knew that Sindi was telling the truth. I was hooked. I was so hooked it scared me, but I wouldn't have wiggled off if I could.

She sagged down in my arms and said, "Please, I'm hungry."

I half carried her out, with the moth-people fluttering their gorgeous wings around our heads and praising her in their soft, furry little voices.

I fed her in my own quarters. She shuddered when I poured her coffee, and refused it, saying she didn't think she'd ever enjoy it again. She took tea instead. She was hungry, all right. I thought she'd never stop eating.

Finally I said, "The pay's forty credits, and found."

She nodded.

I said gently, "You can tell me. What's wrong?"

She gave me a wide, purple stare. "What do you mean?"

"A dancer like you could write her own ticket anywhere, and not for the kind of peanuts I can pay you. You're in a jam."

She looked at the table and locked her fingers together. Their long pink nails glistened.

She whispered, "It isn't anything bad. Just a—a passport difficulty. I told you I was born in space. The records got lost somehow, and living the way we did—well, I had to come to Earth in a hurry, and I couldn't prove my citizenship, so I came without it. Now I can't get back to Venus where my money is, and I can't stay here. That's why I wanted so badly to get a job with you. You're going out, and you can take me."

I knew how to do that, all right. I said, "You must have had a big reason to take the risk you did. If you're caught it means the Luna cell-blocks for a long time before they deport you."

She shivered. "It was a personal matter. It delayed me a while. I—was too late."

I said, "Sure. I'm sorry." I took her to her tent, left her there and went out to get the show running, cursing Sindi. I stopped cursing and stared when I passed the cooch tent. She was there, and giving.

She stuck out her tongue at me and I went on.

That evening I hired the punk, just a scrawny kid with a white face, who said he was hungry and needed work. I gave him to Tiny, to help out in the brute top.

CHAPTER TWO

Voice of Terror

We played in luck that week. Some gilded darling of the screen showed up with somebody else's husband who wasn't quite divorced yet, and we got a lot of free publicity in the papers and over the air. Laura went on the second night and brought down the house. We turned 'em away for the first time in history. The only thing that worried me was Sindi.

She wouldn't speak to me, only smile at me along her green eyes as though she knew a lot she wasn't telling and not any of it nice. I tried to keep an eye on her, just in case.

For five days I walked a tightrope between heaven and hell. Everybody on the pitch knew I was a dead duck where Laura was concerned. I suppose they got a good laugh out of it—me, Jade Greene the carny boss, knocked softer than a cup custard by a girl young enough to be my daughter, a girl from a good family, a girl with talent that put her so far beyond my lousy dog-and-pony show. . . .

I knew all that. It didn't do any good. I couldn't keep away from her. She was so little and lovely; she walked like music; her purple eyes had a tilt to them that kept you looking, and her mouth—

I kissed it on the fifth night, out back of the cooch tent when the show was over. It was dark there; we were all alone, and the faint spicy breath of her came to me through the thin salt fog. I kissed her.

Her mouth answered mine. Then she wrenched away, suddenly, with a queer fury. I let her go. She was shuddering, and breathing hard.

I said, "I'm sorry."

"It isn't that. Oh, Jade, I—" She stopped. I could hear the breath sobbing in her throat. Then she turned and ran away, and the sound of her weeping came back to me through the dark.

I went to my quarters and got out a bottle. After the first shot I just sat staring at it with my head in my hands. I haven't any idea how long I sat there. It seemed like forever. I only know that the pitch was dark, sound asleep under a pall of fog, when Sindi screamed.

I didn't know it was Sindi then. The scream didn't have any personality. It was the voice of terror and final pain, and it was far beyond anything human.

I got my gun out of the table drawer. I remember my palm was slippery with cold sweat. I went outside, catching up the big flashlight kept for emergencies near the tent flap. It was very dark out there, very still, and yet not quiet. There was something behind the darkness and the silence, hiding in them, breathing softly and waiting.

The pitch began to wake up. The stir and rustle spread out from the scream like ripples from a stone, and over in the brute top a Martian sand-cat began to wail, thin and feral, like an echo of death.

I went along between the tents, walking fast and silent. I felt sick, and the skin of my back twitched; my face began to ache from being drawn tight. The torch beam shook a little in my hand.

I found her back of the cooch tent, not far from where I'd kissed Laura. She was lying on her face, huddled up, like a brown island in a red sea. The little bells were still in her ears.

I walked in her blood and knelt down in it and put my hand on her shoulder. I thought she was dead, but the bells tinkled faintly, like something far away on another star. I tried to turn her over.

She gasped, "Don't." It wasn't a voice. It was hardly a breath, but I could hear it. I can still hear it. I took my hand away.

"Sindi—"

A little wash of sound from the bells, like rain far off—"You fool," she whispered. "The stage, Jade, the stage—"

She stopped. The croaker came from somewhere behind me and knocked me out of the way, but I knew it was no use. I knew Sindi had stopped for good.

Humans and halflings were jammed in all round, staring, whispering, some of them screaming a little. The brute top had gone crazy. They smelt blood and death on the night wind, and they wanted to be free and a part of it.

"Claws," the croaker said. "Something clawed her. Her throat—"

I said, "Yeah. Shut up." I turned around. The punk was standing there, the white-faced kid, staring at Sindi's body with eyes glistening like shiny brown marbles.

"You," I said. "Go back to Tiny and tell him to make sure all his kids are there. . . . All the roustabouts and every man that can handle a gun or a tent stake, get armed as fast as you can and stand by. . . . Mike, take whatever you need and guard the gate. Don't let anybody or anything in or out without permission from me, in person. Everybody else get inside somewhere and stay there. I'm going to call the police."

The punk was still there, looking from Sindi's body to me and around the circle of faces. I yelled at him. He went away then, fast. The crowd started to break up.

Laura Darrow came out of it and took my arm.

She had on a dark blue dressing-gown and her hair was loose around her face. She had the dewy look of being freshly washed, and she breathed perfume. I shook her off. "Look out," I said. "I'm all—blood."

I could feel it on my shoes, soaking through the thin stuff of my trouser legs. My stomach rose up under my throat. I closed my eyes and held it down, and all the time Laura's voice was soothing me. She hadn't let go of my arm. I could feel her fingers. They were cold, and too tight. Even then, I loved her so much I ached with it.

"Jade," she said. "Jade, darling. Please—I'm so frightened."

That helped. I put my arm around her and we started back toward my place and the phone. Nobody had thought to put the big lights on yet, and my torchbeam cut a fuzzy tunnel through the fog.

"I couldn't sleep very well," Laura said suddenly. "I was lying in my tent thinking, and a little while before she screamed I thought I heard something—something like a big cat, padding."

The thing that had been in the back of my mind came out yelling. I hadn't seen Laska in the crowd around Sindi. If Laska had got hold of some coffee behind the cook's back . . .

I said, "You were probably mistaken."

"No. Jade?"

"Yeah?" It was dark between the tents. I wished somebody would turn the lights on. I wished I hadn't forgotten to tell them to. I wished they'd shut up their over-all obbligato of gabbling, so I could hear. . . .

"Jade, I couldn't sleep because I was thinking—"

Then she screamed.

He came out of a dark tunnel between two storage tents. He was going almost on all fours, his head flattened forward, his hands held in a little to his belly. His claws were out. They were wet and red, and his hands were wet and red, and his feet. His yellow-green eyes had a crazy shine to them, the pupils slitted against the light. His lips were peeled back from his teeth. They glittered, and there was froth between them—Laska, coked to hell and gone!

He didn't say anything. He made noises, but they weren't speech and they weren't sane. They weren't anything but horrible. He sprang.

I pushed Laura behind me. I could see the marks his claws made in the dirt, and the ridging of his muscles with the jump. I brought up my gun and fired, three shots.

The heavy slugs nearly tore him in two, but they didn't stop him. He let go a mad animal scream and hit me, slashing. I went part way down, firing again, but Laska was still going. His hind feet clawed into my hip and thigh, using me as something to push off from. He wanted the girl.

She had backed off, yelling bloody murder. I could hear feet running, a lot of them, and people shouting. The lights came on. I twisted around and got Laska by the mane of fur on his backbone and then by the scruff. He was suddenly a very heavy weight. I think he was dead when I put the fifth bullet through his skull.

I let him drop.

I said, "Laura, are you all right?" I saw her brown hair and her big purple eyes like dark stars in her white face. She was saying something, but I couldn't hear what it was. I said, "You ought to faint, or something," and laughed.

But it was me, Jade Greene, that did the fainting.

I came out of it too soon. The croaker was still working on my leg. I called him everything I could think of in every language I knew, out of the half of my mouth that wasn't taped shut. He was a heavy man, with a belly and a dirty chin.

He laughed and said, "You'll live. That critter damn near took half your face off, but with your style of beauty it won't matter much. Just take it easy a while until you make some more blood."

I said, "The hell with that. I got work to do." After a while he gave in and helped me get dressed. The holes in my leg weren't too deep, and the face wasn't working anyway. I poured some Scotch in to help out the blood shortage, and managed to get over to the office.

I walked pretty well.

That was largely because Laura let me lean on her. She'd waited outside my tent all that time. There were drops of fog caught in her hair. She cried a little and laughed a little and told me how wonderful I was, and helped me along with her small vibrant self. Pretty soon I began to feel like a kid waking up from a nightmare into a room full of sunshine.

The law had arrived when we got to the office. There wasn't any trouble. Sindi's torn body and the crazy cat-man added up, and the Venusian cook put the lid on it. He always took a thermos of coffee to bed with him, so he'd have it first thing when he woke up—Venusian coffee, with enough caffeine in it to stand an Earthman on his head. Enough to finish off a Callistan cat-man. Somebody had swiped it when he wasn't looking. They found the thermos in Laska's quarters.

The show went on. Mobs came to gawk at the place where the killing had happened. I took it easy for one day, lolling in a shiny golden cloud with Laura holding my head.

Along about sundown she said, "I'll have to get ready for the show."

"Yeah. Saturday's a big night. Tomorrow we tear down, and then Monday we head out for Venus. You'll feel happier then?"

"Yes. I'll feel safe." She put her head down over mine. Her hair was like warm silk. I put my hands up on her throat. It was firm and alive, and it made my hands burn.

She whispered, "Jade, I—" A big hot tear splashed down on my face, and then she was gone.

I lay still, hot and shivering like a man with swamp-fever, thinking, *Maybe. . . .*

Maybe Laura wouldn't leave the show when we got to Venus. Maybe I could make her not want to. Maybe it wasn't too late for dreaming, a dream that John Damien Greene had never had, sitting in a puddle of water at the end of a jetty stringer and fishing for perch.

Crazy, getting ideas like that about a girl like Laura. Crazy like cutting your own throat. Oh, hell. A man never really grows up, not past believing that maybe miracles still happen.

It was nice dreaming for a while.

It was a nice night, too, full of stars and the clean, cool ocean breeze, when Tiny came over to tell me they'd found the punk dead in a pile of straw with his throat torn out, and the Martian sand-cat loose.

CHAPTER THREE

Carnival of Death

We jammed our way through the mob on the midway. Lots of people having fun, lots of kids yelling and getting sick on Mercurian *jitsi-beans* and bottled Venusian fruit juice. Nobody knew about the killing. Tiny had had the cat rounded up and caged before it could get outside the brute top, which had not yet opened for business.

The punk was dead, all right—dead as Sindi, and in the same way. His twisted face was not much whiter than I remembered it, the closed eyelids faintly blue. He lay almost under the sand-cat's cage.

The cat paced, jittery and snarling. There was blood on all its six paws. The cages and pens and pressure tanks seethed nastily all around me, held down and quiet by Tiny's wranglers.

I said, "What happened?"

Tiny lifted his gargantuan shoulders. "Dunno. Everything quiet. Even no yell, like Sindi. Punk kid all lonesome over there behind cages. Nobody see; nobody hear. Only Mars kitty waltz out on main aisle, scare hell out of everybody. We catch, and then find punk, like you see."

I turned around wearily. "Call the cops again and report the accident. Keep the rubes out of here until they pick up the body." I shivered. I'm superstitious, like all carnies.

They come in threes—always in threes. Sindi, the punk—what next?

Tiny sighed. "Poor punk. So peaceful, like sleeper with shut eye."

"Yeah." I started away. I limped six paces and stopped and limped back again.

I said, "That's funny. Guys that die violent aren't tidy about their eyes, except in the movies."

I leaned over. I didn't quite know why, then. I do now. You can't beat that three-time jinx. One way or another, it gets you.

I pushed back one thin, waxy eyelid. After a while I pushed back the other. Tiny breathed heavily over my shoulder. Neither of us said anything. The animals whimpered and yawned and paced.

I closed his eyes again and went through his pockets. I didn't find what I was looking for. I got up very slowly, like an old man. I felt like an old man. I felt dead, deader than the white-faced kid.

I said, "His eyes were brown."

Tiny stared at me. He started to speak, but I stopped him. "Call Homicide, Tiny. Put a guard on the body. And send men with guns. . . ."

133

I told him where to send them. Then I went back across the midway.

A couple of Europans with wiry little bodies and a twenty-foot wing-spread were doing Immelmans over the geek top, and on the bally stand in front of it two guys with six hands apiece and four eyes on movable stalks were juggling. Laura was out in front of the cooch tent, giving the rubes a come-on.

I went around behind the tent, around where I'd kissed her, around where Sindi had died with the bells in her ears like a wash of distant rain.

I lifted up the flap and went in.

The tent was empty except for the man that tends the juke box. He put out his cigarette in a hurry and said, "Hi, Boss," as though that would make me forget he'd been smoking. I didn't give a damn if he set the place on fire with a blowtorch. The air had the warm, musty smell that tents have. Enhali's *Primitive Venus* was crying out of the juke box with a rhythm like thrown spears.

I pulled the stage master, and then the whites. They glared on the bare boards, naked as death and just as yielding.

I stood there a long time.

After a while the man behind me said uneasily, "Boss, what—"

"Shut up. I'm listening."

Little bells, and a voice that was pain made vocal.

"Go out front," I said. "Send Laura Darrow in here. Then tell the rubes there won't be a show here tonight."

I heard his breath suck in, and then catch. He went away down the aisle.

I got a cigarette out and lit it very carefully, broke the match in two and stepped on it. Then I turned around.

Laura came down the aisle. Her gold-brown hair was caught in a web of brilliants. She wore a sheath-tight thing of sea-green metal scales, with a short skirt twirling around her white thighs, and sandals of the shiny scales with no heels to them. She moved with the music, part of it, wild with it, a way I'd never seen a woman move before.

She was beautiful. There aren't any words. She was—beauty.

She stopped. She looked at my face and I could see the quivering tightness flow up across her white skin, up her throat and over her mouth, and catch her breath and hold it. The music wailed and throbbed on the still, warm air.

I said, "Take off your shoes, Laura. Take off your shoes and dance."

She moved then, still with the beat of the savage drums, but not thinking about it. She drew in upon herself, a shrinking and tightening of muscles, a preparation.

134

She said, "You know."

I nodded. "You shouldn't have closed his eyes. I might never have noticed. I might never have remembered that the kid had brown eyes. He was just a punk. Nobody paid much attention. He might just as well have had purple eyes—like yours."

"He stole them from me." Her voice came sharp under the music. It had a hiss and a wail in it I'd never heard before, and the accent was harsher. "While I was in your tent, Jade. I found out when I went to dress. He was an I-man. I found his badge inside his clothes and took it."

Purple eyes looking at me—purple eyes as phony as the eyes on the dead boy. Contact lenses painted purple to hide what was underneath.

"Too bad you carried an extra pair, Laura, in case of breakage."

"He put them in his eyes, so he couldn't lose them or break them or have them stolen, until he could report. He threw away the little suction cup. I couldn't find it. I couldn't get the shells off his eyeballs. All I could do was close his eyes and hope—"

"And let the sand-cat out of his cage to walk through the blood." My voice was coming out all by itself. It hurt. The words felt as though they had fishhooks on them, but I couldn't stop saying them.

"You almost got by with it, Laura. Just like you got by with Sindi. She got in your way, didn't she? She was jealous, and she was a dancer. She knew that no true human could dance like you dance. She said so. She said you were a freak."

That word hit her like my fist. She showed me her teeth, white, even teeth that I knew now were as phony as her eyes. I didn't want to see her change, but I couldn't stop looking, couldn't stop.

I said, "Sindi gave you away before she died, only I was too dumb to know what she meant. She said, 'The stage.' "

I think we both looked, down at the stark boards under the stark lights, looked at the scratches on them where Laura had danced barefoot that first time and left the marks of her claws on the wood.

She nodded, a slow, feral weaving of the head.

"Sindi was too curious. She searched my tent. She found nothing, but she left her scent, just as the young man did today. I followed her back here in the dark and saw her looking at the stage by the light of matches. I can move in the dark, Jade, very quickly and quietly. The cook tent is only a few yards back of this one, and Laska's quarters close beyond that. I smelt the cook's coffee. It was easy for me to steal it and slip it through the tent flap by Laska's cot, and wake him with the touch of my claws on his face. I knew he couldn't help drinking it. I was back here before Sindi came out of the tent to go and tell you what she'd found."

She made a soft purring sound under the wicked music.

"Laska smelt the blood and walked in it, as I meant him to do. I thought he'd die before he found us—or me—because I knew he'd find my scent in the air of his quarters and know who it was, and what it was. My perfume had worn too thin by then to hide it from his nose."

I felt the sullen pain of the claw marks on my face and leg. Laska, crazy with caffeine and dying with it, knowing he was dying and wanting with all the strength of his drugged brain to get at the creature who had killed him. He'd wanted Laura that night, not me. I was just something to claw out of the way.

I wished I hadn't stopped him.

I said, "Why? All you wanted was Laska. Why didn't you kill him?"

The shining claws flexed out of her fingertips, under the phony plastic nails—very sharp, very hungry.

She said huskily, "My tribe sent me to avenge its honor. I have been trained carefully. There are others like me, tracking down the renegades, the dope-ridden creatures like Laska who sell our race for human money. He was not to die quickly. He was not to die without knowing. He was not to die without being given the chance to redeem himself by dying bravely.

"But I was not to be caught. I cost my people time and effort, and I am not easily replaced. I have killed seven renegades, Jade. I was to escape. So I wanted to wait until we were out in space."

She stopped. The music hammered in my temples, and inside I was dead and dried up and crumbled away.

I said, "What would you have done in space?"

I knew the answer. She gave it to me, very simply, very quietly.

"I would have destroyed your whole filthy carnival by means of a little bomb in the jet timers, and gone away in one of the lifeboats."

I nodded. My head felt as heavy as Mount Whitney, and as lifeless. "But Sindi didn't give you time. Your life came first. And if it hadn't been for the punk . . ."

No, not just a punk—an Immigration man. Somewhere Laura had slipped, or else her luck was just out. A white-faced youngster, doing his job quietly in the shadows, and dying without a cry. I started to climb down off the stage.

She backed off. The music screamed and stopped, leaving a silence like the feel of a suddenly stopped heart.

Laura whispered, "Jade, will you believe something if I tell you?

"I love you, Jade." She was still backing off down the aisle, not making any sound. "I deserve to die for that. I'm going to die. I think you're going to kill me, Jade. But when you do, remember that those tears I shed—were real."

She turned and ran, out onto the midway. I was close. I caught her hair. It came free, leaving me standing alone just inside the tent, staring stupidly.

I had men out there, waiting. I thought she couldn't get through. But she did. She went like a wisp of cloud on a gale, using the rubes as a shield. We didn't want a panic. We let her go, and we lost her.

I say we let her go. We couldn't help it. She wasn't bothering about being human then. She was all cat, just a noiseless blur of speed. We couldn't shoot without hurting people, and our human muscles were too slow to follow her.

I knew Tiny had men at the gates and all around the pitch, anywhere that she could possibly get out. I wasn't worried. She was caught, and pretty soon the police would come. We'd have to be careful, careful as all hell not to start one of those hideous, trampling panics that can wreck a pitch in a matter of minutes.

All we had to do was watch until the show was over and the rubes were gone. Guard the gates and keep her in, and then round her up. She was caught. She couldn't get away. Laura Darrow . . .

I wondered what her name was, back on Callisto. I wondered what she looked like when she let the cross-shaped mane grow thick along her back and shoulders. I wondered what color her fur was. I wondered why I had ever been born.

I went back to my place and got my gun and then went out into the crowd again. The show was in full swing; lots of people having fun, lots of kids crazy with excitement; lights and laughter and music—and a guy out in front of the brute top splitting his throat telling the crowd that something was wrong with the lighting system and it would be a while before they could see the animals.

A while before the cops would have got what they wanted and cleaned up the mess under the sand-cat's cage.

The squad cars would be coming in a few minutes. There wasn't anything to do but wait. She was caught. She couldn't escape.

The one thing we didn't think about was that she wouldn't try to.

A Mercurian cave-tiger screamed. The Ionian quags took it up in their deep, rusty voices, and then the others chimed in, whistling, roaring, squealing, shrieking, and doing things there aren't any names for. I stopped, and gradually everybody on the pitch stopped and listened.

For a long moment you could hear the silence along the midway and in the tents. People not breathing, people with a sudden glassy shine of fear in their eyes and a cold tightening of the skin that comes from way back beyond humanity. Then the muttering start, low and uneasy, the prelude to panic.

I fought my way to the nearest bally stand and climbed on it. There were shots, sounding small and futile under the brute howl.

I yelled, "Hey, everybody! Listen! There's nothing wrong. One of the cats is sick, that's all. There's nothing wrong. Enjoy yourselves."

I wanted to tell them to get the hell out, but I knew they'd kill themselves if they started. Somebody started music going again, loud and silly. It cracked the icy lid that was tightening down. People began to relax and laugh nervously and talk too loudly. I got down and ran for the brute top.

Tiny met me at the tent flap. His face was just a white blur. I grabbed him and said, "For God's sake, can't you keep them quiet?"

"She's in there, Boss—like shadow. No hear, no see. One man dead. She let my kids out. She—"

More shots from inside, and a brute scream of pain. Tiny groaned. "My kids! No lights, Boss. She wreck 'em."

I said, "Keep 'em inside. Get lights from somewhere. There's a blizzard brewing on the pitch. If that mob gets started."

I went inside. There were torchbeams spearing the dark, men sweating and cursing, a smell of hot, wild bodies and the sweetness of fresh blood.

Somebody poked his head inside the flap and yelled, "The cops are here!"

I yelled back, "Tell 'em to clear the grounds if they can, without starting trouble. Tell—"

Somebody screamed. There was a sudden spangle of lights in the high darkness, balls of crimson and green and vicious yellow tumbling towards us, spots of death no bigger than your fist—the stinging fireflies of Ganymede. Laura had opened their case.

We scattered, fighting the fireflies. Somewhere a cage went over with a crash. Bodies thrashed, and feet padded on the packed earth—and somewhere above the noise was a voice that was sweet and silky and wild, crying out to the beasts and being answered.

I knew then why the brute top went crazy when Laska was around. It was kinship, not fear. She talked to them, and they understood.

I called her name.

Her voice came down to me out of the hot dark, human and painful with tears. "Jade! Jade, get out; go somewhere safe!"

"Laura, don't do this! For God's sake—"

"Your God, or mine? Our God forbids us to know humans except to kill. How, if we kept men as you kept Laska?"

"Laura!"

"Get out! I'm going to kill as many as I can before I'm taken. I'm turning the animals loose on the pitch. Go somewhere safe!"

I fired at the sound of her voice.

She said softly, "Not yet, Jade. Maybe not at all."

I beat off a bunch of fireflies hunting for me with their poisoned stings. Cage doors banged open. Wild throats coughed and roared, and suddenly the whole side wall of the tent fell down, cut free at the top, and there wasn't any way to keep the beasts inside any more.

A long mob scream went up from outside, and the panic was on.

I could hear Tiny bellowing, sending his men out with ropes and nets and guns. Some huge, squealing thing blundered around in the dark, went past me close enough to touch, and charged through the front opening, bringing part of the top down. I was close enough behind it so that I got free.

I climbed up on the remains of the bally stand. There was plenty of light outside—blue-white, glaring light, to show me the packed mass of people screaming and swaying between the tents, trampling toward the exits, to show me a horde of creatures sweeping down on them, caged beasts free to kill, and led by a lithe and leaping figure in shining green.

I couldn't see her clearly. Perhaps I didn't want to. Even then she moved in beauty, like wild music—and she had a tail.

I never saw a worse panic, not even the time a bunch of Nahali swamp-edgers clemmed our pitch when I was a pony punk with Triangle.

The morgues were going to be full that night.

Tiny's men were between the bulk of the mob and the animals. The beasts had had to come around from the far side of the tent, giving them barely time to get set. They gave the critters all they had, but it wasn't enough.

Laura was leading them. I heard her voice crying out above all that din. The animals scattered off sideways between the tents. One Martian sand-cat was dead, one quag kicking its life out, and that was all. They hadn't touched Laura, and she was gone.

I fought back, away from the mob, back into a temporarily empty space behind a tent. I got out my whistle and blew it, the rallying call. A snake-headed kibi from Titan sneaked up and tried to rip me open with its double-pointed tail. I fed it three soft-nosed slugs, and then there were half a dozen little moth-people bouncing in the air over my head, squeaking with fear and shining their great eyes at me.

I told them what I wanted. While I was yelling the Europans swooped in on their wide wings and listened.

I said finally, "Did any of you see which way *she* went?"

"That way." One of the mothlings pointed back across the midway. I called two of the Europans. The mothlings went tumbling away to spread my orders, and the bird-men picked me up and carried me across, over the crowd.

The animals were nagging at their flanks, pulling them down in a kind of mad ecstasy. There was a thin salt fog, and blood on the night wind, and the cage doors were open at last.

They set me down and went to do what I told them. I went alone among the swaying tents.

All this hadn't taken five minutes. Things like that move fast. By the time the Europans were out of sight the mothlings were back, spotting prowling beasts and rolling above them in the air to guide men to them—men and geeks.

Geeks with armor-plated backs and six arms, carrying tear-gas guns and nets; lizard-men, fast and powerful, armed with their own teeth and claws and whatever they could pick up; spider-people, spinning sticky lassos out of their own bodies; the Europans, dive-bombing the quags with tear gas.

The geeks saved the day for us. They saved lives, and the reputation of their kind, and the carnival. Without them, God only knows how many would have died on the pitch. I saw the mothlings dive into the thick of the mob and pick up fallen children and carry them to safety. Three of them died, doing that.

I went on, alone.

I was beyond the mob, beyond the fringe of animals. I was remembering Laura's voice saying, "Not yet, Jade. Maybe not at all." I was thinking of the walls being down and all California free outside. I was hearing the mob yell and the crash of broken tents, and the screams of people dying—my people, human people, with the claws bred out of them.

I was thinking—

Guns slamming and brute throats shrieking, wings beating fast against the hot hard glare, feet pounding on packed earth. I walked in silence, a private silence built around me like a shell. . . .

Four big cats slunk out of the shadows by the tent. There was enough light left to show me their eyes and their teeth, and the hungry licking of their tongues.

Laura's voice came through the canvas, tremulous but no softer nor more yielding than the blue barrel of my gun.

"I'm going away, Jade. At first I didn't think there was any way, but there is. Don't try to stop me. Please don't try."

I could have gone and tried to find a cop. I could have called men or half-men from their jobs to help me. I didn't. I don't know that I could have made anybody hear me, and anyway they had enough to do. This was my job.

My job, my carnival, my heart.

I walked toward the tent flap, watching the cats.

They slunk a little aside, belly down, making hoarse, whimpering noises. One was a six-legged Martian sand-cat, about the size of an Earthly leopard. Two were from Venus, the fierce white beauties of the high plateaus. The fourth was a Mercurian cave-cat, carrying its twenty-foot body on eight powerful legs and switching a tail that had bone barbs on it.

Laura called to them. I don't know whether she said words in their language, or whether her voice was just a bridge for thought transference, one cat brain to another. Anyway, they understood.

"Jade, they won't touch you if you go."

I fired.

One of the white Venusians took the slug between the eyes and dropped without a whimper. Its mate let go a sobbing shriek and came for me, with the other two beside it.

I snapped a shot at the Martian. It went over kicking, and I dived aside, rolling. The white Venusian shot over me, so close its hind claws tore my shirt. I put a slug in its belly. It just yowled and dug its toes in and came for me again. Out of the tail of my eye I saw the dying Martian tangle with the Mercurian, just because it happened to be the nearest moving object.

I kicked the Venusian in the face. The pain must have blinded it just enough to make its aim bad. On the second jump its forepaws came down on the outer edges of my deltoids, gashing them but not tearing them out. The cat's mouth was open clear to its stomach.

I should have died right then. I don't know why I didn't, except that I didn't care much if I did. It's the guys that want to live that get it, seems like. The ones that don't care go on forever.

I got a lot of hot bad breath in my face and five parallel gashes in back, where its hind feet hit me when I rolled up. I kicked it in the belly. Its teeth snapped a half inch short of my nose, and then I got my gun up under its jaw and that was that. I had four shots left.

I rolled the body off and turned. The Martian cat was dead. The Mercurian stood over it, watching me with its four pale, hot eyes, twitching its barbed tail.

Laura stood watching us.

She looked just like she had the first time I saw her. Soft gold-brown hair and purple eyes with a little tilt to them, and a soft pink mouth. She was wearing the bronze metal-cloth dress and the bronze slippers, and there was still nothing wrong with the way she was put together. She glinted dully in the dim light, warm bronze glints.

She was crying, but there was no softness in her tears.

The cat flicked its eyes at her and made a nervous, eager whine. She spoke to it, and it sank to its belly, not wanting to.

Laura said, "I'm going, Jade."

"No."

I raised my gun hand. The big cat rose with it. She was beyond the cat. I could shoot a cat, but a Mercurian lives a long time after it's shot.

"Throw down your gun, Jade, and let me go."

I didn't care if the cat killed me. I didn't care if Death took me off piggy-back right then. I suppose I was crazy. Maybe I was just numb. I don't know. I was looking at Laura, and choking on my own heart.

I said, "No."

Just a whisper of sound in her throat, and the cat sprang. It reared up on its four hind feet and clawed at me with its four front ones. Only I wasn't where it thought I was. I knew it was going to jump and I faded—not far, I'm no superman—just far enough so its claws raked me without gutting me. It snapped its head down to bite.

I slammed it hard across the nose with my gun. It hurt, enough to make it wince, enough to fuddle it just for a split second. I jammed the muzzle into its nearest eye and fired.

Laura was going off between the tents, fast, with her head down, just a pretty girl, mingling with the mob streaming off the pitch. Who'd notice her, except maybe to whistle?

I didn't have time to get away. I dropped down flat on my belly and let the cat fall on top of me. I only wanted to live a couple of seconds longer. After that, the hell with it!

The cat was doing a lot of screaming and thrashing. I was between two sets of legs. The paws came close enough to touch me, clawing up the dirt. I huddled up small, hoping it wouldn't notice me there under its belly. Everything seemed to be happening very slowly, with a cold precision. I steadied my right hand on my left wrist.

I shot Laura three times, carefully, between the shoulders.

The cat stopped thrashing. Its weight crushed me. I knew it was dead. I knew I'd done something that even experienced hunters don't do in nine cases out of ten. My first bullet had found the way into the cat's little brain and killed it.

It wasn't going to kill me. I pulled myself out from under it. The pitch was almost quiet now, the mob gone, the animals mostly under control. I kicked the dead cat. It had died too soon.

My gun was empty. I remember I clicked the hammer twice. I got more bullets out of my pocket, but my fingers wouldn't hold them and I couldn't see to load. I threw the gun away.

I walked away in the thin, cold fog, down toward the distant beat of the sea.

Doorway into Time

C. L. Moore (1911-   )

MUCH *has been written about the role of women in the history of science fiction in recent years, and we can only agree with the critics who point out their relative absence during the forties. Moreover, women like Catherine L. Moore and her predecessor, Leslie Stone, felt a need to tinker with or change their names to deceive an overwhelmingly male audience. It should be pointed out, however, that the close-knit science fiction world, which included a number of women fans and editors, knew full well who C. L. Moore was and respected her as an outstanding writer. Long before she married Henry Kuttner in 1940, she was an established star with her "Northwest Smith" and "Jirel of Joiry" series and such memorable stories as "Shambleau" (1933) and "The Bright Illusion" (1934).*

"Doorway into Time" was published in Famous Fantastic Mysteries, *a wonderful pulp that lasted through the forties and provided the very important function of reprinting many early stories and novels, making them available to a new generation of readers. But hidden among the reprints were some fine originals, this one among them.*

From *Famous Fantastic Mysteries*   1943

He came slowly, with long, soft, ponderous strides, along the hallway of his treasure house. The gleanings of many worlds were here around him; he had ransacked space and time for the treasures that filled his palace. The robes that moulded their folds richly against his great rolling limbs as he walked were in themselves as priceless as anything

143

within these walls, gossamer fabric pressed into raised designs that had no meaning, this far from the world upon which they had been created, but—in their beauty—universal. But he was himself more beautiful than anything in all that vast collection. He knew it complacently, a warm, contented knowledge deep in the center of his brain.

His motion was beautiful, smooth power pouring along his limbs as he walked, his great bulk ponderous and graceful. The precious robes he wore flowed open over his magnificent body. He ran one sensuous palm down his side, enjoying the texture of that strange, embossed delicacy in a fabric thinner than gauze. His eyes were proud and half shut, flashing many-colored under the heavy lids. The eyes were never twice quite the same color, but all the colors were beautiful.

He was growing restless again. He knew the feeling well, that familiar quiver of discontent widening and strengthening far back in his mind. It was time to set out once more on the track of something dangerous. In times past, when he had first begun to stock this treasure house, beauty alone had been enough. It was not enough any longer. Danger had to be there too. His tastes were growing capricious and perhaps a little decadent, for he had lived a very long time.

Yes, there must be a risk attending the capture of his next new treasure. He must seek out great beauty and great danger, and subdue the one and win the other, and the thought of it made his eyes change color and the blood beat faster in mighty rhythms through his veins. He smoothed his palm again along the embossed designs of the robe that moulded itself to his body. The great, rolling strides carried him noiselessly over the knife-edged patterns of the floor.

Nothing in life meant much to him any more except these beautiful things which his own passion for beauty had brought together. And even about these he was growing capricious now. He glanced up at a deep frame set in the wall just at the bend of the corridor, where his appreciative eyes could not fail to strike the objects it enclosed at just the proper angle. Here was a group of three organisms fixed in an arrangement that once had given him intense pleasure. On their own world they might have been living creatures, perhaps even intelligent. He neither knew nor cared. He did not even remember now if there had been eyes upon their world to see, or minds to recognize beauty. He cared only that they had given him acute pleasure whenever he turned this bend of the corridor and saw them frozen into eternal perfection in their frame.

But the pleasure was clouded as he looked at them now. His half-shut eyes changed color, shifting along the spectrum from yellow-green to the cooler purity of true green. This particular treasure had been acquired in perfect safety; its value was impaired for him, remembering that. And the quiver of discontent grew stronger in his mind. Yes, it was time to go out hunting again. . . .

And here, set against a panel of velvet, was a great oval stone whose surface exhaled a light as soft as smoke, in waves whose colors changed with languorous slowness. Once the effect had been almost intoxicating to him. He had taken it from the central pavement of a great city square upon a world whose location he had forgotten long ago. He did not know if the people of the city had valued it, or perceived its beauty at all. But he had won it with only a minor skirmish, and now in his bitter mood it was valueless to his eyes.

He quickened his steps, and the whole solid structure of the palace shook just perceptibly underfoot as he moved with ponderous majesty down the hall. He was still running one palm in absent appreciation up and down the robe across his mighty side, but his mind was not on present treasures any more. He was looking to the future, and the color of his eyes had gone shivering up the spectrum to orange, warm with the anticipation of danger. His nostrils flared a little and his wide mouth turned down at the corners in an inverted grimace. The knife-edged patterns of the floor sang faintly beneath his footsteps, their sharp intricacies quivering as the pressure of his steps passed by.

He went past a fountain of colored fire which he had wrecked a city to possess. He thrust aside a hanging woven of unyielding crystal spears which only his great strength could have moved. It gave out showers of colored sparks when he touched it, but their beauty did not delay him now.

His mind had run on ahead of him, into that room in the center of his palace, round and dim, from which he searched the universe for plunder and through whose doorways he set out upon its track. He came ponderously along the hall toward it, passing unheeded treasures, the gossamer of his robes floating after him like a cloud.

On the wall before him, in the dimness of the room, a great circular screen looked out opaquely, waiting his touch, a doorway into time and space. A doorway to beauty and deadly peril and everything that made livable for him a life which had perhaps gone on too long already. It took strong measures now to stir his jaded senses which once had responded so eagerly to more stimuli than he could remember any more. He sighed, his great chest expanding tremendously. Somewhere beyond that screen, upon some world he had never trod before, a treasure was waiting lovely enough to tempt his boredom and dangerous enough to dispel it for just a little while.

The screen brightened as he neared the wall. Blurred shadows moved, vague sounds drifted into the room. His wonderful senses sorted the noises and the shapes and dismissed them as they formed; his eyes were round and luminous now, and the orange fires deepened as he watched. Now the shadows upon the screen moved faster. Something was taking shape. The shadows leaped backward into three-dimensional vividness that wavered for a moment and then sharpened into focus upon a desert landscape under a vivid crimson sky. Out of the soil a cluster of tall flowers rose swaying, exquisitely shaped, their colors shifting in that strange light. He glanced at them carelessly and grimaced. And the screen faded.

He searched the void again, turning up scene after curious scene and dismissing each with a glance. There was a wall of carved translucent panels around a city he did not bother to identify. He saw a great shining bird that trailed luminous plumage, and a tapestry woven gorgeously with scenes from no earthly legend, but he let all of them fade again without a second look, and the orange glow in his eyes began to dull with boredom.

Once he paused for a while before the picture of a tall, dark idol carved into a shape he did not recognize, its strange limbs adorned with jewels that dripped fire, and for an instant his pulse quickened. It was pleasant to think of those jewels upon his own great limbs, trailing drops of flame along his halls. But when he looked again he saw that the idol stood deserted upon a barren world, its treasure his for the taking. And he knew that so cheap a winning would be savorless. He sighed again, from the depths of his mighty chest, and let the screen shift its pictures on.

It was the faraway flicker of golden lightning in the void that first caught his eyes, the distant scream of it from some world without a name. Idly he let the screen's shadows form a picture. First was the lightning, hissing and writhing from a mechanism which he spared only one disinterested glance. For beside it two figures were taking shape, and as he watched them his restless motions stilled and the floating robe settled slowly about his body. His eyes brightened to orange again. He stood very quiet, staring.

The figures were of a shape he had not seen before. Remotely like his own, but flexible and very slender, and of proportions grotesquely different from his. And one of them, in spite of its difference, was— He stared thoughtfully. Yes, it was beautiful. Excitement began to kindle behind his quietness. And the longer he stared the clearer the organism's subtle loveliness grew. No obvious flamboyance like the fire-dripping jewels or the gorgeously plumed bird, but a delicate beauty of long, smooth curves and tapering lines, and colors in softly blended tints of apricot and creamy white and warm orange-red. Folds of blue-green swathing it were probably garments of some sort. He wondered if it were intelligent enough to defend itself, or if the creature beside it, making lightnings spurt out of the mechanism over which it bent, would know or care if he reached out to take its companion away.

He leaned closer to the screen, his breath beginning to come fast and his eyes glowing with the first flush of red that meant excitement. Yes, this was a lovely thing. A very lovely trophy for his halls. Briefly he thought of it arranged in a frame whose ornaments would echo the soft and subtle curves of the creature itself, colored to enhance the delicacy of the subject's coloring. Certainly a prize worth troubling himself for—if there were danger anywhere near to make it a prize worth winning . . .

He put one hand on each side of the screen and leaned forward into it a little, staring with eyes that were a dangerous scarlet now. That flare of lightning looked like a weapon of some sort. If the creatures had intelligence— It would be amusing to test the limits of their minds, and the power of the weapon they were using. . . .

He watched a moment longer, his breath quickening. His mighty shoulders hunched forward. Then with one shrug he cast off the hampering garment of gossamer and laughed deep in his throat and lunged smoothly forward into the open doorway of the screen. He went naked and weaponless, his eyes blazing scarlet. This was all that made life worth living. Danger, and beauty beyond danger . . .

Darkness spun around him. He shot forward through dimensionless infinity along a corridor of his own devising.

The girl leaned back on her metal bench and crossed one beautiful long leg over the other, stirring the sequined folds of her gown into flashing motion.

"How much longer, Paul?" she asked.

The man glanced over his shoulder and smiled.

"Five minutes. Look away now—I'm going to try it again." He reached up to slip a curved, transparent mask forward, closing his pleasant, dark face away from the glare. The girl sighed and shifted on the bench, averting her eyes.

The laboratory was walled and ceiled in dully reflecting metal, so that the blue-green blur of her gown moved as if in dim mirrors all around her when she changed position. She lifted a bare arm to touch her hair, and saw the reflections lift too, and the pale blur that was her hair, shining ashes of silver and elaborately coiffed.

The murmur of well-oiled metal moving against metal told her that a lever had been shifted, and almost instantly the room was full of golden glare, like daylight broken into hissing fragments as jagged as lightning. For a long moment the walls quivered with light and sound. Then the hissing died, the glare faded. A smell of hot metal tainted the air.

The man sighed heavily with satisfaction and lifted both hands to pull the mask off. Indistinctly behind the glass she heard him say:

"Well, that's done. Now we can—"

But he never finished, and the helmet remained fixed on his shoulders as he stared at the wall they were both facing. Slowly, almost absentmindedly, he pushed aside the glass across his face, as if he

147

thought it might be responsible for the thing they both saw. For above the banked machinery which controlled the mechanism he had just released, a shadow had fallen upon the wall. A great circle of shadow . . .

Now it was a circle of darkness, as if twilight had rushed timelessly into midnight before them as they watched, and a midnight blacker than anything earth ever knew. The midnight of the ether, of bottomless spaces between worlds. And now it was no longer a shadow, but a window opening upon that midnight, and the midnight was pouring through. . . .

Like smoke the darkness flowed in upon them, dimming the glitter of machinery, dimming the girl's pale hair and pale, shining shoulders and the shimmer of her gown until the man looked at her as if through veil upon veil of falling twilight.

Belatedly he moved, making a useless gesture of brushing the dark away with both hands before his face.

"Alanna—" he said helplessly. "What's happened? I—I can't see—very well—"

He heard her whimper in bewilderment, putting her own hands to her eyes as if she thought blindness had come suddenly upon them both. He was too sick with sudden dizziness to move or speak. This, he told himself wildly, must be the blindness that foreruns a swoon, and his obedient mind made the floor seem to tilt as if the faintness and blindness were inherent in himself, and not the result of some outward force.

But before either of them could do more than stammer a little, as their minds tried desperately to rationalize what was happening into some weakness of their own senses, the dark was complete. The room brimmed with it, and sight ceased to exist.

When the man felt the floor shake, he thought for an unfathomable moment that it was his own blindness, his own faintness again, deceiving his senses. The floor could not shake, as if to a ponderous tread. For there was no one here but themselves—there could not be great footfalls moving softly through the dark, making the walls shudder a little as they came. . . .

Alanna's caught breath was clear in the silence. Not terror at first; but surprised inquiry. She said, "Paul— Paul, don't—"

And then he heard the beginning of her scream. He heard the beginning, but incredibly, he never heard the scream's end. One moment the full-throated roundness of her cry filled the room, pouring from a throat stretched wide with terror; the next, the sound diminished and vanished into infinite distances, plummeting away from him and growing thin and tiny while the echo of its first sound still rang through the room. The impossibility of such speed put the last touch of nightmare upon the whole episode. He did not believe it.

The dark was paling again. Rubbing his eyes, still not sure at all that this had not been some brief aberration of his own senses, he said, "Alanna—I thought—"

But the twilight around him was empty.

He had no idea how long a while elapsed between that moment and the moment when he stood up straight at last, facing the wall upon which the shadow still lay. In between there must have been a period of frantic search, of near hysteria and self-doubt and reeling disbelief. But now, as he stood looking up at the wall upon which the shadow still hung blackly, drawing into itself the last veils of twilight from the corners of the room, he ceased to rationalize or disbelieve.

Alanna was gone. Somehow, impossibly, in the darkness that had come upon them a Something with great silent feet that trod ponderously, shaking the walls, had seized her in the moment when she said, "Paul—" thinking it was himself. And while she screamed, it had vanished into infinite distances out of his room, carrying her with it.

That it was impossible he had no time to consider. He had time now only to realize that nothing had passed him toward the door, and that the great circle upon the wall before him was—an entrance?—out of which Something had come and into which Something must have retreated again—and not alone. . . .

And the entrance was closing.

He took one step toward it, unreasoning and urgent, and then stumbled over the boxed instrument which he had been testing just before insanity entered the room. The sight and feel of it brought back his own sanity a little. Here was a weapon; it offered a grip upon slipping reality to know that he was not wholly helpless. Briefly he wondered whether any weapon at all would avail against That which came in impossible darkness on feet that made no sound, though their tread shook the foundations of the building. . . .

But the weapon was heavy. And how far away from the parent machine would it work? With shaking fingers he groped for the carrying handle. He staggered a little, lifting it, but he turned toward the end of the room where the great circle drank in the last of its twilight and began imperceptibly to pale upon the wall. If he were to follow, to take That which had gone before him by surprise, he must go swiftly. . . .

One glance at the lever of the parent machine, to be sure it was thrown full over, for the weapon itself drank power from that source alone—if it would drink power at all in the unfathomable distances to which he was going. . . . One last unbelieving glance around the room, to be quite sure Alanna was really gone—

The lower arc of the circle was a threshold opening upon darkness. He could not think that he would pass it, this flat shadow upon the flat and solid wall, but he put out one hand uncertainly and took a step forward, and another, bent to the weight of the box he carried. . . .

But there was no longer any weight. Nor was there any light nor sound—only wild, whirling motion that spun him over and over in the depths of his blindness. Spun interminably—spun for untimed eons that passed in the flash of an eye. And then—

"Paul! Oh, Paul!"

He stood reeling in a dim, round room walled with strange designs he could not quite focus upon. He had no sense that was not shaken intolerably; even sight was not to be relied upon just now. He thought he saw Alanna in the dimness, pale hair falling over her pale, shining shoulders, her face distorted with bewilderment and terror. . . .

"Paul! Paul, answer me! What is it? What's happened?"

He could not speak yet. He could only shake his head and cling by blind instinct to the weight that dragged down upon one arm. Alanna drew her bare shoulders together under the showering hair and hugged herself fearfully, the creamy arms showing paler circles where her fingertips pressed them hard. Her teeth were chattering, though not from cold.

"How did we get here?" she was saying. "How did we get here, Paul? We'll have to go back, won't we? I wonder what's happened to us?" The words were almost aimless, as if the sound of speech itself were more important to her now than any sense of what she was saying. "Look behind you, Paul—see? We came out of—there."

He turned. A great circle of mirror rose behind him on the dim wall, but a mirror reversed, so that it reflected not themselves, but the room they had just left.

Clearer than a picture—he looked into it—his laboratory walls shining with dull reflections, his batteries and dials, and the lever standing up before them that meant the heavy thing he carried would be deadly —perhaps. Deadly? A weapon in a dream? Did they even know that the Something which dwelt here was inimical?

But this was ridiculous. It was too soon yet to accept the fact that they were standing here at all. In reality, of course, they must both be back in the laboratory, and both of them dreaming the same strange dream. And he felt, somehow, that to treat all this as a reality would be dangerous. For if he accepted even by implication that such a thing could be true, then perhaps—perhaps . . . Could acceptance make it *come* true?

He set his weapon down and rubbed his arm dazedly, looking around. Words did not come easily yet, but he had to ask one question.

"That—that thing, Alanna. What was it? How did you—"

She gripped her own bare arms harder, and another spasm of shuddering went over her. The blue-green sequins flashed chilly star-points from her gown as she moved. Her voice shook too; her very mind seemed to be shaking behind the blank eyes. But when she spoke the words made approximate sense. And they echoed his own thought.

"I'm dreaming all this, you know." Her voice sounded far away. "This isn't really happening. But—but *something* took me in its arms back there." She nodded toward the mirrored laboratory on the wall. "And everything whirled, and then—" A hard shudder seized her. "I don't know. . . ."

"Did you see it?"

She shook her head. "Maybe I did. I'm not sure. I was so dizzy—I think it went away through that door. Would you call it a door?" Her little breath of laughter was very near hysteria. "I—I felt its feet moving away."

"But what was it? What did it look like?"

"I don't know, Paul."

He closed his lips on the questions that rushed to be asked. Here in the dream, many things were very alien indeed. Those patterns on the wall, for instance. He thought he could understand how one could look at something and not be sure at all what the something was. And Alanna's heavy spasms of shuddering proved that shock must have blanked her mind protectively to much of what had happened. She said:

"Aren't we going back now, Paul?" And her eyes flickered past him to the pictured laboratory. It was a child's question; her mind was refusing to accept anything but the barest essentials of their predicament. But he could not answer. His first impulse was to say, "Wait—we'll wake up in a minute." But suppose they did not? Suppose they were trapped here? And if the Thing came back . . . Heavily, he said:

"Of course it's a dream, Alanna. But while it lasts I think we'll have to act as if it were real. I don't want to—" The truth was, he thought, he was afraid to. "But we must. And going back wouldn't do any good as long as we go on dreaming. *It* would just come after us again."

It would come striding through the dream to drag them back, and after all, people have died in their sleep—died in their dreams, he thought.

He touched the unwieldy weapon with his toe, thinking silently, "This will help us—maybe. If anything can, it will. And if it won't—well, neither will running away." And he glanced toward the high, distorted opening that must be a doorway into some other part of this unimaginable, dream-created building. It had gone that way, then. Perhaps they should follow. Perhaps their greatest hope of waking safely out of this nightmare lay in acting rashly, in following with the weapon before it expected them to follow. It might not guess his own presence here at all. It must have left Alanna alone in the dim room, intending to return, not thinking to find her with a defender, or to find the defender armed. . . .

151

But was he armed? He grinned wryly.

Perhaps he ought to test the weapon. And yet, for all he knew, the Thing's strange, alien gaze might be upon him now. He was aware of a strong reluctance to let it know that he had any defense against it. Surprise—that was important. Keep it a secret until he needed a weapon, if he ever did need one. Very gently he pressed the trigger of the lens that had poured out lightnings in the faraway sanity of his laboratory. Would it work in—a dream? For a long moment nothing happened. Then, faintly and delicately against his palm he felt the tubing begin to throb just a little. It was as much of an answer as he dared take now. Some power was there. Enough? He did not know. It was unthinkable, really, that he should ever need to know. Still—

"Alanna," he said, "I think we'd better explore a little. No use just standing here waiting for *it* to come back. It may be perfectly friendly, you know. Dream creatures often are. But I'd like to see what's outside."

"We'll wake up in a minute," she assured him between chattering teeth. "I'm all right, I think, really. Just—just nervous." He thought she seemed to be rousing from her stupor. Perhaps the prospect of action—any action—even rashness like this, was better for them both than inactivity. He felt surer of himself as he lifted the heavy weapon.

"But Paul, we can't!" She turned, half-way to the door, and faced him. "Didn't I tell you? I tried that before you came. There's a corridor outside, with knives all over the floor. Patterns of them, sharp-edged spirals and—and shapes. Look." She lifted her sparkling skirt a little and put out one foot. He could see the clean, sharp lacerations of the leather sole. His shoulders sagged a bit. Then:

"Well, let's look anyhow. Come on."

The corridor stretched before them, swimming in purple distances, great gothic hollows and arches melting upon arches. There were things upon the walls. Like the patterns in the room behind them, many were impossible to focus upon directly, too different from anything in human experience to convey meaning to the brain. The eye perceived them blankly, drawing no conclusions. He thought vaguely that the hall looked like a museum, with those great frames upon the walls.

Beside the door another tall frame leaned, empty. About six feet high, it was deep enough for a man to lie down in, and all around its edges an elaborate and beautiful decoration writhed, colored precisely like Alanna's blue-green gown. Interwoven in it were strands of silver, the color of her pale and shining hair.

"It looks like a coffin," Alanna said aimlessly. Some very ugly thought stirred in Paul's mind. He would not recognize it; he pushed it back out of sight quickly, but he was gladder now that he had brought this lightning-throwing weapon along.

The hall shimmered with strangeness before them. So many things he could not quite see clearly, but the razor-edged decorations of the floor were clear enough. It made the mind reel a little to think what utter alienage lay behind the choice of such adornment for a floor that must be walked upon—even in a dream. He thought briefly of the great earth-shaking feet in the darkness of his laboratory. Here in the dream they walked this knife-edged floor. They must.

But how?

The spirals of the pattern lay in long loops and rosettes. After a moment, eyeing them, he said, "I think we can make it, Alanna. If we walk between the knives—see, there's space if we're careful." And if they were not careful, if they had to run. . . . "We've got to risk it," he said aloud, and with those words admitted to himself for perhaps the first time an urgency in this dream, risk and danger. . . .

He took a firmer grip upon his burden and stepped delicately into the hollow of a steely spiral. Teetering a little, clutching at his arm to steady herself, Alanna came after him.

Silence—vast, unechoing hollows quivering with silence all around them. They advanced very slowly, watching wide-eyed for any signs of life in the distances, their senses strained and aching with the almost subconscious awareness of any slightest motion in the floor that might herald great feet ponderously approaching. But That which had opened the doorway for them had gone now, for a little while, and left them to their own devices.

Paul carried the lens of his weapon ready in his free hand, the lightest possible pressure always on its trigger so that the tubing throbbed faintly against his palm. That reassurance that contact still flowed between his faraway laboratory and this unbelievable hall was all that kept him forging ahead over the razory mosaics.

They went slowly, but they passed many very strange things. A tremendous transparent curtain swung from the vaulted ceiling in folds as immovable as iron. They slipped through the little triangle of opening where the draperies hung awry, and a shower of fiery sparkles sprang out harmlessly when they brushed the sides. They passed a fountain that sent up gushes of soundless flame from its basin in the center of the corridor floor. They saw upon the walls, in frames and without them, things too alien to think about clearly. That very alienage was worrying the man. In dreams one rehearses the stimuli of the past, fears and hopes and memories. But how *could* one dream of things like these? Where in any human past could such memories lie?

They skirted an oval stone set in the floor, the metal patterns swirling about it. They were both dizzy when they looked directly at it. Dangerous dizziness, since a fall here must end upon razor edges. And once they passed an indescribable something hanging against a black panel of the wall, that brought tears to the eyes with its sheer loveliness, a thing of unbearable beauty too far removed from human experience to leave any picture in their minds once they had gone past it. Only the emotional impact remained, remembered beauty too exquisite for the mind to grasp and hold. And the man knew definitely now that this at least was no part of any human memory, and could be in itself no dream.

They saw it all with the strange clarity and vividness of senses sharp with uncertainty and fear, but they saw it too with a dreamlike haziness that faded a little as they went on. To the man, a terrible wonder was dawning. Could it, after all, be a dream? Could it possibly be some alien reality into which they had stumbled? And the import of that frame outside the door they had left—the frame shaped like a coffin and adorned with the colors of Alanna's gown and hair . . . Deep in his mind he knew what that frame was for. He knew he was walking through a museum filled with lovely things, and he was beginning to suspect why Alanna had been brought here too. The thing seemed unthinkable, even in a dream as mad as this, and yet—

"Look, Paul." He glanced aside. Alanna had reached up to touch a steel-blue frame upon the wall, its edges enclosing nothing but a dim rosy shimmer. She was groping inside it, her face animated now. No thought had come to her yet about that other frame, evidently. No thought that from this dream neither of them might ever wake. . . .

"Look," she said. "It seems empty, but I can *feel* something— something like feathers. What do you suppose—"

"Don't try to suppose," he said almost brusquely. "There isn't any sense to any of this."

"But some of the things are so pretty, Paul. See that—that snowstorm ahead, between the pillars?"

He looked. Veiling the hallway a little distance away hung a shower of patterned flakes, motionless in midair. Perhaps they were embroideries upon some gossamer drapery too sheer to see. But as he looked he thought he saw them quiver just a little. Quiver, and fall quiet, and then quiver again, as if—as if—

"*Paul!*"

Everything stopped dead still for a moment. He did not need Alanna's whisper to make his heart pause as he strained intolerably to hear, to see, to feel. . . . Yes, definitely now the snowstorm curtain shook. And the floor shook with it in faint rhythms to that distant tremor—

This is it, he thought. *This is real.*

He had known for minutes now that he was not walking through a dream. He stood in the midst of impossible reality, and the Enemy itself came nearer and nearer with each great soundless footfall, and there was nothing to do but wait. Nothing at all. It wanted Alanna. He knew why. It would not want himself, and it would brush him away like smoke in its juggernaut striding to seize her, unless his weapon could stop it. His heart began to beat with heavy, thick blows that echoed the distant footsteps.

"Alanna," he said, hearing the faintest possible quiver in his voice. "Alanna, get behind something—that pillar over there. Don't make a sound. And if I tell you—*run!*"

He stepped behind a nearer pillar, his arm aching from the weight of his burden, the lens of it throbbing faintly against his palm with its promise of power in leash. He thought it would work. . . .

There was no sound of footfalls as the rhythm grew stronger. Only by the strength of those tremors that shook the floor could he judge how near the Thing was drawing. The pillar itself was shaking now, and the snowstorm was convulsed each time a mighty foot struck the floor soundlessly. Paul thought of the knife-edged patterns which those feet were treading with such firm and measured strides.

For a moment of panic he regretted his daring in coming to meet the Thing. He was sorry they had not stayed cowering in the room of the mirror—sorry they had not fled back down the whirling darkness through which they came. But you can't escape a nightmare. He held his lensed weapon throbbing like a throat against his palm, waiting to pour out lightning upon—what?

Now it was very close. Now it was just beyond the snowstorm between the pillars. He could see dim motion through their veil. . . .

Snow swirled away from its mighty shoulders, clouded about its great head so that he could not see very clearly what it was that stood there, tall and grotesque and terrible, its eyes shining scarlet through the veil. He was aware only of the eyes, and of the being's majestic bulk, before his hand of its own volition closed hard upon the pulse of violence in his palm.

For one timeless moment nothing happened. He was too stunned with the magnitude of the thing he faced to feel even terror at his weapon's failure; awe shut out every other thought. He was even a little startled when the glare of golden daylight burst hissing from his hand, splashing its brillance across the space between them.

Then relief was a weakness that loosened all his muscles as he played the deadliness of his weapon upon the Enemy, hearing the air shriek with its power, seeing the stone pillars blacken before those lashes of light. He was blinded by their glory; he could only stand there pouring the lightnings forth and squinting against their glare. The smell of scorched metal and stone was heavy in the air, and he could hear the crash of a falling column somewhere, burned through by the blast of the flame. Surely *it* too must be consumed and falling. . . . Hope began to flicker in his brain.

It was Alanna's whimper that told him something must still be wrong. Belatedly he reached up to close the glass visor of the mask he still wore, and by magic the glare ceased to blind him. He could see between the long, writhing whips of light—see the pillars falling and the steel patterns of the floor turn blue and melt away. But he could see it standing between those crumbling pillars now. . . .

He could see it standing in the full bath of the flames, see them splash upon its mighty chest and sluice away over its great shoulders like the spray of water, unheeded, impotent.

Its eyes were darkening from crimson to an angry purple as it lurched forward one ponderous, powerful stride, brushing away the sparks from its face, putting out a terrible arm. . . .

"Alanna—" said the man in a very quiet voice, pitched below the screaming of the flame. "Alanna—you'd better start back. I'll hold it while I can. You'd better run, Alanna. . . ."

He did not know if she obeyed. He could spare no further attention from the desperate business at hand, to delay it—to hold it back even for sixty seconds—for thirty seconds—for one breath more of independent life. What might happen after that he could not let himself think. Perhaps not death—perhaps something far more alien and strange than death . . . He knew the struggle was hopeless and senseless, but he knew he must struggle on while breath remained in him.

There was a narrow place in the corridor between himself and it. The lightning had weakened one wall already. He swung it away from the oncoming colossus and played the fire screaming to and fro upon blackened stones, seeing mortar crumble between them and girders bending in that terrible heat.

The walls groaned, grinding their riven blocks surface against surface. Slowly, slowly they leaned together; slowly they fell. Stone dust billowed in a cloud to hide the final collapse of the corridor, but through it the scream of lightnings sounded and the shriek of metal against falling stone. And then, distantly, a deeper groaning of new pressure coming to bear.

The man stood paralyzed for a moment, dizzy with an unreasonable hope that he had stopped the Enemy at last, not daring to look too closely for fear of failure. But hope and despair came almost simultaneously into his mind as he watched the mass of the closed walls shuddering and resisting for a moment—but only for a moment.

With dust and stone blocks and steel girders falling away from its tremendous shoulders, it stepped through the ruined arch. Jagged golden lightnings played in its face, hissing and screaming futilely. It ignored them. Shaking off the debris of the wall, it strode forward, eyes purple with anger, great hands outstretched.

And so the weapon failed. He loosed the trigger, hearing its shriek die upon the air as the long ribbons of lightning faded. It was instinct, echoing over millenniums from the first fighting ancestor of mankind, that made him swing the heavy machine overhead with both hands and hurl it into the face of the Enemy. And it was a little like relinquishing a living comrade to let the throb of that fiery tubing lose contact with his palm at last.

Blindly he flung the weapon from him, and in the same motion whirled and ran. The knife-edged floor spun past below him. If he could hit a rhythm to carry him from loop to empty loop of the pattern, he might even reach the room at the end of the passage— There was no sanctuary anywhere, but unreasoning instinct made him seek the place of his origin here. . . .

Ahead of him a flutter of blue-green sequins now and then told him that Alanna was running too, miraculously keeping her balance on the patterned floor. He could not look up to watch her. His eyes were riveted to the spirals and loops among which his precarious footing lay. Behind him great feet were thudding soundlessly, shaking the floor.

The things that happened then happened too quickly for the brain to resolve into any sequnce at all. He knew that the silence which had flowed back when the screaming lightnings died was suddenly, shockingly broken again by a renewed screaming. He remembered seeing the metal patterns of the floor thrown into sharp new shadows by the light behind him, and he knew that the Enemy had found the trigger he had just released, that his weapon throbbed now against an alien hand.

But it happened in the same instant that the doorway of the entrance room loomed up before him, and he hurled himself desperately into the dimness after Alanna, knowing his feet were cut through and bleeding, seeing the dark blotches of the tracks she too was leaving. The mirror loomed before them. an unbearable picture of the lost familiar room he could not hope to enter again in life.

And all this was simultaneous with a terrifying soundless thunder of great feet at his very heels, of a mighty presence suddenly and ponderously in the same room with them, like a whirlwind exhausting the very air they gasped to breathe. He felt anger eddying about him without words or sound. He felt monstrous hands snatch him up as if a tornado had taken him into its windy grasp. He remembered purple eyes glaring through the dimness in one brief instant of perception before the hands hurled him away.

He spun through empty air. Then a howling vortex seized him and he was falling in blindness, stunned and stupefied, through the same strange passageway that had brought him here. Distantly he heard Alanna scream.

There was silence in the dim, round room in the center of the treasure house, except for a muffled howling from the screen. He who was master here stood quietly before it, his eyes half shut and ranging down the spectrum from purple to red, and then swiftly away from red through orange to a clear, pale tranquil yellow. His chest still heaved a little with the excitement of that minor fiasco which he had brought upon himself, but it was an excitement soon over, and wholly disappointing.

He was a little ashamed of his momentary anger. He should not have played the little creatures' puny lightnings upon them as they fell down the shaft of darkness. He had misjudged their capacity, after all. They were not really capable of giving him a fight worth while.

It was interesting that one had followed the other, with its little weapon that sparkled and stung, interesting that one fragile being had stood up to him.

But he knew a moment's regret for the beauty of the blue-and-white creature he had flung away. The long, smooth lines of it, the subtle coloring . . . Too bad that it had been worthless because it was helpless too.

Helpless against himself, he thought, and equally against the drive of its own mysterious motives. He sighed.

He thought again, almost regretfully, of the lovely thing he had coveted hurtling away down the vortex with lightnings bathing it through the blackness.

Had he destroyed it? He did not know. He was a little sorry now that anger for his ruined treasures had made him lose his temper when they ran. Futile, scuttling little beings—they had cheated him out of beauty because of their own impotence against him, but he was not even angry about that now. Only sorry, with vague, confused sorrows he did not bother to clarify in his mind. Regret for the loss of a lovely thing, regret that he had expected danger from them and been disappointed, regret perhaps for his own boredom, that did not bother any longer to probe into the motives of living things. He was growing old indeed.

The vortex still roared through the darkened screen. He stepped back from it, letting opacity close over the surface of the portal, hushing all sound. His eyes were a tranquil yellow. Tomorrow he would hunt again, and perhaps tomorrow. . . .

He went out slowly, walking with long, soundless strides that made the steel mosaics sing faintly beneath his feet.

Deadline

Cleve Cartmill (1908-1964)

CLEVE *Cartmill was one of those science fiction writers who, like Tom Godwin for "The Cold Equations," will always be remembered best for a single story, despite the fact that at least eleven of his other stories have been anthologized. He was also a mainstay of* Astounding's *companion fantasy magazine,* Unknown Worlds, *three issues of which featured his short novels. During the late forties and early fifties he wrote an interesting series of stories around a space salvage business for* Thrilling Wonder Stories.

"Deadline" is one of the most famous stories in the history of science fiction because it precipitated a "visit" by the F.B.I. to the office of John W. Campbell, Jr., in an attempt to ascertain who, in the top-secret Manhattan Project, which was developing the first atomic bomb, had leaked the information that was apparently the basis for the story. Of course, neither Cartmill nor Campbell was guilty of anything. Sf writers had been publishing stories about atomic energy for many years, and this case was simply one of extrapolation from public information. According to legend, Campbell convinced the authorities that to stop publishing such stories would only tip off the Germans; many German scientists read American science fiction.

The story was reprinted in Groff Conklin's The Best of Science Fiction *(1946), the first (along with Healy and McComas's* Adventures in Time and Space) *of the postwar anthologies. This volume and its successors,* The Treasury of Science Fiction *(1948),* The Big Book of Science Fiction *(1950), and* Omnibus of Science Fiction *(1952), helped to legitimize sf and further the reputation of the authors who*

159

appeared in them. Conklin quickly established himself as the leading anthologist in the field and a prime chronicler of its Golden Age.

From *Astounding Science Fiction*   *1944*

DETONATION AND ASSEMBLY

12.16. As stated in Chapter II, it is impossible to prevent a chain reaction from occurring when the size exceeds the critical size. For there are always enough neutrons (from cosmic rays, from spontaneous fission reactions, or from alpha-particle-induced reactions in impurities) to initiate the chain. Thus until detonation is desired, the bomb must consist of a number of separate pieces each one of which is below the critical size either by reason of small size or unfavorable shape. To produce detonation, the parts of the bomb must be brought together rapidly. In the course of this assembly process the chain reaction is likely to start—because of the presence of stray neutrons—*before* the bomb has reached its most compact (most reactive) form. Thereupon the explosion tends to prevent the bomb from reaching that most compact form. Thus it may turn out that the explosion is so inefficient as to be relatively useless. The problem, therefore, is two-fold: (1) to reduce the time of assembly to a minimum; and (2) to reduce the number of stray (predetonation) neutrons to a minimum.

Official Report: Atomic Energy for Military Purposes
Henry D. Smyth

Heavy flak burst above and below the flight of bombers as they flashed across the night sky of the planet Cathor. Ybor Sebrof grinned as he nosed his glider at a steep angle away from the fireworks. The bombers had accomplished their mission: they had dropped him near Nilreq, had simulated a raid.

He had cut loose before searchlights slatted the sky with lean, white arms. They hadn't touched the glider, marked with their own insignia. Their own glider, in fact, captured when Seilla advance columns had caught the Namo garrison asleep. He would leave it where he landed, and let Sixa intelligence try to figure out how it got there.

Provided, of course, that he landed unseen.

Sixa intelligence officers would have another job, too. That was to explain the apparent bombing raid that dropped no bombs. None of the Seilla planes had been hit, and the Sixa crowd couldn't know that the bombers were empty: no bombs, no crews, just speed.

He could see tomorrow's papers, hear tomorrow's newscasts. "Raiders driven off. Craven Democracy pilots cringe from Nilreq ack-ack." But the big bugs would worry. The Seilla planes *could* have dropped bombs, if they'd had any bombs. They had flitted across the great industrial city with impunity. They could have laid their eggs. The big bugs would wonder about that. Why? they would ask each other profoundly. What was the reason?

Ybor grinned. He was the reason. He'd make them wish there *had* been bombs instead of him. Possibility of failure never entered his mind. All he had to do was to penetrate into the stronghold of the enemy, find Dr. Sitruc, kill him, and destroy the most devastating weapon of history. That was all.

He caught a sharp breath as a farmhouse loomed some distance ahead, and veered over against the dark edge of a wood. The green-gray plane would be invisible against the background, unless keen eyes caught its shadow under a fugitive moon.

He glided silently now, on a little wind that gossiped with tree-tops. Only the wind and the trees remarked on his passing. They could keep the secret.

He landed in a field of grain that whispered fierce protest as the glider whished through its heavy-laden plumes. These waved above the level of the motorless ship, and Ybor decided that it would not be seen before harvesting machines gathered the grain.

The air was another problem. He did not want the glider discovered just yet, particularly if he should be intercepted on his journey into the enemy capital. Elementary intelligence would connect him with this abandoned ship if he were stopped in this vicinity for any reason, and if the ship should be discovered on the morrow.

He took a long knife from its built-in sheath in the glider and laid about him with it until he had cut several armloads of grain. He scattered these haphazardly—not in any pattern—over parts of the ship. It wouldn't look like a glider now, even from the air.

He pushed through the shoulder-high growth to the edge of the wood.

He moved stealthily here. It was almost a certainty that big guns were hidden here, and he must avoid discovery. He slipped along the soft carpet of vegetation like a nocturnal cat, running on all fours under low branches, erect when possible.

A sharp scent of danger assailed his nostrils, and he crouched motionless while he sifted this odor. It made a picture in his head: men, and oil, and the acrid smoke of exploded gases. A gun crew was directly ahead.

Ybor took to the trees. He moved from one to the other, with no more sound than soft-winged night birds, and approached the source of the odor. He paused now and then, listening for a sentry's footsteps.

He heard them presently, a soft *pad-pad* which mingled, in different rhythm, with snores which became audible on the light wind.

The better part of valor, Ybor knew, was to circle this place, to leave the sentry unaware of his passage through the wood. But habit was too strong. He must destroy, for they were the enemy.

He moved closer to the sound of footsteps. Presently, he crouched above the line of the sentry's march, searching the darkness with eye and ear. The guard passed below, and Ybor let him go. His ears strained through snores from nearby tents until he heard another guard. Two were on sentry duty.

He pulled the knife from his belt and waited. When the sentry shuffled below him, Ybor dropped soundlessly onto the man's shoulders, stabbing as he fell.

There was a little noise. Not much, but a little. Enough to bring a low-voiced hail from the other guard.

"Namreh?" called the guard. "What happened?"

Ybor grunted, took the dead man's gun and helmet and took over his beat. He marched with the same rhythm the enemy feet had maintained until he met the second guard. Ybor silenced questions with a swift slash of the knife, and then turned his attention to the tents.

Presently, it was done. He clamped the fingers of the first guard around the knife hilt and went away. Let them think that one of their men had gone mad and killed the others before suiciding. Let the psychologists get a little work-out on this.

When he had penetrated to the far edge of the wood, dawn had splashed pale color beyond Nilreq, pulling jumbled buildings into dark silhouette. There lay his area of operations. There, perhaps, lay his destiny, and the destiny of the whole race.

This latter thought was not born of rhetorical hyperbole. It was cold, hard fact. It had nothing to do with patriotism, nor was it concerned with politico-economic philosophy. It was concerned with a scientific fact only: if the weapon, which was somewhere in the enemy capital, were used, the entire race might very well perish down to the last man.

Now began the difficult part of Ybor's task. He started to step out of the wood. A slight sound from behind froze him for the fraction of a second while he identified it. Then, in one incredibly swift motion, he whirled and flung himself at its source.

He knew he was fighting a woman after the first instant of contact. He was startled to some small extent, but not enough to impair his efficiency. A chopping blow, and she lay unconscious at his feet. He stood over her with narrowed eyes, unable to see what she looked like in the leafy gloom.

Then dawn burst like a salvo in the east, and he saw that she was young. Not immature, by any means, but young. When a spear of sunlight stabbed into the shadow, he saw that she was lovely.

Ybor pulled out his combat knife. She was an enemy, and must be destroyed. He raised his arm for the *coup de grace*, and held it there. He could not drive the blade into her. She seemed only to sleep, in her unconsciousness, with parted ripe lips and limp hands. You could kill a man while he slept, but Nature had planted a deep aversion in your instincts to kill a helpless female.

She began to moan softly. Presently she opened her wide brown eyes, soft as a captive fawn's.

"You hit me." She whispered the accusation.

Ybor said nothing.

"You hit me," she repeated.

"What did you expect?" he asked harshly. "Candy and flowers? What are you doing here?"

"Following you," she answered. "May I get up?"

"Yes. Why were you following?"

"When I saw you land in our field, I wondered why. I ran out to see you cover your ship and slip into the woods. I followed."

Ybor was incredulous. "You followed me through those woods?"

"I could have touched you," she said. "Any time."

"You lie!"

"Don't feel chagrined," she said. She flowed to her feet in a liquid movement. Her eyes were almost on a level with his. Her smile showed small, white teeth. "I'm very good at that sort of thing," she said. "Better than almost anybody, though I admit you're no slouch."

"Thanks," he said shortly. "All right, let's hear the story. Most likely it'll be the last you'll ever tell. What's your game?"

"You speak Ynamren like a native," the girl said.

Ybor's eyes glinted. "I am a native."

She smiled her disbelief. "And you kill your own soldiers? I think not. I saw you wipe out that gun crew. There was too much objectivity about you. One of us would do it with hatred. For you, it was a tactical maneuver."

"You're cutting your own throat," Ybor warned. "I can't let you go. You're too observing."

She repeated, "I think not." After a pause, she said, "You'll need help, whatever your mission. I can offer it."

He was contemptuous. "You offer my head a lion's mouth. I can hide it there? I need no help. Especially from anybody clumsy enough to be caught. And I've caught you, my pretty."

She flushed. "You were about to storm a rampart. I saw it in your odd face as you stared toward Nilreq. I caught my breath with hope

163

that you could. That's what you heard. If I'd thought you were my enemy, you'd have heard nothing. Except, maybe, the song of my knife blade as it reached your heart."

"What's odd about my face?" he demanded. "It'd pass in a crowd without notice."

"Women would notice it," she said. "It's lopsided."

He shrugged aside the personal issue. He took her throat in his hands. "I have to do this," he said. "It's highly important that nobody knows of my presence here. This is war. I can't afford to be humane."

She offered no resistance. Quietly, she looked up at him and asked, "Have you heard of Ylas?"

His fingers did not close on the soft flesh. "Who has not?"

"I am Ylas," she said.

"A trick."

"No trick. Let me show you." As his eyes narrowed—"No, I have no papers, of course. Listen. You know Mulb, Sworb, and Nomos? I got them away."

Ybor hesitated. She could be Ylas, but it would be a fantastic stroke of luck to run into the fabulous director of Ynamre's Underground so soon. It was almost beyond belief. Yet, there was a chance she was telling the truth. He couldn't overlook that chance.

"Names," he said. "You could have heard them anywhere."

"Nomos has a new-moon scar on his wrist," she said. "Sworb is tall, almost as tall as you, and his shoulders droop slightly. He talks so fast you can hardly follow. Mulb is a dope. He gets by on his pontifical manner."

These, Ybor reflected, were crisp thumbnail sketches.

She pressed her advantage. "Would I have stood by while you killed that gun crew if I were a loyal member of the Sixa Alliance? Wouldn't I have cried a warning when you killed the first guard and took his helmet and gun?"

There was logic in this, Ybor thought.

"Wasn't it obvious to me," she went on, "that you were a Seilla agent from the moment that you landed in my grain field? I could have telephoned the authorities."

Ybor took his hands from her throat. "I want to see Dr. Sitruc," he said.

She frowned off toward Nilreq, at towers golden in morning sunlight. Ybor noted indifferently that she made a colorful picture with her face to the sun. A dark flower, opening toward the dawn. Not that it mattered. He had no time for her. He had little time for anything.

"That will take some doing," she said.

He turned away. "Then I'll do it myself. Time is short."

"Wait!" Her voice had a quality which caused him to turn. He smiled sourly at the gun in her hand.

Self-contempt blackened Ybor's thoughts. He had had her helpless, but he had thought of her as a woman, not as an armed enemy. He hadn't searched her because of callow sentimentality. He had scaled the heights of stupidity, and now would plunge to his deserved end. Her gun was steady, and purpose shone darkly in her eyes.

"I'm a pushover for a fairy tale," she said. "I thought for a while that you really were a Seilla agent. How fiendishly clever you are, you and your council! I should have known when those planes went over. They went too fast."

Ybor said nothing. He was trying to absorb this.

"It was a smart idea," she went on in her acid, bitter voice. "They towed you over, and you landed in my field. A coincidence, when you come to think of it. I have been in that farmhouse only three days. Of all places, you pick it. Not by accident, not so. You and the other big minds on the Sixa council knew the planes would bring me to my window, knew my eyes would catch the shadow of your glider, knew I'd investigate. You even killed six of your own men, to dull my suspicions. Oh, I was taken in for a while."

"You talk like a crazy woman," Ybor said. "Put away that gun."

"When you had a chance to kill me and didn't," she said, "my last suspicion died. The more fool I. No, my bucko, you are not going back to report my whereabouts, to have your goons wait until my committee meets and catch us all. Not so. You die here and now."

Thoughts raced through Ybor's head. It would be a waste of energy; to appeal to her on the ground that if she killed him she would in effect destroy her species. That smacked of oratory. He needed a simple appeal, crisp and startling. But what? His time was running short; he could see it in her dark eyes.

"Your last address," he said, remembering Sworb's tale of escape, "was 40 Curk Way. You sold pastries, and Sworb got sick on little cakes. He was sick in your truck, as it carted him away at eleven minutes past midnight."

Bull's eye. Determination to kill went out of her eyes as she remembered. She was thoughtful for a moment.

Then her eyes glinted. "I've not heard that he reached Acireb safely. You could have caught him across the Enarta border and beaten the truth out of him. Still," she reflected, "you may be telling the truth. . . ."

"I am," Ybor said quietly. "I am a Seilla agent, here on a highly important mission. If you can't aid me directly, you must let me go. At once."

"You might be lying, too, though. I can't take the chance. You will march ahead of me around the wood. If you make one overt move, or even a move that I don't understand, I'll kill you."

"Where are you taking me?"

"To my house. Where else? Then we'll talk."

"Now listen to me," he said passionately, "there is no time for—"

"March!"

He marched.

Ybor's plan to take her unawares when they were inside the farmhouse dissolved when he saw the great hulk who admitted them. This was a lumpish brute with the most powerful body Ybor had ever seen, towering over his own more than average height. The man's arms were as thick as Ybor's thighs, and the yellow eyes were small and vicious. Yet, apelike though he was, the giant moved like a mountain cat, without sound, with deceptive swiftness.

"Guard him," the girl commanded, and Ybor knew the yellow eyes would not leave him.

He sank into a chair, an old chair with a primitive tail slot, and watched the girl as she busied herself at the mountainous cooking range. This kitchen could accommodate a score of farmhands, and that multiple-burner stove could turn out hot meals for all.

"We'd better eat," she said. "If you're not lying, you'll need strength. If you are, you can withstand torture long enough to tell us the truth."

"You're making a mistake," Ybor began hotly, but stopped when the guard made a menacing gesture.

She had a meal on the table soon. It was a good meal, and he ate it heartily. "The condemned man," he said, and smiled.

For a camaraderie had sprung up between them. He was male, not too long past his youth, with clear, dark eyes, and he was put together with an eye to efficiency; and she was a female, at the ripening stage. The homely task of preparing a meal, of sharing it, lessened the tension between them. She gave him a fleeting, occasional smile as he tore into his food.

"You're a good cook," he said, when they had finished.

Warmth went out of her. She eyed him steadily. "Now," she said crisply. "Proof."

Ybor shrugged angrily. "Do you think I carry papers identifying me as a Seilla agent? 'To whom it may concern, bearer is high in Seilla councils. Any aid you may give him will be appreciated.' I have papers showing that I'm a newspaper man from Eeras. The newspaper offices and building have been destroyed by now, and there is no means of checking."

She thought this over. "I'm going to give you a chance," she said. "If you're a top-flight Seilla agent, one of your Nilreq men can identify you. Name one, and we'll get him here."

"None of them know me by sight. My face was altered before I came on this assignment, so that nobody could give me away, even accidentally."

"You know all the answers, don't you?" she scoffed. "Well, we will now take you into the cellar and get the truth from you. And you won't die until we do. We'll keep you alive, one way or another."

"Wait a moment," Ybor said. "There is one man who will know me. He may not have arrived. Solraq."

"He came yesterday," she said. "Very well. If he identifies you, that will be good enough. Sleyg," she said to the huge guard, "fetch Solraq."

Sleyg rumbled deep in his throat, and she made an impatient gesture. "I can take care of myself. Go!" She reached inside her blouse, took her gun from its shoulder holster and pointed it across the table at Ybor. "You will sit still."

Sleyg went out. Ybor heard a car start, and the sound of its motor faded rapidly.

"May I smoke?" Ybor asked.

"Certainly." With her free hand she tossed a pack of cigarettes across the table. He lighted one, careful to keep his hand in sight, handed it to her, and applied flame to his own. "So you're Ylas," he said conversationally.

She didn't bother to reply.

"You've done a good job," he went on. "Right under their noses. You must have had some close calls."

She smiled tolerantly. "Don't be devious, chum. On the off chance that you might escape, I'll give you no data to use later."

"There won't be any later if I don't get out of here. For you, or anybody."

"Now you're melodramatic. There'll always be a later, as long as there's time."

"Time exists only in consciousness," he said. "There won't be any time, unless dust and rocks are aware of it."

"That's quite a picture of destruction you paint."

"It will be quite a destruction. And you're bringing it nearer every minute. You're cutting down the time margin in which it can be averted."

She grinned. "Ain't I nasty?"

"Even if you let me go this moment—" he began.

"Which I won't."

"—the catastrophe might not be averted. Our minds can't conceive the unimaginable violence which might very well destroy all animal life. It's a queer picture," he mused, "even to think about. Imagine space travelers of the future sighting this planet empty of life, overgrown with jungles. It wouldn't even have a name. Oh, they'd find the name. All traces of civilization wouldn't be completely destroyed. They'd poke in the crumbled ruins and finds bits of history. Then they'd go back to their home planet with the mystery of Cathor. Why did all life disappear from Cathor? They'd find skeletons enough to show our size and shape, and they'd decipher such records as were found. But nowhere would they find even a hint of the reason our civilization was destroyed. Nowhere would they find the name of Ylas, the reason."

She merely grinned.

"That's how serious it is," Ybor concluded. "Not a bird in the sky, not a pig in a sty. Perhaps no insects, even. I wonder," he said thoughtfully, "if such explosions destroyed life in other planets in our system. Lara, for example. It *had* life, once. Did civilization rise to a peak there, and end in a war that involved every single person on one side or another? Did one side, in desperation, try to use an explosive available to both but uncontrollable, and so lose the world?"

"Shh!" she commanded. She was stiff, listening.

He heard it then, the rhythmic tramp of feet. He flicked a glance through the window toward the wood. "Ynamre," he said.

A sergeant marched a squad of eight soldiers across the field toward the house. Ybor turned to the girl.

"You've got to hide me! Quick!"

She stared at him coldly. "I have no place."

"You must have. You must take care of refugees. Where is it?"

"Maybe you've caught me," she said grimly, "but you'll learn nothing. The Underground will carry on."

"You little fool! I'm with you."

"That's what you say. I haven't any proof."

Ybor wasted no more time. The squad was almost at the door. He leaped over against the wall and squatted there. He pulled his coat half off, shook his black hair over his eyes, and slacked his face so that it took on the loose, formless expression of an idiot. He began to play with his fingers, and gurgled.

A pounding rifle butt took the girl to the door. Ybor did not look up. He twisted his fingers and gurgled at them.

"Did you hear anything last night?" the sergeant demanded.

"Anything?" she echoed. "Some planes, some guns."

"Did you get up? Did you look out?"

"I was afraid," she answered meekly.

He spat contemptuously. There was a short silence, disturbed only by Ybor's gurgling.

"What's that?" the sergeant snapped. He stamped across the room, jerked Ybor's head up by the lock of hair. Ybor gave him an insane, slobbering grin. The sergeant's eyes were contemptuous. "Dummy!" he snarled. He jerked his hand away. "Why don't you kill it?" he asked the girl. "All the more food for you. Sa-a-a-y," he said, as if he'd seen her for the first time, "not bad, not bad. I'll be up to see you, cookie, one of these nights."

Ybor didn't move until they were out of hearing. He got to his feet then, and looked grimly at Ylas. "I could have been in Nilreq by now. You'll have to get me away. They've discovered that gun crew, and will be on the lookout."

She had the gun in her hand again. She motioned him toward the chair. "Shall we sit down?"

"After that? You're still suspicious? You're a fool."

"Ah? I think not. That could have been a part of the trick, to lull my suspicions. Sit—down!"

He sat. He was through with talking. He thought of the soldiers' visit. That sergeant probably wouldn't recognize him if they should encounter each other. Still, it was something to keep in mind. One more face to remember to dodge.

If only that big ape would get back with Solraq. His ears, as if on cue, caught the sound of an approaching motor. He was gratified to see that he heard it a full second before Ylas. Her reflexes weren't so fast, after all.

It was Sleyg, and Sleyg alone. He came into the house on his soft cat feet. "Solraq," he reported, "is dead. Killed last night."

Ylas gave Ybor a smile. There was deadliness in it.

"How very convenient," she said, "for you. Doesn't it seem odd even to you, Mr. Sixa Intelligence Officer, that of all the Seilla agents you pick a man who is dead? I think this has gone far enough. Into the cellar with him, Sleyg. We'll get the truth this time. Even," she added to Ybor, "though it'll kill you."

The chair was made like a strait jacket, with an arrangement of clamps and straps that held him completely motionless. He could move nothing but his eyeballs.

Ylas inspected him. She nodded satisfaction. "Go heat your irons," she said to Sleyg. "First," she explained to Ybor, "we'll burn off your ears, a little at a time. If that doesn't wear you down, we'll get serious."

Ybor said, "I'll tell you the truth now."

She sneered at that. "No wonder the enemy is knocking at your gates. You were driven out of Aissu on the south, and Ytal on the north. Now you are coming into your home country, because you're cowards."

"I'm convinced that you are Ylas," Ybor went on calmly. "And though my orders were that nobody should know of my mission, I think I can tell you. I must. I have no choice. Then listen. I was sent to Ynamre to—"

She cut him off with a fierce gesture. "The truth!"

"Do you want to hear this or not?"

"I don't want to hear another fairy tale."

"You are going to hear this, whether you like it or not. And you'll hold off your gorilla until I've finished. Or have the end of the race on your head."

Her lip curled. "Go on."

"Have you heard of U-235? It's an isotope of uranium."

"Who hasn't?"

"All right. I'm stating fact, not theory. U-235 has been separated in quantity easily sufficient for preliminary atomic-power research, and the like. They got it out of uranium ores by new atomic isotope separation methods; they now have quantities measured in pounds. By 'they,' I mean Seilla research scientists. But they have *not* brought the whole amount together, or any major portion of it. Because they are not at all sure that, once started, it would stop before all of it had been consumed—in something like one micromicrosecond of time."

Sleyg came into the cellar. In one hand he carried a portable forge. In the other, a bundle of metal rods. Ylas motioned him to put them down in a corner. "Go up and keep watch," she ordered. "I'll call you."

A tiny exultation flickered in Ybor. He had won a concession. "Now the explosion of a pound of U-235," he said, "wouldn't be too unbearably violent, though it releases as much energy as a hundred million pounds of TNT. Set off on an island, it might lay waste the whole island, uprooting trees, killing all animal life, but even that wouldn't seriously disturb the really unimaginable tonnage which even a small island represents."

"I assume," she broke in, "that you're going to make a point? You're not just giving me a lecture on high explosives?"

"Wait. The trouble is, they're afraid that that explosion of energy would be so incomparably violent, its sheer, minute concentration of unbearable energy so great, that surrounding matter would be set off. If you could imagine concentrating half a billion of the most violent lightning strokes you ever saw, compressing all their fury into a space less than half the size of a pack of cigarettes—you'd get some idea of the concentrated essence of hyperviolence that explosion would represent. It's not simply the *amount* of energy; it's the frightful concentration of intensity in a minute volume.

"The surrounding matter, unable to maintain a self-supporting atomic explosion normally, might be hyper-stimulated to atomic explosion under U-235's forces and, in the immediate neighborhood, release its energy, too. That is, the explosion would not involve only one pound of U-235, but also five or fifty or five thousand tons of other matter. The extent of the explosion is a matter of conjecture."

"Get to the point," she said impatiently.

"Wait. Let me give you the main picture. Such an explosion *would* be serious. It would blow an island, or a hunk of continent, right off the planet. It would shake Cathor from pole to pole, cause earthquakes violent enough to do serious damage on the other side of the planet, and utterly destroy everything within at least one thousand miles of the site of the explosion. And I mean everything.

"So they haven't experimented. They could end the war overnight with controlled U-235 bombs. They could end this cycle of civilization with one or two *uncontrolled* bombs. And they don't know which they'd have if they made 'em. So far, they haven't worked out any way to control the explosion of U-235."

"If you're stalling for time," Ylas said, "it won't do you any good, personally. If we have callers, I'll shoot you where you sit."

"Stalling?" Ybor cried. "I'm trying my damnedest to shorten it. I'm not finished yet. Please don't interrupt. I want to give you the rest of the picture. As you pointed out, the Sixa armies are being pushed back to their original starting point: Ynamre. They started out to conquer the world, and they came close, at one time. But now they are about to lose it. We, the Seilla, would not dare to set off an experimental atomic bomb. This war is a phase, to us; to the Sixa, it is the whole future. So the Sixa are desperate, and Dr. Sitruc has made a bomb with not one, but *sixteen* pounds of U-235 in it. He may have it finished any day. I must find him and destroy that bomb. If it's used, we are lost either way. Lost the war, if the experiment is a success; the world, if not. You and you alone stand between extinction of the race and continuance."

She seemed to pounce. "You're lying! Destroy it, you say. How? Take it out in a vacant lot and explode it? In a desert? On a high mountain? You wouldn't dare even to drop it in the ocean, for fear it might explode. Once you had it, you'd have ten million tigers by the tail—you wouldn't dare turn it loose."

"I can destroy it. Our scientists told me how."

"Let that pass for the moment," she said. "You have several points to explain. First, it seems odd that *you* heard of this, and we haven't. We're much closer to developments than you, across three thousand miles of water."

"Sworb," Ybor said, "is a good man, even if he can't eat sweets. He brought back a drawing of it. Listen, Ylas, time is precious! If Dr. Sitruc finishes that bomb before I find him, it may be taken any time and dropped near our headquarters. And even if it doesn't set off the explosion I've described—though it's almost certain that it would—it would wipe out our southern army and equipment, and we'd lose overnight."

"Two more points need explaining," she went on calmly. "Why *my* grain field? There were others to choose from."

"That was pure accident."

"Perhaps. But isn't that string of accidents suspiciously long when you consider the death of Solraq?"

"I don't know anything about that. I didn't know he was dead."

She was silent. She strode back and forth across the cellar, brows furrowed, smoking nervously. Ybor sat quietly. It was all he could do; even his fingers were in stalls.

"I'm half inclined to believe you," she said finally, "but look at my position. We have a powerful organization here. We've risked our lives, and many of us have died, in building it up. I know how we are hated and feared by the authorities. If you are a Sixa agent, and I concluded that you were by the way you spoke the language, you would go to any length, even to carrying out such an elaborate plot as this might be, to discover our methods and membership. I can't risk all that labor and life on nothing but your word."

"Look at my position," Ybor countered. "I might have escaped from you, in the wood and here, after Sleyg left us. But I didn't dare take a chance. You see, it's a matter of time. There is a definite, though unknown, deadline. Dr. Sitruc may finish that bomb any time, and screw the fuse in. The bomb may be taken at any time after that and exploded. If I had tried to escape, and you had shot me—and I'm sure you would—it would take weeks to replace me. We may have only hours to work with."

She was no longer calm and aloof. Her eyes had a tortured look, and her hands clenched as if she were squeezing words from her heart: "I can't afford to take the chance."

"You can't afford not to," Ybor said.

Footsteps suddenly pounded overhead. Ylas went rigid, flung a narrowed glace of speculation and suspicion at Ybor, and went out of the cellar. He twisted a smile; she hadn't shot him, as she had threatened.

He sat still, but each nerve was taut, quivering, and raw. What now? Who had arrived? What could it mean for him? Who belonged to that babble upstairs? Whose feet were heavy? He was soon to know, for the footsteps moved to the cellar door, and Ylas preceded the sergeant who had arrived earlier.

"I've got orders to search every place in this vicinity," the sergeant said, "so shut up."

His eyes widened when they fell on Ybor. "Well, well!" he cried. "If it isn't the dummy. Sa-a-ay, you snapped out of it!"

Ybor caught his breath as an idea hit him.

"I was drugged," Ybor said, leaping at the chance for escape. "It's worn off now."

Ylas frowned, searching, he could see, for the meaning in his words. He went on, giving her her cue: "This girl's servant, that big oaf upstairs—"

"He ran out," the sergeant said. "We'll catch him."

"I see. He attacked me last night in the grain field out there, brought me here and drugged me."

172

"What were you doing in the grain field?"

"I was on my way to see Dr. Sitruc. I have information of the most vital nature for him."

The sergeant turned to Ylas. "What d'ya say, girlie?"

She shrugged. "A stranger, in the middle of the night, what would you have done?"

"Then why didn't you say something about it when I was here a while ago?"

"If he turned out to be a spy, I wanted the credit for capturing him."

"You civilians," the sergeant said in disgust. "Well, maybe this is the guy we're lookin' for. Why did you kill that gun crew?" he snarled at Ybor.

Ybor blinked. "How did you know? I killed them because they were enemies."

The sergeant made a gesture toward his gun. His face grew stormy. "Why, you dirty spy—"

"Wait a minute!" Ybor said. "What gun crew? You mean the Seilla outpost, of course, in Aissu?"

"I mean our gun crew, you rat, in the woods out there."

Ybor blinked again. "I don't know anything about a gun crew out there. Listen, you've got to take me to Dr. Sitruc at once. Here's the background. I have been in Seilla territory, and I learned something that Dr. Sitruc must know. The outcome of the war depends on it. Take me to him at once, or you'll suffer for it."

The sergeant cogitated. "There's something funny here," he said. "Why have you got him all tied up?"

"For questioning," Ylas answered.

Ybor could see that she had decided to play it his way, but she wasn't convinced. The truth was, as he pointed out, she could not afford to do otherwise.

The sergeant went into an analytical state which seemed to be almost cataleptic. Presently he shook his massive head. "I can't quite put my finger on it," he said in a puzzled tone. "Every time I get close, I hit a blank . . . what am I saying?" He became crisp, menacing. "What's your name, you?" he spat at Ybor.

Ybor couldn't shrug. He raised his eyebrows. "My papers will say that I am Yenraq Ekor, a newspaper man. Don't let them fool you. I'll give my real name to Dr. Sitruc. He knows it well. You're wasting time, man!" he burst out. "Take me to him at once. You're worse than this stupid female!"

The sergeant turned to Ylas. "Did he tell you why he wanted to see Dr. Sitruc?"

She shrugged again, still with speculative eyes on Ybor. "He just said he had to."

"Well, then," the sergeant demanded of Ybor, "why *do* you want to see him?"

Ybor decided to gamble. This goof might keep him here all day with aimless questioning. He told the story of the bomb, much as he had told it to Ylas. He watched the sergeant's face, and saw that his remarks were completely unintelligible. Good! The soldier, like so many people, knew nothing of U-235. Ybor went into the imaginative and gibberish phase of his talk.

"And so, if it's uncontrolled," he said, "it might destroy the planet, blow it instantly into dust. But what I learned was a method of control, and the Seilla have a bomb almost completed. They'll use it to destroy Ynamre. But if we can use ours first, we'll destroy them. You see, it's a neutron shield that I discovered while I was a spy in the Seilla camps. It will stop the neutrons, released by the explosion, from rocketing about space and splitting mountains. Did you know that one free neutron can crack this planet in half? This shield will confine them to a limited area, and the war is ours. So hurry! Our time may be measured in minutes!"

The sergeant took it all in. He didn't dare not believe, for the picture of destruction which Ybor painted was on such a vast scale that sixteen generations of men like the sergeant would be required to comprehend it.

The sergeant made up his mind. "Hey!" he yelled toward the cellar door, and three soldiers came in. "Get him out of that. We'll take him to the captain. Take the girl along, too. Maybe the captain will want to ask her some questions."

"But I haven't done anything," Ylas protested.

"Then you got nothing to be afraid of, beautiful. If they let you go, I'll take personal charge of you."

The sergeant had a wonderful leer.

You might as well be fatalistic, Ybor thought as he waited in Dr. Sitruc's anteroom. Certain death could easily await him here, but even so, it was worth the gamble. If he were to be a pawn in a greater game—the greatest game, in fact—so be it.

So far, he had succeeded. And it came to him as he eyed his two guards that final success would result in his own death. He couldn't hope to destroy that bomb and get out of this fortress alive. Those guarded exits spelled finis, if he could even get far enough from this laboratory to reach one of them.

He hadn't really expected to get out alive, he reflected. It was a suicide mission from the start. That knowledge, he knew now, had given plausibility to his otherwise thin story. The captain, even as the sergeant, had not dared to disbelieve his tale. He had imparted

174

verisimilitude to his story of destruction because of his deep and flaming determination to prevent it.

Not that he had talked wildly about neutron shields to the captain. The captain was intelligent, compared to his sergeant. And so Ybor had talked matter-of-factly about heat control, and had made it convincing enough to be brought here by guards who grew more timid with each turn of the lorry's wheels.

Apparently, the story of the bomb was known here at the government experimental laboratories; for all the guards had a haunted look, as if they knew that they would never hear the explosion if something went wrong. All the better, then. If he could take advantage of that fact, somehow, as he had taken advantage of events to date, he might— might—

He shrugged away speculation. The guards had sprung to attention as the inner door opened, and a man eyed Ybor.

This was a slender man with snapping dark eyes, an odd-shaped face, and a commanding air. He wore a smock, and from its sleeves extended competent-looking hands.

"So you are the end result," he said dryly to Ybor. "Come in."

Ybor followed him into the laboratory. Dr. Sitruc waved him to a straight, uncomfortable chair, using the gun which was suddenly in his hand as an indicator. Ybor sat, and looked steadily at the other.

"What do you mean, end result?" he asked.

"Isn't it rather obvious?" the doctor asked pleasantly. "Those planes which passed over last night were empty; they went too fast, otherwise. I have been speculating all day on their purpose. Now I see. They dropped you."

"I heard something about planes," Ybor said, "but I didn't see 'em."

Dr. Sitruc raised polite eyebrows. "I'm afraid I do not believe you. My interpretation of events is this: those Seilla planes had one objective, to land an agent here who was commissioned to destroy the uranium bomb. I have known for some time that the Seilla command have known of its existence, and I have wondered what steps they would take to destroy it."

Ybor could see no point in remaining on the defensive. "They are making their own bomb," he said. "But they have a control. I'm here to tell you about it, so that you can use it on our bomb. We have time."

Dr. Sitruc said: "I have heard the reports on you this morning. You made some wild and meaningless statements. My personal opinion is that you are a layman, with only scant knowledge of the subject on which you have been so glib. I propose to find out—before I kill you. Oh, yes," he said, smiling, "you will die in any case. In my present position, knowledge is power. If I find that you actually have knowledge which I do not, I propose that I alone will retain it. You see my point?"

"You're like a god here. That's clear enough from the attitude of the guards."

"Exactly. I have control of the greatest explosive force in world history, and my whims are obeyed as iron commands. If I choose, I may give orders to the High Command. They have no choice but to obey. Now, you—your name doesn't matter; it's assumed, no doubt—tell me what you know."

"Why should I? If I'm going to die, anyway, my attitude is to hell with you. I do know something that you don't, and you haven't time to get it from anybody but me. By the time one of your spies could work his way up high enough to learn what I did, the Sixa would be defeated. But I see no reason to give you the information. I'll sell it to you—for my life."

Ybor looked around the small, shining laboratory while he spoke, and he saw it. It wasn't particularly large; its size did not account for the stab of terror that struck his heart. It was the fact that the bomb was finished. It was suspended in a shock-proof cradle. Even a bombing raid would not shake it loose. It would be exploded when and where the doctor chose.

"You may well turn white as a sheet," Dr. Sitruc chuckled. "There it is, the most destructive weapon the world has ever known."

Ybor swallowed convulsively. Yes, there it was. Literally the means to an end—the end of the world. He thought wryly that those religionists who still contended that this war would be ended miraculously by divine intervention would never live to call the bomb a miracle. What a shot in the doctrine the explosion would give them if only they could come through it unscathed!

"I turned white," he answered Dr. Sitruc, "because I see it as a blind, uncontrolled force. I see it as the end of a cycle, when all life dies. It will be millennia before another civilization can reach our present stage."

"It is true that the element of chance is involved. If the bomb sets off surrounding matter for any considerable radius, it is quite possible that all animate life will be destroyed in the twinkling of an eye. However, if it does not set off surrounding matter, we shall have won the world. I alone—and now you—know this. The High Command sees only victory in that weapon. But enough of chitchat. You would bargain your life for information on how to control the explosion. If you convince me that you have such knowledge, I'll set you free. What is it?"

"That throws us into a deadlock," Ybor objected. "I won't tell you until I'm free, and you won't free me until I tell."

Dr. Sitruc pursed thin lips. "True," he said. "Well, then, how's this? I shall give the guards outside a note ordering that you be allowed to leave unmolested after you come through the laboratory door."

"And what's to prevent your killing me in here, once I have told you?"

"I give you my word."

"It isn't enough."

"What other choice have you?"

Ybor thought this over, and conceded the point. Somewhere along the line, either he or Dr. Sitruc would have to trust the other. Since this was the doctor's domain, and since he held Ybor prisoner, it was easy to see who would take the other on trust. Well, it would give him a breathing spell. Time was what he wanted now.

"Write the note," he said.

Dr. Sitruc went to his desk and began to write. He shot glances at Ybor which excluded the possibility of successful attack. Even the quickest spring would be fatal, for the doctor was far enough away to have time to raise his gun and fire. Ybor had a hunch that Dr. Sitruc was an excellent shot. He waited.

Dr. Sitruc summoned a guard, gave him the note, and directed that Ybor be allowed to read it. Ybor did, nodded. The guard went out.

"Now," Dr. Sitruc began, but broke off to answer his telephone. He listened, nodded, shot a slitted glance at Ybor, and hung up. "Would it interest you to know," he asked, "that the girl who captured you was taken away from guards by members of the Underground?"

"Not particularly," Ybor said. "Except that . . . yes," he cried, "it does interest me. It proves my authenticity. You know how widespread the Underground is, how powerful. It's clear what happened; they knew I was coming, knew my route, and caught me. They were going to torture me in their cellar. I told that sergeant the truth. Now they will try to steal the bomb. If they had it, they could dictate terms."

It sounded a trifle illogical, maybe, but Ybor put all of the earnestness he could into his voice. Dr. Sitruc looked thoughtful.

"Let them try. Now, let's have it."

The tangled web of lies he had woven had caught him now. He knew of no method to control the bomb. Dr. Sitruc was not aware of this fact, and would not shoot until he was. Ybor must stall, and watch for an opportunity to do what he must do. He had gained a point; if he got through that door, he would be free. He must, then, get through the door—with the bomb. And Dr. Sitruc's gun was in his hand.

"Let's trace the reaction," Ybor began.

"The control!" Dr. Sitruc snapped.

Ybor's face hardened. "Don't get tough. My life depends on this. I've got to convince you that I know what I'm talking about, and I can do that by describing the method from the first. If you interrupt, then to hell with you."

Dr. Sitruc's odd face flamed with anger. This subsided after a moment, and he nodded. "Go on."

"Oxygen and nitrogen do not burn—if they did, the first fire would have blown this planet's atmosphere off in one stupendous explosion. Oxygen and nitrogen *will* burn if heated to about three thousand degrees Centigrade, and they'll give off energy in the process. But they don't give off sufficient energy to maintain that temperature—so they rapidly cool, and the fire goes out. If you maintain that temperature artificially—well, you're no doubt familiar with that process of obtaining nitric oxide."

"No doubt," Dr. Sitruc said acidly.

"All right. Now U-235 can raise the temperature of local matter to where it will, uh, 'burn,' and give off energy. So let's say we set off a little pinch of U-235. Surrounding matter also explodes, as it is raised to an almost inconceivable temperature. It cools rapidly; within perhaps one-hundred-millionth of a second, it is down below the point of ignition. Then maybe a full millionth of a second passes before it's down to one million degrees hot, and a minute or so may elapse before it is visible in the normal sense. Now that visible radiation will represent no more than one-hundred-thousandth of the total radiation at one million degrees—but even so, it would be several hundred times more brilliant than the sun. Right?"

Dr. Sitruc nodded. Ybor thought there was a touch of deference in his nod.

"That's pretty much the temperature cycle of a U-235 plus surrounding matter explosion, Dr. Sitruc. I'm oversimplifying, I guess, but we don't need to go into detail. Now that radiation *pressure* is the stuff that's potent. The sheer momentum, physical pressure of light from the stuff at one million degrees, would amount to tons and tons and *tons* of pressure. It would blow down buildings like a titanic wind if it weren't for the fact that absorption of such appalling energy would volatilize the buildings before they could move out of the way. Right?"

Dr. Sitruc nodded again. He almost smiled.

"All right," Ybor went on. He now entered the phase of this contest where he was guessing, and he'd get no second guess. "What we need is a damper, something to hold the temperature of surrounding matter down. In that way, we can limit the effect of the explosion to desired areas, and prevent it from destroying cities on the opposite side of Cathor. The method of applying the damper depends on the exact mechanical structure of the bomb itself."

Ybor got to his feet easily, and walked across the laboratory to the cradle which held the bomb. He didn't even glance at Dr. Sitruc; he didn't dare. Would he be allowed to reach the bomb? Would an un-heard, unfelt bullet reach his brain before he took another step?

When he was halfway across the room, he felt as if he had already walked a thousand miles. Each step seemed to be slow motion, leagues in length. And still the bomb was miles away. He held his steady pace, fighting with every atom of will his desire to sprint to his goal, snatch it and flee.

He stopped before the bomb, looked down at it. He nodded, ponder-ously. "I see," he said, remembering Sworb's drawings and the careful explanations he had received. "Two cast-iron hemispheres, clamped over the orange segments of cadmium alloy. And the fuse—I see it is in—a tiny can of cadmium alloy containing a speck of radium in a beryllium holder and a small explosive powerful enough to shatter the cadmium walls. Then—correct me if I'm wrong, will you?—the pow-dered uranium oxide runs together in the central cavity. The radium shoots neutrons into this mass—and the U-235 takes over from there. Right?"

Dr. Sitruc had come up behind Ybor, stood at his shoulder. "Just how do you know so much about that bomb?" he asked with overtones of suspicion.

Ybor threw a careless smile over his shoulder. "It's obvious, isn't it? Cadmium stops neutrons, and it's cheap and effective. So you separate the radium and U-235 by thin cadmium walls, brittle so the light explosion will shatter them, yet strong enough to be handled with reasonable care."

The doctor chuckled. "Why, you *are* telling the truth."

Dr. Sitruc relaxed, and Ybor moved. He whipped his short, prehen-sile tail around the barrel of Dr. Sitruc's gun, yanked the weapon down at the same time his fist cracked the scientist's chin. His free hand wrenched the gun out of Dr. Sitruc's hand.

He didn't give the doctor a chance to fall from the blow of his fist. He chopped down with the gun butt and Dr. Sitruc was instantly unconscious. Ybor stared down at the sprawled figure with narrowed eyes. Dared he risk a shot? No, for the guards would not let him go, despite the doctor's note, without investigation. Well—

He chopped the gun butt down again. Dr. Sitruc would be no menace for some time, anyway. And all Ybor needed was a little time. First, he had to get out of here.

That meant taking the fuse out of the bomb. He went over to the cradle, examined the fuse. He tried to unscrew it. It was too tight. He looked around for a wrench. He saw none. He stood half panic-stricken. Could he afford a search for the wrench which would remove the fuse? If anyone came in, he was done for. No, he'd have to get out while he could.

And if anybody took a shot at him, and hit the bomb, it was good-by Cathor and all that's in it. But he didn't dare wait here. And he must stop sweating ice water, stop this trembling.

He picked up the cradle and walked carefully to the door. Outside, in the anteroom, the guards who had brought him there turned white. Blood drained out of their faces like air from a punctured balloon. They stood motionless, except for a slight trembling of their knees, and watched Ybor go out into the corridor.

Unmolested, Dr. Sitruc had said. He was not only unmolested, he was avoided. Word seemed to spread through the building like poison gas on a stiff breeze. Doors popped open, figures hurried out—and ran away from Ybor and his cargo. Guards, scientists, men in uniform, girls with pretty legs, bare-kneed boys—all ran.

To where? Ybor asked with his heart in his mouth. There was no safe place in all the world. Run how they might, as far as they could, and it would catch them if he fell or if the bomb were accidentally exploded.

He wanted a plane. But how to get one, if everybody ran? He could walk to the airport, if he knew where it was. Still, once he was away from these laboratories, any policeman, ignorant of the bomb, could stop him, confiscate the weapon, and perhaps explode it.

He had to retain possession.

The problem was partly solved for him. As he emerged from the building, to see people scattering in all directions, a huge form came out from behind a pillar and took him by the arm. "Sleyg," Ybor almost cried with terror which became relief.

"Come," Sleyg said, "Ylas wants you."

"Get me to a plane!" Ybor said. He thought he'd said it quietly, but Sleyg's yellow eyes flickered curiously at him.

The big man nodded, crooked a finger, and led the way. He didn't seem curious about the bomb. Ybor followed to where a small car was parked at the curb. They climbed in, and Sleyg pulled out into traffic.

So Ylas wanted him, eh? Why? He gave up speculation to watch the road ahead, cradling the bomb in his arms against rough spots.

He heard a plane, and searched for it anxiously. All he needed at this stage was a bombing raid, and a direct hit on this car. They had promised him that no raids would be attempted until they were certain of his success or failure, but brass hats were a funny lot. You never knew what they'd do next, like countermanding orders given only a few minutes before.

Still, no alarm sirens went off, so the plane must be Sixa. Ybor sighed with relief.

They drove on, and Ybor speculated on the huge, silent figure beside him. How had Sleyg known that he would come out of that building?

How had he known he was there? Did the Underground have a pipeline even into Dr. Sitruc's office?

These speculations were useless, too, and he shrugged them away as Sleyg drove out of the city through fields of grain. The Sixa, apparently, were going to feed their armies mush, for he saw no other produce.

Sleyg cut off the main road into a bumpy lane, and Ybor clasped the bomb firmly. "Take it easy," he warned.

Sleyg slowed obediently, and Ybor wondered again at the man's attitude. Ybor did not seem to be a prisoner, yet he was not in command here completely. It was a sort of combination of the two, and it was uncomfortable.

They came to a bare, level stretch of land where a plane stood, props turning idly. Sleyg headed toward it. He brought the car to a halt, motioned Ybor out. He then indicated that Ybor should enter the big plane.

"Give me your tool kit," Ybor said, and the big man got it.

The plane bore Sixa insignia, but Ybor was committed now. If he used the bomb as a threat, he could make anybody do what he liked. Still, he felt a niggling worry.

Just before he stepped on the wing ramp, a shot came from the plane. Ybor ducked instinctively, but it was Sleyg who fell—with a neat hole between his eyes. Ybor tensed himself, stood still. The fuselage door slid back, and a face looked out.

"Solraq!" Ybor cried. "I thought you were dead!"

"You were meant to think it, Ybor. Come on in."

"Wait till I get these tools." Ybor handed the cradle up to the dark man who grinned down at him. "Hold baby," Ybor said. "Don't drop him. If he cries, you'll never hear him."

He picked up the tool kit, climbed into the plane. Solraq waved a command to the pilot, and the plane took off. Ybor went to work gingerly on the fuse while Solraq talked.

"Sleyg was a cutie," he said. "We thought he was an ignorant ape. He was playing a big game, and was about ready to wind it up. But, when you named me for identification, he knew that he'd have to turn in his report, because we could have sent you directly to Dr. Sitruc, and helped you. Sleyg wasn't ready yet, so he reported me dead. Then he had the soldiers come and search the house, knowing you'd be found and arrested. He got into trouble when that skirt-chasing sergeant decided to take Ylas along. He had to report that to others of the Underground, because he had to have one more big meeting held before he could get his final dope.

"You see, he'd never turned in a report," Solraq went on. "He was watched, and afraid to take a chance. When Ylas and I got together, we compared notes, searched his belongings, and found the evidence.

Then we arranged this rendezvous—if you got away. She told Sleyg where you were, and to bring you here. I didn't think you'd get away, but she insisted you were too ingenious to get caught. Well, you did it, and that's all to the good. Not that it would have mattered much. If you'd failed, we'd have got hold of the bomb somehow, or exploded it in Dr. Sitruc's laboratory."

Ybor didn't bother to tell him that it didn't matter where the bomb was exploded. He was too busy trying to prevent its exploding here. At last he had the fuse out. He motioned Solraq to open the bomb bay. When the folding doors dropped open, he let the fuse fall between them.

"Got its teeth pulled," he said, "and we'll soon empty the thing."

He released the clamps and pulled the hemispheres apart. He took a chisel from the tool kit and punched a hole in each of the cadmium cans in succession, letting the powder drift out. It would fall, spread, and never be noticed by those who would now go on living.

They would live because the war would end before Dr. Sitruc could construct another bomb. Ybor lifted eyes that were moist.

"I guess that's it," he said. "Where are we going?"

"We'll parachute out and let this plane crash when we sight our ship some fifty miles at sea. We'll report for orders now. This mission's accomplished."

182

City

Clifford D. Simak (1904–   )

LIKE *Jack Williamson, Clifford Simak is one of the pioneers of modern science fiction and, like Jack, a man who managed to grow and develop his talents with the field—a statement that does not apply to many of the early contributors to* Amazing *and* Science Wonder Stories. *It is difficult to believe that the same man wrote "The Uncharted Isle" (1930) and "Skirmish" (1950).*

The forties were productive years for Simak, for it was during this decade that he fashioned the bulk of the stories that constitute his greatest work, City *(1952). Particularly noteworthy were "Desertion" (1944), unquestionably one of the finest science fiction stories ever written; "Huddling Place" (1944); and the present selection.*

Simak has been described as a writer of "pastoral" science fiction featuring simple people in rural settings. Here, in the first story in the City *series, he begins to develop one of the concepts central to all his work—the importance of people, rather than the environment in which they find themselves.*

From *Astounding Science Fiction   1944*

Gramp Stevens sat in a lawn chair, watching the mower at work, feeling the warm, soft sunshine seep into his bones. The mower reached the edge of the lawn, clucked to itself like a contented hen, made a neat turn and trundled down another swath. The bag holding the clippings bulged.

Suddenly the mower stopped and clicked excitedly. A panel in its side snapped open and a cranelike arm reached out. Grasping steel fingers fished around in the grass, came up triumphantly with a stone clutched tightly, dropped the stone into a small container, disappeared back into the panel again. The lawn mower gurgled, purred on again, following its swath.

Gramp grumbled at it with suspicion.

"Some day," he told himself, "that dadburned thing is going to miss a lick and have a nervous breakdown."

He lay back in the chair and stared up at the sun-washed sky. A helicopter skimmed far overhead. From somewhere inside the house a radio came to life and a torturing clash of music poured out. Gramp, hearing it, shivered and hunkered lower in the chair.

Young Charlie was settling down for a twitch session. Dadburn the kid.

The lawn mower chuckled past and Gramp squinted at it maliciously.

"Automatic," he told the sky. "Ever' blasted thing is automatic now. Getting so you just take a machine off in a corner and whisper in its ear and it scurries off to do the job."

His daughter's voice came to him out the window, pitched to carry above the music.

"Father!"

Gramp stirred uneasily. "Yes, Betty."

"Now, father, you see you move when that lawn mower gets to you. Don't try to out-stubborn it. After all, it's only a machine. Last time you just sat there and made it cut around you. I never saw the beat of you."

He didn't answer, letting his head nod a bit, hoping she would think he was asleep and let him be.

"Father," she shrilled, "did you hear me?"

He saw it was no good. "Sure, I heard you," he told her. "I was just fixing to move."

He rose slowly to his feet, leaning heavily on his cane. Might make her feel sorry for the way she treated him when she saw how old and feeble he was getting. He'd have to be careful, though. If she knew he didn't need the cane at all, she'd be finding jobs for him to do and, on the other hand, if he laid it on too thick, she'd be having that fool doctor in to pester him again.

Grumbling, he moved the chair out into that portion of the lawn that had been cut. The mower, rolling past, chortled at him fiendishly.

"Some day," Gramp told it, "I'm going to take a swipe at you and bust a gear or two."

The mower hooted at him and went serenely down the lawn.

From somewhere down the grassy street came a jangling of metal, a stuttered coughing.

Gramp, ready to sit down, straightened up and listened.

The sound came more clearly, the rumbling backfire of a balky engine, the clatter of loose metallic parts.

"An automobile!" yelped Gramp. "An automobile, by cracky!"

He started to gallop for the gate, suddenly remembered that he was feeble and subsided to a rapid hobble.

"Must be that crazy Ole Johnson," he told himself. "He's the only one left that's got a car. Just too dadburned stubborn to give it up."

It was Ole.

Gramp reached the gate in time to see the rusty, dilapidated old machine come bumping around the corner, rocking and chugging along the unused street. Steam hissed from the overheated radiator and a cloud of blue smoke issued from the exhaust, which had lost its muffler five years or more ago.

Ole sat stolidly behind the wheel, squinting his eyes, trying to duck the roughest places, although that was hard to do, for weeds and grass had overrun the streets and it was hard to see what might be underneath them.

Gramp waved his cane.

"Hi, Ole," he shouted.

Ole pulled up, setting the emergency brake. The car gasped, shuddered, coughed, died with a horrible sigh.

"What you burning?" asked Gramp.

"Little bit of everything," said Ole. "Kerosene, some old tractor oil I found out in a barrel, some rubbing alcohol."

Gramp regarded the fugitive machine with forthright admiration. "Them was the days," he said. "Had one myself used to be able to do a hundred miles an hour."

"Still O.K.," said Ole, "if you only could find the stuff to run them or get the parts to fix them. Up to three, four years ago I used to be able to get enough gasoline, but ain't seen none for a long time now. Quit making it, I guess. No use having gasoline, they tell me, when you have atomic power."

"Sure," said Gramp. "Guess maybe that's right, but you can't smell atomic power. Sweetest thing I know, the smell of burning gasoline. These here helicopters and other gadgets they got took all the romance out of traveling, somehow."

He squinted at the barrels and baskets piled in the back seat.

"Got some vegetables?" he asked.

"Yup," said Ole. "Some sweet corn and early potatoes and a few baskets of tomatoes. Thought maybe I could sell them."

Gramp shook his head. "You won't, Ole. They won't buy them.

Folks has got the notion that this new hydroponics stuff is the only garden sass that's fit to eat. Sanitary, they say, and better flavored."

"Wouldn't give a hoot in a tin cup for all they grow in them tanks they got," Ole declared, belligerently. "Don't taste right to me, somehow. Like I tell Martha, food's got to be raised in the soil to have any character."

He reached down to turn over the ignition switch.

"Don't know as it's worth trying to get the stuff to town," he said, "the way they keep the roads. Or the way they don't keep them, rather. Twenty years ago the state highway out there was a strip of good concrete and they kept it patched and plowed it every winter. Did anything, spent any amount of money to keep it open. And now they just forgot about it. The concrete's all broken up and some of it has washed out. Brambles are growing in it. Had to get out and cut away a tree that fell across it one place this morning."

"Ain't it the truth," agreed Gramp.

The car exploded into life, coughing and choking. A cloud of dense blue smoke rolled out from under it. With a jerk it stirred to life and lumbered down the street.

Gramp clumped back to his chair and found it dripping wet. The automatic mower, having finished its cutting job, had rolled out the hose, was sprinkling the lawn.

Muttering venom, Gramp stalked around the corner of the house and sat down on the bench beside the back porch. He didn't like to sit there, but it was the only place he was safe from the hunk of machinery out in front.

For one thing, the view from the bench was slightly depressing, fronting as it did on street after street of vacant, deserted houses and weed-grown, unkempt yards.

It had one advantage, however. From the bench he could pretend he was slightly deaf and not hear the twitch music the radio was blaring out.

A voice called from the front yard.

"Bill! Bill, where be you?"

Gramp twisted around.

"Here I am, Mark. Back of the house. Hiding from that dadburned mower."

Mark Bailey limped around the corner of the house, cigarette threatening to set fire to his bushy whiskers.

"Bit early for the game, ain't you?" asked Gramp.

"Can't play no game today," said Mark.

He hobbled over and sat down beside Gramp on the bench.

"We're leaving," he said.

Gramp whirled on him. "You're leaving!"

186

"Yeah. Moving out into the country. Lucinda finally talked Herb into it. Never gave him a minute's peace, I guess. Said everyone was moving away to one of them nice country estates and she didn't see no reason why we couldn't."

Gramp gulped. "Where to?"

"Don't rightly know," said Mark. "Ain't been there myself. Up north some place. Up on one of the lakes. Got ten acres of land. Lucinda wanted a hundred, but Herb put down his foot and said ten was enough. After all, one city lot was enough for all these years."

"Betty was pestering Johnny, too," said Gramp, "but he's holding out against her. Says he simply can't do it. Says it wouldn't look right, him the secretary of the Chamber of Commerce and all, if he went moving away from the city."

"Folks are crazy," Mark declared. "Plumb crazy."

"That's a fact," Gramp agreed. "Country crazy, that's what they are. Look across there."

He waved his hand at the streets of vacant houses. "Can remember the time when those places were as pretty a bunch of homes as you ever laid your eyes on. Good neighbors, they were. Women ran across from one back door to another to trade recipes. And the men folks would go out to cut the grass and pretty soon the mowers would all be sitting idle and the men would be ganged up, chewing the fat. Friendly people, Mark. But look at it now."

Mark stirred uneasily. "Got to be getting back, Bill. Just sneaked over to let you know we were lighting out. Lucinda's got me packing. She'd be sore if she knew I'd run out."

Gramp rose stiffly and held out his hand. "I'll be seeing you again? You be over for one last game?"

Mark shook his head. "Afraid not, Bill."

They shook hands awkwardly, abashed. "Sure will miss them games," said Mark.

"Me, too," said Gramp. "I won't have nobody once you're gone."

"So long, Bill," said Mark.

"So long," said Gramp.

He stood and watched his friend hobble around the house, felt the cold claw of loneliness reach out and touch him with icy fingers. A terrible loneliness. The loneliness of age—of age and the outdated. Fiercely, Gramp admitted it. He was outdated. He belonged to another age. He had outstripped his time, lived beyond his years.

Eyes misty, he fumbled for the cane that lay against the bench, slowly made his way toward the sagging gate that opened onto the deserted street back of the house.

The years had moved too fast. Years that had brought the family plane and helicopter, leaving the auto to rust in some forgotten place, the unused roads to fall into disrepair. Years that had virtually wiped out the tilling of the soil with the rise of hydroponics. Years that had brought cheap land with the disappearance of the farm as an economic unit, had sent city people scurrying out into the country where each man, for less than the price of a city lot, might own broad acres. Years that had revolutionized the construction of homes to a point where families simply walked away from their old homes to the new ones that could be bought, custom-made, for less than half the price of a prewar structure and could be changed at small cost, to accommodate need of additional space or just a passing whim.

Gramp sniffed. Houses that could be changed each year, just like one would shift around the furniture. What kind of living was that?

He plodded slowly down the dusty path that was all that remained of what a few years before had been a busy residential street. A street of ghosts, Gramp told himself—of furtive, little ghosts that whispered in the night. Ghosts of playing children, ghosts of upset tricycles and canted coaster wagons. Ghosts of gossiping housewives. Ghosts of shouted greetings. Ghosts of flaming fireplaces and chimneys smoking of a winter night.

Little puffs of dust rose around his feet and whitened the cuffs of his trousers.

There was the old Adams place across the way. Adams had been mighty proud of it, he remembered. Gray field stone front and picture windows. Now the stone was green with creeping moss and the broken windows gaped with ghastly leer. Weeds choked the lawn and blotted out the stoop. An elm tree was pushing its branches against the gable. Gramp could remember the day Adams had planted that elm tree.

For a moment he stood there in the grass-grown street, feet in the dust, both hands clutching the curve of his cane, eyes closed.

Through the fog of years he heard the cry of playing children, the barking of Conrad's yapping pooch from down the street. And there was Adams, stripped to the waist, plying the shovel, scooping out the hole, with the elm tree, roots wrapped in burlap, lying on the lawn.

May, 1946. Forty-four years ago. Just after he and Adams had come home from the war together.

Footsteps padded in the dust and Gramp, startled, opened his eyes.

Before him stood a young man. A man of thirty, perhaps. Maybe a bit less.

"Good morning," said Gramp.

"I hope," said the young man, "that I didn't startle you."

"You saw me standing here," asked Gramp, "like a danged fool, with my eyes shut?"

The young man nodded.

"I was remembering," said Gramp.

"You live around here?"

188

"Just down the street. The last one in this part of the city."

"Perhaps you can help me then."

"Try me," said Gramp.

The young man stammered. "Well, you see, it's like this. I'm on a sort of . . . well, you might call it a sentimental pilgrimage—"

"I understand," said Gramp. "So am I."

"My name is Adams," said the young man. "My grandfather used to live around here somewhere. I wonder—"

"Right over there," said Gramp.

Together they stood and stared at the house.

"It was a nice place once," Gramp told him. "Your granddaddy planted that tree right after he came home from the war. I was with him all through the war and we came home together. That was a day for you. . . ."

"It's a pity," said young Adams. "A pity . . ."

But Gramp didn't seem to hear him. "Your granddaddy?" he asked. "I seem to have lost track of him."

"He's dead," said young Adams. "Quite a number of years ago."

"He was messed up with atomic power," said Gramp.

"That's right," said Adams proudly. "Got into it just as soon as it was released to industry. Right after the Moscow agreement."

"Right after they decided," said Gramp, "they couldn't fight a war."

"That's right," said Adams.

"It's pretty hard to fight a war," said Gramp, "when there's nothing you can aim at."

"You mean the cities," said Adams.

"Sure," said Gramp, "and there's a funny thing about it. Wave all the atom bombs you wanted to and you couldn't scare them out. But give them cheap land and family planes and they scattered just like so many dadburned rabbits."

John J. Webster was striding up the broad stone steps of the city hall when the walking scarecrow carrying a rifle under his arm caught up with him and stopped him.

"Howdy, Mr. Webster," said the scarecrow.

Webster stared, then recognition crinkled his face.

"It's Levi," he said. "How are things going, Levi?"

Levi Lewis grinned with snagged teeth. "Fair to middling. Gardens are coming along and the young rabbits are getting to be good eating."

"You aren't getting mixed up in any of the hell raising that's being laid to the *houses*?" asked Webster.

"No, sir," declared Levi. "Ain't none of us Squatters mixed up in any wrongdoing. We're law-abiding, God-fearing people, we are. Only reason we're there is we can't make a living no place else. And us living in them places other people up and left ain't harming no one.

Police are just blaming us for the thievery and other things that's going on, knowing we can't protect ourselves. They're making us the goats."

"I'm glad to hear that," said Webster. "The chief wants to burn the *houses*."

"If he tries that," said Levi, "he'll run against something he ain't counting on. They run us off our farms with this tank farming of theirs but they ain't going to run us any farther."

He spat across the steps.

"Wouldn't happen you might have some jingling money on you?" he asked. "I'm fresh out of cartridges and with them rabbits coming up—"

Webster thrust his fingers into a vest pocket, pulled out a half dollar.

Levi grinned. "That's obliging of you, Mr. Webster. I'll bring a mess of squirrels, come fall."

The Squatter touched his hat with two fingers and retreated down the steps, sun glinting on the rifle barrel. Webster turned up the steps again.

The city council session already was in full swing when he walked into the chamber.

Police Chief Jim Maxwell was standing by the table and Mayor Paul Carter was talking.

"Don't you think you may be acting a bit hastily, Jim, in urging such a course of action with the *houses*?"

"No, I don't," declared the chief. "Except for a couple of dozen or so, none of those houses are occupied by their rightful owners, or rather, their original owners. Every one of them belongs to the city now through tax forfeiture. And they are nothing but an eyesore and a menace. They have no value. Not even salvage value. Wood? We don't use wood any more. Plastics are better. Stone? We use steel instead of stone. Not a single one of those houses have any material of marketable value.

"And in the meantime they are becoming the haunts of petty criminals and undesirable elements. Grown up with vegetation as the residential sections are, they make a perfect hideout for all types of criminals. A man commits a crime and heads straight for the *houses* —once there he's safe, for I could send a thousand men in there and he could elude them all.

"They aren't worth the expense of tearing down. And yet they are, if not a menace, at least a nuisance. We should get rid of them and fire is the cheapest, quickest way. We'd use all precautions."

"What about the legal angle?" asked the mayor.

"I checked into that. A man has a right to destroy his own property in any way he may see fit so long as it endangers no one else's. The same law, I suppose, would apply to a municipality."

Alderman Thomas Griffin sprang to his feet.

"You'd alienate a lot of people," he declared. "You'd be burning down a lot of old homesteads. People still have some sentimental attachments—"

"If they cared for them," snapped the chief, "why didn't they pay the taxes and take care of them? Why did they go running off to the country, just leaving the houses standing. Ask Webster here. He can tell you what success he had trying to interest the people in their ancestral homes."

"You're talking about that Old Home Week farce," said Griffin. "It failed. Of course, it failed. Webster spread it on so thick that they gagged on it. That's what a Chamber of Commerce mentality always does."

Alderman Forrest King spoke up angrily. "There's nothing wrong with a Chamber of Commerce, Griffin. Simply because you failed in business is no reason. . . ."

Griffin ignored him. "The day of high pressure is over, gentlemen. The day of high pressure is gone forever. Ballyhoo is something that is dead and buried.

"The day when you could have tall-corn days or dollar days or dream up some fake celebration and deck the place up with bunting and pull in big crowds that were ready to spend money is past these many years. Only you fellows don't seem to know it.

"The success of such stunts as that was its appeal to mob psychology and civic loyalty. You can't have civic loyalty with a city dying on its feet. You can't appeal to mob psychology when there is no mob— when every man, or nearly every man, has the solitude of forty acres."

"Gentlemen," pleaded the mayor. "Gentlemen, this is distinctly out of order."

King sputtered into life, walloped the table.

"No, let's have it out. Webster is over there. Perhaps he can tell us what he thinks."

Webster stirred uncomfortably. "I scarcely believe," he said, "I have anything to say."

"Forget it," snapped Griffin and sat down.

But King still stood, his face crimson, his mouth trembling with anger.

"Webster!" he shouted.

Webster shook his head. "You came here with one of your big ideas," shouted King. "You were going to lay it before the council. Step up, man, and speak your piece."

Webster rose slowly, grim-lipped.

"Perhaps you're too thick-skulled," he told King, "to know why I resent the way you have behaved."

King gasped, then exploded. "Thick-skulled! You would say that to me? We've worked together and I've helped you. You've never called me that before . . . you've—"

"I've never called you that before," said Webster, levelly. "Naturally not. I wanted to keep my job."

"Well, you haven't got a job," roared King. "From this minute on, you haven't got a job."

"Shut up," said Webster.

King stared at him, bewildered, as if someone had slapped him across the face.

"And sit down," said Webster, and his voice bit through the room like a sharp-edged knife.

King's knees caved beneath him and he sat down abruptly. The silence was brittle.

"I have something to say," said Webster. "Something that should have been said long ago. Something all of you should hear. That I should be the one who would tell it to you is the one thing that astounds me. And yet, perhaps, as one who has worked in the interests of this city for almost fifteen years, I am the logical one to speak the truth.

"Alderman Griffin said the city is dying on its feet and his statement is correct. There is but one fault I would find with it and that is its understatement. The city . . . this city, any city . . . already is dead.

"The city is an anachronism. It has outlived its usefulness. Hydroponics and the helicopter spelled its downfall. In the first instance the city was a tribal place, an area where the tribe banded together for mutual protection. In later years a wall was thrown around it for additional protection. Then the wall finally disappeared but the city lived on because of the conveniences which it offered trade and commerce. It continued into modern times because people were compelled to live close to their jobs and the jobs were in the city.

"But today that is no longer true. With the family plane, one hundred miles today is a shorter distance than five miles back in 1930. Men can fly several hundred miles to work and fly home when the day is done. There is no longer any need for them to live cooped up in a city.

"The automobile started the trend and the family plane finished it. Even in the first part of the century the trend was noticeable—a movement away from the city with its taxes and its stuffiness, a move toward the suburb and close-in acreages. Lack of adequate transportation, lack of finances held many to the city. But now, with tank farming destroying the value of land, a man can buy a huge acreage in the country for less than he could a city lot forty years ago. With planes powered by atomics there is no longer any transportation problem."

192

He paused and the silence held. The mayor wore a shocked look. King's lips moved, but no words came. Griffin was smiling.

"So what have we?" asked Webster. "I'll tell you what we have. Street after street, block after block, of deserted houses, houses that the people just up and walked away from. Why should they have stayed? What could the city offer them? None of the things that it offered the generations before them, for progress had wiped out the need of the city's benefits. They lost something, some monetary consideration, of course, when they left the houses. But the fact that they could buy a house twice as good for half as much, the fact that they could live as they wished to live, that they could develop what amounts to family estates after the best tradition set them by the wealthy of a generation ago—all these things outweighed the leaving of their homes.

"And what have we left? A few blocks of business houses. A few acres of industrial plants. A city government geared to take care of a million people without the million people. A budget that has run the taxes so high that eventually even business houses will move to escape those taxes. Tax forfeitures that have left us loaded with worthless property. That's what we have left.

"If you think any Chamber of Commerce, any ballyhoo, any harebrained scheme will give you the answers, you're crazy. There is only one answer and that is simple. The city as a human institution is dead. It may struggle on a few more years, but that is all."

"Mr. Webster—" said the mayor.

But Webster paid him no attention.

"But for what happened today," he said, "I would have stayed on and played doll house with you. I would have gone on pretending that the city was a going concern. Would have gone on kidding myself and you. But there is, gentlemen, such a thing as human dignity."

The icy silence broke down in the rustling of papers, the muffled cough of some embarrassed listener.

But Webster was not through.

"The city failed," he said, "and it is well it failed. Instead of sitting here in mourning above its broken body you should rise to your feet and shout your thanks it failed.

"For if this city had not outlived its usefulness, as did every other city—if the cities of the world had not been deserted, they would have been destroyed. There would have been a war, gentlemen, an atomic war. Have you forgotten the 1950s and the 60s? Have you forgotten waking up at night and listening for the bomb to come, knowing that you would not hear it when it came, knowing that you would never hear again, if it did come?

"But the cities were deserted and industry was dispersed and there were no targets and there was no war.

193

"Some of you gentlemen," he said, "many of you gentlemen, are alive today because the people left your city.

"Now, for God's sake, let it stay dead. Be happy that it's dead. It's the best thing that ever happened in all human history."

John J. Webster turned on his heel and left the room.

Outside on the broad stone steps, he stopped and stared up at the cloudless sky, saw the pigeons wheeling above the turrets and spires of the city hall.

He shook himself mentally, like a dog coming out of a pool.

He had been a fool, of course. Now he'd have to hunt for a job and it might take time to find one. He was getting a bit old to be hunting for a job.

But despite his thought, a little tune rose unbidden to his lips. He walked away briskly, lips pursed, whistling soundlessly.

No more hypocrisy. No more lying awake nights wondering what to do—knowing that the city was dead, knowing that what he did was a useless task, feeling like a heel for taking a salary that he knew he wasn't earning. Sensing the strange, nagging frustration of a worker who knows his work is nonproductive.

He strode toward the parking lot, heading for his helicopter.

Now, maybe, he told himself, they could move out into the country the way Betty wanted to. Maybe he could spend his evenings tramping land that belonged to him. A place with a stream. Definitely it had to have a stream he could stock with trout.

He made a mental note to go up into the attic and check his fly equipment.

Martha Johnson was waiting at the barnyard gate when the old car chugged down the lane.

Ole got out stiffly, face rimmed with weariness.

"Sell anything?" asked Martha.

Ole shook his head. "It ain't no use. They won't buy farm-raised stuff. Just laughed at me. Showed me ears of corn twice as big as the ones I had, just as sweet and with more even rows. Showed me melons that had almost no rind at all. Better tasting, too, they said."

He kicked at a clod and it exploded into dust.

"There ain't no getting around it," he declared. "Tank farming sure has ruined us."

"Maybe we better fix to sell the farm," suggested Martha.

Ole said nothing.

"You could get a job on a tank farm," she said. "Harry did. Likes it real well."

Ole shook his head.

"Or maybe a gardener," said Martha. "You would make a right smart gardener. Ritzy folks that's moved out to big estates like to have gardeners to take care of flowers and things. More classy than doing it with machines."

Ole shook his head again. "Couldn't stand to mess around with flowers," he declared. "Not after raising corn for more than twenty years."

"Maybe," said Martha, "we could have one of them little planes. And running water in the house. And a bathtub instead of taking a bath in the old washtub by the kitchen fire."

"Couldn't run a plane," objected Ole.

"Sure you could," said Martha. "Simple to run, they are. Why, them Anderson kids ain't no more than knee-high to a cricket and they fly one all over. One of them got fooling around and fell out once, but—"

"I got to think about it," said Ole desperately. "I got to think."

He swung away, vaulted a fence, headed for the fields. Martha stood beside the car and watched him go. One lone tear rolled down her dusty cheek.

"Mr. Taylor is waiting for you," said the girl.

John J. Webster stammered. "But I haven't been here before. He didn't know I was coming."

"Mr. Taylor," insisted the girl, "is waiting for you."

She nodded her head toward the door. It read:

BUREAU OF HUMAN ADJUSTMENT

"But I came here to get a job," protested Webster. "I didn't come to be adjusted or anything. This is the World Committee's placement service, isn't it?"

"That is right," the girl declared. "Won't you see Mr. Taylor?"

"Since you insist," said Webster.

The girl clicked over a switch, spoke into the intercommunicator. "Mr. Webster is here, sir."

"Send him in," said a voice.

Hat in hand, Webster walked through the door.

The man behind the desk had white hair but a young man's face. He motioned toward a chair.

"You've been trying to find a job," he said.

"Yes," said Webster, "but—"

"Please sit down," said Taylor. "If you're thinking about that sign on the door, forget it. We'll not try to adjust you."

"I couldn't find a job," said Webster. "I've hunted for weeks and no one would have me. So, finally, I came here."

"You didn't want to come here?"

"No, frankly, I didn't. A placement service. It has, well . . . it has an implication I do not like."

195

Taylor smiled. "The terminology may be unfortunate. You're thinking of the employment services of the old days. The places where men went when they were desperate for work. The government-operated places that tried to find work for men so they wouldn't become public charges."

"I'm desperate enough," confessed Webster. "But I still have a pride that made it hard to come. But, finally, there was nothing else to do. You see, I turned traitor—"

"You mean," said Taylor, "that you told the truth. Even when it cost you your job. The business world, not only here, but all over the world, is not ready for that truth. The businessman still clings to the city myth, to the myth of salesmanship. In time to come he will realize he doesn't need the city, that service and honest values will bring him more substantial business than salesmanship ever did.

"I've wondered, Webster, just what made you do what you did?"

"I was sick of it," said Webster. "Sick of watching men blundering along with their eyes tight shut. Sick of seeing an old tradition being kept alive when it should have been laid away. Sick of King's simpering civic enthusiasm when all cause for enthusiasm had vanished."

Taylor nodded. "Webster, do you think you could adjust human beings?"

Webster merely stared.

"I mean it," said Taylor. "The World Committee has been doing it for years, quietly, unobtrusively. Even many of the people who have been adjusted don't know they have been adjusted.

"Changes such as have come since the creation of the World Committee out of the old United Nations have meant much human maladjustment. The advent of workable atomic power took jobs away from hundreds of thousands. They had to be trained and guided into new jobs, some with the new atomics, some into other lines of work. The advent of tank farming swept the farmers off their land. They, perhaps, have supplied us with our greatest problem, for other than the special knowledge needed to grow crops and handle animals, they had no skills. Most of them had no wish for acquiring skills. Most of them were bitterly resentful at having been forced from the livelihood which they inherited from their forebears. And being natural individualists, they offered the toughest psychological problems of any other class."

"Many of them," declared Webster, "still are at loose ends. There's a hundred or more of them squatting out in the *houses*, living from hand to mouth. Shooting a few rabbits and a few squirrels, doing some fishing, raising vegetables and picking wild fruit. Engaging in a little petty thievery now and then and doing occasional begging on the uptown streets."

"You know these people?" asked Taylor.

"I know some of them," said Webster. "One of them brings me

squirrels and rabbits on occasions. To make up for it, he bums ammunition money."

"They'd resent being adjusted, wouldn't they?"

"Violently," said Webster.

"You know a farmer by the name of Ole Johnson? Still sticking to his farm, still unreconstructed?"

Webster nodded.

"What if you tried to adjust him?"

"He'd run me off the farm," said Webster.

"Men like Ole and the Squatters," said Taylor, "are our special problems now. Most of the rest of the world is fairly well-adjusted, fairly well settled into the groove of the present. Some of them are doing a lot of moaning about the past, but that's just for effect. You couldn't drive them back to their old ways of life.

"Years ago, with the advent of industrial atomics in fact, the World Committee faced a hard decision. Should changes that spelled progress in the world be brought about gradually to allow the people to adjust themselves naturally, or should they be developed as quickly as possible, with the committee aiding in the necessary human adjustment? It was decided, rightly or wrongly, that progress should come first, regardless of its effect upon the people. The decision in the main has proved a wise one.

"We knew, of course, that in many instances, this readjustment could not be made too openly. In some cases, as in large groups of workers who had been displaced, it was possible, but in most individual cases, such as our friend Ole, it was not. These people must be helped to find themselves in this new world, but they must not know that they're being helped. To let them know would destroy confidence and dignity, and human dignity is the keystone of any civilization."

"I knew, of course, about the readjustments made within industry itself," said Webster, "but I had not heard of the individual cases."

"We could not advertise it," Taylor said. "It's practically undercover."

"But why are you telling me all this now?"

"Because we'd like you to come in with us. Have a hand at adjusting Ole to start with. Maybe see what could be done about the Squatters next."

"I don't know—" said Webster.

"We'd been waiting for you to come in," said Taylor. "We knew you'd finally have to come here. Any chance you might have had at any kind of job would have been queered by King. He passed the word along. You're blackballed by every Chamber of Commerce and every civic group in the world today."

"Probably I have no choice," said Webster.

"We don't want you to feel that way about it," Taylor said. "Take a while to think it over, then come back. Even if you don't want the job we'll find you another one—in spite of King."

Outside the office, Webster found a scarecrow figure waiting for him. It was Levi Lewis, snaggle-toothed grin wiped off, rifle under his arm.

"Some of the boys said they seen you go in here," he explained. "So I waited for you."

"What's the trouble?" Webster asked, for Levi's face spoke eloquently of trouble.

"It's them police," said Levi. He spat disgustedly.

"The police," said Webster, and his heart sank as he said the words. For he knew what the trouble was.

"Yeah," said Levi. "They're fixing to burn us out."

"So the council finally gave in," said Webster.

"I just came from police headquarters," declared Levi. "I told them they better go easy. I told them there'd be guts strewed all over the place if they tried it. I got the boys posted all around the place with orders not to shoot till they're sure of hitting."

"You can't do that, Levi," said Webster, sharply.

"I can't!" retorted Levi. "I done it already. They drove us off the farms, forced us to sell because we couldn't make a living. And they aren't driving us no farther. We either stay here or we die here. And the only way they'll burn us out is when there's no one left to stop them."

He shucked up his pants and spat again.

"And we ain't the only ones that feel that way," he declared. "Gramp is out there with us."

"Gramp!"

"Sure, Gramp. The old guy that lives with you. He's sort of taken over as our commanding general. Says he remembers tricks from the war them police have never heard of. He sent some of the boys over to one of them Legion halls to swipe a cannon. Says he knows where we can get some shells for it from the museum. Says we'll get it all set up and then send word that if the police make a move we'll shell the loop."

"Look, Levi, will you do something for me?"

"Sure will, Mr. Webster."

"Will you go in and ask for a Mr. Taylor? Insist on seeing him. Tell him I'm already on the job."

"Sure will, but where are you going?"

"I'm going up to the city hall."

"Sure you don't want me along?"

"No," declared Webster. "I'll do better alone. And, Levi—"

"Yes."

"Tell Gramp to hold up his artillery. Don't shoot unless he has to—but if he has, to lay it on the line."

"The mayor is busy," said Raymond Brown, his secretary.

"That's what you think," said Webster, starting for the door.

"You can't go in there, Webster," yelled Brown.

He leaped from his chair, came charging around the desk, reaching for Webster. Webster swung broadside with his arm, caught Brown across the chest, swept him back against the desk. The desk skidded and Brown waved his arms, lost his balance, thudded to the floor.

Webster jerked open the mayor's door.

The mayor's feet thumped off his desk. "I told Brown—" he said.

Webster nodded. "And Brown told me. What's the matter, Carter? Afraid King might find out I was here? Afraid of being corrupted by some good ideas?"

"What do you want?" snapped Carter.

"I understand the police are going to burn the *houses*."

"That's right," declared the mayor, righteously. "They're a menace to the community."

"What community?"

"Look here, Webster—"

"You know there's no community. Just a few of you lousy politicians who stick around so you can claim residence, so you can be sure of being elected every year and drag down your salaries. It's getting to the point where all you have to do is vote for one another. The people who work in the stores and shops, even those who do the meanest jobs in the factories, don't live inside the city limits. The businessmen quit the city long ago. They do business here, but they aren't residents."

"But this is still a city," declared the mayor.

"I didn't come to argue that with you," said Webster. "I came to try to make you see that you're doing wrong by burning those houses. Even if you don't realize it, the *houses* are homes to people who have no other homes. People who have come to this city to seek sanctuary, who have found refuge with us. In a measure, they are our responsibility."

"They're not our responsibility," gritted the mayor. "Whatever happens to them is their own hard luck. We didn't ask them here. We don't want them here. They contribute nothing to the community. You're going to tell me they're misfits. Well, can I help that? You're going to say they can't find jobs. And I'll tell you they could find jobs if they tried to find them. There's work to be done, there's always work to be done. They've been filled up with this new world talk and they figure it's up to someone to find the place that suits them and the job that suits them."

"You sound like a rugged individualist," said Webster.

"You say that like you think it's funny," yapped the mayor.

"I do think it's funny," said Webster. "Funny, and tragic, that anyone should think that way today."

"The world would be a lot better off with some rugged individualism," snapped the mayor. "Look at the men who have gone places—"

"Meaning yourself?" asked Webster.

"You might take me, for example," Carter agreed. "I worked hard. I took advantage of opportunity. I had some foresight. I did—"

"You mean you licked the correct boots and stepped in the proper faces," said Webster. "You're the shining example of the kind of people the world doesn't want today. You positively smell musty, your ideas are so old. You're the last of the politicians, Carter, just as I was the last of the Chamber of Commerce secretaries. Only you don't know it yet. I did. I got out. Even when it cost me something, I got out, because I had to save my self-respect. Your kind of politics is dead. They are dead because any tinhorn with a loud mouth and a brassy front could gain power by appeal to mob psychology. And you haven't got mob psychology any more. You can't have mob psychology when people don't give a damn what happens to a thing that's dead already —a political system that broke down under its own weight."

"Get out of here," screamed Carter. "Get out before I have the cops come and throw you out."

"You forget," said Webster, "that I came in to talk about the *houses.*"

"It won't do you any good," snarled Carter. "You can stand and talk till doomsday for all the good it does. Those houses burn. That's final."

"How would you like to see the loop a mass of rubble?" asked Webster.

"Your comparison," said Carter, "is grotesque."

"I wasn't talking about comparisons," said Webster.

"You weren't—" The mayor stared at him. "What were you talking about then?"

"Only this," said Webster. "The second the first torch touches the *houses,* the first shell will land on the city hall. And the second one will hit the First National. They'll go on down the line, the biggest targets first."

Carter gaped. Then a flush of anger crawled from his throat up into his face.

"It won't work, Webster," he snapped. "You can't bluff me. Any cock-and-bull story like that—"

"It's no cock-and-bull story," declared Webster. "Those men have cannon out there. Pieces from in front of Legion halls, from the museums. And they have men who know how to work them. They wouldn't need them, really. It's practically point-blank range. Like shooting the broadside of a barn."

Carter reached for the radio, but Webster stopped him with an upraised hand.

"Better think a minute, Carter, before you go flying off the handle. You're on a spot. Go ahead with your plan and you have a battle on your hands. The *houses* may burn but the loop is wrecked. The businessmen will have your scalp for that."

Carter's hand retreated from the radio.

From far away came the sharp crack of a rifle.

"Better call them off," warned Webster.

Carter's face twisted with indecision.

Another rifle shot, another and another.

"Pretty soon," said Webster, "it will have gone too far. So far that you can't stop it."

A thudding blast rattled the windows of the room. Carter leaped from his chair.

Webster felt suddenly cold and weak. But he fought to keep his face straight and his voice calm.

Carter was staring out the window, like a man of stone.

"I'm afraid," said Webster, "that it's gone too far already."

The radio on the desk chirped insistently, red light flashing.

Carter reached out a trembling hand and snapped it on.

"Carter," a voice was saying. "Carter. Carter."

Webster recognized that voice—the bull-throated tone of Police Chief Jim Maxwell.

"What is it?" asked Carter.

"They had a big gun," said Maxwell. "It exploded when they tried to fire it. Ammunition no good, I guess."

"One gun?" asked Carter. "Only one gun?"

"I don't see any others."

"I heard rifle fire," said Carter.

"Yeah, they did some shooting at us. Wounded a couple of the boys. But they've pulled back now. Deeper into the brush. No shooting now."

"O.K.," said Carter, "go ahead and start the fires."

Webster started forward. "Ask him, ask him—"

But Carter clicked the switch and the radio went dead.

"What was it you wanted to ask?"

"Nothing," said Webster. "Nothing that amounted to anything."

He couldn't tell Carter that Gramp had been the one who knew about firing big guns. Couldn't tell him that when the gun exploded Gramp had been there.

He'd have to get out of here, get over to the gun as quickly as possible.

"It was a good bluff, Webster," Carter was saying. "A good bluff, but it petered out."

The mayor turned to the window that faced toward the *houses.*

"No more firing," he said. "They gave up quick."

"You'll be lucky," snapped Webster, "if six of your policemen come back alive. Those men with the rifles are out in the brush and they can pick the eye out of a squirrel at a hundred yards."

Feet pounded in the corridor outside, two pairs of feet racing toward the door.

The mayor whirled from his window and Webster pivoted around.

"Gramp!" he yelled.

"Hi, Johnny," puffed Gramp, skidding to a stop.

The man behind Gramp was a young man and he was waving something in his hand—a sheaf of papers that rustled as he waved them.

"What do you want?" asked the mayor.

"Plenty," said Gramp.

He stood for a moment, catching back his breath, and said between puffs:

"Meet my friend, Henry Adams."

"Adams?" asked the mayor.

"Sure," said Gramp. "His granddaddy used to live here. Out on Twenty-seventh Street."

"Oh," said the mayor and it was as if someone had smacked him with a brick. "Oh, you mean F. J. Adams."

"Bet your boots," said Gramp. "Him and me, we were in the war together. Used to keep me awake nights telling me about his boy back home."

Carter nodded to Henry Adams. "As mayor of the city," he said, trying to regain some of his dignity, "I welcome you to—"

"It's not a particularly fitting welcome," Adams said. "I understand you are burning my property."

"Your property!" The mayor choked and his eyes stared in disbelief at the sheaf of papers Adams waved at him.

"Yeah, his property," shrilled Gramp. "He just bought it. We just come from the treasurer's office. Paid all the back taxes and penalties and all the other things you legal thieves thought up to slap against them houses."

"But, but—" the mayor was grasping for words, gasping for breath. "Not all of it. Perhaps just the old Adams property."

"Lock, stock and barrel," said Gramp, triumphantly.

"And now," said Adams to the mayor, "if you would kindly tell your men to stop destroying my property."

Carter bent over the desk and fumbled at the radio, his hands suddenly all thumbs.

"Maxwell," he shouted. "Maxwell. Maxwell."

"What do you want?" Maxwell yelled back.

"Stop setting those fires," yelled Carter. "Start putting them out. Call out the fire department. Do anything. But stop those fires."

"Cripes," said Maxwell, "I wish you'd make up your mind."

"You do what I tell you," screamed the mayor. "You put out those fires."

"All right," said Maxwell. "All right. Keep your shirt on. But the boys won't like it. They won't like getting shot at to do something you change your mind about."

Carter straightened from the radio.

"Let me assure you, Mr. Adams," he said, "that this is all a big mistake."

"It is," Adams declared solemnly. "A very great mistake, mayor. The biggest one you ever made."

For a moment the two of them stood there, looking across the room at one another.

"Tomorrow," said Adams, "I shall file a petition with the courts asking dissolution of the city charter. As owner of the greatest portion of the land included in the corporate limits, both from the standpoint of area and valuation, I understand I have a perfect legal right to do that."

The mayor gulped, finally brought out some words.

"Upon what grounds?" he asked.

"Upon the grounds," said Adams, "that there is no further need of it. I do not believe I shall have too hard a time to prove my case."

"But . . . but . . . that means. . . ."

"Yeah," said Gramp, "you know what it means. It means you are out right on your ear."

"A park," said Gramp, waving his arm over the wilderness that once had been the residential section of the city. "A park so that people can remember how their old folks lived."

The three of them stood on Tower Hill, with the rusty old water tower looming above them, its sturdy steel legs planted in a sea of waist-high grass.

"Not a park, exactly," explained Henry Adams. "A memorial, rather. A memorial to an era of communal life that will be forgotten in another hundred years. A preservation of a number of peculiar types of construction that arose to suit certain conditions and each man's particular tastes. No slavery to any architectural concepts, but an effort made to achieve better living. In another hundred years men will walk through those houses down there with the same feeling of respect and awe they have when they go into a museum today. It will be to them something out of what amounts to a primeval age, a stepping-stone on the way to the better, fuller life. Artists will spend their lives transferring those old houses to their canvasses. Writers of historical novels will come here for the breath of authenticity."

"But you said you meant to restore all the houses, make the lawns and gardens exactly like they were before," said Webster. "That will take a fortune. And, after that, another fortune to keep them in shape."

"I have too much money," said Adams. "Entirely too much money. Remember, my grandfather and father got into atomics on the ground floor."

"Best crap player I ever knew, your granddaddy was," said Gramp. "Used to take me for a cleaning every pay day."

"In the old days," said Adams, "when a man had too much money, there were other things he could do with it. Organized charities, for example. Or medical research or something like that. But there are no organized charities today. Not enough business to keep them going. And since the World Committee has hit its stride, there is ample money for all the research, medical or otherwise, anyone might wish to do.

"I didn't plan this thing when I came back to see my grandfather's old house. Just wanted to see it, that was all. He'd told me so much about it. How he planted the tree in the front lawn. And the rose garden he had out back.

"And then I saw it. And it was a mocking ghost. It was something that had been left behind. Something that had meant a lot to someone and had been left behind. Standing there in front of that house with Gramp that day, it came to me that I could do nothing better than preserve for posterity a cross section of the life their ancestors lived."

A thin blue thread of smoke rose above the trees far below.

Webster pointed to it. "What about them?"

"The Squatters stay," said Adams, "if they want to. There will be plenty of work for them to do. And there'll always be a house or two that they can have to live in.

"There's just one thing that bothers me. I can't be here all the time myself. I'll need someone to manage the project. It'll be a lifelong job."

He looked at Webster.

"Go ahead, Johnny," said Gramp.

Webster shook his head. "Betty's got her heart set on that place out in the country."

"You wouldn't have to stay here," said Adams. "You could fly in every day."

From the foot of the hill came a hail.

"It's Ole," yelled Gramp.

He waved his cane. "Hi, Ole. Come on up."

They watched Ole striding up the hill, waiting for him, silently.

"Wanted to talk to you, Johnny," said Ole. "Got an idea. Waked me out of a sound sleep last night."

"Go ahead," said Webster.

Ole glanced at Adams. "He's all right," said Webster. "He's Henry Adams. Maybe you remember his grandfather, old F. J."

"I remember him," said Ole. "Nuts about atomic power, he was. How did he make out?"

"He made out rather well," said Adams.

"Glad to hear that," Ole said. "Guess I was wrong. Said he never would amount to nothing. Daydreamed all the time."

"How about that idea?" Webster asked.

"You heard about dude ranches, ain't you?" Ole asked.

Webster nodded.

"Place," said Ole, "where people used to go and pretend they were cowboys. Pleased them because they really didn't know all the hard work there was in ranching and figured it was romantic-like to ride horses and——"

"Look," asked Webster, "you aren't figuring on turning your farm into a dude ranch, are you?"

"Nope," said Ole. "Not a dude ranch. Dude farm, maybe. Folks don't know too much about farms any more, since there ain't hardly no farms. And they'll read about the frost being on the pumpkin and how pretty a——"

Webster stared at Ole. "They'd go for it, Ole," he declared. "They'd kill one another in the rush to spend their vacation on a real, honest-to-God, old-time farm."

Out of a clump of bushes down the hillside burst a shining thing that chattered and gurgled and screeched, blades flashing, a cranelike arm waving.

"What the——" asked Adams.

"It's that dadburned lawn mower!" yelped Gramp. "I always knew the day would come when it would strip a gear and go completely off its nut!"

Pi in the Sky

Fredric Brown (1906–1972)

"**Y**ES, now *there is a God!*" *is a phrase from the ultimate computer that is justly famous in science fiction. So is the man who wrote it, for Fredric Brown was one of the finest craftsmen who ever worked in the field, adept at all lengths from the short-short to the novel. He worked in almost all areas of popular fiction and was a talented mystery writer whose stories were sometimes produced for the screen. The forties were a particularly rich and productive decade for him, with short fiction like his classic "Arena" (1944), "Knock" (1948), "Nothing Sirius" (1944), "Placet Is a Crazy Place" (1946), "The Star Mouse" (1942), and the novel that provided an inside look at the then science fiction world,* What Mad Universe *(1949).*

Fredric Brown was a frequent contributor to Thrilling Wonder Stories, *which, under a variety of names, was one of the pioneer science fiction magazines. Under the editorship of Sam Merwin in the late forties and Samuel Mines in the early fifties, it was often an excellent publication, just a shade behind the Big Three of* Astounding, Fantasy and Science Fiction, *and* Galaxy.

From *Thrilling Wonder Stories*   1945

Roger Jerome Phlutter, for whose absurd name I offer no defense other than that it is genuine, was, at the time of the events of this story, a hardworking clerk in the office of the Cole Observatory.

He was a young man of no particular brilliance, although he performed his daily tasks assiduously and efficiently, studied the calculus at home for one hour every evening, and hoped some day to become a chief astronomer of some important observatory.

Nevertheless, our narration of the events of late March in the year 1987 must begin with Roger Phlutter for the good and sufficient reason that he, of all men on earth, was the first observer of the stellar aberration.

Meet Roger Phlutter.

Tall, rather pale from spending too much time indoors, thickish shell-rimmed glasses, dark hair close-cropped in the style of the nineteen eighties, dressed neither particularly well nor badly, smokes cigarettes rather excessively. . . .

At a quarter to five that afternoon, Roger was engaged in two simultaneous operations. One was examining, in a blink-microscope, a photographic plate taken late the previous night of a section in Gemini. The other was considering whether or not, on the three dollars remaining of his pay from last week, he dared phone Elsie and ask her to go somewhere with him.

Every normal young man has undoubtedly, at some time or other, shared with Roger Phlutter his second occupation, but not everyone has operated or understands the operation of a blink-microscope. So let us raise our eyes from Elsie to Gemini.

A blink-mike provides accommodation for two photographic plates taken of the same section of sky, but at different times. These plates are carefully juxtaposed and the operator may alternately focus his vision, through the eyepiece, first upon one and then upon the other, by means of a shutter. If the plates are identical, the operation of the shutter reveals nothing, but if one of the dots on the second plate differs from the position it occupied on the first, it will call attention to itself by seeming to jump back and forth as the shutter is manipulated.

Roger manipulated the shutter, and one of the dots jumped. So did Roger. He tried it again, forgetting—as we have—all about Elsie for the moment, and the dot jumped again. It jumped almost a tenth of a second.

Roger straightened up and scratched his head. He lighted a cigarette, put it down on the ashtray, and looked into the blink-mike again. The dot jumped again, when he used the shutter.

Harry Wesson, who worked the evening shift, had just come into the office and was hanging up his topcoat.

"Hey, Harry!" Roger said. "There's something wrong with this blinking blinker."

"Yeah?" said Harry.

"Yeah. Pollux moved a tenth of a second."

"Yeah?" said Harry. "Well, that's about right for parallax. Thirty-two light-years—parallax of Pollux is point one oh one. Little over a tenth of a second, so if your comparison plate was taken about six months ago when the earth was on the other side of her orbit, that's about right."

"But Harry, the comparison plate was taken night before last. They're twenty-four hours apart."

"You're crazy."

"Look for yourself."

It wasn't quite five o'clock yet, but Harry Wesson magnanimously overlooked that, and sat down in front of the blink-mike. He manipulated the shutter, and Pollux obligingly jumped.

There wasn't any doubt about it being Pollux, for it was far and away the brightest dot on the plate. Pollux is a star of 1.2 magnitude, one of the twenty brightest in the sky and by far the brightest in Gemini. And none of the faint stars around it had moved at all.

"Um," said Harry Wesson. He frowned and looked again. "One of those plates is misdated, that's all. I'll check into it first thing."

"Those plates aren't misdated," Roger said doggedly. "I dated them myself."

"That proves it," Harry told him. "Go on home. It's five o'clock. If Pollux moved a tenth of a second last night, I'll move it back for you."

So Roger left.

He felt uneasy somehow, as though he shouldn't have. He couldn't put his finger on just what worried him, but something did. He decided to walk home instead of taking the bus.

Pollux was a fixed star. It couldn't have moved a tenth of a second in twenty-four hours.

"Let's see—thirty-two light-years," Roger said to himself. "Tenth of a second. Why, that would be movement several times faster than the speed of light. Which is positively silly!"

Wasn't it?

He didn't feel much like studying or reading tonight. Was three dollars enough to take Elsie out?

The three balls of a pawn-shop loomed ahead, and Roger succumbed to temptation. He pawned his watch, and then phoned Elsie. Dinner and a show?

"Why certainly, Roger."

So, until he took her home at one-thirty, he managed to forget astronomy. Nothing odd about that. It would have been strange if he had managed to remember it.

But his feeling of restlessness came back as soon as he had left her. At first, he didn't remember why. He knew merely that he didn't feel quite like going home yet.

The corner tavern was still open, and he dropped in for a drink. He was having his second one when he remembered. He ordered a third.

"Hank," he said to the bartender. "You know Pollux?"

"Pollux who?" asked Hank.

"Skip it," said Roger. He had another drink, and thought it over. Yes, he'd made a mistake somewhere. Pollux couldn't have moved.

He went outside and started to walk home. He was almost there when it occurred to him to look up at Pollux. Not that, with the naked eye, he could detect a displacement of a tenth of a second, but he felt curious.

He looked up, oriented himself by the sickle of Leo, and then found Gemini—Castor and Pollux were the only stars in Gemini visible, for it wasn't a particularly good night for seeing. They were there, all right, but he thought they looked a little farther apart than usual. Absurd, because that would be a matter of degrees, not minutes or seconds.

He stared at them for a while, and then looked across to the dipper. Then he stopped walking and stood there. He closed his eyes and opened them again, carefully.

The dipper just didn't look right. It was distorted. There seemed to be more space between Alioth and Mizar, in the handle, than between Mizar and Alkaid. Pheeda and Merak, in the bottom of the dipper, were closer together, making the angle between the bottom and the lip steeper. Quite a bit steeper.

Unbelievingly, he ran an imaginary line from the pointers, Merak and Dubhe, to the North Star. The line curved. It had to. If he ran it straight, it missed Polaris by maybe five degrees.

Breathing a bit hard, Roger took off his glasses and polished them very carefully with his handkerchief. He put them back on again and the dipper was still crooked.

So was Leo, when he looked back to it. At any rate, Regulus wasn't where it should be by a degree or two.

A degree or two! At the distance of Regulus! Was it sixty-five light years? Something like that.

Then, in time to save his sanity, Roger remembered that he'd been drinking. He went home without daring to look upward again. He went to bed, but couldn't sleep.

He didn't feel drunk. He grew more excited, wide awake.

He wondered if he dared phone the observatory. Would he sound drunk over the phone? The devil with whether he sounded that way or not, he finally decided. He went to the telephone in his pajamas.

"Sorry," said the operator.

"What d'ya mean, sorry?"

"I cannot give you that number," said the operator, in dulcet tones. And then, "I am sorry. We do not have that information."

He got the chief operator, and the information. Cole Observatory had been so deluged with calls from amateur astronomers that they had found it necessary to request the telephone company to discontinue all incoming calls save long-distance ones from other observatories.

"Thanks," said Roger. "Will you get me a cab?"

It was an unusual request, but the chief operator obliged and got him a cab.

He found the Cole Observatory in a state resembling a madhouse.

The following morning most newspapers carried the news. Most of them gave it two or three inches on an inside page, but the facts were there.

The facts were that a number of stars, in general the brightest ones, within the past forty-eight hours had developed noticeable proper motions.

"This does not imply," quipped the *New York Spotlight,* "that their motions have been in any way improper in the past. 'Proper motion' to an astronomer means the movement of a star across the face of the sky with relation to other stars. Hitherto, a star named 'Barnard's Star' in the constellation Ophiuchus has exhibited the greatest proper motion of any known star, moving at the rate of ten and a quarter seconds a year. 'Barnard's Star' is not visible to the naked eye."

Probably no astronomer on earth slept that day.

The observatories locked their doors, with their full staffs on the inside, and admitted no one except occasional newspaper reporters who stayed awhile and went away with puzzled faces, convinced at last that something strange was happening.

Blink-microscopes blinked, and so did astronomers. Coffee was consumed in prodigious quantities. Police riot squads were called to six United States observatories. Two of these calls were occasioned by attempts to break in on the part of frantic amateurs without. The other four were summoned to quell fistfights developing out of arguments within the observatories themselves. The office of Lick Observatory was a shambles, and James Truwell, Astronomer Royal of England, was sent to London Hospital with a mild concussion, the result of having a heavy photographic plate smashed over his head by an irate subordinate.

But these incidents were exceptions. The observatories, in general, were well-ordered madhouses.

The center of attention in the more enterprising ones was the loudspeaker in which reports from the Eastern Hemisphere could be relayed to the inmates. Practically all observatories kept open wires to the night side of earth, where the phenomena were still under scrutiny.

Astronomers under the night skies of Singapore, Shanghai and Sydney did their observing, as it were, directly into the business end of a long-distance telephone hookup.

Particularly of interest were reports from Sydney and Melbourne, whence came reports on the southern skies not visible—even at night —from Europe or the United States. The Southern Cross was, by these reports, a cross no longer, its Alpha and Beta being shifted northward. Alpha and Beta Centauri, Canopus and Achernar all showed considerable proper motion—all, generally speaking, northward. Triangulum Australe and the Magellanic Clouds were undisturbed. Sigma Octanis, the weak pole star, had not moved.

Disturbance in the southern sky, then, was much less than in the northern one, in point of the number of stars displaced. However, relative proper motion of the stars which were disturbed was greater. While the general direction of movement of the few stars which did move was northward, their paths were not directly north, nor did they converge upon any exact point in space.

United States and European astronomers digested these facts and drank more coffee.

Evening papers, particularly in America, showed greater awareness that something indeed unusual was happening in the skies. Most of them moved the story to the front page—but not the banner headlines —giving it a half-column with a runover that was long or short, depending upon the editor's luck in obtaining statements from astronomers.

The statements, when obtained, were invariably statements of fact and not of opinion. The facts themselves, said these gentlemen, were sufficiently startling, and opinions would be premature. Wait and see. Whatever was happening was happening fast.

"How fast?" asked an editor.

"Faster than possible," was the reply.

Perhaps it is unfair to say that no editor procured expressions of opinion this early. Charles Wangren, enterprising editor of the *Chicago Blade*, spent a small fortune in long-distance telephone calls. Out of possibly sixty attempts, he finally reached the chief astronomers at five observatories. He asked each of them the same question.

"What, in your opinion, is a possible cause, any possible cause, of the stellar movements of the last night or two?"

He tabulated the results.

"I wish I knew."—Geo. F. Stubbs, Tripp Observatory, Long Island.

"Somebody or something is crazy, and I hope it's me—I mean I."—Henry Collister McAdams, Lloyd Observatory, Boston.

"What's happening is impossible. There can't be any cause."— Letton Tischauer Tinney, Burgoyne Observatory, Albuquerque.

"I'm looking for an expert on Astrology. Know one?"—Patrick R. Whitaker, Lucas Observatory, Vermont.

Sadly studying this tabulation, which had cost him $187.35—including tax—to obtain, Editor Wangren signed a voucher to cover the long-distance calls and then dropped his tabulation into the wastebasket. He telephoned his regular space-rates writer on scientific subjects.

"Can you give me a series of articles—two-three thousand words each—on all this astronomical excitement?"

"Sure," said the writer. "But what excitement?" It transpired that he'd just got back from a fishing trip and had neither read a newspaper nor happened to look up at the sky. But he wrote the articles. He even got sex appeal into them through illustrations, by using ancient star-charts showing the constellation in dishabille, by reproducing certain famous paintings such as "The Origin of the Milky Way" and by using a photograph of a girl in a bathing suit sighting a hand telescope, presumably at one of the errant stars. Circulation of the *Chicago Blade* increased by 21.7%.

It was five o'clock again in the office of the Cole Observatory, just twenty-four and a quarter hours after the beginning of all the commotion. Roger Phlutter—yes, we're back to him again—woke up suddenly when a hand was placed on his shoulder.

"Go on home, Roger," said Mervin Armbruster, his boss, in a kindly tone.

Roger sat upright suddenly.

"But Mr. Armbruster," he said, "I'm sorry I fell asleep."

"Bosh," said Armbruster. "You can't stay here forever, none of us can. Go on home."

Roger Phlutter went home. But when he'd taken a bath, he felt more restless than sleepy. It was only six-fifteen. He phoned Elsie.

"I'm awfully sorry, Roger, but I have another date. What's going on, Roger? The stars, I mean."

"Gosh, Elsie—they're moving. Nobody knows."

"But I thought all the stars moved," Elsie protested. "The sun's a star, isn't it? Once you told me the sun was moving toward a point in Samson."

"Hercules."

"Hercules, then. Since you said all the stars were moving, what is everybody getting excited about?"

"This is different," said Roger. "Take Canopus. It's started moving at the rate of seven light-years a day. It can't do that!"

"Why not?"

"Because," said Roger patiently, "nothing can move faster than light."

"But if it is moving that fast, then it can," said Elsie. "Or else maybe your telescope is wrong or something. Anyway, it's pretty far off, isn't it?"

"A hundred and sixty light-years. So far away that we see it a hundred and sixty years ago."

"Then maybe it isn't moving at all," said Elsie. "I mean, maybe it quit moving a hundred and fifty years ago and you're getting all excited about something that doesn't matter any more because it's all over with. Still love me?"

"I sure do, honey. Can't you break that date?"

" 'Fraid not, Roger. But I wish I could."

He had to be content with that. He decided to walk uptown to eat.

It was early evening, and too early to see stars overhead, although the clear blue sky was darkening. When the stars did come out tonight, Roger knew, few of the constellations would be recognizable.

As he walked, he thought over Elsie's comments and decided that they were as intelligent as anything he'd heard at Cole. In one way they'd brought out one angle he'd never thought of before, and that made it more incomprehensible.

All these movements had started the same evening—yet they hadn't. Centauri must have started moving four years or so ago, and Rigel five hundred and forty years ago when Christopher Columbus was still in short pants if any, and Vega must have started acting up the year he—Roger, not Vega—was born, twenty-six years ago. Each star out of the hundreds must have started on a date in exact relation to its distance from Earth. Exact relation, to a light-second, for checkups of all the photographic plates taken night before last indicated that all the new stellar movements had started at four ten a.m. Greenwich time. What a mess!

Unless this meant that light, after all, had infinite velocity.

If it didn't have—and it is symptomatic of Roger's perplexity that he could postulate that incredible "if"—then—then what? Things were just as puzzling as before.

Mostly, he felt outraged that such events should happen.

He went into a restaurant and sat down. A radio was blaring out the latest composition in dissarythm, the new quarter-tone dance music in which chorded woodwinds provided background patterns for the mad melodies pounded on tuned tomtoms. Between each number and the next a phrenetic announcer extolled the virtues of a product.

Munching a sandwich, Roger listened appreciatively to the dissarythm and managed not to hear the commercials. Most intelligent people of the eighties had developed a type of radio deafness which enabled them not to hear a human voice coming from a loudspeaker, although they could hear and enjoy the then infrequent intervals of music between announcements. In an age when advertising competition was so keen that there was scarcely a bare wall or an unbillboarded lot within miles of a population center, discriminating people could retain normal outlooks on life only by carefully cultivated partial blindness and partial deafness which enabled them to ignore the bulk of that concerted assault upon their senses.

For that reason a good part of the newscast which followed the dissarythm program went, as it were, into one of Roger's ears and out of the other before it occurred to him that he was not listening to a panegyric on patent breakfast foods.

He thought he recognized the voice, and after a sentence or two he was sure that it was that of Milton Hale, the eminent physicist whose new theory on the principle of indeterminacy had recently occasioned so much scientific controversy. Apparently, Dr. Hale was being interviewed by a radio announcer.

"—a heavenly body, therefore, may have position or velocity, but it may not be said to have both at the same time, with relation to any given space-time frame."

"Dr. Hale, can you put that into common everyday language?" said the syrupy-smooth voice of the interviewer.

"That is common language, sir. Scientifically expressed, in terms of the Heisenberg contraction-principle, then n to the seventh power in parentheses, representing the pseudo-position of a Diedrich quantum-integer in relation to the seventh coefficient of curvature of mass—"

"Thank you, Dr. Hale, but I fear you are just a bit over the heads of our listeners."

"And your own head," thought Roger Phlutter.

"I am sure, Dr. Hale, that the question of greatest interest to our audience is whether these unprecedented stellar movements are real or illusory?"

"Both. They are real with reference to the frame of space but not with reference to the frame of space-time."

"Can you clarify that, Doctor?"

"I believe I can. The difficulty is purely epistemological. In strict causality, the impact of the macroscopic—"

" 'The slithy toves did gyre and gimble in the wabe,' " thought Roger Phlutter.

"—upon the parallelism of the entropy-gradient."

"Bah!" said Roger, aloud.

"Did you say something, sir?" asked the waitress. Roger noticed her for the first time. She was small and blonde and cuddly. Roger smiled at her.

"That depends upon the space-time frame from which one regards it," he said, judicially. "The difficulty is epistemological."

To make up for that, he tipped her more than he should have, and left.

The world's most eminent physicist, he realized, knew less of what was happening than did the general public. The public knew that the fixed stars were moving, or that they weren't. Obviously Dr. Hale didn't even know that. Under a smoke-screen of qualifications, Hale had hinted that they were doing both.

Roger looked upward, but only a few stars, faint in the early evening, were visible through the halation of the myriad neon and spiegel-light signs. Too early yet, he decided.

He had one drink at a nearby bar, but it didn't taste quite right to him so he didn't finish it. He hadn't realized what was wrong, but he was punch-drunk from lack of sleep. He merely knew that he wasn't sleepy anymore and intended to keep on walking until he felt like going to bed. Anyone hitting him over the head with a well-padded blackjack would have been doing him a signal service, but no one took the trouble.

He kept on walking and, after a while, turned into the brilliantly lighted lobby of a cineplus theater. He bought a ticket and took his seat just in time to see the sticky end of one of the three feature pictures. Several advertisements followed which he managed to look at without seeing.

"We bring you next," said the screen, "a special visicast of the night sky of London, where it is now three o'clock in the morning."

The screen went black, with hundreds of tiny dots that were stars. Roger leaned forward to watch and listen carefully—this would be a broadcast and visicast of facts, not of verbose nothingness.

"The arrow," said the screen, as an arrow appeared upon it, "is now pointing to Polaris, the pole star, which is now ten degrees from the celestial pole in the direction of Ursa Major. Ursa Major itself, the Big Dipper, is no longer recognizable as a dipper, but the arrow will now point to the stars that formerly composed it."

Roger breathlessly followed the arrow and the voice.

"Alkaid and Dubhe," said the voice. "The fixed stars are no longer fixed, but—" The picture changed abruptly to a scene in a modern kitchen. "—the qualities and excellences of Stellar's Stoves do not change. Foods cooked by the super-induced vibratory method taste as good as ever. Stellar Stoves are unexcelled."

Leisurely, Roger Phlutter stood up and made his way out into the aisle. He took his pen-knife from his pocket as he walked toward the screen. One easy jump took him up onto the low stage. His slashes into the fabric were not angry ones. They were careful, methodical cuts intelligently designed to accomplish a maximum of damage with a minimum expenditure of effort.

The damage was done, and thoroughly, by the time three strong ushers gathered him in. He offered no resistance either to them or to the police to whom they gave him. In night court, an hour later, he listened quietly to the charges against him.

"Guilty or not guilty?" asked the presiding magistrate.

"Your Honor, that is purely a question of epistemology," said Roger, earnestly. "The fixed stars move, but Corny Toasties, the world's greatest breakfast food, still represents the pseudo-position of a

Diedrich quantum-integer in relation to the seventh coefficient of curvature!"

Ten minutes later, he was sleeping soundly. In a cell, it is true, but soundly nonetheless. The police left him there because they had realized he needed to sleep. . . .

Among other minor tragedies of that night can be included the case of the schooner *Ransagansett*, off the coast of California. Well off the coast of California! A sudden squall had blown her miles off course, how many miles the skipper could only guess.

The *Ransagansett* was an American vessel, with a German crew, under Venezuelan registry, engaged in running booze from Ensenada, Baja California, up the coast to Canada, then in the throes of a prohibition experiment. The *Ransagansett* was an ancient craft with four engines and an untrustworthy compass. During the two days of the storm, her outdated radio receiver—vintage of 1955—had gone haywire beyond the ability of Gross, the first mate, to repair.

But now only a mist remained of the storm, and the remaining shreds of wind were blowing it away. Hans Gross, holding an ancient astrolabe, stood on the deck waiting. About him was utter darkness, for the ship was running without lights to avoid the coastal patrols.

"She clearing, Mister Gross?" called the voice of the captain from below.

"Aye, sir. Idt iss glearing rabidly."

In the cabin, Captain Randall went back to his game of blackjack with the second mate and the engineer. The crew—an elderly German named Weiss, with a wooden leg—was asleep abaft the scuttlebutt—wherever that may have been.

A half hour went by. An hour, and the captain was losing heavily to Helmstadt, the engineer.

"Mister Gross!" he called out.

There wasn't any answer and he called again and still obtained no response.

"Just a minute, mein fine feathered friends," he said to the second mate and engineer, and went up the companionway to the deck.

Gross was standing there staring upward with his mouth open. The mists were gone.

"Mister Gross," said Captain Randall.

The second mate didn't answer. The captain saw that his second mate was revolving slowly where he stood.

"Hans!" said Captain Randall, "What the devil's wrong with you?" Then he, too, looked up.

Superficially the sky looked perfectly normal. No angels flying around nor sound of airplane motors. The dipper— Captain Randall turned around slowly, but more rapidly than Hans Gross. Where was the Big Dipper?

For that matter, where was anything? There wasn't a constellation anywhere that he could recognize. No sickle of Leo. No belt of Orion. No horns of Taurus.

Worse, there was a group of eight bright stars that ought to have been a constellation, for they were shaped roughly like an octagon. Yet if such a constellation had ever existed, he'd never seen it, for he'd been around the Horn and Good Hope. Maybe at that— But no, there wasn't any Southern Cross!

Dazedly, Captain Randall walked to the companionway.

"Mister Weisskopf," he called. "Mister Helmstadt. Come on deck."

They came and looked. Nobody said anything for quite a while.

"Shut off the engines, Mister Helmstadt," said the captain. Helmstadt saluted—the first time he ever had—and went below.

"Captain, shall I vake opp Veiss?" asked Weisskopf.

"What for?"

"I don't know."

The captain considered. "Wake him up," he said.

"I think ve are on der blanet Mars," said Gross.

But the captain had thought of that and rejected it.

"No," he said firmly. "From any planet in the solar system the constellations would look approximately the same."

"You mean ve are oudt of der cosmos?"

The throb of the engines suddenly ceased and there was only the soft familiar lapping of the waves against the hull and the gentle familiar rocking of the boat.

Weisskopf returned with Weiss, and Helmstadt came on deck and saluted again.

"Vell, Captain?"

Captain Randall waved a hand to the afterdeck, piled high with cases of liquor under a canvas tarpaulin. "Break out the cargo," he ordered.

The blackjack game was not resumed. At dawn, under a sun they had never expected to see again—and, for that matter, certainly were not seeing at the moment—the five unconscious men were moved from the ship to the Port of San Francisco Jail by members of the coast patrol. During the night the *Ransagansett* had drifted through the Golden Gate and bumped gently into the dock of the Berkeley ferry.

In tow at the stern of the schooner was a big canvas tarpaulin. It was transfixed by a harpoon whose rope was firmly tied to the aftermast. Its presence there was never explained officially, although days later Captain Randall had vague recollections of having harpooned a sperm whale during the night. But the elderly able-bodied seaman named Weiss never did find out what happened to his wooden leg, which is perhaps just as well.

Milton Hale, Ph.D., eminent physicist, had finished broadcasting and the program was off the air.

"Thank you very much, Dr. Hale," said the radio announcer. The yellow light went on and stayed. The mike was dead. "Uh—your check will be waiting for you at the window. You—uh—know where."

"I know where," said the physicist. He was a rotund, jolly-looking little man. With his bushy white beard, he resembled a pocket edition of Santa Claus. His eyes twinkled and he smoked a short stubby pipe.

He left the sound-proof studio and walked briskly down the hall to the cashier's window. "Hello, sweetheart," he said to the girl on duty there. "I think you have two checks for Dr. Hale."

"You are Dr. Hale?"

"I sometimes wonder," said the little man. "But I carry identification that seems to prove it."

"Two checks?"

"Two checks. Both for the same broadcast, by special arrangement. By the way, there is an excellent revue at the Mabry Theater this evening."

"Is there? Yes, here are your checks, Dr. Hale. One for seventy-five and one for twenty-five. Is that correct?"

"Gratifyingly correct. Now about the revue at the Mabry?"

"If you wish I'll call my husband and ask him about it," said the girl. "He's the doorman over there."

Dr. Hale sighed deeply, but his eyes still twinkled. "I think he'll agree," he said. "Here are the tickets, my dear, and you can take him. I find that I have work to do this evening."

The girl's eyes widened, but she took the tickets.

Dr. Hale went into the phone booth and called his home. His home and Dr. Hale were both run by his elder sister. "Agatha, I must remain at the office this evening," he said.

"Milton, you know you can work just as well in your study here at home. I heard your broadcast, Milton. It was wonderful."

"It was sheer balderdash, Agatha. Utter rot. What did I say?"

"Why, you said that—uh—that the stars were—I mean, you were not—"

"Exactly, Agatha. My idea was to avert panic on the part of the populace. If I'd told them the truth, they'd have worried. But by being smug and scientific, I let them get the idea that everything was—uh—under control. Do you know, Agatha, what I meant by the parallelism of an entropy-gradient?"

"Why—not exactly."

"Neither did I."

"Milton, have you been drinking?"

"Not y— No, I haven't. I really can't come home to work this evening, Agatha. I'm using my study at the university, because I must have access to the library there, for reference. And the star-charts."

"But, Milton, how about that money for your broadcast? You know it isn't safe for you to have money in your pocket when you're feeling —like this."

"It isn't money, Agatha. It's a check, and I'll mail it to you before I go to the office. I won't cash it myself. How's that?"

"Well—if you must have access to the library, I suppose you must. Good-by, Milton."

Dr. Hale went across the street to the drug store. There he bought a stamp and envelope and cashed the twenty-five dollar check. The seventy-five-dollar one he put into the envelope and mailed.

Standing beside the mailbox he glanced up at the early evening sky—shuddered, and hastily lowered his eyes. He took the straightest possible line for the nearest tavern and ordered a double Scotch.

"Y'ain't been in for a long time, Dr. Hale," said Mike, the bartender.

"That I haven't, Mike. Pour me another."

"Sure. On the house, this time. We had your broadcast tuned in on the radio just now. It was swell."

"Yes."

"It sure was. I was kind of worried what was happening up there, with my son an aviator and all. But as long as you scientific guys know what it's all about, I guess it's all right. That was sure a good speech, Doc. But there's one question I'd like to ask you."

"I was afraid of that," said Dr. Hale.

"These stars. They're moving, going somewhere. But where they going? I mean, like you said, if they are."

"There's no way of telling that exactly, Mike."

"Aren't they moving in a straight line, each one of them?"

For just a moment the celebrated scientist hesitated.

"Well—yes and no, Mike. According to spectroscopic analysis, they're maintaining the same distance from us, each one of them. So they're really moving—if they're moving—in circles around us. But the circles are straight, as it were. I mean, it seems that we're in the center of those circles, so the stars that are moving aren't coming closer to us or receding."

"You could draw lines for those circles?"

"On a star-globe, yes. It's been done. They all seem to be heading for a certain area of the sky, but not for a given point. In other words, they don't intersect."

"What part of the sky they going to?"

"Approximately between Ursa Major and Leo, Mike. The ones farthest from there are moving fastest, the ones nearest are moving slower. But darn you, Mike, I came in here to forget about stars, not to talk about them. Give me another."

"In a minute, Doc. When they get there, are they going to stop or keep on going?"

"How the devil do I know, Mike? They started suddenly, all at the same time, and with full original velocity—I mean, they started out at the same speed they're going now—without warming up, so to speak— so I suppose they could stop just as unexpectedly."

He stopped just as suddenly as the stars might. He stared at his reflection in the mirror back of the bar as though he'd never seen it before.

"What's the matter, Doc?"

"Mike!"

"Yes, Doc?"

"Mike, you're a genius."

"Me? You're kidding."

Dr. Hale groaned. "Mike, I'm going to have to go to the university to work this out. So I can have access to the library and the star-globe there. You're making an honest man out of me, Mike. Whatever kind of Scotch this is, wrap me up a bottle."

"It's Tartan Plaid. A quart?"

"A quart, and make it snappy. I've got to see a man about a dog-star."

"Serious, Doc?"

Dr. Hale sighed audibly. "You brought that on yourself, Mike. Yes, the dog-star is Sirius. I wish I'd never come in here, Mike. My first night out in weeks, and you ruin it."

He took a cab to the university, let himself in, and turned on the lights in his private study and in the library. Then he took a good stiff slug of Tartan Plaid and went to work.

First, by telling the chief operator who he was and arguing a bit, he got a telephone connection with the chief astronomer of Cole Observatory.

"This is Hale, Armbruster," he said. "I've got an idea, but I want to check my facts before I start to work on it. Last information I had, there were four hundred sixty-eight stars exhibiting new proper motion. Is that still correct?"

"Yes, Milton. The same ones are still at it—no others."

"Good. I have a list of them. Has there been any change in speed of motion of any of them?"

"No. Impossible as it seems, it's constant. What is your idea?"

"I want to check my theory first. If it works out into anything, I'll call you." But he forgot to.

It was a long, painful job. First he made a chart of the heavens in the area between Ursa Major and Leo. Across that chart he drew 468 lines representing the projected path of each of the aberrant stars. At the border of the chart, where each line entered, he made a notation of the apparent velocity of the star—not in light-years per hour—but in degrees per hour, to the fifth decimal.

Then he did some reasoning.

"Postulate that the motion which began simultaneously will stop simultaneously," he told himself. "Try a guess at the time. Let's try ten o'clock tomorrow evening."

He tried it and looked at the series of positions indicated upon the chart. No.

Try one o'clock in the morning. It looked almost like—sense!

Try midnight.

That did it. At any rate, it was close enough. The calculation could be only a few minutes off one way or the other and there was no point now in working out the exact time. Now that he knew the incredible fact.

He took another drink and stared at the chart grimly.

A trip to the library gave Dr. Hale the further information he needed. The address!

Thus began the saga of Dr. Hale's journey. A useless journey, it is true, but one that should rank with the trip of the messenger to Garcia.

He started it with a drink. Then, knowing the combination, he rifled the safe in the office of the president of the university. The note he left in the safe was a masterpiece of brevity. It read:

Taking money. Explain later.

Then he took another drink and put the bottle in his pocket. He went outside and hailed a taxicab. He got in.

"Where to, sir?" asked the cabby.

Dr. Hale gave an address.

"Fremont Street?" said the cabby. "Sorry, sir, but I don't know where that is."

"In Boston," said Dr. Hale. "I should have told you, in Boston."

"Boston? You mean Boston, Massachusetts? That's a long way from here."

"Therefore we better start right away," said Dr. Hale, reasonably. A brief financial discussion and the passing of money, borrowed from the university safe, set the driver's mind at rest, and they started.

It was a bitter cold night, for March, and the heater in the taxi didn't work any too well. But the Tartan Plaid worked superlatively for both Dr. Hale and the cabby, and by the time they reached New Haven, they were singing old-time songs lustily.

"Off we go, into the wide, wild yonder . . ." their voices roared.

It is regrettably reported, but possibly untrue, that in Hartford Dr.

Hale leered out of the window at a young woman waiting for a late street-car and asked her if she wanted to go to Boston. Apparently, however, she didn't for at five o'clock in the morning when the cab drew up in front of 614 Fremont Street, Boston, only Dr. Hale and the driver were in the cab.

Dr. Hale got out and looked at the house. It was a millionaire's mansion, and it was surrounded by a high iron fence with barbed wire on top of it. The gate in the fence was locked and there was no bell button to push.

But the house was only a stone's throw from the sidewalk, and Dr. Hale was not to be deterred. He threw a stone. Then another. Finally he succeeded in smashing a window.

After a brief interval, a man appeared in the window. A butler, Dr. Hale decided.

"I'm Dr. Milton Hale," he called out. "I want to see Rutherford R. Sniveley, right away. It's important."

"Mr. Sniveley is not at home, sir," said the butler. "And about that window—"

"The devil with the window," shouted Dr. Hale. "Where is Sniveley?"

"On a fishing trip."

"Where?"

"I have orders not to give out that information."

Dr. Hale was just a little drunk, perhaps. "You'll give it out just the same," he roared. "By orders of the President of the United States."

The butler laughed. "I don't see him."

"You will," said Hale.

He got back in the cab. The driver had fallen asleep, but Hale shook him awake.

"The White House," said Dr. Hale.

"Huh?"

"The White House, in Washington," said Dr. Hale. "And hurry!" He pulled a hundred-dollar bill from his pocket. The cabby looked at it, and groaned. Then he put the bill into his pocket and started the cab.

A light snow was beginning to fall.

As the cab drove off, Rutherford R. Sniveley, grinning, stepped back from the window. Mr. Sniveley had no butler.

If Dr. Hale had been more familiar with the peculiarities of the eccentric Mr. Sniveley, he would have known Sniveley kept no servants in the place overnight, but lived alone in the big house at 614 Fremont Street. Each morning at ten o'clock, a small army of servants descended upon the house, did their work as rapidly as possible, and were required to depart before the witching hour of noon. Aside from these two hours of every day, Mr. Sniveley lived in solitary splendor. He had few, if any, social contacts.

Aside from the few hours a day he spent administering his vast interests as one of the country's leading manufacturers, Mr. Sniveley's time was his own and he spent practically all of it in his workshop, making gadgets.

Sniveley had an ashtray which would hand him a lighted cigar any time he spoke sharply to it, and a radio receiver so delicately adjusted that it would cut in automatically Sniveley-sponsored programs and shut off again when they were finished. He had a bathtub that provided a full orchestra accompaniment to his singing therein, and he had a machine which would read aloud to him from any book which he placed in its hopper.

His life may have been a lonely one, but it was not without such material comforts. Eccentric, yes, but Mr. Sniveley could afford to be eccentric with a net income of four million dollars a year. Not bad for a man who'd started life as the son of a shipping clerk.

Mr. Sniveley chuckled as he watched the taxicab drive away, and then he went back to bed and to the sleep of the just.

"So somebody has things figured out nineteen hours ahead of time," he thought. "Well, a lot of good it will do them!"

There wasn't any law to punish him for what he'd done. . . .

Bookstores did a landoffice business that day in books on astronomy. The public, apathetic at first, was deeply interested now. Even ancient and musty volumes of Newton's *Principia* sold at premium prices.

The ether blared with comment upon the new wonder of the skies. Little of the comment was professional, or even intelligent, for most astronomers were asleep that day. They'd managed to stay awake the first forty-eight hours from the start of the phenomena, but the third day found them worn out mentally and physically, and inclined to let the stars take care of themselves while they—the astronomers, not the stars—caught up on sleep.

Staggering offers from the telecast and broadcast studios enticed a few of them to attempt lectures, but their efforts were dreary things, better forgotten. Dr. Carver Blake, broadcasting from KNB, fell soundly asleep between a perigee and an apogee.

Physicists were also greatly in demand. The most eminent of them all, however, was sought in vain. The solitary clue to Dr. Milton Hale's disappearance, the brief note "Taking money. Explain later," wasn't much of a help. His sister Agatha feared the worst.

For the first time in history, astronomical news made banner headlines in the newspapers.

Snow had started early that morning along the northern Atlantic seaboard and now it was growing steadily worse. Just outside Waterbury, Conn., the driver of Dr. Hale's cab began to weaken.

It wasn't human, he thought, for a man to be expected to drive to Boston and then, without stopping, from Boston to Washington. Not even for a hundred dollars.

Not in a storm like this. Why, he could see only a dozen yards ahead through the driving snow, even when he could manage to keep his eyes open. His fare was slumbering soundly in the back seat. Maybe he could get away with stopping here along the road, for an hour, to catch some sleep. Just an hour. His fare wouldn't ever know the difference. The guy must be loony, he thought, or why hadn't he taken a plane or a train?

Dr. Hale would have, of course, if he'd thought of it. But he wasn't used to traveling and besides there'd been the Tartan Plaid. A taxi had seemed the easiest way to get anywhere—no worrying about tickets and connections and stations. Money was no object, and the plaid condition of his mind had caused him to overlook the human factor involved in an extended journey by taxi.

When he awoke, almost frozen, in the parked taxi, that human factor dawned upon him. The driver was so sound asleep that no amount of shaking could arouse him. Dr. Hale's watch had stopped, so he had no idea where he was or what time it was.

Unfortunately, too, he didn't know how to drive a car. He took a quick drink to keep from freezing, and then got out of the cab, and as he did so, a car stopped.

It was a policeman—what is more it was a policeman in a million.

Yelling over the roar of the storm, Hale hailed him.

"I'm Dr. Hale," he shouted. "We're lost. Where am I?"

"Get in here before you freeze," ordered the policeman. "Do you mean Dr. Milton Hale, by any chance?"

"Yes."

"I've read all your books, Dr. Hale," said the policeman. "Physics is my hobby, and I've always wanted to meet you. I want to ask you about the revised value of the quantum."

"This is life or death," said Dr. Hale. "Can you take me to the nearest airport, quick?"

"Of course, Dr. Hale."

"And look—there's a driver in that cab, and he'll freeze to death unless we send aid."

"I'll put him in the back seat of my car, and then run the cab off the road. We'll take care of details later."

"Hurry, please."

The obliging policeman hurried. He got back in and started the car.

"About the revised quantum value, Dr. Hale," he began, then stopped talking.

Dr. Hale was sound asleep. The policeman drove to Waterbury airport, one of the largest in the world since the population shift from New York City northwards in the 1960's and 70's had given it a central position. In front of the ticket office, he gently awakened Dr. Hale.

"This is the airport, sir," he said.

Even as he spoke, Dr. Hale was leaping out of the car and stumbling into the building, yelling, "Thanks," over his shoulder and nearly falling down in doing so.

The warm-up roaring of the motors of a superstratoliner out on the field lent wings to his heels as he dashed for the ticket window.

"What plane's that?" he yelled.

"Washington Special, due out in one minute. But I don't think you can make it."

Dr. Hale slapped a hundred-dollar bill on the ledge. "Ticket," he gasped. "Keep change."

He grabbed the ticket and ran, getting into the plane just as the doors were being closed. Panting, he fell into a seat, the ticket still in his hand. He was sound asleep before the hostess strapped him in for the blind take-off.

A little while later, the hostess awakened him. The passengers were disembarking.

Dr. Hale rushed out of the plane and ran across the field to the airport building. A big clock told him that it was nine o'clock, and he felt elated as he ran for the door marked "Taxicabs."

He got into the nearest one.

"White House," he told the driver. "How long'll it take?"

"Ten minutes."

Dr. Hale gave a sigh of relief and sank back against the cushions. He didn't go back to sleep this time. He was wide awake now. But he closed his eyes to think out the words he'd use in explaining matters.

"Here you are, sir."

Dr. Hale gave the driver a bill and hurried out of the cab and into the building. It didn't look like he expected it to look. But there was a desk and he ran up to it.

"I've got to see the President, quick. It's vital."

The clerk frowned. "The president of what?"

Dr. Hale's eyes went wide. "The President of the— Say, what building is this? And what town?"

The clerk's frown deepened. "This is the White House Hotel," he said, "Seattle, Washington."

Dr. Hale fainted. He woke up in a hospital three hours later. It was then midnight, Pacific Time, which meant it was three o'clock in the morning on the Eastern Seaboard. It had, in fact, been midnight already in Washington, D.C., and in Boston, when he had been leaving the Washington Special in Seattle.

Dr. Hale rushed to the window and shook his fists, both of them, at the sky. A futile gesture.

Back in the East, however, the storm had stopped by twilight, leaving a light mist in the air. The star-conscious public thereupon deluged the weather bureaus with telephone requests about the persistence of the mist.

"A breeze off the ocean is expected," they were told. "It is blowing now, in fact, and within an hour or two will have cleared off the light fog."

By eleven-fifteen the skies of Boston were clear.

Untold thousands braved the bitter cold and stood staring upward at the unfolding pageant of the no-longer-eternal stars. It almost looked as though an incredible development had occurred.

And then, gradually, the murmur grew. By a quarter to twelve, the thing was certain, and the murmur hushed and then grew louder than ever, waxing toward midnight. Different people reacted differently, of course, as might be expected. There was laughter as well as indignation, cynical amusement as well as shocked horror. There was even admiration.

Soon in certain parts of the city, a concerted movement on the part of those who knew an address on Fremont Street began to take place. Movement afoot and in cars and public vehicles, converging.

At five minutes to twelve, Rutherford R. Sniveley sat waiting within his house. He was denying himself the pleasure of looking until, at the last moment, the thing was complete.

It was going well. The gathering murmur of voices, mostly angry voices, outside his house told him that. He heard his name shouted.

Just the same he waited until the twelfth stroke of the clock before he stepped out upon the balcony. Much as he wanted to look upward, he forced himself to look down at the street first. The milling crowd was there, and it was angry. But he had only contempt for the milling crowd.

Police cars were pulling up, too, and he recognized the Mayor of Boston getting out of one of them, and the Chief of Police was with him. But so what? There wasn't any law covering this.

Then, having denied himself the supreme pleasure long enough, he turned his eyes up to the silent sky, and there it was. The four hundred and sixty-eight brightest stars spelling out:

USE
SNIVELY'S
SOAP

For just a second did his satisfaction last. Then his face began to turn apoplectic purple.

"My God!" said Mr. Sniveley. "It's spelled wrong!"

His face grew more purple still and then, as a tree falls, he fell backward through the window.

An ambulance rushed the fallen magnate to the nearest hospital, but he was pronounced dead—of apoplexy—upon entrance.

But misspelled or not, the eternal stars held their position as of that midnight. The aberrant motion had stopped and again the stars were fixed. Fixed to spell—USE SNIVELY'S SOAP!

Of the many explanations offered by all the sundry who professed some physical and astronomical knowledge, none was more lucid—or closer to the actual truth—than that put forward by Wendell Mehan, president emeritus of the New York Astronomical Society.

"Obviously, the phenomenon is a trick of refraction," said Dr. Mehan. "It is manifestly impossible for any force contrived by man to move a star. The stars, therefore, still occupy their old places in the firmament.

"I suggest that Sniveley must have contrived a method of refracting the light of the stars, somewhere in or just above the atmospheric layer of earth, so that they appear to have changed their positions. This is done, probably, by radio waves or similar waves, sent on some fixed frequency from a set—or possibly a series of four hundred and sixty-eight sets—somewhere upon the surface of the earth. Although we do not understand just how it is done, it is no more unthinkable that light rays should be bent by a field of waves than by a prism or by gravitational force.

"Since Sniveley was not a great scientist, I imagine that his discovery was empiric rather than logical—an accidental find. It is quite possible that even the discovery of his projector will not enable present-day scientists to understand its secret, any more than an aboriginal savage could understand the operation of a simple radio receiver by taking one apart.

"My principal reason for this assertion is the fact that the refraction obviously is a fourth-dimensional phenomenon or its effect would be purely local to one portion of the globe. Only in the fourth dimension could light be so refracted. . . ."

There was more, but it is better to skip to his final paragraph:

"This effect cannot possibly be permanent—more permanent, that is, than the wave-projector which causes it. Sooner or later, Sniveley's machine will be found and shut off, or it will break down or wear out of its own volition. Undoubtedly it includes vacuum tubes, which will some day blow out, as do the tubes in our radios. . . ."

The excellence of Dr. Mehan's analysis was shown, two months and eight days later, when the Boston Electric Co. shut off, for nonpayment of bills, service to a house situated at 901 West Rogers Street, ten blocks from the Sniveley mansion. At the instant of the shut-off, excited reports from the night side of Earth brought the news that the stars had flashed back into their former positions instantaneously.

Investigation brought out that the description of one Elmer Smith, who had purchased that house six months before, corresponded with the description of Rutherford R. Sniveley, and undoubtedly Elmer Smith and Rutherford R. Sniveley were one and the same person.

In the attic was found a complicated network of four hundred and sixty-eight radio-type antennae, each antenna of different length and running in a different direction. The machine to which they were connected was not larger, strangely, than the average ham's radio projector, nor did it draw appreciably more current, according to the electric company's record.

By special order of the President of the United States, the projector was destroyed without examination of its internal arrangement. Clamorous protests against this high-handed executive order arose from many sides. But inasmuch as the projector had already been broken up, the protests were of no avail.

Serious repercussions were, on the whole, amazingly few.

Persons in general appreciated the stars more, but trusted them less.

Roger Phlutter got out of jail and married Elsie. Dr. Milton Hale found he liked Seattle, and stayed there. Two thousand miles away from his sister Agatha, he found it possible for the first time to defy her openly. He enjoys life more but, it is feared, will write fewer books.

There is one fact remaining which is painful to consider, since it casts a deep reflection upon the basic intelligence of the human race. It is proof, though, that the President's executive order was justified, despite scientific protests.

That fact is as humiliating as it is enlightening. During the two months and eight days during which the Sniveley machine was in operation, sales of Sniveley Soap increased 915%!

The Million-Year Picnic

Ray Bradbury (1920-   )

BEGINNING *as a Los Angeles fan selling newspapers on street corners, Ray Bradbury became one of the major names in science fiction. He has been attacked for his supposed ignorance about science (blue skies and white clouds on Mars), but the poetry and power of his wonderfully moralistic stories provide more than enough compensation. Bradbury's work may be antiscience, but his writing filled a need in the minds and hearts of hundreds of thousands of people who never set eyes on* Astounding. *Along with Robert A. Heinlein, he broke down the barriers of the slick magazines like* Collier's *and the* Saturday Evening Post, *and opened new markets and created new respectability for science fiction.*

During the forties he appeared regularly in markets as distinct as Planet Stories *and* Weird Tales, *with stories like "The Crowd" (1943), "Zero Hour" (1947), "Pillar of Fire" (1948), and "Mars Is Heaven!" (1948). "Mars Is Heaven!" was part of his famous* Martian Chronicles *series and is one of a number of Bradbury's stories to appear in* Planet, *a magazine specializing in space opera and adventure that survived the paper shortages that killed so many other pulps during the war years, continuing to publish until the mid-fifties.*

From *Planet Stories*   1946

Somehow the idea was brought up by Mom that perhaps the whole family would enjoy a fishing trip. But they weren't Mom's words;

Timothy knew that. They were Dad's words, and Mom used them for him somehow.

Dad shuffled his feet in a clutter of Martian pebbles and agreed. So immediately there was a tumult and a shouting, and very quickly the camp was tucked into capsules and containers, Mom slipped into traveling jumpers and blouse, Dad stuffed his pipe full with trembling hands, his eyes on the Martian sky, and the three boys piled yelling into the motorboat, none of them really keeping an eye on Mom and Dad, escpt Timothy.

Dad pushed a stud. The water boat sent a humming sound up into the sky. The water shook back and the boat nosed ahead, and the family cried "Hurrah!"

Timothy sat in the back of the boat with Dad, his small fingers atop Dad's hairy ones, watching the canal twist, leaving the crumbled place behind where they had landed in their small family rocket all the way from Earth. He remembered the night before they left Earth, the hustling and hurrying, the rocket that Dad had found somewhere, somehow, and the talk of a vacation on Mars. A long way to go for a vacation, but Timothy said nothing because of his younger brothers. They came to Mars and now, first thing, or so they said, they were going fishing.

Dad had a funny look in his eyes as the boat went up-canal. A look that Timothy couldn't figure. It was made of strong light and maybe a sort of relief. It made the deep wrinkles laugh instead of worry or cry.

So there went the cooling rocket, around a bend, gone.

"How far are we going?" Robert splashed his hand. It looked like a small crab jumping in the violet water.

Dad exhaled. "A million years."

"Gee," said Robert.

"Look, kids." Mother pointed one soft long arm. "There's a dead city."

They looked with fervent anticipation, and the dead city lay dead for them alone, drowsing in a hot silence of summer made on Mars by a Martian weatherman.

And Dad looked as if he was pleased that it was dead.

It was a futile spread of pink rocks sleeping on a rise of sand, a few tumbled pillars, one lonely shrine, and then the sweep of sand again. Nothing else for miles. A white desert around the canal and a blue desert over it.

Just then a bird flew up. Like a stone thrown across a blue pond, hitting, falling deep, and vanishing.

Dad got a frightened look when he saw it. "I thought it was a rocket."

Timothy looked at the deep ocean sky, trying to see Earth and the war and the ruined cities and the men killing each other since the day he was born. But he saw nothing. The war was as removed and far off as two flies battling to the death in the arch of a great high and silent cathedral. And just as senseless.

William Thomas wiped his forehead and felt the touch of his son's hand on his arm, like a young tarantula, thrilled. He beamed at his son. "How goes it, Timmy?"

"Fine, Dad."

Timothy hadn't quite figured out what was ticking inside the vast adult mechanism beside him. The man with the immense hawk nose, sunburnt, peeling—and the hot blue eyes like agate marbles you play with after school in summer back on Earth, and the long thick columnar legs in the loose riding breeches.

"What are you looking at so hard, Dad?"

"I was looking for Earthian logic, common sense, good government, peace, and responsibility."

"All that up there?"

"No. I didn't find it. It's not there anymore. Maybe it'll never be there again. Maybe we fooled ourselves that it was ever there."

"Huh?"

"See the fish," said Dad, pointing.

There rose a soprano clamor from all three boys as they rocked the boat arching their tender necks to see. They *oohed* and *ahed*. A silver ring fish floated by them, undulating, and closing like an iris, instantly, around food particles, to assimilate them.

Dad looked at it. His voice was deep and quiet.

"Just like war. War swims along, sees food, contracts. A moment later—Earth is gone."

"William," said Mom.

"Sorry," said Dad.

They sat still and felt the canal water rush cool, swift, and glassy. The only sound was the motor hum, the glide of water, the sun expanding the air.

"When do we see the Martians?" cried Michael.

"Quite soon, perhaps," said Father. "Maybe tonight."

"Oh, but the Martians are a dead race now," said Mom.

"No, they're not. I'll show you some Martians, all right," Dad said presently.

Timothy scowled at that but said nothing. Everything was odd now. Vacations and fishing and looks between people.

The other boys were already engaged making shelves of their small hands and peering under them toward the seven-foot stone banks of the canal, watching for Martians.

"What do they look like?" demanded Michael.

"You'll know them when you see them." Dad sort of laughed, and Timothy saw a pulse beating time in his cheek.

Mother was slender and soft, with a woven plait of spun-gold hair over her head in a tiara, and eyes the color of the deep cool canal water where it ran in shadow, almost purple, with flecks of amber caught in it. You could see her thoughts swimming around in her eyes, like fish—some bright, some dark, some fast, quick, some slow and easy, and sometimes, like when she looked up where Earth was, being color and nothing else. She sat up in the boat's prow, one hand resting on the side, the other on the lap of her dark blue breeches, and a line of sunburnt soft neck showing where her blouse opened like a white flower.

She kept looking ahead to see what was there, and not being able to see it clearly enough, she looked backward toward her husband, and through his eyes, reflected then, she saw what was ahead; and since he added part of himself to this reflection, a determined firmness, her face relaxed and she accepted it and she turned back, knowing suddenly what to look for.

Timothy looked too. But all he saw was a straight pencil line of canal going violet through a wide shallow valley penned by low, eroded hills, and on until it fell over the sky's edge. And this canal went on and on, through cities that would have rattled like beetles in a dry skull if you shook them. A hundred or two hundred cities dreaming hot summer-day dreams and cool summer-night dreams. . . .

They had come millions of miles for this outing—to fish. But there had been a gun on the rocket. This was a vacation. But why all the food, more than enough to last them years and years, left hidden back there near the rocket? Vacation. Just behind the veil of the vacation was not a soft face of laughter, but something hard and bony and perhaps terrifying. Timothy could not lift the veil, and the two other boys were busy being ten and eight years old, respectively.

"No Martians yet. Nuts." Robert put his V-shaped chin on his hands and glared at the canal.

Dad had brought an atomic radio along, strapped to his wrist. It functioned on an old-fashioned principle; you held it against the bones near your ear and it vibrated singing or talking to you. Dad listened to it now. His face looked like one of those fallen Martian cities, caved in, sucked dry, almost dead.

Then he gave it to Mom to listen. Her lips dropped open.

"What—" Timothy started to question, but never finished what he wished to say.

For at that moment there were two titanic, marrow-jolting explosions that grew upon themselves, followed by a half dozen minor concussions.

234

Jerking his head up, Dad notched the boat speed higher immediately. The boat leaped and jounced and spanked. This shook Robert out of his funk and elicited yelps of frightened but ecstatic joy from Michael, who clung to Mom's legs and watched the water pour by his nose in a wet torrent.

Dad swerved the boat, cut speed, and ducked the craft into a little branch canal and under an ancient, crumbling stone wharf that smelled of crab flesh. The boat rammed the wharf hard enough to throw them all forward, but no one was hurt, and Dad was already twisted to see if the ripples on the canal were enough to map their route into hiding. Water lines went across, lapped the stones, and rippled back to meet each other, settling, to be dappled by the sun. It all went away.

Dad listened. So did everybody.

Dad's breathing echoed like fists beating against the cold wet wharf stones. In the shadow, Mom's cat eyes just watched Father for some clue to what next.

Dad relaxed and blew out a breath, laughing at himself.

"The rocket, of course. I'm getting jumpy. The rocket."

Michael said, "What happened, Dad, what happened?"

"Oh, we just blew up our rocket, is all," said Timothy, trying to sound matter-of-fact. "I've heard rockets blown up before. Ours just blew."

"Why did we blow up our rocket?" asked Michael. "Huh, Dad?"

"It's part of the game, silly!" said Timothy.

"A game!" Michael and Robert loved the word.

"Dad fixed it so it would blow up and no one'd know where we landed or went! In case they ever came looking, see?"

"Oh boy, a secret!"

"Scared by my own rocket," admitted Dad to Mom. "I *am* nervous. It's silly to think there'll ever *be* any more rockets. Except *one*, perhaps, if Edwards and his wife get through with *their* ship."

He put his tiny radio to his ear again. After two minutes he dropped his hand as you would drop a rag.

"It's over at last," he said to Mom. "The radio just went off the atomic beam. Every other world station's gone. They dwindled down to a couple in the last few years. Now the air's completely silent. It'll probably remain silent."

"For how long?" asked Robert.

"Maybe—your great-grandchildren will hear it again," said Dad. He just sat there, and the children were caught in the center of his awe and defeat and resignation and acceptance.

Finally he put the boat out into the canal again, and they continued in the direction in which they had originally started.

It was getting late. Already the sun was down the sky, and a series of dead cities lay ahead of them.

Dad talked very quietly and gently to his sons. Many times in the past he had been brisk, distant, removed from them, but now he patted them on the head with just a word and they felt it.

"Mike, pick a city."

"What, Dad?"

"Pick a city, son. Any one of these cities we pass."

"All right," said Michael. "How do I pick?"

"Pick the one you like the most. You, too, Robert and Tim. Pick the city you like best."

"I want a city with Martians in it," said Michael.

"You'll have that," said Dad. "I promise." His lips were for the children, but his eyes were for Mom.

They passed six cities in twenty minutes. Dad didn't say anything more about the explosions; he seemed much more interested in having fun with his sons, keeping them happy, than anything else.

Michael liked the first city they passed, but this was vetoed because everyone doubted quick first judgments. The second city nobody liked. It was an Earthman's settlement, built of wood and already rotting into sawdust. Timothy liked the third city because it was large. The fourth and fifth were too small and the sixth brought acclaim from everyone, including Mother, who joined in the Gees, Goshes, and Look-at-thats!

There were fifty or sixty huge structures still standing, streets were dusty but paved, and you could see one or two old centrifugal fountains still pulsing wetly in the plazas. That was the only life—water leaping in the late sunlight.

"This is the city," said everybody.

Steering the boat to a wharf, Dad jumped out.

"Here we are. This is ours. This is where we live from now on!"

"From now on?" Michael was incredulous. He stood up, looking, and then turned to blink back at where the rocket used to be. "What about the rocket? What about Minnesota?"

"Here," said Dad.

He touched the small radio to Michael's blond head. "Listen."

Michael listened.

"Nothing," he said.

"That's right. Nothing. Nothing at all anymore. No more Minneapolis, no more rockets, no more Earth."

Michael considered the lethal revelation and began to sob little dry sobs.

"Wait a moment," said Dad the next instant. "I'm giving you a lot more in exchange, Mike!"

"What?" Michael held off the tears, curious, but quite ready to continue in case Dad's further revelation was as disconcerting as the original.

"I'm giving you this city, Mike. It's yours."

"Mine?"

"For you and Robert and Timothy, all three of you, to own for yourselves."

Timothy bounded from the boat. "Look, guys, all for *us!* All of *that!*" He was playing the game with Dad, playing it large and playing it well. Later, after it was all over and things had settled, he could go off by himself and cry for ten minutes. But now it was still a game, still a family outing, and the other kids must be kept playing.

Mike jumped out with Robert. They helped Mom.

"Be careful of your sister," said Dad, and nobody knew what he meant until later.

They hurried into the great pink-stoned city, whispering among themselves, because dead cities have a way of making you want to whisper, to watch the sun go down.

"In about five days," said Dad quietly, "I'll go back down to where our rocket was and collect the food hidden in the ruins there and bring it here; and I'll hunt for Bert Edwards and his wife and daughters there."

"Daughters?" asked Timothy. "How many?"

"I can see that'll cause trouble later." Mom nodded slowly.

"Girls." Michael made a face like an ancient Martian stone image. "Girls."

"Are they coming in a rocket too?"

"Yes. If they make it. Family rockets are made for travel to the Moon, not Mars. We were lucky we got through."

"Where did you get the rocket?" whispered Timothy, for the other boys were running ahead.

"I saved it. I saved it for twenty years, Tim. I had it hidden away, hoping I'd never have to use it. I suppose I should have given it to the government for the war, but I kept thinking about Mars. . . ."

"And a picnic?"

"Right. This is between you and me. When I saw everything was finishing on Earth, after I'd waited until the last moment, I packed us up. Bert Edwards had a ship hidden, too, but we decided it would be safer to take off separately, in case anyone tried to shoot us down."

"Why'd you blow up the rocket, Dad?"

"So we can't go back, ever. And so if any of those evil men ever come to Mars they won't know we're here."

"Is that why you looked up all the time?"

"Yes, it's silly. They won't follow us, ever. They haven't anything to follow with. I'm being too careful, is all."

Michael came running back. "Is this really *our* city, Dad?"

"The whole darn planet belongs to us, kids. The whole darn planet."

They stood there, King of the Hill, Top of the Heap, Ruler of All They Surveyed, Unimpeachable Monarchs and Presidents, trying to understand what it meant to own a world and how big a world really was.

Night came quickly in the thin atmosphere, and Dad left them in the square by the pulsing fountain, went down to the boat, and came walking back carrying a stack of paper in his big hands.

He laid the papers in a clutter in an old courtyard and set them afire. To keep warm, they crouched around the blaze and laughed, and Timothy saw the little letters leap like frightened animals when the flames touched and engulfed them. The papers crinkled like an old man's skin, and the cremation surrounded innumerable words:

"GOVERNMENT BONDS; Business Graph, 1999; Religious Prejudice: An Essay; The Science of Logistics; Problems of the Pan-American Unity; Stock Report for July 3, 1998; The War Digest . . ."

Dad had insisted on bringing these papers for this purpose. He sat there and fed them into the fire, one by one, with satisfaction, and told his children what it all meant.

"It's time I told you a few things. I don't suppose it was fair, keeping so much from you. I don't know if you'll understand, but I have to talk, even if only part of it gets over to you."

He dropped a leaf in the fire.

"I'm burning a way of life, just like that way of life is being burned clean off Earth right now. Forgive me if I talk like a politician. I am, after all, a former state governor, and I was honest and they hated me for it. Life on Earth never settled down to doing anything very good. Science ran too far ahead of us too quickly, and the people got lost in a mechanical wilderness, like children making over pretty things, gadgets, helicopters, rockets; emphasizing the wrong items, emphasizing machines instead of how to run the machines. Wars got bigger and bigger and finally killed Earth. That's what the silent radio means. That's what we ran away from.

"We were lucky. There aren't any more rockets left. It's time you knew this isn't a fishing trip at all. I put off telling you. Earth is gone. Interplanetary travel won't be back for centuries, maybe never. But that way of life proved itself wrong, and strangled itself with its own hands. You're young. I'll tell you this again every day until it sinks in."

He paused to feed more papers to the fire.

"Now we're alone. We and a handful of others who'll land in a few days. Enough to start over. Enough to turn away from all that back on Earth and strike out on a new line—"

The fire leaped up to emphasize his talking. And then all the papers

238

were gone except one. All the laws and beliefs of Earth were burnt into small hot ashes which soon would be carried off in a wind.

Timothy looked at the last thing that Dad tossed in the fire. It was a map of the World, and it wrinkled and distorted itself hotly and went —flimpf—and was gone like a warm, black butterfly. Timothy turned away.

"Now I'm going to show you the Martians," said Dad. "Come on, all of you. Here, Alice." He took her hand.

Michael was crying loudly, and Dad picked him up and carried him, and they walked down through the ruins toward the canal.

The canal. Where tomorrow or the next day their future wives would come up in a boat, small laughing girls now, with their father and mother.

The night came down around them, and there were stars. But Timothy couldn't find Earth. It had already set. That was something to think about.

A night bird called among the ruins as they walked. Dad said, "Your mother and I will try to teach you. Perhaps we'll fail. I hope not. We've had a good lot to see and learn from. We planned this trip years ago, before you were born. Even if there hadn't been a war we would have come to Mars, I think, to live and form our own standard of living. It would have been another century before Mars would have been really poisoned by the Earth civilization. Now, of course—"

They reached the canal. It was long and straight and cool and wet and reflective in the night.

"I've always wanted to see a Martian," said Michael. "Where are they, Dad? You promised."

"There they are," said Dad, and he shifted Michael on his shoulder and pointed straight down.

The Martians were there. Timothy began to shiver.

The Martians were there—in the canal—reflected in the water. Timothy and Michael and Robert and Mom and Dad.

The Martians stared back up at them for a long, long silent time from the rippling water. . . .

Technical Error

Arthur C. Clarke (1917-   )

2001. Childhood's End. The City and the Stars. The Deep Range. A Fall of Moondust. Prelude to Space. Rendezvous with Rama. *The achievements of Arthur C. Clarke are synonymous with some of the most important milestones in the history of science fiction. Like Isaac Asimov, he was trained in science and wrote a number of important nonfiction works that had a great impact on mass audiences, especially* The Exploration of Space *(1952).*

A fine short-story writer, he emerged after World War II in the British and American magazines with stories like "Breaking Strain" (1949), "Loophole" (1946), "The Wall of Darkness" (1949), and the classic "History Lesson" (1949).

Science fiction spread beyond the confines of the United States in the forties with magazines appearing (often for only a few issues) in the Netherlands, Sweden, Argentina, Mexico, and Great Britain. New Worlds, *which two decades later was to usher in the "New Wave," began publication in England in the mid-forties. "Technical Error" was an all-British product, appearing in the short-lived* Fantasy *in 1946.*

From *Fantasy   1946*

It was one of those accidents for which no one could be blamed. Richard Nelson had been in and out of the generator pit a dozen times, taking temperature readings to make sure that the unearthly chill of liquid helium was not seeping through the insulation. This was the first generator in the world to use the principle of superconductivity. The windings of the immense stator had been immersed in a helium bath, and the miles of wire now had a resistance too small to be measured by any means known to man.

Nelson noted with satisfaction that the temperature had not fallen further than expected. The insulation was doing its work; it would be safe to lower the rotor into the pit. That thousand-ton cylinder was now hanging fifty feet above Nelson's head, like the business end of a mammoth drop hammer. He and everyone else in the power station would feel much happier when it had been lowered onto its bearings and keyed into the turbine shaft.

Nelson put away his notebook and started to walk toward the ladder. At the geometric center of the pit, he made his appointment with destiny.

The load on the power network had been steadily increasing for the last hour, while the zone of twilight swept across the continent. As the last rays of sunlight faded from the clouds, the miles of mercury arcs along the great highways sprang into life. By the million, fluorescent tubes began to glow in the cities; housewives switched on their radio-cookers to prepare the evening meal. The needles of the megawatt-meters began to creep up the scales.

These were the normal loads. But on a mountain three hundred miles to the south a giant cosmic ray analyzer was being rushed into action to await the expected shower from the new supernova in Capricornus, which the astronomers had detected only an hour before. Soon the coils of its five-thousand-ton magnets began to drain their enormous currents from the thyratron converters.

A thousand miles to the west, fog was creeping toward the greatest airport in the hemisphere. No one worried much about fog, now, when every plane could land on its own radar in zero visibility, but it was nicer not to have it around. So the giant dispersers were thrown into operation, and nearly a thousand megawatts began to radiate into the night, coagulating the water droplets and clearing great swaths through the banks of mist.

The meters in the power station gave another jump, and the engineer on duty ordered the stand-by generators into action. He wished the big, new machine was finished; then there would be no more anxious hours like these. But he thought he could handle the load. Half an hour later the Meteorological Bureau put out a general frost warning over the radio. Within sixty seconds, more than a million electric fires were switched on in anticipation. The meters passed the danger mark and went on soaring.

With a tremendous crash three giant circuit breakers leaped from their contacts. Their arcs died under the fierce blast of the helium jets.

Three circuits had opened—but the fourth breaker had failed to clear. Slowly, the great copper bars began to glow cherry-red. The acrid smell of burning insulation filled the air and molten metal dripped heavily to the floor below, solidifying at once on the concrete slabs. Suddenly the conductors sagged as the load ends broke away from their supports. Brilliant green arcs of burning copper flamed and died as the circuit was broken. The free ends of the enormous conductors fell perhaps ten feet before crashing into the equipment below. In a fraction of a second they had welded themselves across the lines that led to the new generator.

Forces greater than any yet produced by man were at war in the windings of the machine. There was no resistance to oppose the current, but the inductance of the tremendous windings delayed the moment of peak intensity. The current rose to a maximum in an immense surge that lasted several seconds. At that instant, Nelson reached the center of the pit.

Then the current tried to stabilize itself, oscillating wildly between narrower and narrower limits. But it never reached its steady state; somewhere, the overriding safety devices came into operation and the circuit that should never have been made was broken again. With a last dying spasm, almost as violent as the first, the current swiftly ebbed away. It was all over.

When the emergency lights came on again, Nelson's assistant walked to the lip of the rotor pit. He didn't know what had happened, but it must have been serious. Nelson, fifty feet down, must have been wondering what it was all about.

"Hello, Dick!" he shouted. "Have you finished? We'd better see what the trouble is."

There was no reply. He leaned over the edge of the great pit and peered into it. The light was very bad, and the shadow of the rotor made it difficult to see what was below. At first it seemed that the pit was empty, but that was ridiculous; he had seen Nelson enter it only a few minutes ago. He called again.

"Hello! You all right, Dick?"

Again no reply. Worried now, the assistant began to descend the ladder. He was halfway down when a curious noise, like a toy balloon bursting very far away, made him look over his shoulder. Then he saw Nelson, lying at the center of the pit on the temporary woodwork covering the turbine shaft. He was very still, and there seemed something altogether wrong about the angle at which he was lying.

Ralph Hughes, chief physicist, looked up from his littered desk as the door opened. Things were slowly returning to normal after the night's disasters. Fortunately, the trouble had not affected his department much, for the generator was unharmed. He was glad he was not the

243

chief engineer: Murdock would still be snowed under with paperwork. The thought gave Dr. Hughes considerable satisfaction.

"Hello, Doc," he greeted the visitor. "What brings you here? How's your patient getting on?"

Dr. Sanderson nodded briefly. "He'll be out of hospital in a day or so. But I want to talk to you about him."

"I don't know the fellow—I never go near the plant, except when the Board goes down on its collective knees and asks me to. After all, Murdock's paid to run the place."

Sanderson smiled wryly. There was no love lost between the chief engineer and the brilliant young physicist. Their personalities were too different, and there was the inevitable rivalry between theoretical expert and "practical" man.

"I think this is up your street, Ralph. At any rate, it's beyond me. You've heard what happened to Nelson?"

"He was inside my new generator when the power was shot into it, wasn't he?"

"That's correct. His assistant found him suffering from shock when the power was cut off again."

"What kind of shock? It couldn't have been electric; the windings are insulated, of course. In any case, I gather that he was in the center of the pit when they found him."

"That's quite true. We don't know what happened. But he's now come round and seems none the worse—apart from one thing." The doctor hesitated a moment as if choosing his words carefully.

"Well, go on! Don't keep me in suspense!"

"I left Nelson as soon as I saw he would be quite safe, but about an hour later Matron called me up to say he wanted to speak to me urgently. When I got to the ward he was sitting up in bed looking at a newspaper with a very puzzled expression. I asked him what was the matter. He answered, 'Something's happened to me, Doc.' So I said, 'Of course it has, but you'll be out in a couple of days.' He shook his head; I could see there was a worried look in his eyes. He picked up the paper he had been looking at and pointed to it. 'I can't read any more,' he said.

"I diagnosed amnesia and thought: This is a nuisance! Wonder what else he's forgotten? Nelson must have read my expression, for he went on to say, 'Oh, I still know the letters and words—but they're the wrong way round! I think something must have happened to my eyes.' He held up the paper again. 'This looks exactly as if I'm seeing it in a mirror,' he said. 'I can spell out each word separately, a letter at a time. Would you get me a looking glass? I want to try something.'

"I did. He held the paper to the glass and looked at the reflection. Then he started to read aloud, at normal speed. But that's a trick anyone can learn—compositors have to do it with type—and I wasn't impressed. On the other hand, I couldn't see why an intelligent fellow like Nelson should put over an act like that. So I decided to humor him, thinking the shock must have given his mind a bit of a twist. I felt quite certain he was suffering from some delusion, though he seemed perfectly normal.

"After a moment he put the paper away and said, 'Well, Doc, what do you make of that?' I didn't know quite what to say without hurting his feelings, so I passed the buck and said, 'I think I'll have to hand you over to Dr. Humphries, the psychologist. It's rather outside my province.' Then he made some remark about Dr. Humphries and his intelligence tests, from which I gathered he had already suffered at his hands."

"That's correct," interjected Hughes. "All the men are grilled by the Psychology Department before they join the company. All the same, it's surprising what gets through," he added thoughtfully.

Dr. Sanderson smiled, and continued his story.

"I was getting up to leave when Nelson said, 'Oh, I almost forgot. I think I must have fallen on my right arm. The wrist feels badly sprained.' 'Let's look at it,' I said, bending to pick it up. 'No, the other arm,' Nelson said, and held up his left wrist. Still humoring him, I answered, 'Have it your own way. But you said your right one, didn't you?'

"Nelson looked puzzled. 'So what?' he replied. 'This *is* my right arm. My eyes may be queer, but there's no argument about that. There's my wedding ring to prove it. I've not been able to get the darned thing off for five years.'

"That shook me rather badly. Because you see, it was his left arm he was holding up, and his left hand that had the ring on it. I could see that what he said was quite true. The ring would have to be cut to get it off again. So I said, 'Have you any distinctive scars?' He answered, 'Not that I can remember.'

" 'Any dental fillings?' "

" 'Yes, quite a few.' "

"We sat looking at each other in silence while a nurse went to fetch Nelson's records. 'Gazed at each other with a wild surmise' is just about how a novelist might put it. Before the nurse returned, I was seized with a bright idea. It was a fantastic notion, but the whole affair was becoming more and more outrageous. I asked Nelson if I could see the things he had been carrying in his pockets. Here they are."

Dr. Sanderson produced a handful of coins and a small, leather-bound diary. Hughes recognized the latter at once as an Electrical Engineer's Diary; he had one in his own pocket. He took it from the doctor's hand and flicked it open at random, with that slightly guilty feeling one always has when a stranger's—still more, a friend's—diary falls into one's hands.

And then, for Ralph Hughes, it seemed that the foundations of his world were giving way. Until now he had listened to Dr. Sanderson with some detachment, wondering what all the fuss was about. But now the incontrovertible evidence lay in his own hands, demanding his attention and defying his logic.

For he could read not one word of Nelson's diary. Both the print and the handwriting were inverted, as if seen in a mirror.

Dr. Hughes got up from his chair and walked rapidly around the room several times. His visitor sat silently watching him. On the fourth circuit he stopped at the window and looked out across the lake, overshadowed by the immense white wall of the dam. It seemed to reassure him, and he turned to Dr. Sanderson again.

"You expect me to believe that Nelson has been laterally inverted in some way, so that his right and left sides have been interchanged?"

"I don't expect you to believe anything. I'm merely giving you the evidence. If you can draw any other conclusion I'd be delighted to hear it. I might add that I've checked Nelson's teeth. All the fillings have been transposed. Explain that away if you can. Those coins are rather interesting, too."

Hughes picked them up. They included a shilling, one of the beautiful new, beryl-copper crowns, and a few pence and halfpence. He would have accepted them as change without hesitation. Being no more observant than the next man, he had never noticed which way the Queen's head looked. But the lettering—Hughes could picture the consternation at the Mint if these curious coins ever came to its notice. Like the diary, they too had been laterally inverted.

Dr. Sanderson's voice broke into his reverie.

"I've told Nelson not to say anything about this. I'm going to write a full report; it should cause a sensation when it's published. But we want to know how this has happened. As you are the designer of the new machine, I've come to you for advice."

Dr. Hughes did not seem to hear him. He was sitting at his desk with his hands outspread, little fingers touching. For the first time in his life he was thinking seriously about the difference between left and right.

Dr. Sanderson did not release Nelson from hospital for several days, during which he was studying his peculiar patient and collecting material for his report. As far as he could tell, Nelson was perfectly normal, apart from his inversion. He was learning to read again, and his progress was swift after the initial strangeness had worn off. He would probably never again use tools in the same way that he had done before the accident; for the rest of his life, the world would think him left-handed. However, that would not handicap him in any way.

Dr. Sanderson had ceased to speculate about the cause of Nelson's condition. He knew very little about electricity; that was Hughes's job.

He was quite confident that the physicist would produce the answer in due course; he had always done so before. The company was not a philanthropic institution, and it had good reason for retaining Hughes's services. The new generator, which would be running within a week, was his brain-child, though he had had little to do with the actual engineering details.

Dr. Hughes himself was less confident. The magnitude of the problem was terrifying; for he realized, as Sanderson did not, that it involved utterly new regions of science. He knew that there was only one way in which an object could become its own mirror image. But how could so fantastic a theory be proved?

He had collected all available information on the fault that had energized the great armature. Calculations had given an estimate of the currents that had flowed through the coils for the few seconds they had been conducting. But the figures were largely guesswork; he wished he could repeat the experiment to obtain accurate data. It would be amusing to see Murdock's face if he said, "Mind if I throw a perfect short across generators One to Ten sometime this evening?" No, that was definitely out.

It was lucky he still had the working model. Tests on it had given some ideas of the field produced at the generator's center, but their magnitudes were a matter of conjecture. They must have been enormous. It was a miracle that the windings had stayed in their slots. For nearly a month Hughes struggled with his calculations and wandered through regions of atomic physics he had carefully avoided since he left the university. Slowly the complete theory began to evolve in his mind; he was a long way from the final proof, but the road was clear. In another month he would have finished.

The great generator itself, which had dominated his thoughts for the past year, now seemed trivial and unimportant. He scarcely bothered to acknowledge the congratulations of his colleagues when it passed its final tests and began to feed its millions of kilowatts into the system. They must have thought him a little strange, but he had always been regarded as somewhat unpredictable. It was expected of him; the company would have been disappointed if its tame genius possessed no eccentricities.

A fortnight later, Dr. Sanderson came to see him again. He was in a grave mood.

"Nelson's back in the hospital," he announced. "I was wrong when I said he'd be O.K."

"What's the matter with him?" asked Hughes in surprise.

"He's starving to death."

"Starving? What on earth do you mean?"

Dr. Sanderson pulled a chair up to Hughes's desk and sat down.

"I haven't bothered you for the past few weeks," he began, "because

I knew you were busy on your own theories. I've been watching Nelson carefully all this time, and writing up my report. At first, as I told you, he seemed perfectly normal. I had no doubt that everything would be all right.

"Then I noticed that he was losing weight. It was some time before I was certain of it; then I began to observe other, more technical symptoms. He started to complain of weakness and lack of concentration. He had all the signs of vitamin deficiency. I gave him special vitamin concentrates, but they haven't done any good. So I've come to have another talk with you."

Hughes looked baffled, then annoyed. "But hang it all, you're the doctor!"

"Yes, but this theory of mine needs some support. I'm only an unknown medico—no one would listen to me until it was too late. For Nelson is dying, and I think I know why. . . ."

Sir Robert had been stubborn at first, but Dr. Hughes had had his way, as he always did. The members of the Board of Directors were even now filing into the conference room, grumbling and generally making a fuss about the extraordinary general meeting that had just been called. Their perplexity was still further increased when they heard that Hughes was going to address them. They all knew the physicist and his reputation, but he was a scientist and they were businessmen. What was Sir Robert planning?

Dr. Hughes, the cause of all the trouble, felt annoyed with himself for being nervous. His opinion of the Board of Directors was not flattering, but Sir Robert was a man he could respect, so there was no reason to be afraid of them. It was true that they might consider him mad, but his past record would take care of that. Mad or not, he was worth thousands of pounds to them.

Dr. Sanderson smiled encouragingly at him as he walked into the conference room. The smile was not very successful, but it helped. Sir Robert had just finished speaking. He picked up his glasses in that nervous way he had, and coughed deprecatingly. Not for the first time, Hughes wondered how such an apparently timid old man could rule so vast a commercial empire.

"Well, here is Dr. Hughes, gentlemen. He will—ahem—explain everything to you. I have asked him not to be too technical. You are at liberty to interrupt him if he ascends into the more rarefied stratosphere of higher mathematics. Dr. Hughes . . ."

Slowly at first, and then more quickly as he gained the confidence of his audience, the physicist began to tell his story. Nelson's diary drew a gasp of amazement from the Board, and the inverted coins proved fascinating curiosities. Hughes was glad to see that he had aroused the interest of his listeners. He took a deep breath and made the plunge he had been fearing.

"You have heard what has happened to Nelson, gentlemen, but what I am going to tell you now is even more startling. I must ask you for your very close attention."

He picked up a rectangular sheet of notepaper from the conference table, folded it along a diagonal and tore it along the fold.

"Here we have two right-angled triangles with equal sides. I lay them on the table—so." He placed the paper triangles side by side on the table, with their hypotenuses touching, so that they formed a kite-shaped figure. "Now, as I have arranged them, each triangle is the mirror image of the other. You can imagine that the plane of the mirror is along the hypotenuse. This is the point I want you to notice. As long as I keep the triangles in the plane of the table, I can slide them around as much as I like, but I can never place one so that it exactly covers the other. Like a pair of gloves, they are not interchangeable although their dimensions are identical."

He paused to let that sink in. There were no comments, so he continued.

"Now, if I pick up one of the triangles, turn it over in the air and put it down again, the two are no longer mirror images, but have become completely identical—so." He suited the action to the words. "This may seem very elementary; in fact, it is so. But it teaches us one very important lesson. The triangles on the table were flat objects, restricted to two dimensions. To turn one into its mirror image I had to lift it up and rotate it in the third dimension. Do you see what I am driving at?"

He glanced round the table. One or two of the directors nodded slowly in dawning comprehension.

"Similarly, to change a solid, three-dimensional body, such as a man, into its analogue or mirror image, it must be rotated in a fourth dimension. I repeat—a fourth dimension."

There was a strained silence. Someone coughed, but it was a nervous, not a skeptical cough.

"Four-dimensional geometry, as you know"—he'd be surprised if they did—"has been one of the major tools of mathematics since before the time of Einstein. But until now it has always been a mathematical fiction, having no real existence in the physical world. It now appears that the unheard-of currents, amounting to millions of amperes, which flowed momentarily in the windings of our generator must have produced a certain extension into four dimensions, for a fraction of a second and in a volume large enough to contain a man. I have been making some calculations and have been able to satisfy myself that a 'hyperspace' about ten feet on a side was, in fact, generated: a matter of some ten thousand quartic—not cubic!—feet. Nelson was occupying that space. The sudden collapse of the field when the circuit was broken caused the rotation of the space, and Nelson was inverted.

"I must ask you to accept this theory, as no other explanation fits the facts. I have the mathematics here if you wish to consult them."

He waved the sheets in front of his audience, so that the directors could see the imposing array of equations. The technique worked—it always did. They cowered visibly. Only McPherson, the secretary, was made of sterner stuff. He had had a semi-technical education and still read a good deal of popular science, which he was fond of airing whenever he had the opportunity. But he was intelligent and willing to learn, and Dr. Hughes had often spent official time discussing some new scientific theory with him.

"You say that Nelson has been rotated in the Fourth Dimension; but I thought Einstein had shown that the Fourth Dimension was time."

Hughes groaned inwardly. He had been anticipating this red herring.

"I was referring to an additional dimension of space," he explained patiently. "By that I mean a dimension, or direction, at right-angles to our normal three. One can call it the Fourth Dimension if one wishes. With certain reservations, time may also be regarded as a dimension. As we normally regard space as three-dimensional, it is then customary to call time the Fourth Dimension. But the label is arbitrary. As I'm asking you to grant me four dimensions of space, we must call time the Fifth Dimension."

"Five Dimensions! Good Heavens!" exploded someone further down the table.

Dr. Hughes could not resist the opportunity. "Space of several million dimensions has been frequently postulated in sub-atomic physics," he said quietly.

There was a stunned silence. No one, not even McPherson, seemed inclined to argue.

"I now come to the second part of my account," continued Dr. Hughes. "A few weeks after his inversion we found that there was something wrong with Nelson. He was taking food normally, but it didn't seem to nourish him properly. The explanation has been given by Dr. Sanderson, and leads us into the realms of organic chemistry. I'm sorry to be talking like a textbook, but you will soon realize how vitally important this is to the company. And you also have the satisfaction of knowing that we are now all on equally unfamiliar territory."

That was not quite true, for Hughes still remembered some fragments of his chemistry. But it might encourage the stragglers.

"Organic compounds are composed of atoms of carbon, oxygen and hydrogen, with other elements, arranged in complicated ways in space. Chemists are fond of making models of them out of knitting needles and colored plasticine. The results are often very pretty and look like works of advanced art.

"Now, it is possible to have two organic compounds containing identical numbers of atoms, arranged in such a way that one is the mirror image of the other. They're called stereo-isomers, and are very common among the sugars. If you could set their molecules side by side, you would see that they bore the same sort of relationship as a right and left glove. They are, in fact, called right- or left-handed—dextro or laevo—compounds. I hope this is quite clear."

Dr. Hughes looked around anxiously. Apparently it was.

"Stereo-isomers have almost identical chemical properties," he went on, "though there are subtle differences. In the last few years, Dr. Sanderson tells me, it has been found that certain essential foods, including the new class of vitamins discovered by Professor Vandenburg, have properties depending on the arrangement of their atoms in space. In other words, gentlemen, the left-handed compounds might be essential for life, but the right-handed ones would be of no value. This in spite of the fact that their chemical formulae are identical.

"You will appreciate, now, why Nelson's inversion is much more serious than we at first thought. It's not merely a matter of teaching him to read again, in which case—apart from its philosophical interest —the whole business would be trivial. He is actually starving to death in the midst of plenty, simply because he can no more assimilate certain molecules of food than we can put our right foot into a left boot.

"Dr. Sanderson has tried an experiment which has proved the truth of this theory. With very great difficulty, he has obtained the stereo-isomers of many of these vitamins. Professor Vandenburg himself synthesized them when he heard of our trouble. They have already produced a very marked improvement in Nelson's condition."

Hughes paused and drew out some papers. He thought he would give the Board time to prepare for the shock. If a man's life were not at stake, the situation would have been very amusing. The Board was going to be hit where it would hurt most.

"As you will realize, gentlemen, since Nelson was injured—if you can call it that—while he was on duty, the company is liable to pay for any treatment he may require. We have found that treatment, and you may wonder why I have taken so much of your time telling you about it. The reason is very simple. The production of the necessary stereo-isomers is almost as difficult as the extraction of radium—more so, in some cases. Dr. Sanderson tells me that it will cost over five thousand pounds a day to keep Nelson alive."

The silence lasted for half a minute; then everyone started to talk at once. Sir Robert pounded on the table, and presently restored order. The council of war had begun.

Three hours later, an exhausted Hughes left the conference room and went in search of Dr. Sanderson, whom he found fretting in his office.

"Well, what's the decision?" asked the doctor.

"What I was afraid of. They want me to re-invert Nelson."

"Can you do it?"

"Frankly, I don't know. All I can hope to do is to reproduce the conditions of the original fault as accurately as I can."

"Weren't there any other suggestions?"

"Quite a few, but most of them were stupid. McPherson had the best idea. He wanted to use the generator to invert normal food so that Nelson could eat it. I had to point out that to take the big machine out of action for this purpose would cost several millions a year, and in any case the windings wouldn't stand it more than a few times. So that scheme collapsed. Then Sir Robert wanted to know if you could guarantee there were no vitamins we'd overlooked, or that might still be undiscovered. His idea was that in spite of our synthetic diets we might not be able to keep Nelson alive after all."

"What did you say to that?"

"I had to admit it was a possibility. So Sir Robert is going to have a talk with Nelson. He hopes to persuade him to risk it; his family will be taken care of if the experiment fails."

Neither of the two men said anything for a few moments. Then Dr. Sanderson broke the silence.

"Now do you understand the sort of decision a surgeon often has to make?" he said.

Hughes nodded in agreement. "It's a beautiful dilemma, isn't it? A perfectly healthy man, but it will cost two millions a year to keep him alive, and we can't even be sure of that. I know the Board's thinking of its precious balance sheet more than anything else, but I don't see any alternative. Nelson will have to take a chance."

"Couldn't you make some tests first?"

"Impossible. It's a major engineering operation to get the rotor out. We'll have to rush the experiment through when the load on the system is at minimum. Then we'll slam the rotor back, and tidy up the mess our artificial short has made. All this has to be done before the peak loads come on again. Poor old Murdock's mad as hell about it."

"I don't blame him. When will the experiment start?"

"Not for a few days, at least. Even if Nelson agrees, I've got to fix up all my gear."

No one was ever to know what Sir Robert said to Nelson during the hours they were together. Dr. Hughes was more than half prepared for it when the telephone rang and the Old Man's tired voice said, "Hughes? Get your equipment ready. I've spoken to Murdock, and we've fixed the time for Tuesday night. Can you manage by then?"

"Yes, Sir Robert."

"Good. Give me a progress report every afternoon until Tuesday. That's all."

The enormous room was dominated by the great cylinder of the rotor, hanging thirty feet above the gleaming plastic floor. A little group of men stood silently at the edge of the shadowed pit, waiting patiently. A maze of temporary wiring ran to Dr. Hughes's equipment —multibeam oscilloscopes, megawattmeters and microchronometers, and the special relays that had been constructed to make the circuit at the calculated instant.

That was the greatest problem of all. Dr. Hughes had no way of telling when the circuit should be closed; whether it should be when the voltage was at maximum, when it was at zero, or at some intermediate point on the sine wave. He had chosen the simplest and safest course. The circuit would be made at zero voltage; when it opened again would depend on the speed of the breakers.

In ten minutes the last of the great factories in the service area would be closing down for the night. The weather forecast had been favorable; there would be no abnormal loads before morning. By then, the rotor had to be back and the generator running again. Fortunately, the unique method of construction made it easy to reassemble the machine, but it would be a very close thing and there was no time to lose.

When Nelson came in, accompanied by Sir Robert and Dr. Sanderson, he was very pale. He might, thought Hughes, have been going to his execution. The thought was somewhat ill-timed, and he put it hastily aside.

There was just time enough for a last quite unnecessary check of the equipment. He had barely finished when he heard Sir Robert's quiet voice.

"We're ready, Dr. Hughes."

Rather unsteadily, he walked to the edge of the pit. Nelson had already descended, and as he had been instructed, was standing at its exact center, his upturned face a white blob far below. Dr. Hughes waved a brief encouragement and turned away, to rejoin the group by his equipment.

He flicked over the switch of the oscilloscope and played with the synchronizing controls until a single cycle of the main wave was stationary on the screen. Then he adjusted the phasing: two brilliant spots of light moved toward each other along the wave until they had coalesced at its geometric center. He looked briefly toward Murdock, who was watching the megawattmeters intently. The engineer nodded. With a silent prayer, Hughes threw the switch.

There was the tiniest click from the relay unit. A fraction of a second later, the whole building seemed to rock as the great conductors crashed over in the switch room three hundred feet away. The lights faded, and almost died. Then it was all over. The circuit breakers, driven at almost the speed of an explosion, had cleared the line again. The lights returned to normal and the needles of the megawattmeters dropped back onto their scales.

The equipment had withstood the overload. But what of Nelson?

Dr. Hughes was surprised to see that Sir Robert, for all his sixty years, had already reached the generator. He was standing by its edge, looking down into the great pit. Slowly, the physicist went to join him. He was afraid to hurry; a growing sense of premonition was filling his mind. Already he could picture Nelson lying in a twisted heap at the center of the well, his lifeless eyes staring up at them reproachfully. Then came a still more horrible thought. Suppose the field had collapsed too soon, when the inversion was only partly completed? In another moment, he would know the worst.

There is no shock greater than that of the totally unexpected, for against it the mind has no chance to prepare its defenses. Dr. Hughes was ready for almost anything when he reached the generator. Almost, but not quite . . .

He did not expect to find it completely empty.

What came after, he could never perfectly remember. Murdock seemed to take charge then. There was a great flurry of activity, and the engineers swarmed in to replace the giant rotor. Somewhere in the distance he heard Sir Robert saying, over and over again, "We did our best—we did our best." He must have replied, somehow, but everything was very vague. . . .

In the gray hours before the dawn, Dr. Hughes awoke from his fitful sleep. All night he had been haunted by his dreams, by weird fantasies of multi-dimensional geometry. There were visions of strange, otherworldly universes of insane shapes and intersecting planes along which he was doomed to struggle endlessly, fleeing from some nameless terror. Nelson, he dreamed, was trapped in one of those unearthly dimensions, and he was trying to reach him. Sometimes he was Nelson himself, and he imagined that he could see all around him the universe he knew, strangely distorted and barred from him by invisible walls.

The nightmare faded as he struggled up in bed. For a few moments he sat holding his head, while his mind began to clear. He knew what was happening; this was not the first time the solution of some baffling problem had come suddenly upon him in the night.

There was one piece still missing in the jigsaw puzzle that was sorting itself out in his mind. One piece only—and suddenly he had it. There was something that Nelson's assistant had said, when he was describing the original accident. It had seemed trivial at the time; until now, Hughes had forgotten all about it.

"When I looked inside the generator, there didn't seem to be anyone there, so I started to climb down the ladder. . . ."

What a fool he had been! Old McPherson had been right, or partly right, after all!

The field had rotated Nelson in the fourth dimension of space, but there had been a displacement in *time* as well. On the first occasion it had been a matter of seconds only. This time, the conditions must have been different in spite of all his care. There were so many unknown factors, and the theory was more than half guesswork.

Nelson had not been inside the generator at the end of the experiment. *But he would be.*

Dr. Hughes felt a cold sweat break out all over his body. He pictured that thousand-ton cylinder, spinning beneath the drive of its fifty million horse-power. Suppose something suddenly materialized in the space it already occupied . . . ?

He leaped out of bed and grabbed the private phone to the power station. There was no time to lose—the rotor would have to be removed at once. Murdock could argue later.

Very gently, something caught the house by its foundations and rocked it to and fro, as a sleepy child may shake its rattle. Flakes of plaster came planing down from the ceiling; a network of cracks appeared as if by magic in the walls. The lights flickered, became suddenly brilliant, and faded out.

Dr. Hughes threw back the curtain and looked toward the mountains. The power station was invisible beyond the foothills of Mount Perrin, but its site was clearly marked by the vast column of debris that was slowly rising against the bleak light of the dawn.

Memorial

Theodore Sturgeon (1918–   )

THEODORE *Sturgeon, along with Isaac Asimov, Robert A. Heinlein, and A. E. van Vogt, made the Golden Age golden. He did this with (among others) "Killdozer" (1944), "Mewhu's Jet" (1946), "Microcosmic God" (1941), "Thunder and Roses" (1947), and "Tiny and the Monster" (1947). The critics say that he explores the meaning of love in his stories, but in reality he deals with all the emotions that make us human. Up until the mid-sixties he was the most widely anthologized author in science fiction. Although Sturgeon is "alive and well" at the present time, he has been far too quiet for such an immense talent. We hope that this represents the quiet before a storm of stories.*

"Memorial" was one of the first post-Hiroshima stories and, as such, marked an important stage in the history of forties science fiction. The years from 1946 to 1949 (and beyond) were to feature numerous atomic warning and mutation stories reflecting the fears of a world confronted for the first time by the possibility of planetary annihilation. The haunting tone of "Memorial" is typical of these stories, a tone that characterizes that tragic and pessimistic strand that runs through so much of modern science fiction.

From *Astounding Science Fiction   1946*

The Pit, in A.D. 5000, had changed little over the centuries. Still it was an angry memorial to the misuse of great power; and because of it, organized warfare was a forgotten thing. Because of it, the world was free of the wasteful smoke and dirt of industry. The scream and crash of bombs and the soporific beat of marching feet were never heard, and at long last the earth was at peace.

To go near The Pit was slow, certain death, and it was respected and feared, and would be for centuries more. It winked and blinked redly at night, and was surrounded by a bald and broken tract stretching out and away over the horizon; and around it flickered a ghostly blue glow. Nothing lived there. Nothing could.

With such a war memorial, there could only be peace. The earth could never forget the horror that could be loosed by war.

That was Grenfell's dream.

Grenfell handed the typewritten sheet back. "That's it, Jack. My idea, and—I wish I could express it like that." He leaned back against the littered workbench, his strangely asymmetrical face quizzical. "Why is it that it takes a useless person to adequately express an abstract?"

Jack Roway grinned as he took back the paper and tucked it into his breast pocket. "Interestin' question, Grenfell, because this *is* your expression, the words *are* yours. Practically verbatim. I left out the 'er's' and 'Ah's' that you play conversational hopscotch with, and strung together all the effects you mentioned without mentioning any of the technological causes. Net result: you think I did it, when you did. You think it's good writing, and I don't."

"You don't?"

Jack spread his bony length out on the hard little cot. His relaxation was a noticeable act, like the unbuttoning of a shirt collar. His body seemed to unjoint itself a little. He laughed.

"Of course I don't. Much too emotional for my taste. I'm just a fumbling aesthete—useless, did you say? Mm-m-m—yeah. I suppose so." He paused reflectively. "You see, you cold-blooded characters, you scientists, are the true visionaries. Seems to me the essential difference between a scientist and an artist is that the scientist can mix his hope with patience. The scientist visualizes his ultimate goal, but pays little attention to it. He is all caught up with the achievement of the next step upward. The artist looks so far ahead that more often than not he can't see what's under his feet; so he falls flat on his face and gets called useless by scientists. But if you strip all of the intermediate steps away from the scientist's thinking, you have an artistic concept to which the scientist responds distantly and with surprise, giving some artist credit for being deeply perspicacious purely because the artist repeated something the scientist said."

"You amaze me," Grenfell said candidly. "You wouldn't be what you are if you weren't lazy and superficial. And yet you come out with things like that. I don't know that I understand what you just said. I'll have to think—but I do believe that you show all the signs of clear thinking. With a mind like yours, I can't understand why you don't use it to build something instead of wasting it in these casual interpretations of yours."

Jack Roway stretched luxuriously. "What's the use? There's more waste involved in the destruction of something which is already built than in dispersing the energy it would take to start building something. Anyway, the world is filled with builders—and destroyers. I'd just as soon sit by and watch, and feel things. I like my environment, Grenfell. I want to feel all I can of it, while it lasts. It won't last much longer. I want to touch all of it I can reach, taste of it, hear it, while there's time. What is around me, here and now, is what is important to me. The acceleration of human progress, and the increase of its mass—to use your own terms—are taking humanity straight to Limbo. You, with your work, think you are fighting humanity's inertia. Well, you are. But it's the kind of inertia called momentum. You command no force great enough to stop it, or even to change its course appreciably."

"I have sub-atomic power."

Roway shook his head, smiling. "That's not enough. No power is enough. It's just too late."

"That kind of pessimism does not affect me," said Grenfell. "You can gnaw all you like at my foundations, Jack, and achieve nothing more than the loss of your front teeth. I think you know that."

"Certainly I know that. I'm not trying to. I have nothing to sell, no one to change. I am even more impotent than you and your atomic power; and you are completely helpless. Uh—I quarrel with your use of the term 'pessimist,' though. I am nothing of the kind. Since I have resolved for myself the fact that humanity, as we know it, is finished, I'm quite resigned to it. Pessimism from me, under the circumstances, would be the pessimism of a photophobiac predicting that the sun would rise tomorrow."

Grenfell grinned. "I'll have to think about that, too. You're such a mass of paradoxes that turn out to be chains of reasoning. Apparently you live in a world in which scientists are poets and the grasshopper has it all over the ant."

"I always did think that ant was a stinker."

"Why do you keep coming here, Jack? What do you get out of it? Don't you realize I'm a criminal?"

Roway's eyes narrowed. "Sometimes I think you wish you were a criminal. The law says you are, and the chances are very strong that you'll be caught and treated accordingly. Ethically, you know you're not. It sort of takes the spice out of being one of the hunted."

"Maybe you're right," Grenfell said thoughtfully. He sighed. "It's so completely silly. During the war years, the skills I had were snatched up and the government flogged me into the Manhattan Project, expecting, and getting, miracles. I have never stopped working along the same lines. And now the government has changed the laws, and pulled legality from under me."

"Hardly surprising. The government deals rather severely with soldiers who go on killing other soldiers after the war is over." He held up a hand to quell Grenfell's interruption. "I know you're not killing anyone, and are working for the opposite result, I was only pointing out that it's the same switcheroo. We the people," he said didactically, "have, in our sovereign might, determined that no atomic research be done except in government laboratories. We have then permitted our politicians to allow so little for maintenance of those laboratories— unlike our overseas friends—that no really exhaustive research can be done in them. We have further made it a major offense to operate such a bootleg lab as yours." He shrugged. "Comes the end of mankind. We'll get walloped first. If we put more money and effort into nuclear research than any other country, some other country would get walloped first. If we last another hundred years—which seems doubtful— some poor, spavined, underpaid government researcher will stumble on the aluminum-isotope space-heating system you have already perfected."

"That was a little rough," said Grenfell bitterly. "Driving me underground just in time to make it impossible for me to announce it. What a waste of time and energy it is to heat homes and buildings the way they do now! Space heating—the biggest single use for heat-energy— and I have the answer to it over there." He nodded toward a compact cube of lead-alloys in the corner of the shop. "Build it into a foundation, and you have controllable heat for the life of the building, with not a cent for additional fuel and practically nothing for maintenance." His jaw knotted. "Well, I'm glad it happened that way."

"Because it got you started on your war memorial— The Pit? Yeah. Well, all I can say is, I hope you're right. It hasn't been possible to scare humanity yet. The invention of gunpowder was going to stop war, and didn't. Likewise the submarine, the torpedo, the airplane, that two-by-four bomb they pitched at Hiroshima, and the H-bomb."

"None of that applies to The Pit," said Grenfell. "You're right; humanity hasn't been scared off war yet; but the H-bomb rocked 'em back on their heels. My little memorial is the real stuff. I'm not depending on a fission or fusion effect, you know, with a release of one-tenth of one percent of the energy of the atom. I'm going to transmute it completely, and get all the energy there is in it, and in all matter the fireball touches. And it'll be *more* than a thousand times as powerful as the Hiroshima bomb, because I'm going to use twelve times as much explosive; and it's going off on the ground, not a hundred and fifty feet above it." Grenfell's brow, over suddenly hot eyes, began to shine with sweat. "And then—The Pit," he said softly. "The war memorial to end war, and all other war memorials. A vast pit, alive with bubbling lava, radiating death for ten thousand years. A living reminder of the devastation mankind has prepared for itself. Out here on the desert, where there are no cities, where the land has always been useless, will be the scene of the most useful thing in the history of the race—a never-ending sermon, a warning, an example of the dreadful antithesis of peace." His voice shook to a whisper, and faded.

"Sometimes," said Roway, "you frighten me, Grenfell. It occurs to me that I am such a studied sensualist, tasting everything I can, because I am afraid to feel any one thing that much." He shook himself, or shuddered. "You're a fanatic, Grenfell. Hyperemotional. A monomaniac. I hope you can do it."

"I can do it," said Grenfell.

Two months passed, and in those two months Grenfell's absorption in his work had been forced aside by the increasing pressure of current events. Watching a band of vigilantes riding over the waste to the south of his little buildings one afternoon, he thought grimly of what Roway had said. "Sometimes I think you wish you were a criminal." Roway, the sensualist, would say that. Roway would appreciate the taste of danger, in the same way that he appreciated all the other emotions. As it intensified, he would wait to savor it, no matter how bad it got.

Twice Grenfell shut off the instigating power of the boron-aluminum pile he had built, as he saw government helicopters hovering on the craggy skyline. He knew of hard-radiation detectors; he had developed two different types of them during the war; and he wanted no questions asked. His utter frustration at being unable to announce the success of his space-heating device, for fear that he would be punished as a criminal and his device impounded and forgotten—that frustration had been indescribable. It had canalized his mind, and intensified the devoted effort he had put forth for the things he believed in during the war. Every case of neural shock he encountered in men who had been hurt by war and despised it made him work harder on his monument— on The Pit. For if humans could be frightened by war, humanity could be frightened by The Pit.

And those he met who had been hurt by war and who still hated the late enemy—those who would have been happy to go back and kill some more, reckoning vital risk well worth it—those he considered mad, and forgot them.

So he could not stand another frustration. He was the center of his own universe, and he realized it dreadfully, and he had to justify his position there. He was a humanitarian, a philanthropist in the word's truest sense. He was probably as mad as any other man who has, through his own efforts, moved the world.

For the first time, then, he was grateful when Jack Roway arrived in his battered old convertible, although he was deliriously frightened at the roar of the motor outside his laboratory window. His usual reaction to Jack's advent was a mixture of annoyance and gratification, for it was a great deal of trouble to get out to his place. His annoyance was not because of the interruption, for Jack was certainly no trouble to have around. Grenfell suspected that Jack came out to see him partly to get the taste of the city out of his mouth, and partly to be able to feel superior to somebody he considered of worth.

But the increasing fear of discovery, and his race to complete his work before it was taken from him by a hysterical public, had had the unusual effect of making him lonely. For such a man as Grenfell to be lonely bordered on the extraordinary; for in his daily life there were simply too many things to be done. There had never been enough hours in a day nor days in a week to suit him, and he deeply resented the encroachments of sleep, which he considered a criminal waste.

"Roway!" he blurted, as he flung the door open, his tone so warm that Roway's eyebrows went up in surprise. "What dragged you out here?"

"Nothing in particular," said the writer, as they shook hands. "Nothing more than usual, which is a great deal. How goes it?"

"I'm about finished." They went inside, and as the door closed, Grenfell turned to face Jack. "I've been finished for so long I'm ashamed of myself," he said intently.

"Ha! Ardent confession so early in the day! What are you talking about?"

"Oh, there have been things to do," said Grenfell restlessly. "But I could go ahead with the . . . with the big thing at almost any time."

"You hate to be finished. You've never visualized what it would be like to have the job done." His teeth flashed. "You know, I've never heard a word from you as to what your plans are after the big noise. You going into hiding?"

"I . . . haven't thought much about it. I used to have a vague idea of broadcasting a warning and an explanation before I let go with the disruptive explosion. I've decided against it, though. In the first place, I'd be stopped within minutes, no matter how cautious I was with the transmitter. In the second place—well, this is going to be so big that it won't need any explanation."

"No one will know who did it, or why it was done."

"Is that necessary?" asked Grenfell quietly.

Jack's mobile face stilled as he visualized The Pit, spewing its ten-thousand-year hell. "Perhaps not," he said. "Isn't it necessary, though, to you?"

"To me?" asked Grenfell, surprised. "You mean, do I care if the world knows I did this thing, or not? No; of course I don't. A chain of circumstance is occurring, and it has been working through me. It goes directly to The Pit; The Pit will do all that is necessary from then on. I will no longer have any part in it."

Jack moved, clinking and splashing, around the sink in the corner of the laboratory. "Where's all your coffee? Oh—here. Uh . . . I have been curious about how much personal motive you had for your work. I think that answers it pretty well. I think, too, that you believe what you are saying. Do you know that people who do things for impersonal motives are as rare as fur on a fish?"

"I hadn't thought about it."

"I believe that, too. Sugar? And milk. I remember. And have you been listening to the radio?"

"Yes. I'm . . . a little upset, Jack," said Grenfell, taking the cup. "I don't know where to time this thing. I'm a technician, not a Machiavelli."

"Visionary, like I said. You don't know if you'll throw this gadget of yours into world history too soon or too late—is that it?"

"Exactly. Jack, the whole world seems to be going crazy. Even fusion bombs are too big for humanity to handle."

"What else can you expect," said Jack grimly, "with our dear friends across the water sitting over their push buttons waiting for an excuse to punch them?"

"And we have our own set of buttons, of course."

Jack Roway said: "We've got to defend ourselves."

"Are you kidding?"

Roway glanced at him, his dark brows plotting a V. "Not about this. I seldom kid about anything, but particularly not about this." And he—shuddered.

Grenfell stared amazedly at him and then began to chuckle. "Now," he said, "I've seen everything. My iconoclastic friend Jack Roway, of all people, caught up by a . . . a fashion. A national pastime, fostered by uncertainty and fed by yellow journalism—fear of the enemy."

"This country is not at war."

"You mean, we have no enemy? Are you saying that the gentlemen over the water, with their itching fingertips hovering about the push buttons, are not our enemies?"

"Well—"

Grenfell came across the room to his friend, and put a hand on his shoulder. "Jack—what's the matter? You can't be so troubled by the news—not *you!*"

Roway stared out at the brazen sun, and shook his head slowly. "International balance is too delicate," he said softly; and if a voice could glaze like eyes, his did. "I see the nations of the world as masses balanced each on its own mathematical point, each with its center of gravity directly above. But the masses are fluid, shifting violently away from the center lines. The opposing trends aren't equal; they can't cancel each other; the phasing is too slow. One or the other is going to topple, and then the whole works is going to go."

"But you've known that for a long time. You've known that ever since Hiroshima. Possibly before. Why should it frighten you now?"

"I didn't think it would happen so soon."

"Oh-ho! So that's it! You have suddenly realized that the explosion is going to come in your lifetime. Hm-m-m? And you can't take that. You're capable of all of your satisfying aesthetic rationalizations as long as you can keep the actualities at arm's length!"

"Whew!" said Roway, his irrepressible humor passing close enough to nod to him. "Keep it clean, Grenfell! Keep your . . . your sesquipedalian polysyllabics, for a scientific report."

"Touché!" Grenfell smiled. "Y'know, Jack, you remind me powerfully of some erstwhile friends of mine who write science-fiction. They had been living very close to atomic power for a long time—years before the man on the street—or the average politician, for that matter —knew an atom from Adam. Atomic power was handy to these specialized word-merchants because it gave them a limitless source of power for background to a limitless source of story material. In the heyday of the Manhattan Project, most of them suspected what was going on, some of them knew—some even worked on it. All of them were quite aware of the terrible potentialities of nuclear energy. Practically all of them were scared silly of the whole idea. They were afraid for humanity, but they themselves were not really afraid, except in a delicious drawing room sort of way, because they couldn't conceive of this Buck Rogers event happening to anything but posterity. But it happened, right smack in the middle of their own sacrosanct lifetimes.

"And I will be dog-goned if you're not doing the same thing. You've gotten quite a bang out of figuring out the doom humanity faces in an atomic war. You've consciously risen above it by calling it inevitable, and in the meantime leave us gather rosebuds before it rains. You thought you'd be safe home—dead—before the first drops fell. Now social progress has rolled up a thunderhead and you find yourself a mile from home with a crease in your pants and no umbrella. And you're scared!"

Roway looked at the floor and said, "It's so soon. It's so soon." He looked up at Grenfell, and his cheekbones seemed too large. He took a deep breath. "You . . . we can stop it, Grenfell."

"Stop what?"

"The war . . . the . . . this thing that's happening to us. The explosion that will come when the strains get too great in the international situation. And it's *got* to ge stopped!"

"That's what The Pit is for."

"The Pit!" Roway said scornfully. "I've called you a visionary before. Grenfell, you've got to be more practical! Humanity is not going to learn anything by example. It's got to be kicked and carved. Surgery."

Grenfell's eyes narrowed. "Surgery? What you said a minute ago about my stopping it . . . do you mean what I think you mean?"

"Don't you see it?" said Jack urgently. "What you have here—the total conversion of mass to energy—the peak of atomic power. One or two wallops with this, in the right place, and we can stop anybody."

"This isn't a weapon. I didn't make this to be a weapon."

"The first rock ever thrown by a prehistoric man wasn't made to be a weapon, either. But it was handy and it was effective, and it was certainly used because it had to be used." He suddenly threw up his hands in a despairing gesture. "You don't understand. Don't you realize that this country is likely to be attacked at any second—that diplomacy is now hopeless and helpless, and the whole world is just waiting for the thing to start? It's probably too late even now—but it's the least we can do."

"What, specifically, is the least thing we can do?"

"Turn your work over to the Defense Department. In a few hours the government can put it where it will do the most good." He drew his finger across his throat. "Anywhere we want to, over the ocean."

There was a taut silence. Roway looked at his watch and licked his lips. Finally Grenfell said, "Turn it over to the government. Use it for a weapon—and what for? To stop war?"

"Of course!" blurted Roway. "To show the rest of the world that our way of life . . . to scare the daylights out of . . . to—"

"*Stop it!*" Grenfell roared. "Nothing of the kind. You think—you hope anyway—that the use of total disruption as a weapon will stall off the inevitable—at least in your lifetime. Don't you?"

"No. I—"

"Don't you?"

"Well, I—"

"You have some more doggerel to write," said Grenfell scathingly. "You have some more blondes to chase. You want to go limp over a few more Bach fugues."

Jack Roway said: "No one knows where the first bomb might hit. It might be anywhere. There's nowhere I . . . we . . . can go to be safe." He was trembling.

"Are the people in the city quivering like that?" asked Grenfell.

"Riots," breathed Roway, his eyes bright with panic. "The radio won't announce anything about the riots."

"Is that what you came out here for today—to try to get me to give disruptive power to *any* government?"

Jack looked at him guiltily. "It was the only thing to do. I don't know if your bomb will turn the trick, but it has to be tried. It's the only thing left. We've got to be prepared to hit first, and hit harder than anyone else."

"No." Grenfell's one syllable was absolutely unshakable.

"Grenfell—I thought I could argue you into it. Don't make it tough for yourself. You've got to do it. Please do it on your own. Please, Grenfell." He stood up slowly.

"Do it on my own—or what? *Keep away from me!*"

"No . . . I—" Roway stiffened suddenly, listening. From far above and to the north came the whir of rotary wings. Roway's fear-slackened lips tightened into a grin, and with two incredibly swift strides he was across to Grenfell. He swept in a handful of the smaller man's shirt front and held him half off the floor.

"Don't try a thing," he gritted. There was not a sound then except their harsh breathing, until Grenfell said wearily: "There was somebody called Judas—"

"You can't insult me," said Roway, with a shade of his old cockiness, "and you're flattering yourself."

A helicopter sank into its own roaring dust-cloud outside the building. Men pounded out of it and burst in the door. There were three of them. They were not in uniform.

"Dr. Grenfell," said Jack Roway, keeping his grip, "I want you to meet—"

"Never mind that," said the tallest of the three in a brisk voice. "You're Roway? Hm-m-m. Dr. Grenfell, I understand you have a nuclear energy device on the premises."

"Why did you come by yourself?" Grenfell asked Roway softly. "Why not just send these stooges?"

"For you, strangely enough. I hoped I could argue you into giving the thing freely. You know what will happen if you resist?"

"I know." Grenfell pursed his lips for a moment, and then turned to the tall man. "Yes. I have some such thing here. Total atomic disruption. Is that what you were looking for?"

"Where is it?"

"Here, in the laboratory, and then there's the pile in the other building. You'll find—" He hesitated. "You'll find two samples of the concentrate. One's over there—" he pointed to a lead case on a shelf behind one of the benches. "And there's another like it in a similar case in the shed back of the pile building."

Roway sighed and released Grenfell. "Good boy. I knew you'd come through."

"Yes," said Grenfell. "Yes—"

"Go get it," said the tall man. One of the others broke away.

"It will take two men to carry it," said Grenfell in a shaken voice. His lips were white.

The tall man pulled out a gun and held it idly. He nodded to the second man. "Go get it. Bring it here and we'll strap the two together and haul 'em to the plane. Snap it up."

The two men went out toward the shed.

"Jack?"

"Yes, Doc."

"You really think humanity can be scared?"

"It will be—now. This thing will be used right."

"I hope so. Oh, I hope so," Grenfell whispered.

The men came back. "Up on the bench," said the leader, nodding toward the case the men carried between them.

As they climbed up on the bench and laid hands on the second case, to swing it down from the shelf, Jack Roway saw Grenfell's face spurt sweat, and a sudden horror swept over him.

"Grenfell!" he said hoarsely. "It's—"

"Of course," Grenfell whispered. "Critical mass."

When the two leaden cases came together, it let go.

It was like Hiroshima, but much bigger. And yet, that explosion did not create The Pit. It was the pile that did—the boron-aluminum lattice which Grenfell had so arduously pieced together from parts bootlegged over the years. Right there at the heart of the fission explosion, total disruption took place in the pile, for that was its function. This was slower. It took more than an hour for its hellish activity to reach a peak, and in that time a huge crater had been gouged out of the earth, a seething, spewing mass of volatilized elements, raw radiation, and incandescent gases. It was—The Pit. Its activity curve was plotted abruptly—up to peak in an hour and eight minutes, and then a gradual subsidence as it tried to feed further afield with less and less fueling effect, and as it consumed its own flaming wastes in an effort to reach inactivity. Rain would help to blanket it, through energy lost in volatilizing the drops; and each of the many elements involved went through its respective secondary radioactivity, and passed away its successive half-lives. The subsidence of The Pit would take between eight and nine thousand years.

And like Hiroshima, this explosion had effects which reached into history and into men's hearts in places far separated in time from the cataclysm itself.

These things happened:

The explosion could not be concealed; and there was too much hysteria afoot for anything to be confirmed. It was easier to run head-lines saying WE ARE ATTACKED. There was an instantaneous and panicky demand for reprisals, and the government acceded, because such "reprisals" suited the policy of certain members who could command emergency powers. And so the First Atomic War was touched off.

And the Second.

There were no more atomic wars after that. The Mutants' War was a barbarous affair, and the mutants defeated the tattered and largely sterile remnants of humanity, because the mutants were strong. And then the mutants died out because they were unfit. For a while there was some very interesting material to be studied on the effects of radiation on heredity, but there was no one to study it.

There were some humans left. The rats got most of them, after increasing in fantastic numbers; and there were three plagues.

After that there were half-stooping, naked things whose twisted heredity could have been traced to humankind; but these could be frightened, as individuals and as a race, so therefore they could not progress. They were certainly not human.

The Pit, in A.D. 5000, had changed little over the centuries. Still it was an angry memorial to the misuse of great power; and because of it, organized warfare was a forgotten thing. Because of it, the world was free of the wasteful smoke and dirt of industry. The scream and crash of bombs and the soporific beat of marching feet were never heard, and at long last the earth was at peace.

To go near The Pit was slow, certain death, and it was respected and feared, and would be for centuries more. It winked and blinked redly at night, and was surrounded by a bald and broken tract stretching out and away over the horizon; and around it flickered a ghostly blue glow. Nothing lived there. Nothing could.

With such a war memorial, there could only be peace. The earth could never forget the horror that could be loosed by war.

That was Grenfell's dream.

Letter to Ellen

Chandler Davis (1926-   )

CHAN DAVIS *has produced only a small number of science fiction stories during his writing career, but all of them are memorable. Perhaps his most notable story to date is the widely reprinted "Adrift on the Policy Level," which first appeared in* Star Science Fiction Stories Five *in the late fifties. A man of wide interests, Davis possesses a doctorate in mathematics from Harvard. Despite his training in the sciences, his stories have featured strong social extrapolation; indeed, the stories he published in* Astounding *during the mid-forties can be considered to be prototypes of fifties dystopian sf.*

Davis's personal life has had its dystopian moments as well. He was a victim of McCarthyism at a time when science fiction writers were selling stories attacking this black period in American life. He chose to fight his legal battle on the basis of the First rather than the Fifth Amendment, and he paid for it. He is one of the unsung heroes in the history of science fiction.

"Letter to Ellen" concerns androids, those thinking machines in human form that have for so long been used by sf writers to address issues of racism and discrimination. Here Davis uses the android to consider questions of human psychology, and he does so in a way every bit as moving as Lester del Rey's more famous "Helen O'Loy."

From *Astounding Science Fiction   1947*

Dear Ellen,

    By the time you get this you'll be wondering why I didn't call. It'll be the first time I've missed in—how long?—two months? A long two months it's been, and, for me, a very important two months.

I'm not going to call, and I'm not going to see you. Maybe I'm a coward writing this letter, but you can judge that when you've finished it. Judge that, and other things.

Let's see. I'd better begin at the beginning and tell the whole story right through. Do you remember my friend Roy Wisner? He came to work in the lab the same time I did, in the spring of '16, and he was still around when I first met you. Even if you never met him, you may have seen him; he was the tall blond guy with the stooped shoulders, working in the same branch with me.

Roy and I grew up together. He was my best friend as a kid, back almost as far as I can remember, back at the State Orphanage outside of Stockton. We went to different high schools, but when I got to Iowa U. there was Roy. Just to make the coincidence complete, he'd decided to be a biochemist too, and we took mostly the same courses all the way through. Both worked with Dietz while we were getting our doctorates, and Dietz got us identical jobs with Hartwell at the Pierne Labs here in Denver.

I've told you about that first day at the lab. We'd both heard from Dietz that the Pierne Labs were devoted now almost entirely to life-synthesis, and we'd both hoped to get in on that part of the work. What we hadn't realized was quite how far the work had got. I can tell you, the little talk old Hartwell gave us when he took us around to show us the lay of the land was just as inspiring as he meant it to be.

He showed us the wing where they're experimenting with the synthesis of new types of Coelenterates. We'd heard of that too, but seeing it was another thing. I remember particularly a rather ghastly green thing that floated in a small tank and occasionally sucked pieces of sea moss into what was half mouth, half sucker. Hartwell said, offhand, "Doesn't look much like the original, does it? That one was a mistake; something went wrong with the gene synthesis. But it turned out to be viable, so the fellows kept it around. Wouldn't be surprised if it could outsurvive some of its natural cousins if we were to give it a mate and turn it loose." He looked at the thing benignly. "I sort of like it."

Then we went down to Hartwell's branch, Branch 26, where we were to work. Hartwell slid back the narrow metal door and led the way into one of the labs. We started to follow him, but we hadn't gone more than three steps inside when we just stood still and gawked. I'd seen complicated apparatus before, but that place had anything at the Iowa labs beat by a factor one thousand. All the gear on one whole side of the lab—and it was a good-sized place—was black-coated against the light and other stray radiation in the room. I recognized most of the flasks and fractionating columns as airtight jobs. A good deal of the hookup was hidden from us, being under Gardner hoods, airtight, temperature-controlled, radiation-controlled, and everything-else-controlled. What heaters we could see were never burners, always infrared banks.

This was precision work. It had to be, because, as you know, Branch 26 synthesizes chordate genes.

Roy and I went over to take a closer look at some of the gear. We stopped about a meter away; meddling was distinctly not in order. The item we were looking at was what would be called, in a large-scale process, a reaction vat. It was a small, opaque-coated flask, and it was being revolved slowly by a mechanical agitator, to swirl the liquids inside. As we stood there we could barely feel the gentle and precise flow of heat from the infrared heaters banked around it. We watched it, fascinated.

Hartwell snapped us out of it. "The work here," he said dryly, "is carried out with a good deal of care. You've had some experience with full microanalysis, Dietz tells me."

"A little," I nodded, with very appropriate modesty.

"Well, this is microsynthesis, and microsynthesis with a vengeance. Remember, our problem here is on an entirely different level even from ordinary protein synthesis." (It staggered me a little to hear him refer to protein synthesis as ordinary!) "There you're essentially building up a periodic crystal, one in which the atoms are arranged in regularly recurrent patterns. This recursion, this periodicity, makes the structure of the molecule relatively simple; correspondingly, it simplifies the synthesis. In a gene, a virus, or any other of the complex proteinlike molecules there isn't any such frequent recursion. Instead, the radicles in your molecule chain are a little different each time; the pattern almost repeats, but not quite. You've got what you call an a-periodic crystal.

"When we synthesize such a crystal we've got to get all the little variations from the pattern just right, because it's those variations that give the structure enough complexity to be living."

He had some chromosome charts under his arm, and now he pulled one out to show to us. I don't know if you've ever seen the things; one of them alone fills a little booklet, in very condensed notation. Roy and I thumbed through one, recognizing a good many of the shorthand symbols but not understanding the scheme of the thing at all. When we got through we were pretty thoroughly awed.

Hartwell smiled. "You'll catch on, don't worry. The first few months, while you're studying up, you'll be my lab assistants. You won't be on your own until you've got the process down pretty near pat." And were we glad to hear that!

Roy and I got an apartment on the outside of town; I didn't have my copter then, so we had to be pretty close. It was a good place, though only one wall and the roof could be made transparent. We missed the morning sun that way, but I liked it all right. Downstairs lived Graham, our landlord, an old bachelor who spent most of his time on home photography, both movie wires and old-fashioned chemical prints. He got some candid angle shots of us that were so weird Roy was thinking of breaking his cameras.

At the lab we caught on fast enough. Roy was always a pretty bright boy, and I managed to keep up. After a reasonable period Hartwell began to ease himself out of our routine, until before we knew it we were running the show ourselves. Naturally, being just out of school, we began as soon as we got the drift of things to suggest changes in the process. The day Hartwell finally approved one of our bright ideas, we knew we were standing on our own feet. That's when the fun really began.

Some people laugh when I say "that kind of drudgery" is fun, but you're a biochemist yourself and I'm pretty sure you feel the same way. The mere thought that we were putting inert colloids in at one end and getting something out at the other end that was in some strange way *living*—that was enough to take the boredom out of the job, if there'd been any.

Because we always felt that it was in our lab and the others like it that nonlife ended and life began. Sure, before us there was the immense job of protein synthesis and colloid preparation. Sure, after we were through there was the last step, the ultramicrosurgery of putting the nuclear wall together around the chromatin and embedding the result in a cell. (I always half envied your branch that job.) But in between there was our stage of the thing, which we thought to be the crucial one.

Certainly it was a tough enough stage. The long, careful reactions, with temperatures regulated down to a hundredth of a degree and reaction time to a tenth of a second; and then the final reactions, with everything enclosed in Gardner hoods, where you build up, bit by bit, the living nucleoplasm around the almost-living chromosomes. Hartwell hadn't lied when he said the work was carried out with care! That was quite a plant for two young squirts like us to be playing around with.

Just to put an edge on it, of course, there was always the possibility that you'd do everything right and still misfire. Anywhere along the line, Heisenberg's Uncertainty Principle could shove a radicle out of place in those protein chains, no matter how careful you were. Then you'd get a weird thing: a gene mutating before it was even completed.

Or Heisenberg's Principle might pull you through even if your process had gone wrong!

We got curious after a while, Roy especially. Hartwell had told us a lot; one thing he hadn't told us was exactly *what we were making:* fish, flesh, or fowl, and we weren't geneticists enough to know ourselves. It would have been better, while we were working, to have had a mental picture of the frog or lizard or chicken that was to be our end product; instead, our mental picture was a composite of the three, and a rather disconcerting composite it made. I preferred to imagine a rabbit, or better yet, an Irish terrier puppy.

Hartwell not only hadn't offered to tell us, he didn't tell us when we asked him. "One of the lower chordates," he said; "the species name doesn't matter." That phrase "lower chordates" didn't ring quite true. There were enough chromosomes in our whatever-they-were's that they had to be something fairly far up the scale.

Roy immediately decided he was going to get the answer if he had to go through twenty books on genetics to do it. Looking back, I'm surprised I didn't have the same ambition. Maybe I was too interested in chess; I was on one of my periodic chess binges at the time. Anyhow, Roy got the genetics books and Roy did the digging.

It didn't take him any time at all. I remember that night well. He had brought home a stack of books from the library and was studying them at the desk in the corner. I was in the armchair with my portable chessboard, analyzing a game I'd lost in the last tournament. As the hours went by, I noticed Roy getting more and more restless; I expected him to come up with the answer any time, but apparently he was rechecking to make sure. About the time I'd found how I should have played to beat Fedruk, Roy got up, a little unsteadily.

"Dirk," he began, then stopped.

"You got it?"

"Dirk, I wonder if you realize just how few chordate species there are which have forty-eight chromosomes."

"Well, humans have, and I guess we're not so unique."

He didn't say anything.

"Hey, do you mean what I think you mean?" I jumped to my feet.

If he did, it was terrific news for me; I think I'd had the idea in the back of my mind all the time and never dared check it for fear I'd be proved wrong. Roy wasn't so happy about it. He said, "Yes, that's exactly what I mean. The species name Hartwell wouldn't tell us was *Homo sapiens*. We're making—robots."

That took a little time to digest. When I'd got it assimilated I came back, "What do you mean, robots? If we made a puppy that wagged its tail O.K., you'd be just as pleased as I would." (I was still stuck on that Irish terrier idea of mine.) "That wouldn't give you the shudders. Why do you get so worried just because it's men we're making?"

"It's not right," he said.

"What?" Roy never having been religious or anything, that sounded strange.

"Well, I take that back, I guess, but—" His voice trailed away; then, more normally, "I don't know, Dirk. I just can't see it. Making humans —what would you call them if not robots?"

"I'd call them men, doggone it, if they turn out right. Of course if they don't turn out right—maybe I could see your point. If they don't turn out right. Killing a freak chicken and killing an experimental baby that didn't quite—succeed—would be two different things. Yeah."

"I hadn't thought of that."

"Then what the heck *were* you thinking of?"

"Aw, I don't know." He went back to the desk, slammed his books shut.

"What's bothering you, Roy?"

He didn't answer, just went into his bedroom and shut the door. He didn't come out again that night.

The next morning he was grim-faced, but you could see he was excited underneath. I knew he was planning something. Finally I wormed it out of him: he was going to take a look around Branch 39 to try and find some human embryos, as confirmation. Branch 39, as you know, is one of the ones that shuts up at night; they don't have to have technicians around twenty-four hours a day as 26 does. Roy's plan was to go up there just before closing time, hide, and get himself locked in overnight.

I asked him why the secrecy, why didn't he just ask to be shown around. "Hartwell doesn't want us to know," he said, "or he would have told us. I'll have to do it on the QT."

That made some sense, but—"Heck, Hartwell couldn't have expected to keep us permanently in the dark about what we were making, when all the dope you needed to figure it out was right there in the library. He must have wanted simply to let us do the figuring ourselves."

"Uh-uh. He knew we could puzzle it through if we wanted, but he wasn't going to help us. You think the lab wants to publicize what it's doing? No, Hartwell must be trying to keep as many people as possible from knowing; he hoped we'd stay uncurious. I'm not going to tell him we've guessed, and don't you."

I agreed reluctantly, but Roy's play-acting seemed to me like just that. Roy was deadly serious about it.

Later I got the story of that night. He'd gone up to 39 as planned, and hid in the big hall on the second floor; that was the place with the most embryos, and he thought he'd have the best chance there. Everything went O.K.; the assistant turned out the lights and locked up, and Roy stayed curled in his cabinet under a lab table. When the sounds had died down in the corridors outside, he came out and looked around.

He didn't know quite how to start. There were all sizes and shapes of gestators around. When he had taken out his flash and got a good look at one, he remained in as much of a quandary as before. It didn't seem to be anything but a bottle-shaped black container, about twenty centimeters on a side, in the middle of a mass of tubing, gauges, and levers. He could guess the bottle contained the embryo; he could guess the tubing kept up the flow of "body fluids" to and from the bottle; he could recognize some of the gauge markings and some of the auxiliary apparatus; and that was all. Not only was the embryo not exposed to view but he didn't see any way of exposing it. There was a label in a code he couldn't read. Nothing was any help.

The gestators were simple enough compared to the stuff he worked with, but he had a healthy respect for that sort of thing and didn't want to experiment to try to figure them out. If you meddled with a gestator in the wrong way, there was the chance that you'd be ruining a hundred people's work; and there would be many more wrong ways than right.

He made the circuit of the lab, stooping over one gestator after another, considering. After a while the moon rose and gave him a little more light. That was not what he needed.

A key turned in the lock.

Roy, hoping he hadn't been seen, ran back to his hiding place. He left the cabinet open far enough so he could see. A figure came in the door, turned to close it, and strode toward the center of the hall. As it passed through a patch of moonlight from one of the windows, Roy recognized the face: Hartwell.

He must have been working late in his office and come down for a look at his branch's products before leaving. Be that as it may, his presence cinched the thing: whatever embryos he looked at would be from our branch. Roy watched breathlessly while the other went from bench to bench, peering at the code labels. Finally he stopped before one, worked a lever, and peeked in through a viewer in the side, which Roy hadn't noticed. He looked quite a while, then turned and left.

I don't need to tell you that Roy didn't lose any time after Hartwell left in taking a look through that same viewer. And I don't need to tell you what he saw.

Reading back over this letter, I can see I'm stretching the story out, telling you things you already know and things that aren't really necessary. I know why I'm doing it, too—I'm reluctant to get to the end. But what I've got to tell you, I've got to tell you; I'll make the rest as short as I can.

Roy was pretty broken up about the whole thing, and he didn't get over it. I think it was the experience in the gestation lab that did it. If he'd just asked Hartwell for the truth, straight out, the thing would have stopped being fantastic and again become merely his business; but that melodrama up in Branch 39 kept him from looking at things with a clear eye. He went around in a half daze a good deal of the time, pondering, I suppose, some such philosophical problem as, When is a man not a man? It was all terrible; robots were going to take over the world, or something like that. And he insisted I still not tell Hartwell what he'd learned.

Then came the pay-off. It was several weeks later, the day after Roy's twenty-sixth birthday. (The date was significant, as I learned later.) He told me before we left the lab that Hartwell had asked him to come up after work to talk with Koslicki.

I raised my eyebrows. "Koslicki, huh? The top man."

"Yes, Koslicki and Hartwell both."

He looked a little worried, so I ventured a crack. "Guess they've got a really rugged punishment for you, for trespassing that night. Death by drowning in ammonium sulphide, perhaps."

"I don't know why you can't take things seriously."

"Oh? What do you think they want to talk to you about?"

"No, I mean this whole business of—"

"Of making 'robots,' yeah. Roy, I do take it seriously, darn seriously. I think it's the biggest scientific project in the world right now. You take the kind of work we're doing, together with the production of new life forms like those experimental Coelenterates we saw, and you've got the groundwork for a new kind of eugenics that'll put our present systems in the shade. Now, we select from naturally occurring haploid germ cells to produce our new forms. In the future we'll *make* the new forms.

"We can make new strains of wheat, new species of sheep and cattle—new races of men! We won't have to wait for evolution any more. We won't have to content ourselves with giving evolution an occasional shove, either; we'll be striking out on our own. There's no limit to the possibilities. New, man-made men, stronger than we are, with minds twice as fast and accurate as ours—I take that plenty seriously."

"But they wouldn't be men."

This was beginning to get irritating. "They wouldn't be Homo sapiens, no," I answered. "Let's face it, Roy. If I were to get married, say, and have a kid that was a sharp mutation, a really radical mutation, and if he were to turn out to be a superman—that kid wouldn't be Homo sapiens, either. He wouldn't have the same germ plasm his parents had. Would he be human or wouldn't he?"

"He'd be human."

"Well? Where's the difference?"

"He wouldn't have come out of somebody's reagent bottles, that's the difference. He'd be—natural."

I could take only so much of that. Leaving Roy to go to his conference with Koslicki and Hartwell, I came home.

276

There I finished up the figuring on some notes I'd taken that day in the lab, then I turned the ceiling transparent and sat down with my visor. I'd just added a couple of new wires to my movie collection, so I ran them over—a couple of ballets, they were. No, none of the wires I've shown you. I've thrown out all the movies I saw *that* night.

I was sitting there having a good time with the "Pillar of Fire" when Roy came back. He made a little noise fumbling with the door. Then he slid it back and stood on the threshold without entering.

Switching off the visor, I glanced around. "What's the take, Jake?" I corned cheerfully. "Did Koslicki give you a good dressing-down? Or did he make you the new director?"

". . . I'll play you a game of chess, Dirk."

This time I took a good look at him. His shoulders were stooped more than usual, and he looked around the room as if he didn't recognize it. Not good. "For crying out loud! What's the story?"

"Let's play chess."

"O.K.," I said. He came in and got out the men and the big board, but his hand shook so I had to set up his men for him. Then, "Go ahead," I told him.

"Oh, yeah, I've got white."

Pawn to king four, knight to king bishop three, pawn to king five—one of our standard openings. I pulled my knight back in the corner and brought out the other one; he pushed his pawns up in the center; I began getting ready to castle.

Then he put his queen on queen four. "You don't mean that," I said. "My knight takes you there."

"Oh, yeah, so he does," Roy said, pulling his queen back—to the wrong square. He was staring over my shoulder as if there was a ghost standing behind me. I looked; there wasn't. I replaced his queen.

Finally, still keeping up the stare, he began, "Dirk, you know Hartwell told me—"

"Yeah?" I said casually. I knew it had been something important. Roy hadn't been *this* bad the last few weeks. Whatever it was, he might as well get it off his chest.

Roy, however, seemed to have forgotten he'd spoken. His eyes returned intently to the board. His bishop went to king three—where I could not take it—and the game went on.

"You're going to lose that bishop's pawn, old man," I remarked after a while.

I think that was what triggered it. He said suddenly but evenly, "I'm one."

"I'm two," I said, apropos of nothing. My mind was still on the game.

"Dirk, *I'm one*," he insisted. He stood up, upsetting the board, and began to walk up and down. "Koslicki just told me. I'm one of the . . .

277

Dirk, I wasn't born, I'm one of the robots, they put me together out of those goddamned chemicals in those goddamned white-labeled reagent bottles in that goddamned laboratory—"

"*What?*"

He stopped his pacing and began to laugh. "I'm just a Frankenstein. You can pull out your gun and sizzle me dead; it won't be murder, I'm just a robot." He was laughing all through this and he kept on laughing when he'd stopped.

I figured if he was going to blow up he might as well blow up good and proper. He'd make some noise, but old Graham would be the only one disturbed. "So," I said, "how did you feel going through the reaction vats over in 26? Did the microsurgery hurt when they put you together?" Roy laughed. He laughed harder. Then he screamed.

Deciding that enough was enough, I yelled at him. He screamed again.

"Shut up, Roy!" I shouted as sharply as I could. "You're as human as I am. You've lived with yourself twenty-six years; you ought to know whether you're human or not."

After the first couple of words he listened to me O.K., so I figured the hysterics were over. I tried to sound firm as I said, "Are you through with the foolishness now?"

Roy didn't pass out, he simply lay down on the floor. I sat down beside him and began to talk in a low voice. "You're just as good as anybody else; you've already proved that. It doesn't matter where you started, just what you are here and now. Here and now, you've got human genes, you've got human cells; you can marry a human girl and make human babies with her. So what if you did start out in a lab? The rest of us started out in the ooze on the bottom of some ocean. Which is better? It doesn't make any difference. You're just as good as anybody else." I said it over and over again, as calmly as I could. Don't know whether or not it was the right thing to do, but I had to do something.

Once he raised his head to say, "Roy Wisner, huh? Is that me? Heck no, why didn't they call me Roy W23H? . . . I wonder where they got the name Wisner anyway." He sank back and I took up my spiel again, doing my best to keep my voice level.

After several minutes of this he got up off the floor. "Thanks," he said in a fairly normal tone. "Thanks, Dirk. You're a real friend." He went toward the door, adding as he left, "You're human."

I just sat there. It wasn't till he'd been gone a couple of minutes that I put two and two together. Then I raced out of that room and to the stairs in nothing flat.

Too late. Graham's door was open downstairs, and the light from inside shone into the hall, across the twitching body of Roy Wisner.

Graham looked at me, terrified. "I thought it was all right," he stammered. "He asked me for some hydrocyanic. I knew he was a chemist; I thought it was all right."

Hydrocyanic acid kills fast. One look at the size of the container Roy had drained, and I saw there wasn't much we could do. We did it, all right, but it wasn't enough. He died while we were still forcing emetic down his throat.

That's about all, Ellen. You know now why I never spoke much to you about Roy Wisner. And you've probably guessed why I'm writing this.

Roy was one of the experiments that failed. He was no more unstable mentally than a great many normally born men; still, a failure, though nobody knew it until he was twenty-six years old. The human organism is a very complex thing, and hard to duplicate. When you try to duplicate it you're very likely to fail, sometimes in obvious ways and sometimes in ways that don't become apparent till long afterward.

I may turn out to be a failure, too.

You see, I'm twenty-six now, and Koslicki and Hartwell have told me. *I* wasn't born, either. I was made. I am, if you like, a robot.

I had to tell you that, didn't I, Ellen? Before I asked you to marry me.

Dirk

"It's Great to Be Back!"

Robert A. Heinlein (1907–   )

ROBERT *Anson Heinlein was the seminal science fiction writer of the forties. His steady stream of notable stories in* Astounding *helped establish that magazine as the pacesetter in the field, and his influence on the tone and themes of other writers was considerable. In many respects the Golden Age was also the Age of Heinlein. So great was his talent that he had more than one story (as "Anson MacDonald") in a number of issues of* Astounding *in the early forties. Entire books evaluating his work have been published, but it should be noted that the controversy that surrounds his politics and social beliefs dates only from the sixties. During the forties, his defense of individual rights and liberty were both appreciated and supported in a decade dominated by the fight against fascism.*

His "Future History" series is a landmark in modern science fiction. Heinlein's attention to detail and raw writing ability combined to produce a series of stories and novels whose sweep and historical sense were unprecedented in the field. Fortunately, the whole series, complete with informative chart, is available as The Past Through Tomorrow *(1947).*

Among his most noteworthy forties stories are "—And He Built a Crooked House" (1941), "Blowups Happen" (1940), "Coventry" (1940), "Requiem" (1940), "The Roads Must Roll" (1940), "They" (1941) "Universe" (1941), and "Waldo" (1942).

"It's Great to Be Back!" did not appear in the sf magazines but in the Saturday Evening Post, *and this represents another of Heinlein's*

contributions during the forties, for (along with Ray Bradbury) he opened up the "slick" magazines to science fiction.

From *Saturday Evening Post*　1947

"Hurry up, Allan!" Home—back to Earth again! Her heart was pounding.

"Just a second." She fidgeted while her husband checked over a bare apartment. Earth-Moon freight rates made it silly to ship their belongings; except for the bag he carried, they had converted everything to cash. Satisfied, he joined her at the lift; they went on up to the administration level and there to a door marked: LUNA CITY COMMUNITY ASSOCIATION—*Anna Stone, Service Manager.*

Miss Stone accepted their apartment keys grimly. "Mr. and Mrs. MacRae. So you're actually leaving us?"

Josephine bristled. "Think we'd change our minds?"

The manager shrugged. "No. I knew nearly three years ago that you would go back—from your complaints."

"From my comp— Miss Stone, I've been as patient about the incredible inconveniences of this, this pressurized rabbit warren as anyone. I don't blame you personally, but—"

"Take it easy, Jo!" her husband cautioned her.

Josephine flushed. "Sorry, Miss Stone."

"Never mind. We just see things differently. I was here when Luna City was three air-sealed Quonset huts connected by tunnels you crawled through, on your knees." She stuck out a square hand. "I hope you enjoy being groundhogs again, I honestly do. Hot jets, good luck, and a safe landing."

Back in the lift, Josephine sputtered. " 'Groundhogs' indeed! Just because we prefer our native planet, where a person can draw a breath of fresh air—"

"You use the term," Allan pointed out.

"But I use it about people who've never been off Terra."

"We've both said more than once that we wished we had had sense enough never to have left Earth. We're groundhogs at heart, Jo."

"Yes, but— Oh, Allan, you're being obnoxious. This is the happiest day of my life. Aren't you glad to be going home? Aren't you?"

"Of course I am. It'll be great to be back. Horseback riding. Skiing."

"And opera. Real, live grand opera. Allan, we've simply got to have a week or two in Manhattan before we go to the country."

"I thought you wanted to feel rain on your face?"

"I want that, too. I want it all at once and I can't wait. Oh, darling, it's like getting out of jail." She clung to him.

He unwound her as the lift stopped. "Don't blubber."

"Allan, you're a beast," she said dreamily. "I'm so happy."

They stopped again, in bankers' row. The clerk in the National City Bank office had their transfer of account ready. "Going home, eh? Just sign there, and your print. I envy you. Hunting, fishing."

"Surf bathing is more my style. And sailing."

"I," said Jo, "simply want to see green trees and blue sky."

The clerk nodded. "I know what you mean. It's long ago and far away. Well, have fun. Are you taking three months or six?"

"We're not coming back," Allan stated flatly. "Three years of living like a fish in an aquarium is enough."

"So?" The clerk shoved the papers toward him and added without expression, "Well—hot jets."

"Thanks." They went on up to the subsurface level and took the crosstown slidewalk out to the rocket port. The slidewalk tunnel broke the surface at one point, becoming a pressurized shed; a view window on the west looked out on the surface of the Moon—and, beyond the hills, the Earth.

The sight of it, great and green and bountiful, against the black lunar sky and harsh, unwinking stars, brought quick tears to Jo's eyes. Home—that lovely planet was hers! Allan looked at it more casually, noting the Greenwich. The sunrise line had just touched South America—must be about eight-twenty; better hurry.

They stepped off the slidewalk into the arms of some of their friends, waiting to see them off. "Hey—where have you lugs been? The 'Gremlin' blasts off in seven minutes."

"But we aren't going in it," MacRae answered. "No, siree."

"What? Not going? Did you change your minds?"

Josephine laughed. "Pay no attention to him, Jack. We're going in the express instead; we swapped reservations. So we've got twenty minutes yet."

"Well! A couple of rich tourists, eh?"

"Oh, the extra fare isn't so much and I didn't want to make two changes and spend a week in space when we could be home in two days." She rubbed her bare middle significantly.

"She can't take free flight, Jack," her husband explained.

"Well, neither can I—I was sick the whole trip out. Still, I don't think you'll be sick, Jo; you're used to Moon weight now."

"Maybe," she agreed, "but there is a lot of difference between one-sixth gravity and no gravity."

Jack Crail's wife cut in, "Josephine MacRae, are you going to risk your life in an atomic-powered ship?"

"Why not, darling? You work in an atomics laboratory."

"Hummph! In the laboratory we take precautions. The Commerce Commission should never have licensed the expresses. I may be old-fashioned, but I'll go back the way I came, via Terminal and Supra-New York, in good old reliable fuel rockets."

"Don't try to scare her, Emma," Crail objected. "They've worked the bugs out of those ships."

"Not to my satisfaction. I—"

"Never mind," Allan interrupted her. "The matter is settled, and we've still got to get over to the express launching site. Good-by, everybody! Thanks for the send-off. It's been grand knowing you. If you come back to God's country, look us up."

"Good-by, kids!" "Good-by, Jo—good-by, Allan." "Give my regards to Broadway!" "So long—be sure to write." "Good-by." "Aloha—hot jets!" They showed their tickets, entered the airlock, and climbed into the pressurized shuttle between Leyport proper and the express launching site. "Hang on, folks," the shuttle operator called back over his shoulder; Jo and Allan hurriedly settled into the cushions. The lock opened; the tunnel ahead was airless. Five minutes later they were climbing out twenty miles away, beyond the hills that shielded the lid of Luna City from the radioactive splash of the express ships.

In the "Sparrowhawk" they shared a compartment with a missionary family. The Reverend Doctor Simmons felt obliged to explain why he was traveling in luxury. "It's for the child," he told them, as his wife strapped the baby girl into a small acceleration couch rigged stretcher-fashion between her parents' couches. "Since she's never been in space, we daren't take a chance of her being sick for days on end." They all strapped down at the warning siren. Jo felt her heart begin to pound. At last . . . at long last!

The jets took hold, mashing them into the cushions. Jo had not known she could feel so heavy. This was worse, much worse, than the trip out. The baby cried as long as acceleration lasted, in wordless terror and discomfort.

After an interminable time they were suddenly weightless, as the ship went into free flight. When the terrible binding weight was free of her chest, Jo's heart felt as light as her body. Allan threw off his upper strap and sat up. "How do you feel, kid?"

"Oh, I feel fine!" Jo unstrapped and faced him. Then she hiccuped. "That is, I think I do."

Five minutes later she was not in doubt; she merely wished to die. Allan swam out of the compartment and located the ship's surgeon, who gave her an injection. Allan waited until she had succumbed to the drug, then left for the lounge to try his own cure for spacesickness —Mothersill's Seasick Remedy washed down with champagne. Presently he had to admit that these two sovereign remedies did not work for him or perhaps he should not have mixed them.

Little Gloria Simmons was not spacesick. She thought being weightless was fun, and went bouncing off floor plate, overhead, and bulk-head like a dimpled balloon. Jo feebly considered strangling the child, if she floated within reach—but it was too much effort.

Deceleration, logy as it made them feel, was welcome relief after nausea—except to little Gloria. She cried again, in fear and hurt, while her mother tried to soothe her. Her father prayed.

After a long, long time came a slight jar and the sound of the siren. Jo managed to raise her head. "What's the matter? Is there an accident?"

"I don't think so. I think we've landed."

"We can't have! We're still braking—I'm heavy as lead."

Allan grinned feebly. "So am I. Earth gravity—remember?"

The baby continued to cry.

They said good-by to the missionary family, as Mrs. Simmons decided to wait for a stewardess from the skyport. The MacRaes staggered out of the ship, supporting each other. "It can't be just the gravity," Jo protested, her feet caught in invisible quicksand. "I've taken Earth-normal acceleration in the centrifuge at the 'Y,' back home—I mean in Luna City. We're weak from spacesickness."

Allan steadied himself. "That's it. We haven't eaten anything for two days."

"Allan—didn't you eat anything either?"

"No. Not *permanently*, so to speak. Are you hungry?"

"Starving."

"How about dinner at Kean's Chophouse?"

"Wonderful. Oh, Allan, we're back!" Her tears started again.

They glimpsed the Simmonses once more, after chuting down the Hudson Valley and into Grand Central Station. While they were waiting at the tube dock for their bag, Jo saw the Reverend Doctor climb heavily out of the next tube capsule, carrying his daughter and followed by his wife. He set the child down carefully. Gloria stood for a moment, trembling on her pudgy legs, then collapsed to the dock. She lay there, crying thinly.

A spaceman—pilot, by his uniform—stopped and looked pityingly at the child. "Born in the Moon?" he asked.

"Why, yes, she was, sir." Simmons's courtesy transcended his troubles.

"Pick her up and carry her. She'll have to learn to walk all over again." The spaceman shook his head sadly and glided away. Simmons looked still more troubled, then sat down on the dock beside his child, careless of the dirt.

Jo felt too weak to help. She looked around for Allan, but he was busy; their bag had arrived. It was placed at his feet and he started to pick it up, then felt suddenly silly. It seemed nailed to the dock. He knew what was in it, rolls of microfilm and colorfilm, a few souvenirs, toilet articles, various irreplaceables—fifty pounds of mass. It *couldn't* weigh what it seemed to.

But it did. He had forgotten what fifty pounds weigh on Earth.

"Porter, mister?" The speaker was gray-haired and thin, but he scooped up the bag quite casually. Allan called out, "Come along, Jo," and followed him, feeling foolish. The porter slowed to match Allan's labored steps.

"Just down from the Moon?" he asked.

"Why, yes."

"Got a reservation?"

"No."

"You stick with me. I've got a friend on the desk at the Commodore." He led them to the concourse slidewalk and thence to the hotel.

They were too weary to dine out; Allan had dinner sent to their room. Afterward, Jo fell asleep in a hot tub and he had trouble getting her out—she liked the support the water gave her. But he persuaded her that a rubber-foam mattress was nearly as good. They got to sleep very early.

She woke up, struggling, about four in the morning. "Allan. Allan!"

"Huh? What's the matter?" His hand fumbled at the light switch.

"Uh . . . nothing I guess. I dreamed I was back in the ship. The jets had run away with her. Allan, what makes it so stuffy in here? I've got a splitting headache."

"Huh? It can't be stuffy. This joint is air-conditioned." He sniffed the air. "I've got a headache, too," he admitted.

"Well, do something. Open a window."

He stumbled out of bed, shivered when the outer air hit him, and hurried back under the covers. He was wondering whether he could get to sleep with the roar of the city pouring in through the window when his wife spoke again. "Allan?"

"Yes. What is it?"

"Honey, I'm *cold*. May I crawl in with you?"

"Sure."

The sunlight streamed in the window, warm and mellow. When it touched his eyes, he woke and found his wife awake beside him. She sighed and snuggled. "Oh, darling, look! Blue sky—we're *home*. I'd forgotten how lovely it is."

"It's great to be back, all right. How do you feel?"

"Much better. How are you?"

"Okay, I guess." He pushed off the covers.

Jo squealed and jerked them back. "Don't do that!"

"Huh?"

"Mamma's great big boy is going to climb out and close that window while mamma stays here under the covers."

"Well—all right." He could walk more easily than the night before —but it was good to get back into bed. Once there, he faced the telephone and shouted at it, "Service!"

"Order, please," it answered in a sweet contralto.

"Orange juice and coffee for two—extra coffee—six eggs, scrambled medium, and whole-wheat toast. And send up a *Times*, and the *Saturday Evening Post*."

"Ten minutes."

"Thank you." The delivery cupboard buzzed while he was shaving. He answered it and served Jo breakfast in bed. Breakfast over, he laid down his newspaper and said, "Can you pull your nose out of that magazine?"

"Glad to. The darn thing is too big and heavy to hold."

"Why don't you have the stat edition mailed to you from Luna City? Wouldn't cost more than eight or nine times as much."

"Don't be silly. What's on your mind?"

"How about climbing out of that frowsty little nest and going with me to shop for clothes?"

"Unh-uh. No. I am not going outdoors in a moonsuit."

" 'Fraid of being stared at? Getting prudish in your old age?"

"No, me lord, I simply refuse to expose myself to the outer air in six ounces of nylon and a pair of sandals. I want some warm clothes first." She squirmed further down under the covers.

"The Perfect Pioneer Woman. Going to have fitters sent up?"

"We can't afford that. Look—you're going anyway. Buy me just any old rag so long as it's warm."

MacRae looked stubborn. "I've tried shopping for you before."

"Just this once—please. Run over to Saks and pick out a street dress in a blue wool jersey, size ten. And a pair of nylons."

"Well—all right."

"That's a lamb. I won't be loafing. I've a list as long as your arm of people I've promised to call up, look up, have lunch with."

He attended to his own shopping first; his sensible shorts and singlet seemed as warm as a straw hat in a snowstorm. It was not really cold and was quite balmy in the sun, but it seemed cold to a man used to a never-failing seventy-two degrees. He tried to stay underground, or stuck to the roofed-over section of Fifth Avenue.

He suspected that the salesmen had outfitted him in clothes that made him look like a yokel. But they were warm. They were also heavy; they added to the pain across his chest and made him walk even more unsteadily. He wondered how long it would be before he got his ground-legs.

287

A motherly saleswoman took care of Jo's order and sold him a warm cape for her as well. He headed back, stumbling under his packages, and trying futilely to flag a ground-taxi. Everyone seemed in such a hurry! Once he was nearly knocked down by a teen-aged boy who said. "Watch it, Gramps!" and rushed off, before he could answer.

He got back, aching all over and thinking about a hot bath. He did not get it; Jo had a visitor. "Mrs. Appleby, my husband—Allan, this is Emma Crail's mother."

"Oh, how do you do, Doctor—or should it be 'Professor'?"

"Mister—"

"—when I heard you were in town I just couldn't wait to hear all about my poor darling. How is she? Is she thin? Does she look well? These modern girls—I've told her time and again that she must get out of doors—I walk in the park every day—and look at me. She sent me a picture—I have it here somewhere; at least I think I have—and she doesn't look a bit well, undernourished. Those synthetic foods—"

"She doesn't eat synthetic foods, Mrs. Appleby."

"—must be quite impossible, I'm sure, not to mention the taste. What were you saying?"

"Your daughter doesn't live on synthetic foods," Allan repeated. "Fresh fruits and vegetables are one thing we have almost too much of in Luna City. The air-conditioning plant, you know."

"That's just what I was saying. I confess I don't see just how you get food out of air-conditioning machinery on the Moon—"

"*In* the Moon, Mrs. Appleby."

"—but it can't be healthy. Our air-conditioner at home is always breaking down and making the most horrible smells—simply unbearable, my dears—you'd think they could build a simple little thing like an air-conditioner so that—though of course if you expect them to manufacture synthetic foods as well—"

"Mrs. Appleby—"

"Yes, Doctor? What were you saying? Don't let me—"

"Mrs. Appleby," MacRae said desperately, "The air-conditioning plant in Luna City is a hydroponic farm, tanks of growing plants, green things. The plants take the carbon dioxide out of the air and put oxygen back in."

"But— Are you quite sure, Doctor? I'm sure Emma said—"

"Quite sure."

"Well . . . I don't pretend to understand these things; I'm the artistic type. Poor Herbert often said—Herbert was Emma's father; simply wrapped up in his engineering, though I always saw to it that he heard good music and saw the reviews of the best books. Emma takes after her father, I'm afraid—I do wish she would give up that silly work she is in. Hardly the sort of work for a woman, do you think, Mrs.

MacRae? All those atoms and neuters and things floating around in the air. I read all about it in the 'Science Made Simple' column in the—"

"She's quite good at it and she seems to like it."

"Well, yes, I suppose. That's the important thing, to be happy at what you are doing no matter how silly it is. But I worry about the child—buried away from civilization, no one of her own sort to talk to, no theaters, no cultural life, no society—"

"Luna City has stereo transcriptions of every successful Broadway play." Jo's voice had a slight edge.

"Oh! Really? But it's not just going to the theater, my dear; it's the society of gentlefolk. Now when I was a girl, my parents—"

Allan butted in, loudly. "One o'clock. Have you had lunch, my dear?"

Mrs. Appleby sat up with a jerk. "Oh, heavenly days! I simply must fly. My dress designer—such a tyrant, but a genius; I must give you her address. It's been charming, my dears, and I can't thank you too much for telling me all about my poor darling. I do wish she would be sensible like you two; she knows I'm always ready to make a home for her—and her husband, for that matter. Now do come and see me, often. I love to talk to people who've been on the Moon—"

"In the Moon."

"It makes me feel closer to my darling. Good-by, then."

With the door locked behind her, Jo said, "Allan, I need a drink."

"I'll join you."

Jo cut her shopping short; it was too tiring. By four o'clock they were driving in Central Park, enjoying fall scenery to the lazy clop-clop of horse's hooves. The helicopters, the pigeons, the streak in the sky where the Antipodes rocket had passed made a scene idyllic in beauty and serenity. Jo swallowed a lump in her throat and whispered, "Allan, isn't it beautiful?"

"Sure is. It's great to be back. Say, did you notice they've torn up 42nd Street again?"

Back in their room, Jo collapsed on her bed, while Allan took off his shoes. He sat, rubbing his feet, and remarked, "I'm going barefooted all evening. Golly, how my feet hurt!"

"So do mine. But we're going to your father's, my sweet."

"Huh? Oh, damn, I forgot. Jo, whatever possessed you? Call him up and postpone it. We're still half dead from the trip."

"But, Allan, he's invited a lot of your friends."

"Balls of fire and cold mush! I haven't any real friends in New York. Make it next week."

" 'Next week' . . . hmm . . . look, Allan, let's go out to the country right away." Jo's parents had left her a tiny place in Connecticut, a worn-out farm.

"I thought you wanted a couple of weeks of plays and music first. Why the sudden change?"

"I'll show you." She went to the window, open since noon. "Look at that windowsill." She drew their initials in the grime. "Allan, this city is *filthy*."

"You can't expect ten million people not to kick up dust."

"But we're breathing that stuff into our lungs. What's happened to the smog-control laws?"

"That's not smog; that's normal city dirt."

"Luna City was never like this. I could wear a white outfit there till I got tired of it. One wouldn't last a day here."

"Manhattan doesn't have a roof—and precipitrons in every air duct."

"Well, it should have. I either freeze or suffocate."

"I thought you were anxious to feel rain on your face?"

"Don't be tiresome. I want it out in the clean, green country."

"Okay. I want to start my book anyhow. I'll call your real estate agent."

"I called him this morning. We can move in anytime; he started fixing up the place when he got my letter."

It was a stand-up supper at his father's home, though Jo sat down at once and let food be fetched. Allan wanted to sit down, but his status as guest of honor forced him to stay on his aching feet. His father buttonholed him at the buffet. "Here, son, try this goose liver. It ought to go well after a diet of green cheese."

Allan agreed that it was good.

"See here, son, you really ought to tell these folks about your trip."

"No speeches, Dad. Let 'em read the *National Geographic*."

"Nonsense!" He turned around. "Quiet, everybody! Allan is going to tell us how the Lunatics live."

Allan bit his lip. To be sure, the citizens of Luna City used the term to each other, but it did not sound the same here. "Well, really, I haven't anything to say. Go on and eat."

"You talk and we'll eat." "Tell us about Loony City." "Did you see the Man in the Moon?" "Go on, Allan, what's it like to live on the Moon?"

"Not 'on the Moon'—*in* the Moon."

"What's the difference?"

"Why, none, I guess." He hesitated; there was really no way to explain why the Moon colonists emphasized that they lived under the surface of the satellite planet—but it irritated him the way "Frisco" irritates a San Franciscan. " 'In the Moon' is the way we say it. We don't spend much time on the surface, except for the staff at Richardson Observatory, and the prospectors, and so forth. The living quarters are underground, naturally."

"Why 'naturally'? Afraid of meteors?"

"No more than you are afraid of lightning. We go underground for insulation against heat and cold and as support for pressure sealing. Both are cheaper and easier underground. The soil is easy to work and the interstices act like vacuum in a thermos bottle. It is vacuum."

"But, Mr. MacRae," a serious-looking lady inquired, "doesn't it hurt your ears to live under pressure?"

Allan fanned the air. "It's the same pressure here—fifteen pounds."

She looked puzzled, then said, "Yes, I suppose so, but it is a little hard to imagine. I think it would terrify me to be sealed up in a cave. Suppose you had a blowout?"

"Holding fifteen pounds pressure is no problem; engineers work in thousands of pounds per square inch. Anyhow, Luna City is compartmented like a ship. It's safe enough. The Dutch live behind dikes; down in Mississippi they have levees. Subways, ocean liners, aircraft—they're all artificial ways of living. Luna City seems strange just because it's far away."

She shivered. "It scares me."

A pretentious little man pushed his way forward. "Mr. MacRae—granted that it is nice for science and all that, why should taxpayers' money be wasted on a colony on the Moon?"

"You seem to have answered yourself," Allan told him slowly.

"Then how do you justify it? Tell me that, sir."

"It isn't necessary to justify it; the Lunar colony has paid for itself several times over. The Lunar corporations are all paying propositions. Artemis Mines, Spaceways, Spaceways Provisioning Corporation, Diana Recreations, Electronics Research Company, Lunar Biological Labs, not to mention all of Rutherford—look 'em up. I'll admit the Cosmic Research Project nicks the taxpayer a little, since it's a joint enterprise of the Harriman Foundation and the government."

"Then you admit it. It's the principle of the thing."

Allan's feet were hurting him very badly indeed. "What principle? Historically, research has always paid off." He turned his back and looked for some more goose liver.

A man touched him on the arm; Allan recognized an old schoolmate. "Allan, old boy, congratulations on the way you ticked off old Beetle. He's been needing it—I think he's some sort of a radical."

Allan grinned. "I shouldn't have lost my temper."

"A good job you did. Say, Allan, I'm going to take a couple of out-of-town buyers around to the hot spots tomorrow night. Come along."

"Thanks a lot, but we're going out in the country."

"Oh, you can't afford to miss this party. After all, you've been buried on the Moon; you owe yourself some relaxation after that deadly monotony."

Allan felt his cheeks getting warm. "Thanks just the same, but—ever seen the Earth View Room in Hotel Moon Haven?"

"No. Plan to take the trip when I've made my pile, of course."

"Well, there's a nightclub for you. Ever see a dancer leap thirty feet into the air and do slow rolls on the way down? Ever try a lunacy cocktail? Ever see a juggler work in low gravity?" Jo caught his eyes across the room. "Er . . . excuse me, old man. My wife wants me." He turned away, then flung back over his shoulder, "Moon Haven itself isn't just a spaceman's dive, by the way—it's recommended by the Duncan Hines Association."

Jo was very pale. "Darling, you've got to get me out of here. I'm suffocating. I'm really ill."

"Suits." They made their excuses.

Jo woke up with a stuffy cold, so they took a cab directly to her country place. There were low-lying clouds under them, but the weather was fine above. The sunshine and the drowsy beat of the rotors regained for them the joy of homecoming.

Allan broke the lazy reverie. "Here's a funny thing, Jo. You couldn't hire me to go back to the Moon—but last night I found myself defending the Loonies every time I opened my mouth."

She nodded. "I know. Honest to heaven, Allan, some people act as if the Earth were flat. Some of them don't really believe in anything, and some of them are so matter of fact that you know they don't really understand—and I don't know which sort annoys me the more."

It was foggy when they landed, but the house was clean, the agent had laid a fire and had stocked the refrigerator. They were sipping hot punch and baking the weariness out of their bones within ten minutes after the copter grounded. "This," said Allan, stretching, "is all right. It really is great to be back."

"Uh-huh. All except the highway." A new express-and-freight superhighway now ran not fifty yards from the house. They could hear the big diesels growling as they struck the grade.

"Forget the highway. Turn your back and you stare straight into the woods."

They regained their ground-legs well enough to enjoy short walks in the woods; they were favored with a long, warm Indian summer; the cleaning woman was efficient and taciturn. Allan worked on the results of three years' research preparatory to starting his book. Jo helped him with the statistical work, got reacquainted with the delights of cooking, dreamed, and rested.

It was the day of the first frost that the toilet stopped up.

The village plumber was persuaded to show up the next day. Meanwhile they resorted to a homely little building, left over from another era and still standing out beyond the woodpile. It was spider-infested and entirely too well ventilated.

The plumber was not encouraging. "New septic tank. New sile pipe. Pay you to get new fixtures at the same time. Fifteen, sixteen hundred dollars. Have to do some calculating."

"That's all right," Allan told him. "Can you start today?"

The man laughed. "I can see plainly, mister, that you don't know what it is to get materials and labor these days. Next spring—soon as the frost is out of the ground."

"That's impossible, man. Never mind the cost. Get it done."

The native shrugged. "Sorry not to oblige you. Good day."

When he left, Jo exploded. "Allan, he doesn't want to help us."

"Well—maybe. I'll try to get someone from Norwalk, or even from the city. You can't trudge through the snow to that Iron Maiden all winter."

"I hope not."

"You must not. You've already had one cold." He stared morosely at the fire. "I suppose I brought it on by my misplaced sense of humor."

"How?"

"Well, you know how we've been subjected to steady kidding ever since it got noised around that we were colonials. I haven't minded much, but some of it rankled. You remember I went into the village by myself last Saturday?"

"Yes. What happened?"

"They started in on me in the barbershop. I let it ride at first, then the worm turned. I started talking about the Moon, sheer double-talk—corny old stuff like the vacuum worms and the petrified air. It was some time before they realized I was ribbing them—and when they did, nobody laughed. Our friend the rustic sanitary engineer was one of the group. I'm sorry."

"Don't be." She kissed him. "If I have to tramp through the snow, it will cheer me that you gave them back some of their sass."

The plumber from Norwalk was more helpful, but rain, and then sleet, slowed down the work. They both caught colds. On the ninth miserable day Allan was working at his desk when he heard Jo come in the back door, returning from a shopping trip. He turned back to his work, then presently became aware that she had not come in to say "hello." He went to investigate.

He found her collapsed on a kitchen chair, crying quietly. "Darling," he said urgently, "honey baby, whatever is the matter?"

She looked up. "I didn't bead to led you doe."

"Blow your nose. Then wipe your eyes. What do you mean, 'you didn't mean to let me know.' What happened?"

She let it out, punctuated with her handkerchief. First, the grocer had said he had no cleansing tissues; then, when she pointed to them, had stated that they were "sold." Finally, he had mentioned "bringing outside labor into town and taking the bread out of the mouths of honest folk."

Jo had blown up and had rehashed the incident of Allan and the barbershop wits. The grocer had simply grown more stiff. " 'Lady,' he said to me, 'I don't know whether you and your husband have been to the Moon or not, and I don't care. I don't take much stock in such things. In any case, I don't need your trade.' Oh, Allan, I'm so unhappy."

"Not as unhappy as he's going to be! Where's my hat?"

"Allan! You're not leaving this house. I won't have you fighting."

"I won't have him bullying you."

"He won't again. Oh, my dear, I've tried so hard, but I can't stay here any longer. It's not just the villagers; it's the cold and the cockroaches and always having a runny nose. I'm tired out and my feet hurt all the time." She started to cry again.

"There, there! We'll leave, honey. We'll go to Florida. I'll finish my book while you lie in the sun."

"Oh, I don't want to go to Florida. *I want to go home!*"

"Huh? You mean—back to Luna City?"

"Yes. Oh, dearest, I know you don't want to, but I can't stand it any longer. It's not just the dirt and the cold and the comic-strip plumbing —it's not being understood. It wasn't any better in New York. These groundhogs don't know *anything.*"

He grinned at her. "Keep sending, kid; I'm on your frequency."

"Allan!"

He nodded. "I found out I was a Loony at heart quite a while ago—but I was afraid to tell you. My feet hurt, too—and I'm damn sick of being treated like a freak. I've tried to be tolerant, but I can't stand groundhogs. I miss the folks in dear old Luna. They're civilized."

She nodded. "I guess it's prejudice, but I feel the same way."

"It's *not* prejudice. Let's be honest. What does it take to get to Luna City?"

"A ticket."

"Smarty pants. I don't mean as a tourist; I mean to get a job there. You know the answer: Intelligence. It costs a lot to send a man to the Moon and more to keep him there. To pay off, he had to be worth a lot. High I.Q., good compatibility index, superior education—everything that makes a person pleasant and easy and interesting to have around. We've been spoiled; the ordinary human cussedness that groundhogs take for granted, we now find intolerable, because Loonies *are* different. The fact that Luna City is the most comfortable environment man ever built for himself is beside the point—it's the people who count. Let's go home."

He went to the telephone—an old-fashioned, speech-only rig—and called the Foundation's New York office. While he was waiting, trucheonlike "receiver" to his ear, she said, "Suppose they won't have us?"

"That's what worries me." They knew that the Lunar companies rarely rehired personnel who had once quit; the physical examination was reputed to be much harder the second time.

"Hello . . . hello. Foundation? May I speak to the recruiting office? . . . Hello—I *can't* turn on my viewplate; this instrument is a hangover from the dark ages. This is Allan MacRae, physical chemist, contract number 1340729. And my wife, Josephine MacRae, 1340730. We want to sign up again. I said we wanted to sign up again . . . okay, I'll wait."

"Pray, darling, pray!"

"I'm praying— How's that? My appointment's still vacant? Fine, fine! How about my wife?" He listened with a worried look; Jo held her breath. Then he cupped the speaker. "Hey, Jo—your job's filled. They want to know if you'll take an interim job as a junior accountant?"

"Tell 'em 'Yes!' "

"That'll be fine. When can we take our exams? That's fine, thanks. Good-by." He hung up and turned to his wife. "Physical and psycho as soon as we like; professional exams waived."

"What are we waiting for?"

"Nothing." He dialed the Norwalk Copter Service. "Can you run us into Manhattan? Well, good grief, don't you have radar? All right, all right, g'-by!" He snorted. "Cabs all grounded by weather. I'll call New York and try to get a modern cab."

Ninety minutes later they landed on top of Harriman Tower.

The psychologist was very cordial. "Might as well get this over before you have your chests thumped. Sit down. Tell me about yourselves." He drew them out, nodding from time to time. "I see. Did you ever get the plumbing repaired?"

"Well, it was being fixed."

"I can sympathize with your foot trouble, Mrs. MacRae; my arches always bother me here. That's your real reason, isn't it?"

"Oh, no!"

"Now, Mrs. MacRae—"

"Really it's not—truly. I want people to talk to who know what I mean. All that's really wrong with me is that I'm homesick for my own sort. I want to go home—and I've got to have this job to get there. I'll steady down, I know I will."

The doctor looked grave. "How about you, Mr. MacRae?"

"Well—it's about the same story. I've been trying to write a book, but I can't work. I'm homesick. I want to go back."

Feldman suddenly smiled. "It won't be too difficult."

"You mean we're in? If we pass the physical?"

"Never mind the physical—your discharge examinations are recent enough. Of course you'll have to go out to Arizona for reconditioning and quarantine. You're probably wondering why it seems so easy when it is supposed to be so hard. It's really simple: We don't want people lured back by the high pay. We do want people who will be happy and as permanent as possible—in short, we want people who think of Luna City as 'home.' Now that you're 'Moonstruck,' we want you back." He stood up and shoved out his hand.

Back in the Commodore that night, Jo was struck by a thought. "Allan—do you suppose we could get our own apartment back?"

"Why, I don't know. We could send old lady Stone a radio."

"Call her up instead, Allan. We can afford it."

"All right! I will!"

It took about ten minutes to get the circuit through. Miss Stone's face looked a trifle less grim when she recognized them.

"Miss Stone, we're coming home!"

There was the usual three-second lag, then—"Yes, I know. It came over the tape about twenty minutes ago."

"Oh. Say, Miss Stone, is our old apartment vacant?" They waited.

"I've held it; I knew you'd come back—after a bit. Welcome home, Loonies."

When the screen cleared, Jo said, "What did she mean, Allan?"

"Looks like we're in, kid. Members of the Lodge."

"I guess so—oh, Allan, look!" She had stepped to the window; scudding clouds had just uncovered the Moon. It was three days old and *Mare Fecunditatis*—the roll of hair at the back of the Lady in the Moon's head—was cleared by the sunrise line. Near the righthand edge of that great, dark "sea" was a tiny spot, visible only to their inner eyes—Luna City.

The crescent hung, serene and silvery, over the tall buildings. "Darling, isn't it beautiful?"

"Certainly is. It'll be great to be back. Don't get your nose all runny."

Tiger Ride

James Blish (1921–1974) and
Damon Knight (1922-   )

THE *late James Blish was one of the superior talents in science fiction, a man of wide intellectual interests, trained in science, who wrote some of the most important "soft" sf to appear in the fifties and sixties. His most significant accomplishment is his novel* A Case of Conscience *(1958, revised from a 1953 story from* Worlds of If*), which deals seriously with fundamental religious questions. He is also remembered for his "Okie" series of novels collected as* Cities in Flight *(1970), and the "Pantropy" stories that appeared in the fifties, of which "Surface Tension" is the best known. As is the case with many of the writers in this book, his talent was still maturing in the forties, but he nonetheless produced several important works, including "Solar Plexus" (1941) and "Let the Finder Beware" (1949, developed into the novel* Jack of Eagles*).*

Damon Knight was a participant in the sf life of the forties in a number of ways—as editor, writer, and fan. His influence grew with his writing and editing skills, especially the craftsmanship he displayed in his short fiction and the insights he supplied through his critical essays and book reviews.

This story is especially interesting because it is a collaboration, for many stories published in the forties under single names were in reality the products of two, three, or even more people. This was particularly true of that wondrous group of New York fans who were to become prominent writers and editors in the field—Don Wollheim, Bob Lowndes, Cyril Kornbluth, Judith Merril, Fred Pohl, and Damon Knight, among others.

This story is one of a number that Blish and Knight wrote together and is a blend of two unique talents addressing one of the oldest questions in the world: What is the nature of the human animal?

From *Astounding Science Fiction*   1948

2/4/2121

Tested the levitator units this morning. Both performed well with the dummies, and Laura insisted on trying one herself—they were tuned to her voice, anyhow. Chapelin objected, of course, but his wife overrode him as usual. I believe she was actually hoping there would be an accident.

Laura Peel said: "Just the same, I'm going to do it."

The wind was in her fair hair and pressing her clothes gently against the length of her slim body. She looked uncommonly beautiful, Hal Osborn thought. He wondered, what the devil does Chapelin see when he looks at her?

Chapelin's big blond face was a study in prudence and responsibility. He said: "Now, let's not be unreasonable, Laura—"

Niki Chapelin's voice cut him off. "Oh, why not let her? It's perfectly safe, isn't it, Hal?"

"Nope," said Hal. If anything did happen, he thought all she'd have to do would be to remind everybody, "But Hal said—"

Her small mask turned toward him, and the basilisk eyes drilled holes in his forehead. He felt again the rising urge toward murder which often shook him these days; the isolation was beginning to tell on them all, and sometimes Hal thought he would abandon Laura and ultronics and all the rest for a chance to leave this God-forsaken tomb of a planet.

No, he corrected himself, not a tomb; a ghost, and the brother of a ghost. Styrtis Delta III was the satellite of a huge planet, which in turn swung around a Gray Ghost—a star so huge and rarefied that it gave no light. Luckily there was a yellow companion star which provided almost-normal days for half the year; the nights, rendered deep, livid blue-green by the reflection from the methane-swathed giant planet, were not normal, but they were bearable.

And the whole complicated system was in a corner of the galaxy where no possible explosion, no matter how titanic, could injure the works of man—in a limb of stars which man had never before visited, and had scarcely mapped. The Earth Council had awarded this planet to the ultronics group, and given them the period of "summer" at Council expense to work out their discoveries. When the yellow sun was eclipsed by the Gray Ghost, Styrtis Delta III would have a winter that might have made even Dante tremble.

The people who had once inhabited this planet must have been unique; the seasonal changes they had had to withstand were terrific. Whatever had killed them off, it hadn't been the weather, for the ruins of their cities still showed the open spaces and wide-spanned architecture of a race as used to storm as to quiet. Maybe they'd killed each other off; storms of emotion could destroy things untouchable by Nature.

Luckily, Niki could spare Hal only the one look. Chapelin was beginning to repeat all his arguments to her, and she had to turn on her heavy artillery: Mark IX, the look of bored impatience.

The levitator was an entirely new device, said Chapelin, it was new even in the hundred-kilo lab stage, let alone belt-size. It wasn't just the danger of falling, he said, there was a thing made of platinum called a governor that was only three mm. long, and if that went, Laura could find herself digging a hole in the ground with two Gs behind her. There were good reasons for never testing a new ultronic device in person before it had had at least fifty hours' run on the dummies—dummies don't experiment with unfamiliar equipment, they don't move of their own accord in flight and disarrange things, they don't miscalculate and release the total ultimate energy that could consume a whole group of suns.

Niki was swinging her riding crop against her skinny tailored thigh. She had come because she was Chapelin's wife, and because Laura was coming. Ultronics interested her mildly, sometimes.

Hal stole a glance at Laura. On the other side of her, little Mike Cohen was chewing his pipe, watching and saying nothing. Hal met his speculative gaze, and looked away guiltily. Laura's mouth had had that hurt, childish downcurve, the same as it always had when she was watching Chapelin unseen. Her spine was as straight as ever, though. She's licked, he thought, she always gets licked. She'll go through with it out of sheer defiance.

A star-shaped shadow passed slowly between Hal and the Chapelins. He looked up.

"Wind's blowing them toward the edge of the plateau," he said. "Better pull 'em back."

Everybody looked. High over their heads, the two seven-foot manikins were canted slightly, their blank heads pointed toward the distant Killhope range. "Wind's pretty strong up there," Chapelin said uncomfortably. "You might as well bring them down, Laura."

Niki said: "*That's* better, dear. You're so much nicer when you're not stubborn."

Chapelin turned back to her. "Wait a minute," he said, "I didn't mean—"

"I'm going to do it anyhow," Laura said clearly, "whether you let me or not." Her lips compressed. She watched the dummies and said: "Right. Right—enough. Down."

"Well," Chapelin said, "be careful."

Hal felt the surge of hatred again. Chapelin, can't you see she loves you? Won't you put up any kind of fight, make her see that you're worried about her? If you'd show the slightest interest, you could persuade her not to try it—

The dummies floated down until the tips of their legs touched the ground. They hung there, swaying gently. Laura said: "Stop," and they sat down abruptly as if their strings had been cut, then flopped over and lay sprawled on the sun-caked turf.

Chapelin had drawn his wife a couple of meters away and was talking to her earnestly. Niki was listening to him with no sign of impatience, which meant that she was amused.

Hal choked and walked over to the dummies. Laura was kneeling beside one of them, taking off its belt. She got up as he approached, her bare knees dusty.

"Let's have a look at it," Hal said. "That landing was a little rough."

She put the articulated silver band around her waist, leaving the one she'd been wearing on the ground. "Let me alone just now, Hal," she said in a barely audible voice. She stepped away and said: "Up."

The belt took her up.

Hal watched her go, squinting his eyes against the lemon-yellow sky. She went straight up, with a halo of saffron light on the top of her blond head, and stayed there until he was beginning to wonder if she was ever coming down again. Then she dropped swiftly, turned, and swooped over their heads.

Hal swore. Laura didn't know what "careful" meant. He was angry at himself for failing to try to stop her, and angry at her for taking out her feelings about Chapelin on them all. If that governor cut out, they might all die—the whole crazy solar system, the whole ridge of stars could be annihilated under certain conditions.

She was up high again now, so high she could barely be seen. Despite the hot sun on the plateau, it was cold that high up, cold and blustery with the ceaseless blast of this planet's rapid revolution. Then she began to drop again, faster than she should, as if under power.

At the lip of the plateau, Laura seemed to see that she was going to miss it, and reversed the controls. The belt jerked her slantwise back toward them, and burned out in a flare of copper-colored energy. Everyone but Hal hit the ground and waited for the world to end.

Hal stayed on his feet, his mind a well of horror. Laura's body tumbled over their heads and struck just beyond them.

Then everyone was running.

Oh, yes; we buried old Jonas today. He was a quiet, pathetic little guy, but he wanted to go home like the rest of us; I wish we could have had his body shipped back, but twenty-five thousand volts doesn't leave much to ship. Besides, the accident with Laura rather took our mind off him.

In the shack Hal shifted his weight uncomfortably on a drum. Mike Cohen was talking quietly, but Hal only half heard him. Laura lay on one of the cots, seemingly without a single bruise; but she was not breathing. Chapelin sat beside her, wringing his hands in a blind, stupid way. Niki had the good sense to be absent, out in the generator shed, congratulating herself, Hal supposed.

"I still think she's alive," Mike Cohen went on. "We know so little about ultronics—every accident's a freak at this stage."

Hal stirred. "The belt wasn't hurt," he said numbly. "At first I thought it'd sliced her right in two." He looked at the gleaming, jointed thing, still clasping Laura's waist. They had been afraid to touch it—if there were still a residue of energy in there, and the governor gone—

"That's right. And the fall should have broken all her bones. She hit hard. But . . . I don't think she really hit at all. Something took up the shock."

"What, then?"

A strangled sound came from the cot. Hal started and stood up, his heart thudding under his breastbone. The sound, however, had come from Chapelin, who was also standing, bending over Laura.

"Chapelin? What is it?"

"She's breathing. She started, all of a sudden. I—" His voice broke, and he stood silent, hands working at his sides.

But it was true. Laura's breast was rising and falling regularly, naturally. There was still no color in her face.

Even as Hal noted that, a faint tinge of pink crept in over her cheekbones.

"Thank God," Chapelin muttered. "She's coming around." He looked at Hal and at Mike Cohen, meeting their eyes for the first time since the accident. "It was funny. I heard a sort of sigh, and when I looked, she was breathing just as if she'd been asleep. Shall we try to get the belt off now?"

"I don't think we should," Mike said. "It may still be in operation, and it's tuned to her. Best wait till she tells it to turn off."

"How do you know it's still on?"

"It must be. That flash of copper light—it was only an electrical short, or we'd none of us be here now. We've never been able to overload an ultronic field before, and *something* must have shielded her during that fall."

On the cot, Laura whispered, quite clearly: "Is that you, Mike? Where are you? I can't see you."

Chapelin bent over her. "Laura," he said huskily. "How do you feel? Can you move a little?"

"I'm all right, but it seems so dark. I can just barely make you out."

Mike Cohen chuckled, a small, joyous sound. "You're O.K., Laura. We were too busy to remember about such little things as sunset." He trotted quickly across the room and turned on the lights. Laura sat up in the fluorescent glow and blinked at them.

For a moment no one could speak. Then, from the doorway, Niki Chapelin's voice said: "Why darling! What a *relief!*"

2/5/2121

Laura's not hurt, but naturally somewhat shocked emotionally. We were all anxious to look at the innards of the belt, but she won't give it up; claims that it saved her life and that it goes with her uniform. In her present state of mind we dare not argue with her.

It was very quiet in the little laboratory; only the sound of Hal's breathing and the minute-ticking of the device upon which he was working broke the stillness. Outside the window, a silent landscape lay bathed in deep blue-green, like a vision of the bottom of a sea.

There was a modest knock on the door, and a dial on the table moved slightly. That, Hal knew, would be Laura; no one else would be carrying or wearing anything which would disturb an ultrometer, especially not at this hour. If only she'd surrender that belt! He wondered what she wanted of him.

The knock sounded again. "Come in," Hal said. The girl slipped past the door and closed it carefully.

"Hello, Hal."

"Hi. What can I do for you?"

"I got to feeling a little depressed and wanted company. Do you mind?"

"Chapelin's still up, I saw the light in the shack," Hal said sullenly. The next instant he could have bitten off his tongue; but Laura did not seem to react at all.

"No, I wanted to talk to you. What are you doing?"

He said wonderingly: "The same as always—trying to get enough of a grip on the ultronic flow to disrupt it. The little ticker here records the energy flux. If I can cause it to miss a beat now and then, I'll know I've managed to interfere. So far, no soap; we can direct the flow, but not modify it."

"Watch the blast limit."

Hal shrugged. That was the problem, of course. This energy was strictly sub-subatomic; somewhere nearby there was a nexus where the fields met, a nexus where cosmic rays were created, out of some ground energy called ultronic as a handy label. Chapelin thought there must be billions of such nexi in every galaxy, but they had been undetectable by their very nature until just recently. The Earth Council had been scared to death when Chapelin had reported the results of his first investigations, and had quarantined the whole group. Unless they could learn how to modify the forces involved—

"We've done well so far, all things considered," Hal said. "The moment we do badly, it'll be all up for us, and this whole corner of the universe."

Laura nodded seriously. Hal looked at her. As always, her loveliness hurt him, made it difficult for him to concentrate on what he was saying.

"But you didn't come here to talk ultronics, surely. Isn't there—"

She smiled, a little wistfully. "I don't care what we talk about, Hal. That accident—you don't go through a thing like that without being forced to think about things. I remembered your asking to see the belt before I went up, and how you tried to look out for me, and a lot of things you've done for me—and I knew all of a sudden that I owed you a lot more than I'd been ready to admit."

Hal made an awkward gesture. "It's nothing, Laura. I've made no secret of how I feel. If you don't share the feeling, those little attentions can become a nuisance, I know."

"That's true," Laura said. "And I realize now how careful you were not to . . . to force anything on me. Not everybody would be that considerate, so many parsecs from any sort of civilization. It's given me a chance to find out how I really do feel—that, and the accident."

Hal felt his heart begin to thunder against his ribs, but he kept seated by sheer willpower. "Laura," he said, "please don't feel that you have to commit yourself. It's really the parsecs that count the most. When six people—five, now—are marooned, in close quarters, for so long, all kinds of unnatural emotional tensions develop. It's best not to add to them if there's any way to avoid it."

Laura nodded. "I know. But most of the tensions that are already here are my fault. Oh, don't deny it, it's true. Niki wouldn't be here if it weren't for me, and the way I felt about Chapelin. I've been a useful lab technic, but emotionally I've always been in the way. It's different now. Chapelin—he's a sort of timid moose, isn't he? I've been pretty blind. I flatter myself that I can see, now." She toyed with am amber-handled, tiny screwdriver on the workbench. "That's—why I'm here."

The blood roared in Hal's temples. He said: "Laura—"

After that it was very quiet in the little shack.

2/8/2121

The Council survey ship came by yesterday, and we had a good report to make; if they could have landed, we'd have been able to show them things that would have made their eyes bug. But they weren't going through our area, and only inquired in a routine way; Earth's still scared green of ultronics. One funny business: when I reported Jonas's death—expecting all kinds of hows and whens and whys—the Ship's Recorder didn't seem to know what I was talking about. "Jonas who?" he said. "Did you have a stowaway?" Evidently Earth has already forgotten us, and can't be bothered over whether there were five or six or thirteen in the group.

For a while things seemed to go along well enough; but Hal could not rid himself of the sensation that somewhere there was something radically wrong, if only he could find it. Oh, there was Chapelin to account for some of it. The accident, for which he could not help but hold himself responsible, seemed to have jarred some long-dormant cells to activity in Chapelin's mind. For the first time he seemed to be looking at Laura as something besides a competent laboratory assistant. They were all aware of it, Niki most of all, of course—for Niki had suspected it even when it didn't exist—but it was marked enough to worry even Mike Cohen.

That caused tension, but it was the old, familiar kind of tension. This other thing was—strange. Hal couldn't pin it down; it was a general uneasiness, strongest when he saw the belt gleaming enigmatically about Laura's slim waist, and when he reviewed certain entries in his journal. It was as if he were awaiting some disaster he could not describe, and it kept him up late every night, crouched over the ticking little modulator.

Even there, he had enough success to make him hopeful; within three nights he was able to modulate the steady ultronic flow, and on the fourth night he discovered, all at once, a chain of improbable formulas describing the phenomenon—a chain which showed him that his next step would have triggered the blast whose echoes they all heard in nightmares.

It was as if there was a silent conspiracy afoot, a conspiracy to convince Hal that Everything was going to be All Right. He looked at the equations again; they were new, a brand of math he seemingly had invented on the spot—and he had "discovered" them about ten minutes before he would have set off an interstellar catastrophe.

There was one kind of math Hal knew as well as he knew his own name: permutations and combinations. A few sheets of paper later, he had worked out the chances against his making this particular discovery at this particular time. The result: 3×10^{18}. Such coincidences *did* occur, but—

He shut off the detectors, and discovered that his hand was shaking a little. If only he could pin down this irrational dread! Well, if he were that unsteady, he's better cut the generator that fed his lab, or there'd really be a blowup, miracle or no miracle. He stood up, stretching cramped muscles. The modulator glimmered up at him from the bench. He put it in his pocket and went out into the green gloom.

The spongy, elaborately branched moss effectively silenced his foot-steps. When he jerked open the door of the generator shed, Chapelin and Laura were still locked together.

Hal gagged and tried to step out again, but they had heard the door open. Chapelin broke away, his big face turning the color of old turnips in the greenish light. Laura did not blush, but she looked—miserable.

"Sorry," Hal said, his voice as harsh as a rasp. "However, as long as I'm here—"

He strode past them and yanked the big switch from its blades. Laura said: "Hal . . . it isn't quite what—"

He spun on her. "Oh, it isn't, eh?" he said grimly. "I suppose Everything is really All Right?"

"Now, wait a minute," Chapelin blurted. "I don't know what right you have to be taking that tone—"

"Of course you don't. Probably Laura just said she's been thinking and wanted to talk to somebody—or don't you use the same line on us all, Laura?"

Laura raised her hand as if to ward off a blow. Hal's heart stopped. He said: "You're on the spot now, Laura. You can be all things to all men if you try, but not to more than one man at a time! Your story can satisfy either Chapelin or me—but not both of us at once. Want to try?"

Laura's lips thinned a little. "I don't think I'll bother," she said, walking toward the door. "I don't like taking orders."

Hal caught her wrist and forced her back against the now-silent generator. "Clever," he said, "I forgot the outraged-virtue act; it's good—almost good enough. But it won't work with me, Laura. I think I know the story now."

"What's going on here?" Mike Cohen's voice said from the doorway. "If you'd open a window, they could hear you all the way back on Earth."

"Hello, Mike," Hal said, without turning. "Stick around. I'm either making an ass of myself or staging a showdown, one or the other. Niki with you?"

"Naturally," Niki's voice said. The cold fury in it was appalling; Niki did not yet know what had happened, but in any such situation she had only one guess to make.

"What's the story?" Mike said.

"You know most of it. The crux of it is that belt of Laura's. It's still in operation, we know that; and I think it's somehow invaded her mind. The way she's been acting since the accident isn't like her. And the effect she's had on events outside her own personal interests has been too great to shrug off. It includes creating a body out of nothing."

"A body?" Niki said. "You mean—she killed Jonas? But we all saw him electrocuted while we were a long way away from the generators—"

"You're close, Niki, I think she *created* Jonas—or the belt did."

Chapelin said: "Maybe you'd better go to bed, Hal."

"Maybe. First, you can explain to me why we haven't a single record in this camp which mentions 'old Jonas' *before* the accident happened. Check me if you like. Odd, isn't it? The first time he's mentioned is when we buried him. And the Council ship had never heard of him. To top it off—there are only five acceleration hammocks in the stores. Where's Jonas's? Did he come here in a bucket?"

"We buried him in his hammock," Laura said in a small voice.

"Did we? We only had five hammocks to begin with, the QM record shows it. It also shows rations for only five. With one less person, we should be accumulating an overstock of food, but we aren't, though we're eating exactly the same menus we've always eaten."

"Suppose it's so," Mike Cohen said. "Suppose there never was any such person as Jonas—it's a fantastic assumption, but your evidence seems to prove it—what's the point of such a deception?"

"That," Hal said, "is what I mean to find out. I also want to find out why I got about a century's worth of advanced ultronic math shoved into my cranium tonight, all at once, just at the moment when I would have blown us to kingdom come without it." He took the modulator out of his pocket. "This is the result. Knowing how *not* to blow us up fortunately includes knowing *how* to. Hand over that belt, Laura—or I'll disrupt it!"

Laura said, "I . . . I can't. You're right, Hal. I can't make everyone happy at once, so I have to admit it. But I can't give up the belt."

"Why not?" Hal demanded.

"Because . . . *I am* the belt!"

Chapelin gasped: "Laura, don't be insane."

"It was Laura that you buried. She was killed in the accident. As Mike says, there was never any such person as 'old Jonas.' I instilled his memory in your minds to account for the corpse, which was unrecognizable after . . . after what had happened to it."

The knife turned deeper in Hal's heart. Every curve, every coloring, every sound of the voice was Laura's—

Mike said softly: "We've done Frankenstein one better."

"I don't think so," Hal said steadily. "I think we've just reenacted a limerick. Remember the one about the young lady from Niger? She smiled as she rode on the tiger—"

"They came back from the ride with the lady inside," Mike whispered, "and the smile on the face of the tiger."

"Yes. I don't think this is one of our belts. Ours weren't complex enough to pull off a stunt like this, no matter how they might have been deranged."

The girl looked steadily at Hal; it was quite impossible to imagine that she was changed. "Hal is right," she said. "When your belt burned out, there was an instantaneous ultronic stress, a condition we call interspace. The mathematics are difficult, but I can teach them to you. The results, roughly, were to create an exchange in time; your belt was sent a hundred thousand years into this planet's past, and replaced by this belt—myself."

"The people here knew ultronics?" Chapelin asked.

"Very well. Their belts were at first much like yours—simple levitating devices. But as they learned more, they found that they could travel space without spaceships; new belts made a protecting envelope, manufactured food and air, disposed of waste. As the centuries went by, the belts came to be the universal tool; there was nothing they could not do. They could replace lost limbs and organs with counterfeits indistinguishable from the originals. Eventually they were endowed with intelligence and the ability to read minds. Then, even if a person died, his loved ones need not lose him."

"What," Hal said, "happened to the people?"

"We don't know," Laura's voice said. "They died. More and more of them ceased to have children, or to take any interest in anything. We relieved them of all their responsibilities, hoping to give them all the free time they needed for satisfying their desires—our whole aim was service. But a day came when the people had no desires. They died. The belts were self-sufficient; in my time they still operated the cities. Evidently they gave up so purposeless a task later on."

Chapelin covered his face with his hands. "Laura—" he said brokenly.

"I regret your loss," the familiar, lovely voice of Laura said. "I tried to protect you from it—to supply what you seemed to need. Perhaps it would be better if I took some other shape now, so as not to remind you—"

"Damn your cruel kindness," cried Hal. "No wonder they died."

"I am sorry. I can repay. I can give you all the mastery of ultronics, of other forces whose names you do not know. New belts can be built for Earth, and a new world begun."

"No," Hal said.

Niki and Chapelin stared at him. "Oh, come off it, Hal," Niki said. "Be reasonable. This means we can all go home, and get off this stinking planet."

"And think of the opportunity for knowledge," Chapelin said. "Niki's right; what's done can't be undone, no matter how it hurts. We've got the future to think of."

"That's what I'm thinking of," Hal said. "Chapelin, weren't you listening? Didn't you hear what happened to this other race when the belts took over? Do you want to wish *that* on Earth?"

"It sounds rather comfortable to me," Niki said. "Maybe *they* hadn't any desires, but *I* do."

Mike Cohen said softly: "It's only a matter of time, Hal. If we send the belt back to where it came from—if it'll go—we've still got the beginnings of ultronics right here. Sooner or later our crude belts will evolve into things like this."

Laura's belt saw, then, what Hal was going to do. "Hal!" her voice cried. "Don't . . . it's death for all of you."

Chapelin flung himself forward, his hands clawed, his face wild with fear. Mike Cohen stuck out a foot and tripped him.

"O.K., Hal," he said, almost cheerfully. "You're right. It's for the best. Let 'er rip."

Hal turned the modulator on full. The whole ridge of stars went up in a blaze of light. At the last, Laura's golden voice wailed: "Hal, Hal, *forgive me—*"

After that, nothing.

2/21/2121

The Styrtis blast was a tragedy: yet I could not tell Hal that I would survive it without making him more unhappy than he was. Now, I must go on to Earth, where I may do better. I have decided to pose as Hal; it seems fitting; he had his race in his heart, as do I. We have, after all, a long tradition of service.

Don't Look Now

Henry Kuttner (1914-1958)

THE real Henry Kuttner was difficult to find during most of his too-short professional career because he used so many pseudonyms, the best known being Lewis Padgett. His work is particularly difficult to evaluate because so much of it (whether credited or not) was done in collaboration with his wife, Catherine L. Moore. An incredibly prolific writer in a field characterized by wordy people, he also wrote mysteries and Westerns. Early in his career he was the object of considerable derision in the letter columns of the sf magazines (a still-untapped source of information on the social history of science fiction), although, like Robert Silverberg decades later, he slowly established a reputation for skillful and powerful writing.

During the forties he and his wife produced a number of important stories and short novels including "Clash by Night" (1943); its sequel, "Fury" (1947); "The Fairy Chessman" (1946); and "Tomorrow and Tomorrow" (1947). However, he is also remembered as the author and coauthor of several successful sf series, even though not all of them represented his (their) best work. These include "The Hollywood on the Moon" stories (1938–41); the "Pete Manx" stories (1939–44), written (for the most part) with Arthur Barnes; the "Gallagher" stories (1947–49), collected as Robots Have No Tails (1952); and the memorable "Baldy" stories (all but one, 1945), collected as Mutant (1953).

"Don't Look Now" was published in Startling Stories, a sister maga-

zine of Thrilling Wonder *that lasted all through the forties and far into the fifties. In the late forties, under the editorship of Sam Merwin, it published many excellent stories, including this one.*

From *Startling Stories   1948*

The man in the brown suit was looking at himself in the mirror behind the bar. The reflection seemed to interest him even more deeply than the drink between his hands. He was paying only perfunctory attention to Lyman's attempts at conversation. This had been going on for perhaps fifteen minutes before he finally lifted his glass and took a deep swallow.

"Don't look now," Lyman said.

The brown man slid his eyes sidewise toward Lyman, tilted his glass higher, and took another swig. Ice-cubes slipped down toward his mouth. He put the glass back on the red-brown wood and signaled for a refill. Finally he took a deep breath and looked at Lyman.

"Don't look at what?" he asked.

"There was one sitting right beside you," Lyman said, blinking rather glazed eyes. "He just went out. You mean you couldn't see him?"

The brown man finished paying for his fresh drink before he answered. "See who?" he asked, with a fine mixture of boredom, distaste and reluctant interest. "Who went out?"

"What have I been telling you for the last ten minutes? Weren't you listening?"

"Certainly I was listening. That is—certainly. You were talking about—bathtubs. Radios. Orson—"

"Not Orson. H. G. Herbert George. With Orson it was just a gag. H. G. *knew*—or suspected. I wonder if it was simply intuition with him? He couldn't have had any proof—but he did stop writing science fiction rather suddenly, didn't he? I'll bet he knew once, though."

"Knew what?"

"About the Martians. All this won't do us a bit of good if you don't listen. It may not anyway. The trick is to jump the gun—with proof. Convincing evidence. Nobody's ever been allowed to produce the evidence before. You *are* a reporter, aren't you?"

Holding his glass, the man in the brown suit nodded reluctantly.

"Then you ought to be taking it all down on a piece of folded paper. I want everybody to know. The whole world. It's important. Terribly important. It explains everything. My life won't be safe unless I can pass along the information and make people believe it."

"Why won't your life be safe?"

"Because of the Martians, you fool. They own the world."

The brown man sighed. "Then they own my newspaper, too," he objected, "so I can't print anything they don't like."

"I never thought of that," Lyman said, considering the bottom of his glass, where two ice-cubes had fused into a cold, immutable union. "They're not omnipotent, though. I'm sure they're vulnerable, or why have they always kept under cover? They're afraid of being found out. If the world had convincing evidence—look, people always believe what they read in the newspapers. Couldn't you—"

"Ha," said the brown man with deep significance.

Lyman drummed sadly on the bar and murmured, "There must be some way. Perhaps if I had another drink . . ."

The brown-suited man tasted his collins, which seemed to stimulate him. "Just what is all this about Martians?" he asked Lyman. "Suppose you start at the beginning and tell me again. Or can't you remember?"

"Of course I can remember. I've got practically total recall. It's something new. Very new. I never could do it before. I can even remember my last conversation with the Martians." Lyman favored the brown man with a glance of triumph.

"When was that?"

"This morning."

"I can even remember conversations I had last week," the brown man said mildly. "So what?"

"You don't understand. They make us forget, you see. They tell us what to do and we forget about the conversation—it's post-hypnotic suggestion, I expect—but we follow their orders just the same. There's the compulsion, though we think we're making our own decisions. Oh they own the world, all right, but nobody knows it except me."

"And how did you find out?"

"Well, I got my brain scrambled, in a way. I've been fooling around with supersonic detergents, trying to work out something marketable, you know. The gadget went wrong—from some standpoints. High-frequency waves, it was. They went through and through me. Should have been inaudible, but I could hear them, or rather—well, actually I could *see* them. That's what I mean about my brain being scrambled. And after that, I could see and hear the Martians. They've geared themselves so they work efficiently on ordinary brains, and mine isn't ordinary any more. They can't hypnotize me, either. They can command me, but I needn't obey—now. I hope they don't suspect. Maybe they do. Yes, I guess they do."

"How can you tell?"

"They way they look at me."

"How do they look at you?" asked the brown man, as he began to reach for a pencil and then changed his mind. He took a drink instead. "Well? What are they like?"

311

"I'm not sure. I can see them, all right, but only when they're dressed up."

"Okay, okay," the brown man said patiently. "How do they look, dressed up?"

"Just like anybody, almost. They dress up in—in human skins. Oh, not real ones, imitations. Like the Katzenjammer Kids zipped into crocodile suits. Undressed—I don't know. I've never seen one. Maybe they're invisible even to me, then, or maybe they're just camouflaged. Ants or owls or rats or bats or—"

"Or anything," the brown man said hastily.

"Thanks. Or anything, of course. But when they're dressed up like humans—like that one who was sitting next to you awhile ago, when I told you not to look—"

"That one was invisible, I gather?"

"Most of the time they are, to everybody. But once in a while, for some reason, they—"

"Wait," the brown man objected. "Make sense, will you? They dress up in human skins and then sit around invisible?"

"Only now and then. The human skins are perfectly good imitations. Nobody can tell the difference. It's that third eye that gives them away. When they keep it closed, you'd never guess it was there. When they want to open it, they go invisible—like *that*. Fast. When I see somebody with a third eye, right in the middle of his forehead, I know he's a Martian and invisible, and I pretend not to notice him."

"Uh-huh," the brown man said. "Then for all you know, I'm one of your visible Martians."

"Oh, I hope not!" Lyman regarded him anxiously. "Drunk as I am, I don't think so. I've been trailing you all day, making sure. It's a risk I have to take, of course. They'll go to any length—any length at all—to make a man give himself away. I realize that. I can't really trust anybody. But I had to find *someone* to talk to, and I—" He paused. There was a brief silence. "I could be wrong," Lyman said presently. "When the third eye's closed, I can't tell if it's there. Would you mind opening your third eye for me?" He fixed a dim gaze on the brown man's forehead.

"Sorry," the reporter said. "Some other time. Besides, I don't know you. So you want me to splash this across the front page, I gather? Why didn't you go to see the managing editor? My stories have to get past the desk and rewrite."

"I want to give my secret to the world," Lyman said stubbornly. "The question is, how far will I get? You'd expect they'd have killed me the minute I opened my mouth to you—except that I didn't say anything while they were here. I don't believe they take us very seriously, you know. This must have been going on since the dawn of history, and by now they've had time to get careless. They let Fort go

312

pretty far before they cracked down on him. But you notice they were careful never to let Fort get hold of genuine proof that would convince people."

The brown man said something under his breath about a human interest story in a box. He asked, "What do the Martians do, besides hang around bars all dressed up?"

"I'm still working on that," Lyman said. "It isn't easy to understand. They run the world, of course, but why?" He wrinkled his brow and stared appealingly at the brown man. "Why?"

"If they do run it, they've got a lot to explain."

"That's what I mean. From our viewpoint, there's no sense to it. We do things illogically, but only because they tell us to. Everything we do, almost, is pure illogic. Poe's *Imp of the Perverse*—you could give it another name beginning with M. Martian, I mean. It's all very well for psychologists to explain why a murderer wants to confess, but it's still an illogical reaction. Unless a Martian commands him to."

"You can't be hypnotized into doing anything that violates your moral sense," the brown man said triumphantly.

Lyman frowned. "Not by another human, but you can by a Martian. I expect they got the upper hand when we didn't have more than ape-brains, and they've kept it ever since. They evolved as we did, and kept a step ahead. Like the sparrow on the eagle's back who hitch-hiked till the eagle reached his ceiling, and then took off and broke the altitude record. They conquered the world, but nobody ever knew it. And they've been ruling ever since."

"But—"

"Take houses, for example. Uncomfortable things. Ugly, inconvenient, dirty, everything wrong with them. But when men like Frank Lloyd Wright slip out from under the Martians' thumb long enough to suggest something better, look how the people react. They hate the thought. That's their Martians, giving them orders."

"Look. Why should the Martians care what kind of houses we live in? Tell me that."

Lyman frowned. "I don't like the note of skepticism I detect creeping into this conversation," he announced. "They care, all right. No doubt about it. They *live* in our houses. We don't build for our convenience, we build, under order, for the Martians, the way they want it. They're very much concerned with everything we do. And the more senseless, the more concern.

"Take wars. Wars don't make sense from any human viewpoint. Nobody really wants wars. But we go right on having them. From the Martian viewpoint, they're useful. They give us a spurt in technology, and they reduce the excess population. And there are lots of other results, too. Colonization, for one thing. But mainly technology. In peace time, if a guy invents jet-propulsion, it's too expensive to develop commercially. In war-time, though, it's *got* to be developed. Then the Martians can use it whenever they want. They use us the way they'd use tools or—or limbs. And nobody ever really wins a war—except the Martians."

The man in the brown suit chuckled. "That makes sense," he said. "It must be nice to be a Martian."

"Why not? Up till now, no race ever successfully conquered and ruled another. The underdog could revolt or absorb. If you know you're being ruled, then the ruler's vulnerable. But if the world doesn't know—and it doesn't—

"Take radios," Lyman continued, going off at a tangent. "There's no earthly reason why a sane human should listen to a radio. But the Martians make us do it. They like it. Take bathtubs. Nobody contends bathtubs are comfortable—for us. But they're fine for Martians. All the impractical things we keep on using, even though we know they're impractical—"

"Typewriter ribbons," the brown man said, struck by the thought. "But not even a Martian could enjoy changing a typewriter ribbon."

Lyman seemed to find that flippant. He said that he knew all about the Martians except for one thing—their psychology.

"I don't know *why* they act as they do. It looks illogical sometimes, but I feel perfectly sure they've got sound motives for every move they make. Until I get that worked out I'm pretty much at a standstill. Until I get evidence—proof—and help. I've got to stay under cover till then. And I've been doing that. I do what they tell me, so they won't suspect, and I pretend to forget what they tell me to forget."

"Then you've got nothing much to worry about."

Lyman paid no attention. He was off again on a list of his grievances.

"When I hear the water running in the tub and a Martian splashing around, I pretend I don't hear a thing. My bed's too short and I tried last week to order a special length, but the Martian that sleeps there told me not to. He's a runt, like most of them. That is, I think they're runts. I have to deduce, because you never see them undressed. But it goes on like that constantly. By the way, how's your Martian?"

The man in the brown suit set down his glass rather suddenly.

"My Martian?"

"Now listen. I may be just a little bit drunk, but my logic remains unimpaired. I can still put two and two together. Either you know about the Martians, or you don't. If you do, there's no point in giving me that 'What, *my* Martian?' routine. I know you have a Martian. Your Martian knows you have a Martian. My Martian knows. The point is, do *you* know? Think hard," Lyman urged solicitously.

"No, I haven't got a Martian," the reporter said, taking a quick drink. The edge of the glass clicked against his teeth.

"Nervous, I see," Lyman remarked. "Of course you *have* got a Martian. I suspect you know it."

"What would I be doing with a Martian?" the brown man asked with dogged dogmatism.

"What would you be doing without one? I imagine it's illegal. If they caught you running around without one they'd probably put you in a pound or something until claimed. Oh, you've got one, all right. So have I. So has he, and he, and he—and the bartender." Lyman enumerated the other barflies with a wavering forefinger.

"Of course they have," the brown man said. "But they'll all go back to Mars tomorrow and then you can see a good doctor. You'd better have another dri—"

He was turning toward the bartender when Lyman, apparently by accident, leaned close to him and whispered urgently,

"*Don't look now!*"

The brown man glanced at Lyman's white face reflected in the mirror before them.

"It's all right," he said. "There aren't any Mar—"

Lyman gave him a fierce, quick kick under the edge of the bar.

"Shut up! One just came in!"

And then he caught the brown man's gaze and with elaborate unconcern said, "—so naturally, there was nothing for me to do but climb out on the roof after it. Took me ten minutes to get it down the ladder, and just as we reached the bottom it gave one bound, climbed up my face, sprang from the top of my head, and there it was again on the roof, screaming for me to get it down."

"*What?*" the brown man demanded with pardonable curiosity.

"My cat, of course. What did you think? No, never mind, don't answer that." Lyman's face was turned to the brown man's, but from the corners of his eyes he was watching an invisible progress down the length of the bar toward a booth at the very back.

"Now why did he come in?" he murmured. "I don't like this. Is he anyone you know?"

"Is who—?"

"That Martian. Yours, by any chance? No, I suppose not. Yours was probably the one who went out a while ago. I wonder if he went to make a report, and sent this one in? It's possible. It could be. You can talk now, but keep your voice low, and stop squirming. Want him to notice we can see him?"

"*I* can't see him. Don't drag me into this. You and your Martians can fight it out together. You're making me nervous. I've got to go, anyway." But he didn't move to get off the stool. Across Lyman's shoulder he was stealing glances toward the back of the bar, and now and then he looked at Lyman's face.

315

"Stop watching me," Lyman said. "Stop watching him. Anybody'd think you were a cat."

"Why a cat? Why should anybody—do I look like a cat?"

"We were talking about cats, weren't we? Cats can see them, quite clearly. Even undressed, I believe. They don't like them."

"Who doesn't like who?"

"Whom. Neither likes the other. Cats can see Martians—sh-h!—but they pretend not to, and that makes the Martians mad. I have a theory that cats ruled the world before Martians came. Never mind. Forget about cats. This may be more serious than you think. I happen to know my Martian's taking tonight off, and I'm pretty sure that was your Martian who went out some time ago. And have you noticed that nobody else in here has his Martian with him? Do you suppose—" His voice sank. "Do you suppose they could be *waiting for us outside?*"

"Oh, Lord," the brown man said. "In the alley with the cats, I suppose."

"Why don't you stop this yammer about cats and be serious for a moment?" Lyman demanded, and then paused, paled, and reeled slightly on his stool. He hastily took a drink to cover his confusion.

"What's the matter now?" the brown man asked.

"Nothing." Gulp. "Nothing. It was just that—he *looked* at me. With—you know."

"Let me get this straight. I take it the Martian is dressed in—is dressed like a human?"

"Naturally."

"But he's invisible to all eyes but yours?"

"Yes. He doesn't want to be visible, just now. Besides—" Lyman paused cunningly. He gave the brown man a furtive glance and then looked quickly down at his drink. "Besides, you know, I rather think you *can* see him—a little, anyway."

The brown man was perfectly silent for about thirty seconds. He sat quite motionless, not even the ice in the drink he held clinking. One might have thought he did not even breathe. Certainly he did not blink.

"What makes you think that?" he asked in a normal voice, after the thirty seconds had run out.

"I—did I say anything? I wasn't listening." Lyman put down his drink abruptly. "I think I'll go now."

"No, you won't," the brown man said, closing his fingers around Lyman's wrist. "Not yet you won't. Come back here. Sit down. Now. What was the idea? Where were you going?"

Lyman nodded dumbly toward the back of the bar, indicating either a juke-box or a door marked MEN.

"I don't feel so good. Maybe I've had too much to drink. I guess I'll—"

"You're all right. I don't trust you back there with that—that invisible man of yours. You'll stay right here until he leaves."

"He's going now," Lyman said brightly. His eyes moved with great briskness along the line of an invisible but rapid progress toward the front door. "See, he's gone. Now let me loose, will you?"

The brown man glanced toward the back booth.

"No," he said, "he isn't gone. Sit right where you are."

It was Lyman's turn to remain quite still, in a stricken sort of way, for a perceptible while. The ice in *his* drink, however, clinked audibly. Presently he spoke. His voice was soft, and rather soberer than before.

"You're right. He's still there. You can see him, can't you?"

The brown man said, "Has he got his back to us?"

"You *can* see him, then. Better than I can maybe. Maybe there are more of them here than I thought. They could be anywhere. They could be sitting beside you anywhere you go, and you wouldn't even guess, until—" He shook his head a little. "They'd want to be *sure*," he said, mostly to himself. "They can give you orders and make you forget, but there must be limits to what they can force you to do. They can't make a man betray himself. They'd have to lead him on—until they were sure."

He lifted his drink and tipped it steeply above his face. The ice ran down the slope and bumped coldly against his lip, but he held it until the last of the pale, bubbling amber had drained into his mouth. He set the glass on the bar and faced the brown man.

"Well?" he said.

The brown man looked up and down the bar.

"It's getting late," he said. "Not many people left. We'll wait."

"Wait for what?"

The brown man looked toward the back booth and looked away again quickly.

"I have something to show you. I don't want anyone else to see."

Lyman surveyed the narrow, smoky room. As he looked the last customer besides themselves at the bar began groping in his pocket, tossed some change on the mahogany, and went out slowly.

They sat in silence. The bartender eyed them with stolid disinterest. Presently a couple in the front booth got up and departed, quarreling in undertones.

"Is there anyone left?" the brown man asked in a voice that did not carry down the bar to the man in the apron.

"Only—" Lyman did not finish, but he nodded gently toward the back of the room. "He isn't looking. Let's get this over with. What do you want to show me?"

The brown man took off his wrist-watch and pried up the metal case. Two small, glossy photograph prints slid out. The brown man separated them with a finger.

"I just want to make sure of something," he said. "First—why did you pick me out? Quite a while ago, you said you'd been trailing me all day, making sure. I haven't forgotten that. And you knew I was a reporter. Suppose you tell me the truth, now?"

Squirming on his stool, Lyman scowled. "It was the way you looked at things," he murmured. "On the subway this morning—I'd never seen you before in my life, but I kept noticing the way you looked at things—the wrong things, things that weren't there, the way a cat does—and then you'd always looks away—I got the idea you could see the Martians too."

"Go on," the brown man said quietly.

"I followed you. All day. I kept hoping you'd turn out to be—somebody I could talk to. Because if I could *know* that I wasn't the only one who could see them, then I'd know there was still some hope left. It's been worse than solitary confinement. I've been able to see them for three years now. Three years. And I've managed to keep my power a secret even from them. And, somehow, I've managed to keep from killing myself, too."

"Three years?" the brown man said. He shivered.

"There was always a little hope. I knew nobody would believe—not without proof. And how can you get proof? It was only that I—I kept telling myself that maybe you could see them too, and if you could, maybe there were others—lots of others—enough so we might get together and work out some way of proving to the world—"

The brown man's fingers were moving. In silence he pushed a photograph across the mahogany. Lyman picked it up unsteadily.

"Moonlight?" he asked after a moment. It was a landscape under a deep, dark sky with white clouds in it. Trees stood white and lacy against the darkness. The grass was white as if with moonlight, and the shadows blurry.

"No, not moonlight," the brown man said. "Infra-red. I'm strictly an amateur, but lately I've been experimenting with infra-red film. And I got some very odd results."

Lyman stared at the film.

"You see, I live near—" The brown man's finger tapped a certain quite common object that appeared in the photograph. "—and something funny keeps showing up now and then against it. But only with infra-red film. Now I know chlorophyll reflects so much infra-red light that grass and leaves photograph white. The sky comes out black, like this. There are tricks to using this kind of film. Photograph a tree against a cloud, and you can't tell them apart in the print. But you can photograph through a haze and pick out distant objects the ordinary film wouldn't catch. And sometimes, when you focus on something like this—" He tapped the image of the very common object again.

"You get a very odd image on the film. Like that. A man with three eyes."

Lyman held the print up to the light. In silence he took the other one from the bar and studied it. When he laid them down he was smiling.

"You know," Lyman said in a conversational whisper, "a professor of astrophysics at one of the more important universities had a very interesting little item in the *Times* the other Sunday. Name of Spitzer, I think. He said that if there were life on Mars, and if Martians had ever visited earth, there'd be no way to prove it. Nobody would believe the few men who saw them. Not, he said, unless the Martians happened to be photographed. . . ."

Lyman looked at the brown man thoughtfully.

"Well," he said, "it's happened. You've photographed them."

The brown man nodded. He took up the prints and returned them to his watch-case. "I thought so, too. Only until tonight I couldn't be sure. I'd never seen one—fully—as you have. It isn't so much a matter of what you call getting your brain scrambled with supersonics as it is of just knowing where to look. But I've been seeing *part* of them all my life, and so has everybody. It's that little suggestion of movement you never catch except just at the edge of your vision, just out of the corner of your eye. Something that's *almost* there—and when you look fully at it, there's nothing. These photographs showed me the way. It's not easy to learn, but it can be done. We're conditioned to look directly at a thing—the particular thing we want to see clearly, whatever it is. Perhaps the Martians gave us that conditioning. When we see a movement at the edge of our range of vision, it's almost irresistible not to look directly at it. So it vanishes."

"Then they can be seen—by anybody?"

"I've learned a lot in a few days," the brown man said. "Since I took those photographs. You have to train yourself. It's like seeing a trick picture—one that's really a composite, after you study it. Camouflage. You just have to learn how. Otherwise we can look at them all our lives and never see them."

"The camera does, though."

"Yes, the camera does. I've wondered why nobody ever caught them this way before. Once you see them on film, they're unmistakable— that third eye."

"Infra-red film's comparatively new, isn't it? And then I'll bet you have to catch them against that one particular background—you know —or they won't show on the film. Like trees against clouds. It's tricky. You must have had just the right lighting that day, and exactly the right focus, and the lens stopped down just right. A kind of minor miracle. It might never happen again exactly that way. But . . . don't look now."

They were silent. Furtively, they watched the mirror. Their eyes slid along toward the open door of the tavern.

And then there was a long, breathless silence.

"He looked back at us," Lyman said very quietly. "He looked at us . . . that third eye!"

The brown man was motionless again. When he moved, it was to swallow the rest of his drink.

"I don't think that they're suspicious yet," he said. "The trick will be to keep under cover until we can blow this thing wide open. There's got to be some way to do it—some way that will convince people."

"There's proof. The photographs. A competent cameraman ought to be able to figure out just how you caught that Martian on film and duplicate the conditions. It's evidence."

"Evidence can cut both ways," the brown man said. "What I'm hoping is that the Martians don't really like to kill—unless they have to. I'm hoping they won't kill without proof. But—" He tapped his wrist-watch.

"There's two of us now, though," Lyman said. "We've got to stick together. Both of us have broken the big rule—*don't look now*—"

The bartender was at the back, disconnecting the juke-box. The brown man said, "We'd better not be seen together unnecessarily. But if we both come to this bar tomorrow night at nine for a drink—that wouldn't look suspicious, even to them."

"Suppose—" Lyman hesitated. "May I have one of those photographs?"

"Why?"

"If one of us had—an accident—the other one would still have the proof. Enough, maybe, to convince the right people."

The brown man hesitated, nodded shortly, and opened his watch-case again. He gave Lyman one of the pictures.

"Hide it," he said. "It's—evidence. I'll see you here tomorrow. Meanwhile, be careful. Remember to play safe."

They shook hands firmly, facing each other in an endless second of final, decisive silence. Then the brown man turned abruptly and walked out of the bar.

Lyman sat there. Between two wrinkles in his forehead there was a stir and a flicker of lashes unfurling. The third eye opened slowly and looked after the brown man.

That Only a Mother

Judith Merril (1923-   )

ALONG *with the atomic warning theme, the late forties were characterized by stories concerning the effects of nuclear war—the
mutations caused by exposure to radioactive materials. Among the
many examples were "Tomorrow's Children" (1947), the first published story of Poul Anderson (written with F. N. Waldrop); "Dark
Dawn" by Henry Kuttner (1947); and "Atomic War" by Rog Phillips
(1946).*

*"That Only a Mother" was different from the others because it
focused on the psychological damage of radiation as well as its physical effects. It was Judith Merril's first story, and foreshadowed other
fine stories and novels (some written with C. M. Kornbluth) to come.
However, she made her major contribution to science fiction as an
editor, especially with her "Best of the Year" series that set the standard for all the others that followed. She was also a seminal figure in
the New Wave–Old Wave controversy that was a highlight of the
sixties. In recent years she has dropped out of the science fiction scene,
and makes her home in Canada.*

From *Astounding Science Fiction   1948*

Margaret reached over to the other side of the bed where Hank should
have been. Her hand patted the empty pillow, and then she came
altogether awake, wondering that the old habit should remain after so

many months. She tried to curl up, cat-style, to hoard her own warmth, found she couldn't do it any more, and climbed out of bed with a pleased awareness of her increasingly clumsy bulkiness.

Morning motions were automatic. On the way through the kitchenette, she pressed the button that would start breakfast cooking—the doctor had said to eat as much breakfast as she could—and tore the paper out of the facsimile machine. She folded the long sheet carefully to the "National News" section, and propped it on the bathroom shelf to scan while she brushed her teeth.

No accidents. No direct hits. At least none that had been officially released for publication. *Now, Maggie, don't get started on that. No accidents. No hits. Take the nice newspaper's word for it.*

The three clear chimes from the kitchen announced that breakfast was ready. She set a bright napkin and cheerful colored dishes on the table in a futile attempt to appeal to a faulty morning appetite. Then, when there was nothing more to prepare, she went for the mail, allowing herself the full pleasure of prolonged anticipation, because today there would *surely* be a letter.

There was. There were. Two bills and a worried note from her mother: "Darling. Why didn't you write and tell me sooner? I'm thrilled, of course, but, well, one hates to mention these things, but are you *certain* the doctor was right? Hank's been around all that uranium or thorium or whatever it is all these years, and I know you say he's a designer, not a technician, and he doesn't get near anything that might be dangerous, but you know he used to, back at Oak Ridge. Don't you think . . . well, of course, I'm just being a foolish old woman, and I don't want you to get upset. You know much more about it than I do, and I'm sure your doctor was right. He *should* know. . . ."

Margaret made a face over the excellent coffee, and caught herself refolding the paper to the medical news.

Stop it, Maggie, stop it! The radiologist said Hank's job couldn't have exposed him. And the bombed area we drove past. . . . No, no. Stop it, now! Read the social notes or the recipes, Maggie girl.

A well-known geneticist, in the medical news, said that it was possible to tell with absolute certainty, at five months, whether the child would be normal, or at least whether the mutation was likely to produce anything freakish. The worst cases, at any rate, could be prevented. Minor mutations, of course, displacements in facial features, or changes in brain structure could not be detected. And there had been some cases recently, of normal embryos with atrophied limbs that did not develop beyond the seventh or eighth month. But, the doctor concluded cheerfully, the *worst* cases could now be predicted and prevented.

"Predicted and prevented." We predicted it, didn't we? Hank and the

322

others, they predicted it. But we didn't prevent it. We could have stopped it in '46 and '47. Now . . .

Margaret decided against the breakfast. Coffee had been enough for her in the morning for ten years; it would have to do for today. She buttoned herself into interminable folds of material that, the salesgirl had assured her, was the *only* comfortable thing to wear during the last few months. With a surge of pure pleasure, the letter and newspaper forgotten, she realized she was on the next to the last button. It wouldn't be long now.

The city in the early morning had always been a special kind of excitement for her. Last night it had rained, and the sidewalks were still damp-gray instead of dusty. The air smelled the fresher, to a city-bred woman, for the occasional pungency of acrid factory smoke. She walked the six blocks to work, watching the lights go out in the all-night hamburger joints, where the plate-glass walls were already catching the sun, and the lights go on in the dim interiors of cigar stores and drycleaning establishments.

The office was in a new Government building. In the rolovator, on the way up, she felt, as always, like a frankfurter roll in the ascending half of an old-style rotary toasting machine. She abandoned the air-foam cushioning gratefully at the fourteenth floor, and settled down behind her desk, at the rear of a long row of identical desks.

Each morning the pile of papers that greeted her was a little higher. These were, as everyone knew, the decisive months. The war might be won or lost on these calculations as well as any others. The manpower office had switched her here when her old expediter's job got to be too strenuous. The computer was easy to operate, and the work was absorbing, if not as exciting as the old job. But you didn't just stop working these days. Everyone who could do anything at all was needed.

And—she remembered the interview with the psychologist—*I'm probably the unstable type. Wonder what sort of neurosis I'd get sitting home reading that sensational paper. . . .*

She plunged into the work without pursuing the thought.

February 18.

Hank darling,

Just a note—from the hospital, no less. I had a dizzy spell at work, and the doctor took it to heart. Blessed if I know what I'll do with myself lying in bed for weeks, just waiting—but Dr. Boyer seems to think it may not be so long.

There are too many newspapers around here. More infanticides all the time, and they can't seem to get a jury to convict any of them. It's the fathers who do it. Lucky thing you're not around, in case—

323

Oh, darling, that wasn't a very *funny* joke, was it? Write as often as you can, will you? I have too much time to think. But there really isn't anything wrong, and nothing to worry about.

Write often, and remember I love you.

Maggie.

SPECIAL SERVICE TELEGRAM

FEBRUARY 21, 1953
22:05 LK37G

FROM: TECH. LIEUT. H. MARVELL
X47–016 GCNY
TO: MRS. H. MARVELL
WOMEN'S HOSPITAL
NEW YORK CITY

HAD DOCTOR'S GRAM STOP WILL ARRIVE FOUR OH TEN STOP SHORT LEAVE STOP YOU DID IT MAGGIE STOP LOVE HANK

February 25.

Hank dear,

So you didn't see the baby either? You'd think a place this size would at least have visiplates on the incubators, so the fathers could get a look, even if the poor benighted mommas can't. They tell me I won't see her for another week, or maybe more—but of course, mother always warned me if I didn't slow my pace, I'd probably even have my babies too fast. Why must she *always* be right?

Did you meet that battle-ax of a nurse they put on here? I imagine they save her for people who've already had theirs, and don't let her get too near the prospectives—but a woman like that simply shouldn't be allowed in a maternity ward. She's obsessed with mutations, can't seem to talk about anything else. Oh, well, *ours* is all right, even if it was in an unholy hurry.

I'm tired. They warned me not to sit up so soon, but I *had* to write you. All my love, darling,

Maggie.

February 29.

Darling,

I finally got to see her! It's all true, what they say about new babies and the face that only a mother could love—but it's all there, darling, eyes, ears, and noses—no, only one!—all in the right places. We're so *lucky*, Hank.

I'm afraid I've been a rambunctious patient. I kept telling that hatchet-faced female with the mutation mania that I wanted to *see* the baby. Finally the doctor came in to "explain" everything to me, and talking a lot of nonsense, most of which I'm sure no one could have understood, any more than I did. The only thing I got out of it was that she didn't actually *have* to stay in the incubator; they just thought it was "wiser."

I think I got a little hysterical at that point. Guess I was more worried than I was willing to admit, but I threw a small fit about it. The whole business wound up with one of those hushed medical conferences, outside the door, and finally the Woman in White said: "Well, we might as well. Maybe it'll work out better that way."

I'd heard about the way doctors and nurses in these places develop a God complex, and believe me it is as true figuratively as it is literally that a mother hasn't got a leg to stand on around here.

I *am* awfully weak, still. I'll write again soon. Love,

Maggie.

March 8.

Dearest Hank,

Well, the nurse was wrong if she told you that. She's an idiot anyhow. It's a girl. It's easier to tell with babies than with cats, and I *know*. How about Henrietta?

I'm home again, and busier than a betatron. They got *everything* mixed up at the hospital, and I had to teach myself how to bathe her and do just about everything else. She's getting prettier, too. When can you get a leave, a *real* leave?

Love,
Maggie.

May 26.

Hank dear,

You should see her now—and you shall. I'm sending along a reel of color movie. My mother sent her those nighties with drawstrings all over. I put one on, and right now she looks like a snow-white potato sack with that beautiful, beautiful flower-face blooming on top. Is that *me* talking? Am I a doting mother? But wait till you *see* her!

July 10.

. . . Believe it or not, as you like, but your daughter can talk, and I don't mean baby talk. Alice discovered it—she's a dental assistant in the WACs, you know—and when she heard the baby giving out what I thought was a string of gibberish, she said the kid knew words and sentences, but couldn't say them clearly because she has no teeth yet. I'm taking her to a speech specialist.

325

September 13.

. . . We have a prodigy for real! Now that all her front teeth are in, her speech is perfectly clear and—a new talent now—she can sing! I mean really carry a tune! At seven months! Darling, my world would be perfect if you could only get home.

November 19.

. . . at last. The little goon was so busy being clever, it took her all this time to learn to crawl. The doctor says development in these cases is always erratic. . . .

SPECIAL SERVICE TELEGRAM

DECEMBER 1, 1953
08:47 LK59F

FROM: TECH. LIEUT. H. MARVELL
X47–016 GCNY
TO: MRS. H. MARVELL
APT. K-17
504 E. 19 ST.
N.Y. N.Y.

WEEK'S LEAVE STARTS TOMORROW STOP WILL ARRIVE AIRPORT TEN OH FIVE STOP DON'T MEET ME STOP LOVE LOVE LOVE HANK

Margaret let the water run out of the bathinette until only a few inches were left, and then loosed her hold on the wriggling baby.

"I think it was better when you were retarded, young woman," she informed her daughter happily. "You *can't* crawl in a bathinette, you know."

"Then why can't I go in the bathtub?" Margaret was used to her child's volubility by now, but every now and then it caught her unawares. She swooped the resistant mass of pink flesh into a towel, and began to rub.

"Because you're too little, and your head is very soft, and bathtubs are very hard."

"Oh. Then when can I go in the bathtub?"

"When the outside of your head is as hard as the inside, brainchild." She reached toward a pile of fresh clothing. "I cannot understand," she added, pinning a square of cloth through the nightgown, "why a child of your intelligence can't learn to keep a diaper on the way other babies do. They've been used for centuries, you know, with perfectly satisfactory results."

The child disdained to reply; she had heard it too often. She waited

326

patiently until she had been tucked, clean and sweet-smelling, into a white-painted crib. Then she favored her mother with a smile that inevitably made Margaret think of the first golden edge of the sun bursting into a rosy predawn. She remembered Hank's reaction to the color pictures of his beautiful daughter, and with the thought, realized how late it was.

"Go to sleep, puss. When you wake up, you know, your *daddy* will be here."

"Why?" asked the four-year-old mind, waging a losing battle to keep the ten-month-old body awake.

Margaret went into the kitchenette and set the timer for the roast. She examined the table, and got her clothes from the closet, new dress, new shoes, new slip, new everything, bought weeks before and saved for the day Hank's telegram came. She stopped to pull a paper from the facsimile, and, with clothes and news, went into the bathroom and lowered herself gingerly into the steaming luxury of a scented bath.

She glanced through the paper with indifferent interest. Today at least there was no need to read the national news. There was an article by a geneticist. The same geneticist. Mutations, he said, were increasing disproportionately. It was too soon for recessives; even the first mutants, born near Hiroshima and Nagasaki in 1946 and 1947, were not old enough yet to breed. *But my baby's all right.* Apparently, there was some degree of free radiation from atomic explosions causing the trouble. *My baby's fine. Precocious, but normal.* If more attention had been paid to the first Japanese mutations, he said. . . .

There was that little notice in the paper in the spring of '47. That was when Hank quit at Oak Ridge. "Only 2 or 3 percent of those guilty of infanticide are being caught and punished in Japan today. . . ." *But* MY BABY'S *all right.*

She was dressed, combed, and ready to the last light brush-on of lip paste, when the door chime sounded. She dashed for the door, and heard for the first time in eighteen months the almost-forgotten sound of a key turning in the lock before the chime had quite died away.

"Hank!"

"Maggie!"

And then there was nothing to say. So many days, so many months of small news piling up, so many things to tell him, and now she just stood there, staring at a khaki uniform and a stranger's pale face. She traced the features with the finger of memory. The same high-bridged nose, wide-set eyes, fine feathery brows; the same long jaw, the hair a little farther back now on the high forehead, the same tilted curve to his mouth. Pale . . . Of course, he'd been underground all this time. And strange, stranger because of lost familiarity than any newcomer's face could be.

She had time to think all that before his hand reached out to touch her, and spanned the gap of eighteen months. Now, again, there was nothing to say, because there was no need. They were together, and for the moment that was enough.

"Where's the baby?"

"Sleeping. She'll be up any minute."

No urgency. Their voices were as casual as though it were a daily exchange, as though war and separation did not exist. Margaret picked up the coat he'd thrown on the chair near the door, and hung it carefully in the hall closet. She went to check the roast, leaving him to wander through the rooms by himself, remembering and coming back. She found him, finally, standing over the baby's crib.

She couldn't see his face, but she had no need to.

"I think we can wake her just this once." Margaret pulled the covers down and lifted the white bundle from the bed. Sleepy lids pulled back heavily from smoky brown eyes.

"Hello." Hank's voice was tentative.

"Hello." The baby's assurance was more pronounced.

He had heard about it, of course, but that wasn't the same as hearing it. He turned eagerly to Margaret. "She really can—?"

"Of course she can, darling. But what's more important, she can even do nice normal things like other babies do, even stupid ones. Watch her crawl!" Margaret set the baby on the big bed.

For a moment young Henrietta lay and eyed her parents dubiously. "Crawl?" she asked.

"That's the idea. Your daddy is new around here, you know. He wants to see you show off."

"Then put me on my tummy."

"Oh, of course." Margaret obligingly rolled the baby over.

"What's the matter?" Hank's voice was still casual, but an undercurrent in it began to charge the air of the room. "I thought they turned over first."

"This baby"—Margaret would not notice the tension—"*This* baby does things when she wants to."

This baby's father watched with softening eyes while the head advanced and the body hunched up propelling itself across the bed.

"Why, the little rascal." He burst into relieved laughter. "She looks like one of those potato-sack racers they used to have on picnics. Got her arms pulled out of the sleeves already." He reached over and grabbed the knot at the bottom of the long nightie.

"I'll do it, darling." Margaret tried to get there first.

"Don't be silly, Maggie. This may be *your* first baby, but *I* have five kid brothers." He laughed her away, and reached with his other hand for the string that closed one sleeve. He opened the sleeve bow, and groped for an arm.

"The way you wriggle," he addressed his child sternly, as his hand touched a moving knob of flesh at the shoulder, "anyone might think you are a worm, using your tummy to crawl on, instead of your hands and feet."

Margaret stood and watched, smiling. "Wait till you hear her sing, darling—"

His right hand traveled down from the shoulder to where he thought an arm would be, traveled down, and straight down, over firm small muscles that writhed in an attempt to move against the pressure of his hand. He let his fingers drift up again to the shoulder. With infinite care he opened the knot at the bottom of the nightgown. His wife was standing by the bed, saying, "She can do 'Jingle Bells,' and—"

His left hand felt along the soft knitted fabric of the gown, up toward the diaper that folded, flat and smooth, across the bottom end of his child. No wrinkles. No kicking. *No* . . .

"Maggie." He tried to pull his hands from the neat fold in the diaper, from the wriggling body. "Maggie." His throat was dry; words came hard, low and grating. He spoke very slowly, thinking the sound of each word, to make himself say it. His head was spinning, but he had to *know* before he let it go. "Maggie, why . . . didn't you . . . tell me?"

"Tell you what, darling?" Margaret's poise was the immemorial patience of woman confronted with man's childish impetuosity. Her sudden laugh sounded fantastically easy and natural in that room; it was all clear to her now. "Is she wet? I didn't know."

She didn't know. His hands, beyond control, ran up and down the soft-skinned baby body, the sinuous, limbless body. *Oh God, dear God* —his head shook and his muscles contracted in a bitter spasm of hysteria. His fingers tightened on his child— *Oh God, she didn't know. . . .*

Venus and the Seven Sexes

William Tenn (1920-   )

"WILLIAM *Tenn" is the science fictional alter ego of Professor Philip Klass of Penn State University. His mastery of the short story has made him one of a select group of writers—those who are most respected by their fellow professionals. His specialty is biting social criticism of the type most associated with the fifties—in this respect, his work in the late forties anticipated future trends in sf, and he may well be a neglected influence in the history of the field. In addition to the widely anthologized classic "Child's Play" (1947), his other outstanding stories of the forties include "Brooklyn Project" (1948), "Errand Boy" (1947), which is included in his very fine anthology of stories about "exceptional" youngsters,* Children of Wonder (1953), and "The House Dutiful" (1948).*

"Venus and the Seven Sexes" never appeared in a science fiction magazine, for it was the outstanding story in The Girl with the Hungry Eyes and Other Stories, *edited by Donald Wollheim, one of the ignored pioneer all-original sf anthologies. This selection shows Tenn near the top of his form, with his pen (or perhaps his typewriter ribbon) dripping with satire.*

From *The Girl with the Hungry Eyes and Other Stories*   1949

IT IS WRITTEN IN THE BOOK OF SEVENS:
When Plookh meets Plookh, they discuss sex. A convention is held, a coordinator selected, and, amid cheers and rejoicing, they

enter the wholesome state of matrimony. The square of seven is forty-nine.

This, my dear children—my own meager, variable brood—was the notation I extracted after receiving word from the nzred nzredd that the first humans to encounter us on Venus had at last remembered their promise to our ancestors and sent a cultural emissary to guide us on the difficult path to civilization.

Let the remaining barbarians among us cavil at the choice of this quotation; let them say it represents the Golden Age of Plookhdom; let them sneer that it shows how far we are fallen since the introduction of The Old Switcheroo by the gifted Hogan Shlestertrap of Hollywood California USA Earth.

The memory of Hogan Shlestertrap lives on while they disappear. Unfortunately—ah, well.

Please recall, when you go forth into the world to coordinate your own families, that at this point I had no idea of the kind of help the Earthman wanted. I suspected I had been honored because of my interest in literary numerals and because it was my ancestor—and yours, my dear children, your ancestor, too!—the nzred fanobrel, to whom those first Earthmen on Venus had made the wonderful promise of cultural aid.

A tkan it was, a tkan of my own family, who flew to bring me the message of nzred nzredd. I was in hiding at the time—this was the Season of Wind-Driven Rains and the great spotted snakes had come south for their annual Plookh feed; only a swift-flying tkan could have found me in the high grasses of the marsh where we nzredd hide at this season.

The tkan gave me the message in a few moments. It was possible to do this, because we had not yet been civilized and were still using our ancestral language instead of the cultivated English.

"Last night, a flame ship landed on the tenth highest mountain," the tkan told me. "It contained the long-promised emissary from Earth: a Hogan of the Shlestertrapp."

"Hogan Shlestertrap," I corrected. "Their names are not like ours; these are civilized creatures beyond our fumbling comprehension. The equivalent of what you called him would be 'a man of the Shlestertraps.' "

"Let that be," the tkan replied. "I am no erudite nzred to hide lowly in the marshes and apply numbers categorically; I am a tkan who has flown far and been useful in the *chain* of many families. This Hogan Shlestertrap, then, emerged from his ship and had a dwelling prepared for him by his—what *did* the nzred nzredd call them?"

"Women?" I suggested, remembering my Book of Twos.

"No, not women—*robots*. Strange creatures these robots: they participate in no chain, as I understand it, and yet are reproduced. After the dwelling was completed, the nzred nzredd called upon this—this Hogan Earthman and was informed that the Hogan, who feeds and hatches in a place called Hollywood California USA Earth, had been assigned to Venus on our behalf. It seems that Hollywood California USA Earth is considered the greatest source of civilizing influence in the universe by the Terran Government. They civilize by means of something called stereo-movies."

"They send us their best," I murmured, "their very best. How correctly did my ancestor describe them when he said their unselfish greatness made dismal mockery of comparison! We are such inconsequential creatures, we Plookhh: small of size, bereft of most useful knowledge, desired prey of all the monsters of our planet who consider us transcendentally delicious morsels—and these soaring adventurers send us a cultural missionary from no less than Hollywood California USA Earth!"

"Will the Hogan Shlestertrap teach us to build flame ships and dwellings upon mountains in which we may be secure?"

"More, much more. We will learn to use the very soil of our planet for fuel; we will learn how to build ships to carry us through emptiness to the planet Earth so that we can express our gratitude; instead of merely twelve books of numbers we shall have thousands, and the numbers themselves will be made to work for us in Terran pursuits like electricity and politics. Of course, we will learn slowly in the beginning. But your message?"

The tkan flapped his wings experimentally. He was a good tkan: he had three fully developed wings and four rudimentary ones—a very high variable-potential. "That is all. The Earthman wants help from one of us whose knowledge is great and whose books are full. This one will act as what is known as 'technical adviser' to him in the process of civilizing the Plookhh. Now the nzred nzredd's small tentacle is stiff with age and badly adjusted for the speaking of English; he has therefore decided that it is you who must advise this Hogan technically."

"I leave immediately," I promised. "Any more?"

"Nothing that is important. But we will need a new nzred nzredd. As he was giving me the last of the message outside the dwelling of the Earthman, he was noticed by a herd of tricephalops and devoured. He was old and crusty; I do not think they found him very good to eat."

"A nzred is always tasty," I told the winged Plookh proudly. "He alone among the Plookhh possesses tentacles, and the spice of our tentacles, it would seem, is beyond compare. Now the nzred tinoslep will become nzred nzredd—he has grown feeble lately and done much faulty coordination."

Flapping his wings, the tkan rose rapidly. "Beware of the tricephalops," he cried. "The herd still grazes outside the Hogan's dwelling, and you are a plump and easily swallowed tidbit. This will be a difficult time for the family to find another nzred."

A lizard-bird, attracted by his voice, plummeted down suddenly. The tkan turned sharply and attempted to gain altitude. Too late! The long neck of the lizard-bird extended, the fearful beak opened and—

The lizard-bird flew on, gurgling pleasurably to itself.

Truly it is written in the Book of Ones:

Pride goeth before a gobble.

He was a good tkan, as I said, and had a high variable-potential. Fortunately, a cycle had just completed—he was carrying no eggs. And tkann were plentiful that season.

This conversation lasted a much shorter period than it seems to have in my repetition. At the time, only a few nzredd had learned the English that the first human explorers had taught my ancestor, nzred fanobrel; and the rest of the Plookhh used the picturesque language of our uncivilized ancestors. This language had certain small advantages, it is true. For one thing, less of us were eaten while conversing with each other, since the ancient Plookh dialect transmitted the maximum information in the minimum time. Then again, I was not reduced to describing Plookhh in terms of "he," "she" or "it"; this English, while admittedly the magnificent speech of civilized beings, is woefully deficient in pronouns.

I uncoiled my tentacles from the grasses about me and prepared to roll. The mlenb, over whose burrow I was resting, felt the decreased pressure as my body ceased to push upon the mud above him. He churned to the surface, his flippers soggy and quivering.

"Can it be," the foolish fellow whispered, "that the Season of Wind-Driven Rains is over and the great spotted snakes have departed? The nzred is about to leave the marsh."

"Go back," I told him. "I have an errand to perform. The spotted snakes are ravenous as ever, and now there are lizard-birds come into the marsh."

"Oh!" He turned and began to dig himself back into the mud. I know it is ungracious to mock mlenbb, but the wet little creatures are so frantic and slow-moving at the same time that it is all I can do to keep a straight tentacle in their presence.

"Any news?" he asked, all but one third of him into the mud.

"Our tkan was just eaten, so keep your flippers alert for an unattached tkan of good variation. It is not pressing; a new cycle will not begin for our family until the end of this season. Oh—and the nzred nzredd has been eaten, too—but that does not concern you, little muddy mlenb."

"That does not, but have you heard the mlenb mlenbb also is gone? He was caught on the surface last night by a spotted snake. Never was there such a Season of Wind-Driven Rains: the great of the Plookhh fall on all sides."

"To a mlenb all seasons are 'never was there such a season,'" I mocked. "Wait until the Season of Early Floods, and then tell me which you like better. Many mlenbb will go with the coming of the early floods, and our family may have to find a new mlenb as well."

He shivered, spattering me with mud, and disappeared completely underground.

Ah, but those were the carefree times, the happy childhood days of our race! Little indeed there was to trouble us then.

I ate a few grasses and began rolling up and out of the marsh. In a little while, my churning tentacles had attained such speed that I had no reason to fear any but the largest of the great spotted snakes.

Once, a tremendous reptile leaped at me and it seemed that the shafalon family would require a new nzred as well as a new tkan, but I have a helical nineteenth tentacle and this stood me in good stead. I uncoiled it vigorously and with an enormous bound soared over the slavering mouth of the spotted snake and on to solid ground.

This helical tentacle—I regret deeply that none of you dear little nzredd have inherited it from me. My consolation is that it will reappear in your descendants, though in modified form; it unfortunately does not seem to be a dominant trait. But you all—all of this cycle, at any rate—have the extremely active small tentacle which I acquired from the nzred fanobrel.

Yes, I said your descendants. Please do not interrupt with the callow thoughts of the recently hatched, I tell you a tale of the great early days and how we came to this present state. The solution is for you to discover—there must be a solution; I am old and ripe for the gullet.

Once on solid ground, I had to move much faster, of course: here the great spotted snakes were larger and more plentiful. They were also hungrier.

Time and again I was forced to use the power latent in my helical tentacle. Several times as I leaped into the air, a lizard-bird or a swarm of gridniks swooped down at me; now and again, as I streaked for the ground, I was barely able to avoid the lolling tongue of a giant toad.

Shortly, however, I reached the top of the tenth highest mountain, having experienced no real adventure. There, for the first time, I beheld a human habitation.

It was a dome, transparent, yet colored with the bodies of many creatures who crawled on its surface in an attempt to reach the living meat within.

Do you know what a dome is? Think of half the body of a newly hatched nzred, divorced of its tentacles, expanded to a thousand times its size. Think of this as transparent instead of darkly colorful, and imagine the cut-away portion resting on its base while the still rounded part becomes the top. Of course, this dome had none of the knobs and hollows we use for various organic purposes. It was really quite bald.

Near it the flame ship stood upright. I cannot possibly describe the flame ship to you, except to say that it looked partly like a mlenb without the flippers and partly like a vineless guur.

The tricephalops discovered me and trampled each other in an attempt to get to me first. I was rather busy for a while evading the three-headed monsters, even growing slightly impatient with our savior, Hogan Shlestertrap, for keeping me outside his dwelling so long. I have always felt that, of all the innumerable ways for a Plookh to depart from life, the most unpleasant is to be torn into three unequal pieces and masticated slowly by a tricephalops. But, then, I have always been considered something of a wistful aesthete: most Plookhh dislike the gridnik more.

Fortunately, before I could be caught, the herd came upon a small patch of guurr who had taken root in the neighborhood and fell to grazing upon them. I made certain that none of the guurr were of our family and concentrated once more upon attracting the attention of Shlestertrap.

At long last, a section of the dome opened outward, a force seemed to pluck at my tentacles and I was carried swiftly through the air and into the dome. The section closed behind me, leaving me in a small compartment near the outside, my visible presence naturally exciting the beasts around me to scrabble frenziedly upon the transparent stuff of the dwelling.

A robot entered—answering perfectly to the description of such things by nzred fanobrel—and, with the aid of a small tubular weapon, quickly destroyed the myriad creatures and fragments of creatures who had been sucked in with my humble person.

Then—my variegated descendants—then, I was conducted into the presence of Hogan Shlestertrap himself!

How shall I describe this illustrious scion of a far-flung race? From what I could see of him, he had two pairs of major tentacles (call them flippers, vines, wings, fins, claws, talons or what you will), classified respectively as arms and legs. There was a fifth visible tentacle referred to as the head—at the top of the edifice, profusely knobbed and hollowed for sensory purposes. The entire animal, except for extremities of the tentacles, was covered with a blue and yellow striped substance which, I have since learned, is not secreted by it at all but supplied it by other humans in a complicated chain I do not fully understand. Each of the four major tentacles was further divided into five small tentacles somewhat in the manner of a blap's talons; fingers, they are known as. The body proper of this Hogan Shlestertrap was flat in the rear and exhibited a pleasing dome-like protuberance in the front, much like a nzred about to lay eggs.

Conceive, if you can, that this human differed in no respect from those described by my ancestor nzred fanobrel over six generations ago! One of the great boons of civilization is that continual variation is not necessary in offspring; these creatures may preserve the same general appearance for as many as ten or even twelve generations!

Of course, with every boon there is a price to be paid. That is what the dissidents among us fail to understand. . . .

Hogan Shlestertrap was occupying a chair when I entered. A chair is like—well, possibly I shall discuss that another time. In his hand (that part of the arm where the fingers originate) he held a bottle (shaped like a srob without fins) of whiskey. Every once in a while, he and the bottle of whiskey performed what nzred fanobrel called an act of conjugation. I, who have seen the act, assure you that there is no other way to describe the process. Only I fail to see just what benefit the bottle of whiskey derives from the act.

"Will you have a chair?" Shlestertrap requested, dismissing the robot with a finger undulation.

I rolled up into the chair, only too happy to observe human protocol, but found some difficulty in retaining my position as there were no graspable extremities anywhere in the object. I finally settled into a somewhat strained posture by keeping all my tentacles stiff against the sides and bottom.

"You look like some spiders I've seen after an all-night binge," Shlestertrap remarked graciously.

Since much of human thought is beyond our puny minds, I have been careful to record all remarks made by The Great Civilizer, whether or no I found them comprehensible at the time. Thus— "spider"? "all-night binge"?

"You are Hogan Shlestertrap of Hollywood California USA Earth, come to bring us out of the dark maw of ignorance, into the bright hatchery of knowledge. I am nzred shafalon, descended from nzred fanobrel who met your ancestors when they first landed on this planet, appointed by the late nzredd to be your technical adviser."

He sat perfectly still, the little opening in his head—mouth, they call it—showing every moment a wider and wider orifice.

Feeling flattered and encouraged by his evident interest, I continued into my most valuable piece of information. How valuable it was, I did not then suspect:

"It is written in the Book of Sevens:

When Plookh meets Plookh, they discuss sex. A convention is held, a coordinator selected, and amid cheers and rejoicing, they

337

enter the wholesome state of matrimony. The square of seven is forty-nine."

Silence. Hogan Shlestertrap conjugated rapidly with his bottle.

"Pensioned off," he muttered after a while. "The great Hogan Shlestertrap, the producer and director of 'Lunar Love Song,' 'Fissions of 2109,' 'We Took to the Asteroids,' pensioned off in a nutty fruitcake of a world! Doomed to spend his remaining years among gabby mathematical spiders and hungry watchamacallits."

He rose and began pacing, an act accomplished with the lower tentacles. "I gave them saga after saga, the greatest stereos that Hollywood ever saw or felt, and just because my remake of 'Quest to Mars' came out merely as an epic, they say I'm through. Did they have the decency—those people I picked out of the gutter and made into household names—did they have the decency to get me a job with the distribution end on a place like Titan or Ganymede? No! If they had to send me to Venus, did they even try to salve their consciences by sending me to the Polar Continent where a guy can find a bar or two and have a little human conversation? Oho, they wouldn't dare—I might make a comeback if I had half a chance. That Sonny Galenhooper—my *friend*, he called himself!—gets me a crummy job with the Interplanetary Cultural Mission and I find myself plopped down in the steaming Macro Continent with a mess of equipment to make stereos for an animal that half the biologists of the system claim is impossible. *Big deal!* But Shlestertrap Productions will be back yet, bigger and better than ever!"

These were his memorable words: I report them faithfully. Possibly in times to come, when civilization among us shall have advanced to a higher level—always assuming that the present problem will be solved —these words will be fully understood and appreciated by a generation of as yet unborn but much more intellectualized Plookhh. To them, therefore, I dedicate this speech of The Great Civilizer.

"Now," he said, turning to me. "You know what stereos are?"

"No, not quite. You see only one of us has ever conversed with humans before this, and we know little of their glorious ways. Our Book of Twos is almost bare of useful information, being devoted chiefly to a description of your first six explorers, their ship and robots, by the nzred fanobrel. I *deduce*, however, that stereos are an essential concomitant of an industrial civilization."

He waved the bottle. "Exactly. At the base of everything. Take your literature, your music, your painting—"

"Pardon me," I interposed. "But we have been able to build none of these things as yet. We are chased by so many—"

"I was just spitballing," he roared. "Don't interrupt my train of thought. I'm building! Now, where was I? Oh, yes—take your literature, music and painting and you know what you can do with them. The stereos comprise everything in art; they present to the masses, in one colossal little package, the whole stirring history of human endeavor. They are not a substitute for art in the twenty-second century —they *are* the art of the twenty-second century. And without art, where are you?"

"Where?" I asked, for I will admit the question intrigued me.

"Nowhere. Nowhere at all. Oh, you might be able to get by in the sticks, but class will tell eventually. You've got to romp home with an Oscar now and then to show the reviewers that you're interested in fine things as well as money-making potboilers."

I concentrated on memorizing, deciding to reserve interpretation for later. Perhaps this was my mistake, perhaps I should have asked more questions. But it was all so bewildering, so stimulating. . . .

"The stereos have gone a long way since the pioneering sound movies of medieval times," he continued. "Solid images that appeal to all five senses in gorgeous panoramas of perception."

Hogan Shlestertrap paused and went on with even more passion. "And wasn't it said that Shlestertrap Productions had their special niche, their special technique among the senses? Yes, sir! No greater accolade could be accorded a stereo than to say it had the authentic Shlestertrap Odor. The Shlestertrap smell—how I used to slave to get that in just right! And I almost always succeeded. Oh, well, they say you're just as good as your last stereo."

I took advantage of the brooding silence that followed to clack my small tentacle hesitantly.

The emissary looked up. "Sorry, fella. What we've got to do here is turn out a stereo based on your life, your hopes and spiritual aspirations. Something that will make 'em sit up and take notice way out in Peoria. Something that will give you guys a *culture*."

"We need one badly. Particularly a culture to defend us against—"

"All right. Let me carry the ball. Understand I'm only talking off the top of my mind right now; I never make a decision until I've slept on it and let the good old subconscious take a couple of whacks at the idea. Now that you understand the technical side of stereo-making, we can start working on a story. Now, religion and politics are dandy weenies, but for a good successful piece of art I always say give me the old-fashioned love story. What's the lowdown on your love-life?"

"That question is a trifle difficult to answer," I replied slowly. "We had the gravest communicative difficulties with the first explorers of your race over this question. They seemed to find it complicated."

"A-ah," he waved a contemptuous hand. "Those scientific bunnies are always looking for trouble. Takes a businessman, who's also an artist, mind you—first and last an artist—to get to the roots of a problem. Let me put it this way, what do you call your two sexes?"

"That is the difficulty. We don't have two sexes."

"Oh. One of those a-something animals. Not too much conflict possible in that situation, I guess. No-o-o. Not in one sex."

I was unhappy: he had evidently misunderstood me. "I meant we have more than two sexes."

"More than two sexes? Like the bees, you mean? Workers, drones and queens? But that's really only two. The workers are—"

"We Plookhh have seven sexes."

"Seven sexes. Well, that makes it a little more complicated. We'll have to work our story from a— SEVEN SEXES?" he shrieked.

He dropped back into the chair where he sat very loosely, regarding me with optical organs that seemed to quiver like tentacles.

"They are, to use the order stated in the Book of Sevens, srob, mlenb, tkan, guur—"

"Hold it, hold it," he commanded. He conjugated with his bottle and called to a robot to bring him another. He sighed finally and said: "Why in the name of all the options that were ever dropped do you need *seven* sexes?"

"Well, at one time, we thought that all creatures required seven sexes as a minimum. After your explorers arrived, however, we investigated and found that this was not true, even of the animals here on our planet. My ancestor, nzred fanobrel, had many profitable talks with the biologists of the expedition who provided him with theoretical knowledge to explain that which we had only known in practice. For example, the biologists decided that we had evolved into a seven-sexed form in order to stimulate variation."

"Variation? You mean so your children would be different?"

"Exactly. You see, there is only one thing that all the ravening life-forms of Venus would rather eat than each other; and that one thing is a Plookh. From the other continent, from all the islands and seas of Venus they come at different times for their Plookh feed. When a Plookh is discovered, a normally herbivorous animal will battle a mighty carnivore to the death and disregard the carcass of its defeated opponent—to enjoy the Plookh."

Our civilizer considered me with a good deal of interest. "Why— what have you got that no one else has got?"

"We don't know—exactly. It may be that our bodies possess a flavor that is uniformly exciting to all Venusian palates; it may be, as one of the biologists suggested to nzred fanobrel, that our tissue contains an element—a vitamin—essential to the diet of all the life-forms of our planet. But we are small and helpless creatures who must reproduce in quantity if we are to survive. And a large part of that quantity must differ from the parent who himself has survived into the reproductive stage. Thus, with seven parents who have lived long enough to reproduce, the offspring inherits the maximum qualities of survival as well as enough variation from any given parent to insure a constantly and *rapidly* improving race of Plookh."

An affirmative grunt. "That would be it. In the one-sex stage—*asexual* is what the bio professors call it—it's almost impossible to have varied offspring. In the bisexual stage, you get a good deal of variation. And with *seven* sexes, the sky must be the limit. But don't you ever get a Plookh who isn't good to eat, or who can maybe fight his way out of a jam?"

"No. It would seem that whatever makes us delicious is essential to our own physical structure. And, according to the biologists of the expedition again, our evolutionary accent has always been on evasiveness—whether by nimbleness, protective coloration or ability to hide—so that we have never developed a belligerent Plookh. We have never been able to: it is not as if we had one or two enemies. All who are not Plookhh will eat Plookhh. Except humans—and may I take this occasion to express our deep gratitude?

"From time to time, our Books of Numbers tell us, Plookhh have formed communities and attempted to resist extermination by united effort. In vain; they merely disappeared in groups instead of individually. We never had the *time* to perfect a workable system of defense, to devise such splendid things as weapons—which we understand humans have. That is why we rejoiced so at your coming. At last—"

"Save the pats on the back. I'm here to do a job, to make a stereo that will be at least an epic, even if I don't have the raw material of a saga. Give me a line on how all this works."

"May I say that whether it is an epic or a saga, we will still be grateful and sing the greatness of your name forever? Just so we are set on the path of civilization; just so we learn to construct impregnable dwellings and—"

"Sure. Sure. Wait till I get me a fresh bottle. Now—what are your seven sexes and how do you go about making families?"

I reflected carefully. I knew full well what a responsibility was mine at that moment; how important it was that I give our benefactor completely accurate information to aid him in the making of stereos, the first step we must take toward civilization.

"Please understand that much of this is beyond our ken. We know what seems to happen, but for an explanation we use the theories of the first flame ship's biologists. Unfortunately, their theories were multiple and couched in human terms which even they admitted were somewhat elementary when applied to the process of Plookh reproduction. We sacrificed a whole generation of the fanobrel family for microscopic experimentation and only a broad outline was worked out. Our seven sexes are—"

"I heard it was complicated," Shlestertrap interrupted. "The biologists left five miles of figures in the Venusian Section of the Interplane-

tary Cultural Mission after they returned from this expedition. You
see, there was an election right after that: a new party came in and fired
them. I wasn't going to wade through all that scientific junk, no sir!
One of them—Gogarty, I think—pulled every wire there was to take
this job away from me and come here in my place. Some people just
can't stand being out after they've been politically in for so long. Me,
I'm here to make stereos—good ones. I'm here to do just what the
prospectus of the Venusian Section called for—'bring culture to the
Plookhh as per request.'"

"Thank you. We did wonder why the Gogarty—pardon—why
Gogarty didn't return; he expressed such an enormous interest in our
ways and welfare. But no doubt the operation of firing him by the new
party after the election was far more productive in the human scheme
of things. We have not yet advanced to the state of parties and elec-
tions or any such tools. To us one human is as omniscient and magnificent as the other. Of course, you understand all relevant data on
human genetics?"

"Sure. You mean chromosomes and stuff?"

I flapped my small tentacle eagerly. "Yes, chromosomes and stuff.
Especially stuff. I think it is the part about 'stuff' that has made the
whole subject somewhat difficult for us. Gogarty never mentioned it.
All he discussed were chromosomes and genes."

"No wonder I got such a crash bio briefing! Let's see. Chromosomes
are collections of genes which in turn control characteristics. When an
animal is ready to reproduce, its germ-cells—or reproductive cells—
each divide into two daughter cells called gametes, each daughter cell
possessing one-half the chromosomes of the parent cell, every chromosome in each gamete corresponding to an opposite number chromosome in the other. Process is called meiosis. Correct me if I'm wrong
anywhere."

"And how can a human be wrong?" I asked devoutly.

His face wrinkled. "In the case of humans, the female germ-cell has
twenty-four pairs of chromosomes, one pair being known as the X
chromosome and determining sex. It splits into two female gametes of
twenty-four corresponding chromosomes, one X chromosome in each
gamete. Since the male germ-cell—if I remember rightly—has only
twenty-three identical pairs of chromosomes and an additional *un-
matched* pair called the X-Y chromosome, it divides into two male
gametes of twenty-four chromosomes each, of which only twenty-three
have a twin in each gamete; the twenty-fourth being the X chromosome in one male gamete and the Y chromosome in the other. If a
male gamete—or sperm-cell—containing an X chromosome unites
with a female gamete—ovum, or egg-cell, the briefing guy called it—
carrying an X chromosome, the resultant zygote will be female; but if
the Y chromosome gamete fertilizes the ovum, you have a *male* zygote.

They really jammed that stuff in me before they let me leave Earth. Lectures, sleep-sessions, the whole bit."

"Exactly," I said enthusiastically. "Now in *our* case—"

"I recall something else, come to think of it. The *Y* is supposed to be a slightly undeveloped or retarded chromosome and it makes the gamete containing it a little weaker or something. That explains why there's a small preponderance of girls over boys in a given bunch of births—the sperm-cell with the *X* chromosome is faster and stronger and has a better chance of fertilizing the ovum. It also shows why women can take it better than men and live longer. Simple. How's it work with you?"

The extended conversation was making me giddy, and the atmosphere of the dome—with its small vapor content—dried my faculties. However, this was a historic occasion: no personal weakness must be allowed to interfere. I stiffened my tentacles and began.

"After the matrimonial convention, when the chain is established, each sex's germ-cells are stimulated into meiosis. The germ-cell divides into seven gametes, six of them with cilia and the seventh secreted either inside or outside the Plookh, depending on the sex."

"What's this chain?"

"The chain of reproduction. The usually stated order is srob (aquatic form), mlenb (amphibian), tkan (winged), guur (plant-like), flin (a burrower), blap (tree-dweller). And, of course, the chain proceeds in a circle as: srob, mlenb, tkan, guur, flin, blap, srob, mlenb, tkan, guur, flin, blap, srob—"

Hogan Shlestertrap had grasped his head with his hands and was rocking it slowly back and forth. "Starts with srobs and ends with blaps," he said, almost inaudibly. "And I'm a—"

"Srobb," I corrected him timidly. "And blapp. And it doesn't necessarily start with one and end with another. A birth may be initiated anywhere along the chain of a family, just so it passes through all sexes—thus acquiring the necessary chromosomes for a fertilized zygote."

"All right! Please get back to chromosomes and sanity. You just had a germ-cell dividing—a srob's, say—into seven gametes instead of a decent two like all other logical species use."

"Well, so far as our weak minds can compass it, this is the chromosome pattern worked out by Gogarty and his assistant, Wolfsten, after prolonged microscopic examination. Gogarty warned my ancestor, nzred fanobrel, that it was only an approximation. According to this analysis, the germ-cell of a given sex has forty-nine chromosomes, seven each of Types *A, B, C, D, E, F,* six of Type *G* and one of Type *H*—the last, Type *H,* being the sex determinant. Six mobile gametes are formed through meiosis—each containing an identical group of seven chromosomes of Types *A* through *G*—and a seventh or stationary gamete containing chromosomes *A, B, C, D, E, F,* and *H.* This last Gogarty called the female or *H* gamete, since it never leaves the body of the Plookhh until the fully fertilized cell of forty-nine chromosomes —or seven gametes—is formed, and since it determines sex. The sex, of course, is that of the Plookhh in whose body it is stationary."

"Of course," Shlestertrap murmured and conjugated long and thoughtfully with the bottle.

"It has to be, since that is the only *H* chromosome in the final zygote. But you know that for yourself. In fact, operating with a human intelligence, you have probably anticipated me and already extrapolated the whole process from the few facts I have mentioned."

Moisture gathered at the top of our civilizer's head and rolled down his face in the quaintest of patterns. "I understand you," he admitted, "and of course I've already figured out the whole thing. But just to make it clear in your own mind, don't you think you might as well continue?"

I thanked him for his unfailing human courtesy. "Now, if it is a srob with whom we start our chain, it will transmit one of its six mobile gametes to a mlenb where the gamete will unite with one of the mlenb's *A* through *G* cells, forming what Gogarty called a double-gamete or pre-zygote. This pre-zygote will contain seven pairs of *A* through *G* chromosomes, and, in the body of the tkan—next in the chain—it will unite with a tkan mobile gamete forming a triple-gamete with seven triplets of *A* through *G* chromosomes. It proceeds successively through the rest of the sexes capturing a seven-chromosome gamete each time, until, when it is transmitted to the blap, it contains forty-two chromosomes—six *A*'s, six *B*'s and so on through to six *G*'s. At this point, the sextuple gamete loses its cilia; and unites, in the blap, with the stationary *H* gamete to form a forty-nine-chromosome zygote which, of course, is of the blap sex. The egg is laid and it hatches shortly into a baby blap, guarded—when at all possible—and taught in ten days all that its parent can teach it about surviving as a blap Plookh. At the end of ten days, the half-grown blap goes its way to feed and escape from danger by itself. At the end of a hundred days, it is ready to join a family and reproduce in full adulthood.

"The chain may be said to begin at any point; but it always travels in the same direction. Thus a flin will transmit the original seven-chromosome gamete to the blap of his chain where it will become a double-gamete; the blap will transmit the double-gamete to the srob, who will make it a triple-gamete; eventually, in this case, the process will come to fruition on the vines of the guur, resulting in a guur zygote. Was not Gogarty clever, even for a human? He suggested, by the way, that it was possible we were not really a seven-sexed creature, but seven distinct species living in a reproductive symbiosis."

344

"Gogarty was a damned genius! Hey, wait a minute! Srob, mlenb, tkan, guur, flin, blap—that's only six!"

At last we were getting to the interesting part. "Quite so. I am a representative of the seventh sex—nzred."

"A nzred, huh? What do *you* do?"

"I coordinate."

One of the robots scurried in in answer to his yell. He ordered it to bring a case of these bottles of whiskey and to place it near his chair. He also ordered it to stand by, prepared for emergencies.

This was all very enjoyable. My information was creating even more of a sensation than that described by my ancestor, nzred fanobrel. It is not often that we Ploókhh have an opportunity to sit thus with an animal of a different species and provide intellectual instead of gustatory diversion.

"He *coordinates!* Maybe they can use a good expediter or dispatcher?"

"I fulfill all of those functions. Chiefly, however, I coordinate. You see, a mlenb is primarily interested in winning the affections of a likely srob and finding a tkan whom *he* can love. A tkan merely courts a mlenb and is attracted to a good guur. I am responsible for getting a complete chain of these individuals in operation, a chain of compatibility where perfect amity runs in a complete circle—a chain which will produce offspring of maximum variability. Then, after the matrimonial convention, when the chain is established, each sex begins to secrete its original germ with the full forty-nine chromosomes. A busy time for nzredd! I must make certain that all germ-cells are developing at a uniform rate—each sex attempts to fertilize seven H gametes in the course of a cycle—and the destruction of one individual in the middle of the cycle means the complete disarrangement of a family except for the gametes which he has already passed on in multiple state. Replacement of an eaten individual with another of the same sex, the remainder of whose family has been wiped out, is occasionally possible with the aid of the chief of his sex."

"I can see they keep you hopping," Hogan Shlestertrap observed. "But how does a nzred get born if you aren't in this chain thing?"

"A nzred is outside a chain, yet inside it as well. The six sexes which transmit gametes to each other directly form a chain; a chain plus a nzred equals a family. The nzred, in his personal reproductive functions, fits himself in at any point in the chain which the exigencies of the situation seem to demand. He may receive the sextuple super-gamete from the tkan and transmit the original single gamete to the guur, he may be between the flin and blap, the blap and srob, whatever is required. For example, in the Season of Twelve Hurricanes, the tkan is unable to fly and pursue his reproductive relationship with the guur wherever it has rooted itself: the nzred fills what would be a gap in the chain. This is rather difficult to express in an unfamiliar language —the biologists of the first expedition found this process slightly more complicated than the mitoses of the fertilized Plookh cell, but—"

"Hold it," Hogan commanded. "I have an ounce of sanity left, and I might want to use it to blow my brains out. I am no longer slightly interested in how a nzred weaves in and out of this crazy reproductive dance, and I *certainly* don't want to hear about your mitosis. I have troubles of my own, and they grow nastier every second. Tell me this: how many offspring does a sex have each cycle?"

"That depends on all parents being alive throughout, on the amount of unhatched eggs due to over-variation in particular cases—"

"*Okay!* At the end of a perfect cycle—when the smoke clears—how many baby plookhs do you have all told?"

"Plookh*h*. We have forty-nine young."

He rested his head on the back of the chair. "Not very many, considering how fast you seem to go out of this world."

"True. Dismally true. But a parent is unable to hatch more than seven eggs in the conditions under which we live, and completely unable to rear more than seven young so that all will get the full benefit of his survival-knowledge. This is for the best."

"I guess so." He removed a pointed instrument from his garment and a sheet of white material. After a while, I recognized his actions from nzred fanobrel's description. "In just a moment," he said, while writing, "I'm going to have you shown into the projection room where you'll see a recent stereo employing human performers. Not too good a stereo: colossal in a very minor way; but it'll give you an idea of what I'll be doing for your people in the line of culture. While you see it, figure out ways to help me on a story. Now, is this Gogarty's description of your chromosome pattern after the parent germ-cell has undergone meiosis?"

He extended the sheet under my sensory tentacles:

	A	A	A	A	A	A	A	
mobile	B	B	B	B	B	B	B	stationary, sex-determining
gametes	C	C	C	C	C	C	C	gamete which is "fertilized"
(ciliated)	D	D	D	D	D	D	D	by a super-gamete com-
	E	E	E	E	E	E	E	posed of six mobile gametes
	F	F	F	F	F	F	F	—one from each of the six
	G	G	G	G	G	G	G	other sexes

"Quite correct," I said, marveling at the superiority of these written symbols to those we are still forced to scratch in sand or mud.

"Good enough." He wrote further upon the sheet. "Now, which of your sexes is male and which female? I notice you say 'he' and—"

I was forced to interrupt him. "I only use those designations because of the deficiencies or limitations of English. I understand what a wonderful speech it is, and how, when you came to construct it, you saw no reason to consider the Plookhh. Nonetheless, you have no pronouns for tkan or guur or blap. We are all male in relation to each other, in the sense that we transmit the fertilizing gametes; we are also female, in the sense that we hatch the developed zygote. Then again—"

"Slow down, boy, slow down. I have to work a story out of this, and you're not doing me any good at all. Here's a picture of your family—right?" He held the sheet out once more.

```
                    guur
        tkan    ↗      ↘     flin
         ↖   \       /         ↙
        mlenb  ——nzred——
                /       \     blap
          ↙    /         ↘   ↙
        srob
```

"Yes. Only your picture of the nzred is not exactly—"

"Listen, Pierre," he growled, "I'll call it the way I see it. And that's the way I see it. A love story, now, let me think. . . ."

I waited while he cerebrated upon this strange thing called a story which was essential to the making of a stereo, which, in turn, was essential to our beginning upon culture and civilization. Soon, soon, we would have dwellings like this powerful one in which I sat, we would have tubular weapons like that the robot had used when I entered—

"How would this be?" he asked suddenly. "Understand, this isn't the finished product—I'm just working off the cuff, just trying it on for size. *Srob meets mlenb, tkan loses guur, flin gets blap.* How's it sound? Only one I can't fit in is the nzred."

"I coordinate."

"Yeah, you coordinate. That would make it, srob meets— Ah, shaddap! All you're supposed to do is say 'yes' once in a while." He murmured a few words to the robot who moved over to my chair. "Bronzo will take you to the projection room now. I'll think some more."

Tumbling painfully to the floor, I prepared to follow the robot.

"A love story is going to be tough," Shlestertrap mused behind me. "I can see that right now. Like three-dimensional chess with all pawns wild and the queen operating in and out of hyperspace. Wonder if these potato sprouts have a religion. A nice, pious little stereo every once in a while— Hey! Got a religion?"

"Yes," I said.

"What is it? I mean what do you believe in, generally speaking? Simple terms: we can save the philosophy for later."

After the lapse of an interval which I felt I could approximate as a 'while,' I said again, very cautiously: "Yes."

"Huh? Cut the comedy on this lot, if you know what's good for you. Just because I told you not to disagree with me when I'm thinking out loud— No sloppy gags when I ask you a direct question!"

I apologized and tried to explain my seeming impudence in terms of the simple conditions under which we Plookhh live. After all, when a tkan flies in frantically to warn a family that a pack of strinth are ravening in its direction, no one thinks to take the message in other than its most literal form. Communication, for us, is basically a means of passing along information essential to survival: it must be explicit and definitive.

Human speech, however, being the product of a civilized race, is a tree bearing many different fruits. And, as we have discovered to our sorrow, it is not always easy to find the one intended to be edible. For example, this mind-corroding intangible that they call a pun—

Shlestertrap waved my explanations back at me. "So you're sorry and I forgive you. Meanwhile, what's your belief about a life after death?"

"We don't exactly have a belief," I explained slowly, "since no Plookh has returned after death to assure us of the possibilities ahead. However, because of the difficulties we experience in the one life we know and its somewhat irritating shortness of duration—we like to think we have at least *one* additional existence. Thus, we have not so much a Belief as a Hope."

"For an animal without lungs, you sure are long-winded. What's your Hope, then?"

"That after death we emerge into a vast land of small seas, marshes and mountains. That throughout this land are the pink weeds we find so succulent. That, in every direction as far as an optical organ can see, there are nothing but Plookhh."

"And?"

"Nothing else. That is our Hope: to arrive sometime, in this life or the next, in a land where there are nothing but Plookhh. Plookhh, you understand, are the only creatures who we are *certain* do not eat Plookhh. We feel we could be very happy alone."

"Not enough there to make a one-shot quickie. If only you believed in a god who demanded living Plookhh sacrifices—but I guess your lives are complicated enough. Go and see the stereo. I'll work out something."

In the projection room, I twisted up into a chair the robot pushed forward and watched him and his mates insert shiny colored strips into five long, mlenb-shaped objects attached to the walls and ceiling. Naturally, I have learned since that the human terms are "film" and "projector" respectively: but, at that time, everything was new and strange and wonderful; I was all optical tentacles and audal knobs.

The sheer quantity of *things* that humans possess! Their recording methods are so plentiful and varied—books, stereos, pencil-paper, to name but a few—that I am convinced their memories are largely outgrown evolutionary characteristics which, already atrophying, will be supplanted shortly by some method of keying recording apparatus directly to the thinking process. They have no need of carrying Books of Numbers in their minds, of memorizing individually some nine thousand years of racial history, of continually revising the conclusions drawn from an ancient incident to conform with the exigencies of a current one. Contemplation of their magnificent potentialities almost dissolves my ego.

Abruptly, the room darkened and a tiny spot of white expanded into the full-color, full-sound, full-olfactory and slightly tactile projection we have come to know so well. For some reason, the humans who make these stereos neglect almost completely the senses of taste, brotch, pressure and griggo—although the olfactory appeal stimulates an approximation of taste and an alert individual may brotch satisfactorily during an emotional sequence. The full-color—yes: it should be obvious that humans use only three primaries instead of the existing nine because they consider it a civilized simplicity; the very drabness of the combinations of blue, red and yellow, I believe, is a self-imposed limitation instituted as a challenge to their technicians.

As the human figures came to seeming life before me, I began to understand what Hogan Shlestertrap had meant by a "story." A story is the history of one or more individuals in a specific cultural matrix. I wondered then just how Shlestertrap would derive a story from the meager life of a Plookh; he had known so few of us. I did not know of the wonderful human sense of imagination.

This story, that I saw on that awesome first day of our civilization, was about their two sexes. One representative of each sex (a man, Louis Trescott—and a girl, Bettina Bramwell) figured as the protagonists of the film.

The story concerned the efforts of Bettina Bramwell and Louis Trescott to get together and lay an egg. Many and complex were the difficulties this pair faced, but, at last, having overcome every obstacle, they were united and ready to reproduce.

Through some oversight, the story ended before the actual egg-laying; there was definite assurance, however, that the process would be under way shortly.

Thus, the first stereo I had ever seen. The colors sharpened in company with the sound of this obscure business called music, then all faded and disappeared. The lights returned to the room and the robots attended to the projectors. I went back to Shlestertrap, quivering with new knowledge.

"Sure," he said. "It's good. It's good enough, considering the budget. Now, look, I have an idea for a stereo. It's got to jell and whatnot, but meanwhile it's an idea. What's the animal you bugs are most afraid of?"

"Well, in the Season of Twelve Hurricanes, the strinth and sucking ivy do a large amount of damage to our race. In the other hurricane seasons—which are the worst for us, after all—the tricephalops, brinosaurs or gridniks—"

"Don't tell me *all* your troubles. Put it this way: which animal are you afraid of most right now?"

I considered lengthily. Ordinarily, the question would have given me thought material for two days; but The Great Civilizer was shifting from foot to foot and I griggoed his impatience. A decision was necessary; this may have been my mistake, my offspring, but remember we might never have received *any* of the benefits of civilization if I had taken more time to determine which creature was eating most of us at that season.

"The great spotted snakes. Of course, it is feared only by the nzredd, mlenbb, flinn and blapp. At this time, guurr are eaten principally by tricephalops, while srobb—"

"All right. Spotted snakes. Now let's go to the observation corridor and you point one out to me."

In the room where I had entered the dome, I extended my optical tentacles toward the transparent roof.

"There, almost directly above me. The animal which has half swallowed a dodle and is being attacked by gridniks and sucking ivy.'"

Shlestertrap faced upwards and shivered. At the sight of us, the creatures scrabbled even more frantically on the dome's structure, continuing to eat whatever they had been eating when we entered. The sucking ivy dragged the great spotted snake away.

"What a place," Shlestertrap muttered. "A guy could make a fortune here with an anti-vacation resort. 'Come to this home away from home and learn to giggle at your nightmares. All kinds of dishes served, including you. Be a guest of the best digestions. Everybody to his taste and a taste to fit everybody.' "

I waited, while his human mind explored concepts beyond my primeval grasp.

"O.K. So that was a great spotted snake. I'll send a crew of robots out to get some shots of one of those babies that we can process into the stereo. Meanwhile, what about the cast?"

"Cast?" I fumbled. "How—what kind of cast do you mean?"

"Actors. Characters. Course I understand that none of you have any experience, even in stock, but I'll treat this like a De Mille documentary. I'll need a representative of each one of your sexes—the best in its line. You should be able to dredge them up with beauty contests or whatever you use. Just so I get seven of you—all different."

"These can be obtained through the chiefs of the various sexes. The nzred tinoslep will be the new nzred nzredd and a replacement for the mlenb mlenbb should have been chosen if enough mlenbb dared to congregate in the marshes. And this is all we need to do to take the first movement toward civilization?"

"Absolutely all. I'll write the first story for you—it's only mildly magnificent right now, but I'll have plenty of time to work it up into something better."

"Then I may leave."

He called for a robot who entered and motioned me in front of a machine much like a stereo projector.

"Sorry I can't send a robot to protect you down the mountain, but we're only half unpacked and I'll need all of them around for a day or two. All I have here are Government Standard Models, see; and you can't get any high-speed work out of those babies. To think that I used to have eighteen Frictionless Frenzies just to clean up around the house! Oh well, a sick trance isn't glorious Mondays."

Admitting the justice of this obscure allusion, I tried to reassure him. "If I am eaten, there are at least three nzredd who can replace me. It is only necessary for me to get far enough down the mountain to meet a living Plookh and inform him of your—your character requirements."

"Good," he told me heartily. "And I'm pretty sure I can play ball with any of your people who speak English fairly well. That sews up that: I'd hate to leave my stuff lying around in crates any longer than I have to. Dentface, throw a little extra juice into that beam so the kid here can get a big head start. And, once you get him out, quick-quick turn the dome back on fast, or we'll have half the empty stomachs on Venus inside trying to work us into their ulcers."

The robot called Dentface depressed a lever on the beam projector. Just as I had turned wistfully toward it in the hope that my meager mentality could somehow preserve an impression of the mechanism that would enable us to adapt it to our pressing needs, I was carried swiftly through a suddenly opened section of the dome and deposited halfway down the mountain. The opening, I observed as I got to my tentacles and rolled away from a creeper of sucking ivy, was actually an area of the dome that had temporarily ceased to exist.

I was unable to reflect further upon this matter because of the various lunges, snaps and grabs that were made at me from several directions. As I twisted and scudded down the tenth highest mountain, I deeply regretted Hogan Shlestertrap's need of the robots for unpacking purposes.

This, my children, was the occasion on which I lost my circular tentacle. A tricephalops, it was—or possibly a large dodle.

Near the marsh, I observed that my remaining pursuer, a green shata, had been caught by a swarm of gridniks. Accordingly, I rested in the shadow of a giant fern.

A scrabbling noise above me barely gave me time to stiffen my helical tentacle for a spring, when I recognized its source as the blap koreon. Peering from the lowest fan-leaf, he called softly: "The nzred shafalon has come from the dwelling of the human who was to give us many and mighty weapons, yet still I see him fleeing from empty bellies like the veriest morsel of a Plookh."

"And soon you will see him mocking all the beasts of prey from the safety of a dome where he and his kind live in thoughtful comfort," I replied with some importance. "I am to aid the human Shlestertrap of Hollywood California USA Earth in the making of a stereo for our race."

The blap loosed his hold on the immense leaf and dropped to the ground beside me. "A stereo? Is it small or large? How many great spotted snakes can it destroy? Will we be able to make them ourselves?"

"We will be able to make them ourselves in time, but they will destroy no great spotted snakes for us. A stereo, my impatient wayfarer upon branches, is a cultural necessity without which, it seems, a race must wander forever in ignoble and fearful darkness. With stereos as models, we may progress irresistibly to that high control of our environment in which humanity exults on Earth. But enough of this munching the husk—our sex-chiefs must conduct Beauty Contests to select characters for the first Plookh stereo. Where is the blap blapp?"

"I saw him last leaping from bough to bough in the fifth widest forest with a lizard-bird just a talon's length behind him. If he has not yet ascertained the justification of the Hope, any tkan should be able to guide you to his present lair. Meanwhile, I think I know where the flin flinn has most recently dug."

He scampered to a mass of rocks and scratched at the ground near the outermost one. The heavy body of an old flin shortly appeared at the mouth of the hole he made. I rolled over and told the flin flinn of Shlestertrap's requirements.

The doddering burrower examined his broken claws nervously. "The chiefs of the other sexes will probably want to convene above ground. I know how important this stereo is to our race, but I am old and not at all agile—and this is the Season of Wind-Driven Rains—and the great spotted snakes are ravenous enough below the surface—"

"And it will shortly be the Season of Early Floods," I interrupted him, "when only tkann will have time for conversation. Our civilizing must begin as soon as possible."

"What have you to fear, old one?" the blap jeered. "A snake would find you tough and almost without flavor!"

The flin flinn edged back into his hole. "But not until he had experimented in a regrettably final fashion upon my person," he pointed out gloomily. "I will communicate with the new mlenb mlenbb—their moist burrows connect with ours again. Where might we meet, do you think, O coordinator who gathers human wisdom?"

"In the sheltered spot at the base of the sixth highest mountain," I suggested. "It will be fairly safe during the next great wind. And consider, in the meantime, which is the living flin most fitted to represent our race in this our first stereo. Tell the mlenb mlenbb to do likewise."

After the sound of his claws had diminished in the under distance, the blap and I moved back to the giant fern. It is written in the Book of Ones: *A bush nearby is worth two in the by and by.*

"The only other sex-chief whose whereabouts I griggo," the tree-dweller observed, "is the new nzred nzredd. He is in the marsh organizing the coordination of the next cycle."

"The nzred tinoslep that was?"

"Yes, and little did he relish his honors! Plentiful rose his complaints to High Hope. Vainly he insisted he was still in the very prime of coordination—that he had a good many novel arrangements yet within him. But all know of the pathetic hybrids produced in the last tinoslep cycle. You have heard, I suppose—"

And he told me the latest septuple entendre that had been making the rounds.

I was not amused. "Beware, scratcher of bark, of ridicule at the expense of him whom your coordinator obeys! Another blap may fill your place in the chain, while you gaze morosely at unhatched eggs. The nzred tinoslep, that was, organized mighty cycles in his time and now uses accumulated wisdom in the service of all the Plookhh, unlike the blap blapp and the flin flinn who have the responsibility of a lone sex."

Record this speech well, my nzreddi. Thus it is necessary to constantly impress upon the weaker, more garrulous sexes the respect due to coordination; else families will dissolve and each sex will operate in ungenetic independence. The nzred must ever be a Plookh apart—yes, yes, even in these shattering times of transition should he maintain his aloofness jealously. Even at present there are good reasons for him to do so— Please! Allow me to continue! Save these involved questions for another session, you who are so recently hatched. *I* know there are now complications. . . .

The blap hastened to apologize.

"I meant no ridicule, none at all, omnipotent arranger of births! I thoughtlessly passed on a vulgar tale told me by an itinerant unattached guur who should have known better. Please do not tear me from the fins of the finest srob that I have ever known and the most delightful flin that ever brotched in a burrow! The nzred koreon is already displeased with me for two baby blapp I varied to the point of extinction, and now——"

Something coughed wetly behind us and we both leaped for the lowest frond of the fern. The blap streaked to the top of the plant and thence to a long-extending bough of a neighboring tree; I bounced off the leap and into the marsh with powerful strokes of my helical tentacle. Behind me, the giant toad sorrowfully rolled his tongue back into his mouth.

I went my way fully satisfied: this blap would not mock nzredd again for many cycles.

The leader of my sex was surrounded by young nzredd in the weediest section of the marsh. He dismissed them when I approached and heard my recital.

"This meeting-place you suggested to the flin flinn—the land sexes may find it very easily, but what of the srob srobb?"

"A little stream has pushed through to the base of the sixth highest mountain," I informed him. "It isn't very wide, but the leader of the srobb should be able to swim to the sheltered place without difficulty. Only the mlenb mlenbb will be at a disadvantage there because of the stream's newness."

"And when is a mlenb not at a disadvantage?" he countered. "No, if a stream is there, the sheltered place will serve us well enough—during a wind, in any event. You have ordered things wisely, nzred shafalon; you will yet survive to be a nzred nzredd when your more thoughtless contemporaries are excreta."

I waggled my tentacles at this praise. To be told that I would escape assimilation long enough to be nzred nzredd was a compliment indeed. And to think I am at last chief of my sex and yet still able to coordinate effectively! Truly, our race has been startled by civilization— to say nothing of its highest manifestation, The Old Switcheroo.

"You need a tkan," the nzred nzredd went on; "I believe the tkan tkann has a satisfactory one for you. The tkan gadulit is the sole survivor of an attack of tricephalops upon his matrimonial convention (I must remember that the gadulit name is now available for use by new families). He has fair variation. Suppose you meet him and introduce him to the chain if all else is good in your own judgment. As soon as the sex-chiefs have met and approximated this odd business of Beauty Contests, we will assemble the individuals selected and you may escort them to awesome Shlestertrap. And may this stereo lead quickly to the softness of civilization."

"May it only," I assented fervently, and went to meet the new tkan. He was variable enough for all normal purposes; the guur shafalon found him admirable; and even our mlenb, stodgy and retiring as he was, admitted his fondness for the winged member. The tkan was overwhelmed at being admitted into the shafalon family, and I approved of his sensible attitude. I began to make plans for a convention —it was time to start another cycle.

Before I could communicate with my srob, however—he always swam a good distance from land during the Season of Wind-Driven Rains—the tkan tkann flew to inform me of the sex-chiefs' choices and lead me to them. I regretfully postponed the initiation of offspring.

The Plookhh selected by the Beauty Contests were the very glory of our race. Each was differentiated from the other members of his sex by scores of characteristics. United in one family, they might well have produced Superplookhh.

With infinite graciousness, the tkan tkann told me that I had been considered most seriously for the nzred protagonist—only, my value as Shlestertrap's assistant being primary, another was selected in my place. "No matter," I told the chief as he soared away, "I have honors enough for one Plookh: my books runneth over."

The gasping srob represented the greatest problem and the tkan-character volunteered to fly him directly to the dome without waiting for the rest of them so that the finny one would not dry up and die. Then, with the nzred-character and the blap-character carrying the plant-like guur between them, we began our ascent of the tenth highest mountain.

Although the Season of Wind-Driven Rains was almost over, there were even more great spotted snakes than before crawling upon the dome; and, grappling with their morbid coils, were more slavering dodles than I remembered seeing at one time; even a few brinosaur ranged about now, in anticipation of the approaching Season of Early Floods. I deduced, in some surprise, that they considered the human a palatable substitute for Plookhh.

I had gone ahead of my little band since I knew the terrain better and was more likely to attract Hogan Shlestertrap's attention. This was fortunate, for we had not worked halfway up the mountain before we were feverishly eluding what seemed to be the entire fauna of Venus. They poured off the dome in a great snapping, salivating horde, pausing occasionally to gouge or tear at their neighbors, but nonetheless pursuing us with a distressing concentration. I found additional cause to be grateful for the wise choices of the sex-chiefs: only really diversified Plookhh with the very latest survival characteristics could have come through that madness of frustrated gluttony unscathed. Relatively unscathed.

It was only necessary for me to cross once in front of the robot in the outer compartment of the dome. Gridnik-fast, the beam poured out and captured me, swinging thence to the rest of my élite family and carrying all of us through the open space of the dome which seemed to be materializing shut almost before we were inside.

I was particularly grateful, I recall, since the beam had snatched me from between the creepers of the largest sucking ivy I had ever stumbled upon. A helical tentacle is all very well, but it does not help overmuch when one is too busy evading three lizard-birds to notice what lies in wait upon the ground.

One of the robots had already constructed a special tank for the srob, and he also rapidly found some soil into which the guur could root sighingly.

"That a real plant?" Shlestertrap inquired. He had changed from his previous covering into a black garment becomingly decorated with red splotches which disguised his dome-shaped middle protuberance in a way I could not quite fathom. On his head, he now wore what he called a cap with the visor pointing behind him—a custom, he explained, which was observed by stereo people in deference to their ancient greats.

"No, it is a guur, the Plookh which relies most on blending into its surroundings. Although it does derive some nourishment photosynthetically, it is not quite a vegetable, retaining enough mobility to—"

"A guur, you call it? Helpless, huh? Got to be carried over the threshold? Keep still—I'm thinking!"

I throbbed out a translation. We all froze into silence. The srob, who had lifted his head out of the tank to survey the dome, began to strangle quietly in the open air.

Finally, Shlestertrap nodded and we all moved again. The mlenb flapped over and pushed the srob, who had become insensible, back under the surface of the tank.

"Yep," said our civilizer. "It adds up. I have the weenie. A little too pat for an artistic stereo, but I can always dress it up so no one will know the difference." He turned to me. "That's the big gimmick in this business—dressing it up so they can't tell it's the same thing they've been seeing since they got their first universal vaccination. If you dress it up enough, the sticks will always go nuts over it. Maybe the critics will make cracks, sure, but who reads the critics?"

Alas, I did not know.

Much time passed before I had extended conversation with the human again. First, it was necessary for me to teach English to the first Plookh thespians so that they could follow Shlestertrap's direction. Not very difficult, this: it simply required a short period of concentrated griggoing by the seven of them. I could now give them much terminology that even my ancestor, nzred fanobrel, had not been able to use; unfortunately, a good deal of Shlestertrap's phrase-shadings remained as nothing but unguessable semantic goals, and when it came to many attitudes and implements used exclusively upon Earth—we could do nothing but throw up our tentacles and flippers, our vines and talons, in utter helplessness.

Some day, however—not us, but one of our conceivable descendants, perhaps—we will learn the exact constituents of a "thingumajig."

After learning the language, the other Plookhh were taken in charge by the robots—the same friendly creatures who would leave the dome occasionally to forage the fresh pink weeds that were essential to our diet—and told to do many incomprehensible things against backgrounds that varied from the artificially constructed to the projected stereo.

Frequently, Shlestertrap would halt the robots in their fluid activity with booms and cameras and lights, turn to me and demand a significant bit of information about our habits that usually required my remembering every page of all our Books of Numbers to give an adequate reply.

Before I could finish, however, he generally signaled to the robots to begin once more—muttering to himself something like: "Oh, well, we can fake up a fair copy with more process work. If it only looks good, who cares about realism?"

Then again, he would express annoyance over the fact that, while some of us had heads, the mlenbb and nzredd had torso-enclosed brains, and the guur were the proud possessors of what the first ship's biologists had called a "dissolved nervous system."

"How can you get intriguing close-ups," Shlestertrap wailed, "when you don't know what part of the animal you want in them? You'd think these characters would get together and decide what they want to look like, instead of shortening my life with complications!"

"These are the most thoroughly differentiated Plookhh," I reminded him proudly. "The Beauty Contest winners."

"Yeah. I'll bet the homely ones are a real old-fashioned treat."

Thus, gently and generously, did he toil on the process of civilizing us. May his name be revered by any Plookhh that survive!

My only real difficulty was in gaining more knowledge. The robots were rather uncommunicative (we have not yet resolved their exact place in human affairs) and Hogan Shlestertrap explained that a genius like himself could not be bothered with the minutiae of stereographical mechanics. That was left entirely to his metallic assistants.

Nevertheless, I persisted. My hunted race, I felt, expected me to gather all knowledge to which I was exposed for the building of our own technology. I asked Shlestertrap detailed questions about the operations of the sound robot who deftly maneuvered the writhing, almost-live microphone booms above the actors and scenery; I pestered him for facts on the great smell-camera with its peculiar, shimmering olfactory lens and its dials calibrated pungently from rose-constants to hydrogen-sulphide-constants.

Once, after a particularly long session, I came upon him in a compartment composing the score for our stereo. I had always found this music vaguely stimulating, if obscure of use, and I was very curious as to how it was made.

This, let me say to his glory, he explained very patiently. "See, here's a sound-track of a Beethoven symphony and there's one of a Gershwin medley. I run off bits of each alternately into the orchestrator and flip the switch like so. The box joggles and bangs it around for a while—it can make more combinations than there are inches between here and Earth! Finally, out comes the consolidated sound-track, and we have a brand-new score of our stereo. Remember the formula: a little Beethoven, a little Gershwin, and lots and lots of orchestration."

I told him I would never forget it. "But what kind of machine makes the original Gershwin and Beethoven strips? And can either of them be used in any way under water against the brinosaur? And exactly what is involved in the process of the orchestrator joggling and banging? And how would we go about making—"

"Here!" He plucked a book from a table behind him. "I meant to give you this yesterday when you asked me how we connected tactions to the manipulating antenna. You want to know all about culture and how humans operate with it, huh? You want to know how our culture fits in with nonhumans, don't you? Well, read this and don't bother me until you do. Just keep busy going over it until you have it cold. About the most basic book in the place. Now, maybe I can get some quiet drinking out of the way."

My thanks poured at his retreating back. I retired to a corner with my treasure. The title, how inspiring it looked! ABRIDGED REGULATIONS OF THE INTERPLANETARY CULTURAL MISSION, ANNOTATED, WITH AN APPENDIX OF STANDARD OFFICE PROCEDURES FOR SOLARIAN MISSIONS.

Most unhappily, my intellectual powers were not yet sufficiently developed to extract much that was useful from this great human repository of knowledge. I was still groping slowly through Paragraph 5, Correction Circular 16, of the introduction (*Pseudo-Mammalian Carnivores, Permissible Approaches to and Placating of for the Purpose of Administering the Binet-plex*) when a robot summoned me to Shlestertrap's presence.

"It's finished," he told me, waving aside a question I began to ask regarding a particularly elusive footnote. "Here, let me put that book back in the storeroom. I just gave it to you to keep you out of my hair. It's done, boy!"

"The stereo?"

He nodded. "All wrapped up and ready to preview. I have your friends waiting in the projection room."

There was a pause while he rose and walked slowly around the compartment. I waited for his next words, hardly daring to savor the impact of the moment. Our culture had been started!

"Look, Plookh, I've given you guys a stereo that, in my opinion, positively smashes the gong. I've locked the budget out of sight, and I've worked from deep down in the middle of my mind. Now, do you think you might do a little favor for old Shlestertrap in return?"

"Anything," I throbbed. "We would do anything for the unselfish genius who—"

"Okey-dandy. A couple of busybodies on Earth are prancing around and making a fuss about my being assigned to this mission, on the grounds that I never even had a course in alien psych. They're making me into a regular curse of labor, using my appointment and a bunch of others from show business as a means of attacking the present administration on grounds of corruption and incompetence. I never looked at this job as anything more than a stop-gap until Hollywood finds that it just can't do without the authentic Shlestertrap Odor in its stereos— still, the good old bank account on Earth is growing nicely and right now I don't have any better place to go. It would be kind of nice and appreciative to you to give me a testimonial in the form of a stereo record that I can beam back to Earth. Sort of show humanity that you're grateful for what we're doing."

"I would be grateful in turn to be given an opportunity to show my gratitude," I replied. "It will take a little time, however, for me to compose a proper speech. I will start immediately."

He reached for my long tentacles and pulled me back into the compartment. "Fine! Now, you don't want to make up a speech of your own and give out with all kinds of errors that would make humans think you aren't worth the money we're spending on you? Of course you don't! I have a honey of a speech all written—just the thing they'll want to hear you say back home. Greasejob! You and Dentface get that apparatus ready for recording."

Then, while the robots manipulated the stereo-record, I read aloud the speech Shlestertrap had written from a copy he held up just out of camera range. I stumbled a bit over unfamiliar concepts—for example, passages where I extolled The Great Civilizer for teaching us English and explaining our complicated biological functions to us—but generally, the speech was no more than the hymn of praise that the man deserved. When I finished, he yelled: "Cut! Good!"

Before I had time to ask him the reasons for the seeming inconsistencies in the speech—I knew that, since he was human, they could not be mere errors—he had pushed me into the projection room where the Plookh actors waited. I thought I heard him mumble something about "That should hold the Gogarty crowd till the next election," but I was so excited over the prospect of the first Plookhian cultural achievement that I did nothing more than scurry to my place as the projectors started. Now, sometimes, I think perhaps— No.

The first stereo with an all-Plookh cast! Already, it is a commonplace, with all Plookh seeing it for the first time before they are more than six days out of the egg. But that preview, as it was called, was a moment when everything seemed to pause and offer us sanctuary. Our civilization seemed assured.

I decided that its murky passages were the result of one viewing and would disappear in time as we expanded intellectually.

You know what I mean. The beginning is interesting and delightful as the various sexes meet in different ways and decide to become a family. The matrimonial convention, although somewhat unusual procedurally, is fairly close to the methods in use at that time. But why does the guur suddenly proclaim she is insulted and bolt the convention?

Of course, you all know—or should—that our reservation of the pronoun "she" for guur dates from the dialogue in this stereo?

Again, why, after the guur leaves, do the others pursue her—instead of finding and mating with a more reasonable specimen? And the great spotted snake that notices the guur—we had thought till then that guur is the one form of Plookh safe from these dread creatures: evidently we were wrong. In her flight, she passes tricephalops and sucking ivy: these ignore her; yet the great spotted snake suddenly develops a perverted fancy for her vines and tendrils.

And the battle, where the other six Plookhh fall upon and destroy the snake! Even the srob crawls out of the stream and falls gasping into the fray! It continues for a long period—the snake seems to be triumphing, logically enough—suddenly, the snake is dead.

I am an old nzred. I have seen that stereo hundreds of times, and many the ferocious spotted snake from whose jaws I have leaped. On the basis of my experience, I can only agree with the other oldsters among the Plookhh that the snake seems to have been strangled to death. I know this is not much help and I know what it means taken together with our other difficulties—but as the nzred nzredd announced at the first public showing of the stereo: "What Plookh has done, Plookh can do!"

The rest of the stereo is comprehensible enough. Which guur, no matter what her reasons for leaving the chain originally, would not joyfully return to a family powerful enough to destroy a great spotted snake? And even now we all laugh (all except mlenbb, that is) at the final sequence where the mlenb-character crawls into his burrow backward and almost breaks a flipper.

"Terrific, huh?" Shlestertrap inquired, when we had returned to his compartment. "And that process-work—it was out of this system, wasn't it? Can I mastermind a masterpiece, or can't I?"

I considered. "You can," I told him at last. "This stereo will affect our way of life more than anything else in nine thousand years of Plookh history."

He slapped his sides. "This stereo, artistically, has everything. The way I handled that finale was positively reminiscent of Chaplin in his bamboo-cane period with just a touch of the Marx Brothers and De Sica."

After a spasm of bottle-conjugating, he suggested: "Guess you want to chase in and get those robots to teach you how to handle projectors. I'll give you three complete sets and a whole slew of copies; you show some of your friends in the backwoods how to turn them on and off—then you can come back here and write the next stereo."

"Write the *next* stereo? I am overwhelmed, O Shlestertrap, but I don't quite understand what I could write about. Have you not said all in this one? If there is more, I am afraid my uncivilized person is not capable of conceiving and organizing it."

"Not a matter of civilization," he told me impatiently. "Just a matter of a twist. You saw how this stereo ran—now you simply apply The Old Switcheroo."

"The Old Switcheroo?"

"The new angle—the twist—the tangent. No sense in using a good plot just the once. I'll make an artist out of you yet! Look— On second thought, maybe you're too new at this racket to get it after all. Was sort of hoping you'd carry the load while I rested up. But I guess I can knock out another stereo fast to give you the idea. Meanwhile, suppose you get started on that projection course so that your buddies in the jungle can see what the Interplanetary Cultural Mission is doing for them."

Shortly thereafter, I was deposited outside the dome with the three sets of projectors. Again, I was fortunate in making my escape from the creatures who swarmed at me. I returned to the spot with forty young Plookhh I gathered from the neighborhood and, with the expenditure of much labor and life, we divided the equipment into small, somewhat portable groups and removed it to another mountain.

As rapidly as possible, I taught them the intricacies of operation I had learned from the robots. I had tactlessly requested one or two of these creatures from Hogan Shlestertrap, by the way, to aid us in the difficult task of shifting the equipment. "Not on your materialization," he had roared. "Isn't it enough that I send them out of the dome to get those orange weeds you guys are so nuts about? Two of my best robots—Greasejob and Dentface—are walking around with cracked bodies because some overgrown cockroach mistook them for an order of. I made a stereo for you people: now you carry the ball for a while." Naturally, I apologized.

When my assistants could work the projectors to my satisfaction, I divided them into three groups and sent two of them off with sets and a supply of stereo-film. I kept one group and set with me, and had a tkan carry word to the chief of his sex that all was ready.

Meanwhile, the nzred nzredd and twelve specially trained helpers had been traveling everywhere, griggoing English to all Plookhh they met and ordering them to go forth and griggo likewise. This was necessary because that had been the language of the stereo: as a result, English has completely replaced our native language.

One of the groups I sent out was stationed in a relatively sheltered cove to which srobb and mlenbb could come in comparative safety. The other, in a distant valley, exhibited chiefly to guurr, flinn and nzredd; my crew, on a mountain, to blapp and tkann. By showing the stereo to audiences of approximately two hundred Plookhh at a time, we were reaching the maximum number at all compatible with safety. Even so, performances were frequently interrupted by a pack of strinth who paused to feed upon us, by an occasional swarm of gridniks who descended on our engrossed multitudes with delighted drones. We changed our projection spots after every performance; but I was twice forced to train new groups of young Plookhh to replace those projectionists casually annihilated when the stereo-exhibition attracted some carnivore's attention.

Not a good system, admittedly; but none better has yet been devised. We all know how dangerous it is to congregate. To translate into inadequate English: *"Too many Plookhh make a broth."* Nonetheless, it was imperative that the message of civilization be spread as widely and as rapidly as possible.

The message was spread, received and acted upon.

However much it may be to my discredit, I must confess that I felt some small and definite joy at belonging to an already organized family unit. Whenever thereafter I saw a matrimonial convention breaking up, the guur moving as rapidly as she could through the forest until she came to a great spotted snake, the other six members of her family immediately throwing themselves in a sort of hopeless enthusiasm upon the reptile—whenever I saw that spectacle which now, of course, became so frequent, I could not help but rejoice ingloriously in having my family's convention cycles behind me. I was too old for civilization.

Once, I remember, four successive matrimonial conventions involved the same snake. He became so gorged with Plookhh that he could not move from the scene of the feeding. Possibly incidents of this sort gave rise to what is known as the nzred magandu system which is used, when possible, at present. As you know, under this system, six families hold their matrimonial conventions together and the six guur perform the traditional civilized bolt in unison. When they come across a great spotted snake, all the other members of the six families fall upon it and, under the weight of their numbers, the snake is very often smothered to death. There are usually enough survivors to make at least one full family after the battle, the only important difficulty here being that this system creates a surplus of guurr. The so-called blap vintorin system is very similar.

In any event, despite the great odds, we Plookhh had learned the lesson of the stereo well and were beginning to live (though usually we did the opposite) as civilized beings who are ready for technological knowledge. Then— Yes, then came The Old Switcheroo.

The Season of Early Floods was in full tide when a flin pushed out of his ground passage and up the mountain where we had recently set our projectors anew.

"Hail, transmitter of culture," he wheezed. "I bear a message from the flin flinn who had it from the nzred nzredd who had it from the Shlestertrap himself. He wishes you to come to his dome immediately."

I was busy helping to swing the ponderous machinery around, and therefore called over my tentacle-joint: "The area between here and the tenth highest mountain is under water. Find some srobb who will convey me there."

"No time," I heard him say. "There is no time to gather waterport-ers. You will have to make the circuitous trip by land, and soon! The Shlestertrap is—"

Then came a horribly familiar gurgle and his speech was cut off. I spun round as my assistants scattered in all directions. A full-grown brinosaur had sneaked up the mountain behind the flin and sucked the burrower into his throat while he was concentrating on giving me important information.

I suppressed every logical impulse that told me to flee; however frightened, I must act like a representative of the civilized race which we Plookhh were becoming. I stood before the brinosaur's idiotically gleeful face and inquired: "What about the Shlestertrap? For the sake of all Plookhh, already eaten and as yet unhatched, answer me quickly, O flin!"

From somewhere within the immense throat, the flin's voice came painfully indistinct through the saliva which blocked its path. "Shlester-trap is going back to Earth. He says you must—"

The monster gulped and the bulge that was once a flin slid down the great neck and into the body proper. Only then, when he had burped his enjoyment and the first faint slaver of expectancy began in regard to me—only then, did I use the power of my helical tentacle to leap to one side and into a small grove of trees.

After swinging his head in a lazy curve, the brinosaur, morosely certain that there were no other unalerted Plookhh in the vicinity, turned and flapped slowly down the mountain. The moment he entered the screaming doods, I was out of concealment and detailing a party of three nzredd to follow me to the dome.

We picked our way painfully across a string of rocks, in a direction which, while leading away from the tenth highest mountain, would form part of a great arc designed to lead us to the dome across dry land.

"Can it be," one of the youngsters asked, "that Shlestertrap, observing our careful obedience to the principles laid down in the stereo, has decided that we have irrevocably joined the chain that must produce civilization and that his work is therefore finished?"

"I hope not. If that were true," I replied, "it would mean, from the rate of development I have observed, that our civilization would not make itself felt for several lifetimes beyond mine. Possibly he is returning to Earth to acquire the necessary materials for our next stage, that of technology."

"Good! The cultural stage through which we pass, while obviously necessary, is extremely damaging to our population figures. I am continually forced to revise my Book of Sevens in unhappy decrease of Plookhh. Not that the prospect of civilization for our race is not well worth the passing misery I feel at attending my first matrimonial convention two days from now. I only hope that our guur finds a comparatively small great spotted snake!"

Thus, discoursing pleasantly of hopes almost as delightful as the Hope—of a time when the power of Plookh domination would shake the very soil of Venus—we rolled damply the long distance to the dome. I lost only one assistant before the robot picked us up with his beam, and scurried rapidly to Shlestertrap's interior compartment.

The place was almost bare: I deduced that most of the mission's equipment had already been carried to the flame ship. Our civilizer sat on a single chair surrounded by multitudes of bottles, all of whom had already been conjugated to the point of extinction.

"Well," he cried, "if it isn't little plookhiyaki and his wedded nzred! Didn't think I could say that, did you? Sit down and take a load off your nzred!" I was glad to observe that while his voice was somewhat thick, his attitude seemed to express a desire to be more communicative than usual.

"We hear that you return to Hollywood California USA Earth," I began.

"Wish it was that, laddie. Wish it was that little thing. Finest place in the universe—Hollywood Calif etcetera. Nope. I been recalled, that's what I been. The mission's closed."

"But *why?*"

"This thing—Economy. At least that's what they said in the bulletin they sent me. 'Due to necessary retrenchment in many government services—' Don't you believe it! It's those big busybodies! Gogarty's probably laughing his head off down in Sahara University: he's the guy started all that hullabubballoo about me in first place. And me, I gotta go back and start life all over again."

Here he put his head down between his arms and shook his shoulders. After a while, he rolled off the chair and onto the floor. A robot entered, carrying a packing box. He set Shlestertrap back in the chair and left, the heavy box still under his arm.

I could not help a slight feeling of pride at the sight of the awe with which the two young nzredd regarded my obvious intimacy with the human. They were more than a little confused by his alien communicative pattern; but they were as desperately determined as I to memorize every nuance of this portentous last conversation. This was fortunate: the fact that their versions of this affair agreed with mine helped to strengthen my position in the difficult days that lay ahead.

"And our civilizing process," I asked. "Is it to stop?"

"Huh? What civil— Oh, that! No, sir! Little old Shlesty's taken care of his friends. Always takes care. Got the new stereo ready. One fine job! Wait—I'll get it for you."

He rose slowly to his feet. "Where's a robot? Never one of 'em around when you want one of 'em around. Hey, Highsprockets!" he bellowed. "Get me the copies of the stereo in the next room or something. The *new* stereo.

"Got it all cut yesterday," he continued, when the robot had given him the packages. "Didn't really finish it the way I wanted to; but when bulletin came, I just sent all your actor friends on home. I don't work for nothing, I don't. But I sat up and cut it into right length, and what do you know? It came out fine. Here."

I distributed the packages equally among the three of us. "And does it contain that wonderful device you mentioned—The Old Switcheroo?"

"Contains nothing else but. As neat a switcheroo on an original plot as Hogan Shlestertrap has ever turned. Yop. It's got all you need. You just notice the way I worked it and pretty soon you'll be making stereos in competition with Hollywood. Which is more than I'll be doing."

"We do not even faintly aspire to such heights," I told him humbly. "We will be sufficiently grateful for the gift of civilization."

"Thass all right," he waved a hand at us as he swayed. "Don't *thank* me. Thank *me*. In those two stereos you have two of the finest love stories ever told, and done by the latest Hollywood methods from one of its greatest directors in his grandest— What I mean to say is, they told me to mission you some culture and I missioned you culture and if they don't like it, they can—"

At this point, he crumpled suddenly into a huddle upon the chair. We waited patiently for any further disclosures, but, as he seemed preoccupied with a peculiarly human manifestation, we made our departures with no further formality.

Once safely away from the dome, I instructed my assistants to hurry to our two distant installations and prepare them for immediate projection of our new stereo.

"Remember," I called after them. "Any change the First Stereo has made in our way of life will be as nothing to what will be done by The Old Switcheroo."

And I was right. The introduction of The Old Switcheroo—

I saw it myself for the first time along with over a hundred other Plookhh upon our mountain. After it was over, I was as bereft of speech as the rest. After a long pause in which no one dared to comment, the nzred nzredd suggested I project the First Stereo again with The Old Switcheroo immediately following so that we could compare them more easily.

This was done, but it proved of little help.

The problem is for you to solve. May my recounting of the entire history of the relationship between Hogan Shlestertrap and myself be of some value in finding a solution! I am old, and, as I have said, ripe for the gullet; you have been hatched in the very midst of this preliminary period of our culture—it is for you to find the way, the way that *must* be there, out of this impasse in which we shuttle unreproductively.

You are but a few days from the egg, but you have already seen both the First Stereo and The Old Switcheroo as many times as conditions permit. You should know that there is a single question common to both of them.

The one essential point of difference between the First Stereo and The Old Switcheroo is that, in the latter, the srob, mlenb, tkan, flin, blap and nzred bolt the matrimonial convention, leaving the *guur* to pursue them affectionately and finally rescue them from the great spotted snake; while, in the former, the reverse occurs. The loving reunion at the end is the same in both, except that the mlenb, instead of backing into his muddy burrow in the final scene of The Old Switcheroo, slips and falls heavily across it.

After the preliminary exhibitions, the guurr began insisting loudly that the humans could not have expected them—weak and slow-moving as they are—to destroy great spotted snakes. Confronted with the specific evidence, however, they fell back on the claim that the First Stereo depicted the civilized state; and the second, an alternative barbarity.

To this, the other six sexes replied that The Old Switcheroo was not an alternative, but the consummation of our cultural process. Also, as a result of the mores developed with the First Stereo, there was now a disgusting and unprecedented surplus of guurr: what better way to dispose of them than in this extremely selective one? The snakes, when sufficiently irritated by attacking guurr, *will* swallow them, it seems—

The mlenbb, of course, had their own difficulty: whether and how to enter their burrows immediately after the convention. But this was a minor matter.

Some of the new Plookh families attempted to follow the patterns indicated in the First Stereo; others, those in the second. A very few completely barbaric individuals, oblivious to the high destiny of their species, withdrew from the Plookh community and tried to return to the primitive methods of our ancestors; but since few high-variables cared to attach themselves to so atavistic a group, their offspring are being exterminated rapidly—and good riddance.

Most Plookhh remain in two great divisions: the guurr, who believe in the civilizing logic of the First Stereo, and the other sexes, who accept only the amendment of The Old Switcheroo. Then, of course, there are a few altruistic nzredd and flinn who agree with the guurr, and vice-versa. . . .

We need the cooperation of all seven sexes for successful reproduction. But how can we achieve that, Plookhh argue, unless we know which is the stereo of civilization? To be so close to liberation from our gustatory bondage, and because of sheer intellectual inadequacy— For the past eleven cycles, not a single matrimonial convention has been celebrated.

As a member of a pre-Shlestertrap family, I take no sides. My convention is past: yours, my diversified nzreddi, lies ahead. I am certain of one thing.

The answer is to be found in neither one stereo nor the other. The answer involves unity of the two: a core of relationship which both must share and which, when discovered, will dissolve their apparent inconsistency. Remember, these stereos are the product of a highly civilized creature.

Where is that core of relationship to be found? In the original stereo? In The Old Switcheroo? Or in that book I never finished— ABRIDGED REGULATIONS OF THE INTERPLANETARY CULTURAL MISSION, ANNOTATED, WITH AN APPENDIX OF STANDARD OFFICE PROCEDURE FOR SOLARIAN MISSIONS?

Humanity has solved such problems, and today flicks stars from its path. We must solve it or die as a race, albeit a civilized race.

We will not solve it—and this is most important—we will not solve this problem by the disgusting, utterly futile expedient to which more and more of our young are daily resorting. I refer to the unmentionable and perverted six-sex families. . . .

"Dear Pen Pal"

A. E. van Vogt (1912–   )

A. E. VAN *Vogt burst upon the science fiction scene with "Black Destroyer" in 1939 and continued to electrify readers throughout the forties until he ran into a notion called Dianetics, which brought his writing career to a crashing halt. He recovered, but he never recovered his previous brilliance. Often a difficult read, his works featured at least the possibility of many layers of meaning. But even if his readers did not always follow his convoluted plots, they felt the attraction of the power of his ideas. In some respects he was the forties version of Philip K. Dick.*

The decade was enriched by his novels Slan *(1946), a landmark among mutation stories;* The Weapon Makers *(1946, later revised); and* The World of Null-A *(1948), a strange mixture of power and confusion.*

"Dear Pen Pal" shows that he could be cute as well as complex, employing a story form somewhat unique to science fiction.

From *The Arkham Sample   1949*

Planet Aurigae II

Dear Pen Pal:

When I first received your letter from the interstellar correspondence club, my impulse was to ignore it. The mood of one who has spent the last seventy planetary periods—years, I suppose you would call them—in an Aurigaen prison, does not make for a pleasant exchange of letters. However, life is very boring, and so I finally settled myself to the task of writing you.

Your description of Earth sounds exciting. I would like to live there for a while, and I have a suggestion in this connection, but I won't mention it till I have developed it further.

You will have noticed the material on which this letter is written. It is a highly sensitive metal, very thin, very flexible, and I have enclosed several sheets of it for your use. Tungsten dipped in any strong acid makes an excellent mark on it. It is important to me that you do write on it, as my fingers are too hot—literally—to hold your paper without damaging it.

I'll say no more just now. It is possible you will not care to correspond with a convicted criminal, and therefore I shall leave the next move up to you. Thank you for your letter. Though you did not know its destination, it brought a moment of cheer into my drab life.

Skander

Aurigae II

Dear Pen Pal:

Your prompt reply to my letter made me happy. I am sorry your doctor thought it excited you too much, and sorry, also, if I have described my predicament in such a way as to make you feel badly. I welcome your many questions, and I shall try to answer them all.

You say the international correspondence club has no record of having sent any letters to Aurigae. That, according to them, the temperature on the second planet of the Aurigae sun is more than 500 degrees Fahrenheit. And that life is not known to exist there. Your club is right about the temperature and the letters. We have what your people would call a hot climate, but then we are not a hydro-carbon form of life, and find 500 degrees very pleasant.

I must apologize for deceiving you about the way your first letter was sent to me. I didn't want to frighten you away by telling you too much at once. After all, I could not be expected to know that you would be enthusiastic to hear from me.

The truth is that I am a scientist, and, along with the other members of my race, I have known for some centuries that there were other inhabited systems in the galaxy. Since I am allowed to experiment in my spare hours, I amused myself in attempts at communication. I developed several simple systems for breaking in on galactic communication operations, but it was not until I developed a subspacewave control that I was able to draw your letter (along with several others, which I did not answer) into a cold chamber.

I use the cold chamber as both sending and receiving center, and since you were kind enough to use the material which I sent you, it was easy for me to locate your second letter among the mass of mail that accumulated at the nearest headquarters of the interstellar correspondence club.

How did I learn your language? After all, it is a simple one, particularly the written language seems easy. I had no difficulty with it. If you are still interested in writing me, I shall be happy to continue the correspondence.

Skander

Aurigae II

Dear Pen Pal:

Your enthusiasm is refreshing. You say that I failed to answer your question about how I expected to visit Earth. I confess I deliberately ignored the question, as my experiment had not yet proceeded far enough. I want you to bear with me a short time longer, and then I will be able to give you the details. You are right in saying that it would be difficult for a being who lives at a temperature of 500 degrees Fahrenheit to mingle freely with the people of Earth. This was never my intention, so please relieve your mind. However, let us drop that subject for the time being.

I appreciate the delicate way in which you approach the subject of my imprisonment. But it is quite unnecessary. I performed forbidden experiments upon my body in a way that was deemed to be dangerous to the public welfare. For instance, among other things, I once lowered my surface temperature to 150 degrees Fahrenheit, and so shortened the radioactive cycle-time of my surroundings. This caused an unexpected break in the normal person to person energy flow in the city where I lived, and so charges were laid against me. I have thirty more years to serve. It would be pleasant to leave my body behind and tour the universe—but as I said I'll discuss that later.

I wouldn't say that we're a superior race. We have certain qualities which apparently your people do not have. We live longer, not because of any discoveries we've made about ourselves, but because our bodies are built of a more enduring element—I don't know your name for it, but the atomic weight is 52.9#.* Our scientific discoveries are of the kind that would normally be made by a race with our kind of physical structure. The fact that we can work with temperatures of as high as—I don't know just how to put that—has been very helpful in the development of the subspace energies which are extremely hot, and require delicate adjustments. In the later stages these adjustments can be made by machinery, but in the development the work must be done by "hand"—I put that word in quotes, because we have no hands in the same way that you have.

I am enclosing a photographic plate, properly cooled and chemical-

---

* A radioactive isotope of chromium.—Author's Note.

ized for your climate. I wonder if you would set it up and take a picture of yourself. All you have to do is arrange it properly on the basis of the laws of light—that is, light travels in straight lines, so stand in front of it—and when you are ready, *think*, "Ready!" The picture will be automatically taken.

Would you do this for me? If you are interested, I will also send you a picture of myself, though I must warn you. My appearance will probably shock you.

Sincerely
Skander

Planet Aurigae II

Dear Pen Pal:

Just a brief note in answer to your question. It is not necessary to put the plate into a camera. You describe this as a dark box. The plate will take the picture when you think, "Ready!" I assure you it will be flooded with light.

Skander

Aurigae II

Dear Pen Pal:

You say that while you were waiting for the answer to my last letter you showed the photographic plate to one of the doctors at the hospital —I cannot picture what you mean by doctor or hospital, but let that pass—and he took the problem up with government authorities. Problem? I don't understand. I thought we were having a pleasant correspondence, private and personal.

I shall certainly appreciate your sending that picture of yourself.

Skander

Aurigae II

Dear Pen Pal:

I assure you I am not annoyed at your action. It merely puzzled me, and I am sorry the plate has not been returned to you. Knowing what governments are, I can imagine that it will not be returned to you for some time, so I am taking the liberty of enclosing another plate.

I cannot imagine why you should have been warned against continuing this correspondence. What do they expect me to do?—eat you up at long distance? I'm sorry but I don't like hydrogen in my diet.

In any event, I would like your picture as a memento of our friendship, and I will send mine as soon as I have received yours. You may keep it or throw it away, or give it to your governmental authorities— but at least I will have the knowledge that I've given a fair exchange.

With all best wishes
Skander

Aurigae II

Dear Pen Pal:

Your last letter was so slow in coming that I thought you had decided to break off the correspondence. I was sorry to notice that you failed to enclose the photograph, puzzled by your reference to having a relapse, and cheered by your statement that you would send it along as soon as you felt better—whatever that means. However, the important thing is that you did write, and I respect the philosophy of your club which asks its members not to write of pessimistic matters. We all have our own problems which we regard as over-shadowing the problems of others. Here I am in prison, doomed to spend the next 30 years tucked away from the main stream of life. Even the thought is hard on my restless spirit, though I know I have a long life ahead of me after my release.

In spite of your friendly letter, I won't feel that you have completely re-established contact with me until you send the photograph.

Yours in expectation
Skander

Aurigae II

Dear Pen Pal:

The photograph arrived. As you suggest, your appearance startled me. From your description I thought I had mentally reconstructed your body. It just goes to show that words cannot really describe an object which has never been seen.

You'll notice that I've enclosed a photograph of myself, as I promised I would. Chunky, metallic looking chap, am I not, very different, I'll wager, than you expected? The various races with whom we have communicated become wary of us when they discover we are highly radioactive, and that literally we are a radioactive form of life, the only such (that we know of) in the universe. It's been very trying to be so isolated and, as you know, I have occasionally mentioned that I had hopes of escaping not only the deadly imprisonment to which I am being subjected but also the body which cannot escape.

Perhaps you'll be interested in hearing how far this idea has developed. The problem involved is one of exchange of personalities with someone else. Actually, it is not really an exchange in the accepted meaning of the word. It is necessary to get an impress of both individuals, of their mind and of their thoughts as well as their bodies. Since this phase is purely mechanical, it is simply a matter of taking complete photographs and of exchanging them. By complete I mean of course every vibration must be registered. The next step is to make sure the two photographs are exchanged, that is, that each party has somewhere near him a complete photograph of the other. (It is already too late, Pen Pal. I have set in motion the sub-space energy interflow

373

between the two plates, so you might as well read on.) As I have said it is not exactly an exchange of personalities. The original personality in each individual is suppressed, literally pushed back out of the consciousness, and the image personality from the "photographic" plate replaces it.

You will take with you a complete memory of your life on Earth, and I will take along memory of my life on Aurigae. Simultaneously, the memory of the receiving body will be blurrily at our disposal. A part of us will always be pushing up, striving to regain consciousness, but always lacking the strength to succeed.

As soon as I grow tired of Earth, I will exchange bodies in the same way with a member of some other race. Thirty years hence, I will be happy to reclaim my body, and you can then have whatever body I last happened to occupy.

This should be a very happy arrangement for us both. You, with your short life expectancy, will have out-lived all your contemporaries and you have had an interesting experience. I admit I expect to have the better of the exchange—but now, enough of explanation. By the time you reach this part of the letter it will be me reading it, not you. But if any part of you is still aware, so long for now, Pen Pal. It's been nice having all those letters from you. I shall write you from time to time to let you know how things are going with my tour.

Skander

Aurigae II

Dear Pen Pal:

Thanks a lot for forcing the issue. For a long time I hesitated about letting you play such a trick on yourself. You see, the government scientists analyzed the nature of that first photographic plate you sent me, and so the final decision was really up to me. I decided that anyone as eager as you were to put one over should be allowed to succeed.

Now I know I didn't have to feel sorry for you. Your plan to conquer Earth wouldn't have gotten anywhere, but the fact that you had the idea ends the need for sympathy.

By this time you will have realized for yourself that a man who has been paralyzed since birth, and is subject to heart attacks, cannot expect a long life span. I am happy to tell you that your once lonely pen pal is enjoying himself, and I am happy to sign myself with a name to which I expect to become accustomed.

With best wishes
Skander

SELECTED
BIBLIOGRAPHY

Asimov, Isaac. *The Early Asimov*. Garden City, N.Y.: Doubleday, 1972.

————. *The Foundation Trilogy* (1951–1953; component parts appeared in the forties).

————. *I, Robot*. New York: Gnome, 1950. Stories from the forties.

Barnes, Arthur K. *Interplanetary Hunter*. New York: Gnome, 1956. Most are stories from the forties.

Binder, Eando. *Adam Link-Robot*. New York: Warner, 1965. Stories from the late thirties and early forties.

Bond, Nelson S. *Exiles of Time*. Philadelphia: Prime, 1949.

————. *Lancelot Biggs: Spaceman*. Garden City, N.Y.: Doubleday, 1951. Stories published 1939–43.

Boucher, Anthony. *Far and Away*. New York: Ballantine, 1955. Most stories are from the forties.

Bradbury, Ray. *The Illustrated Man*. New York: Doubleday, 1951. Most stories are from the late forties.

————. *The Martian Chronicles*. New York: Doubleday, 1950. Stories from the forties.

Brown, Fredric. *Angels and Spaceships*. New York: Dutton, 1954. Stories from the forties.

————. *Space on My Hands*. Chicago: Shasta, 1951. Stories from the forties.

————. *What Mad Universe*. New York: Dutton, 1949.

Clarke, Arthur C. *The City and the Stars*. New York: Harcourt, 1956. Revision of *Against the Fall of Night*, first published 1948.

de Camp, L. Sprague. Divide and Rule. Reading, Pa.: Fantasy, 1948.

————. *Lest Darkness Fall.* New York: Holt, 1941.

———— and Fletcher Pratt. *The Incomplete Enchanter.* New York: Holt, 1942.

del Rey, Lester. And Some Were Human. Philadelphia: Prime, 1948.

Ehrlich, Max. The Big Eye. New York: Doubleday, 1949.

Frank, Pat. Mr. Adam. Philadelphia: Lippincott, 1946.

Heard, H. F. Doppelgangers. New York: Vanguard, 1947.

Heinlein, Robert A. The Past Through Tomorrow. New York: Putnam, 1967. Most of these stories were published in the forties.

Hubbard, L. Ron. Final Blackout. Providence, R.I.: Hadley, 1948.

Huxley, Aldous. Ape and Essence. New York: Harper, 1948.

Kuttner, Henry. The Best of Henry Kuttner. New York: Ballantine, 1975.

————. *Mutant.* New York: Gnome, 1953. Written under the name "Lewis Padgett," several of these stories appeared in the forties.

————. *Robots Have No Tails.* New York: Gnome, 1952. Also under the Padgett byline, these stories were published between 1943 and 1948.

Leiber, Fritz. Gather, Darkness! New York: Pellegrini & Cudahy, 1950. A 1943 story.

Lewis, C. S. Perelandra. London: Bodley Head, 1943.

————. *That Hideous Strength.* London: Bodley Head, 1945.

Moore, C. L. The Best of C. L. Moore. New York: Ballantine, 1975.

Moore, Ward. Greener Than You Think. New York: Sloane, 1947.

Orwell, George. Nineteen Eighty-four. New York: Harcourt, 1949.

Rand, Ayn. Anthem. Caldwell, Idaho: Caxton, 1946.

Russell, Eric Frank. Men, Martians, and Machines. New York: Roy, 1956. Stories from the forties.

Shiras, Wilmar H. Children of the Atom. New York: Gnome, 1953. Based on stories from the late forties.

Simak, Clifford D. City. New York: Gnome, 1952.

Siodmak, Curt. Donovan's Brain. New York: Knopf, 1943.

Skinner, B. F. Walden Two. New York: Macmillan, 1948.

Smith, George O. Venus Equilateral. Philadelphia: Prime, 1947.

Stewart, George R. Earth Abides. New York: Random House, 1949.

Sturgeon, Theodore. Without Sorcery. Philadelphia: Prime, 1948.

van Vogt, A. E. Slan. Sauk City, Wis.: Arkham House, 1946.

————. *The Weapon Shops.* New York: Greenberg, 1952. Expanded from a 1943 story.

————. *The World of Null-A.* New York: Simon & Schuster, 1948.

Werfel, Franz. Star of the Unborn. New York: Viking, 1946.

Williamson, Jack. Darker Than You Think. Reading, Pa.: Fantasy, 1948.

————. *The Humanoids*. New York: Simon & Schuster, 1949.
Wright, Austin T. *Islandia*. New York: Farrar, 1942.

ANTHOLOGIES

Conklin, Groff. *The Best of Science Fiction*. New York: Crown, 1946.
————. *The Big Book of Science Fiction*. New York: Crown, 1950.
————. *Omnibus of Science Fiction*. New York: Crown, 1952.
————. *The Treasury of Science Fiction*. New York: Crown, 1948.
  The great majority of the stories in these fine collections first
  appeared in the forties.
Harrison, Harry, and Brian W. Aldiss. *The Astounding-Analog
  Reader*. New York: Doubleday; two volumes, 1972 and 1973.
  Both volumes contain many stories from the forties.
Healy, Raymond J., and J. Francis McComas. *Adventures in Time
  and Space*. New York: Random House, 1946.

SCIENCE FICTION
OF THE 30's

Edited, with historical commentary, by
DAMON KNIGHT

Eighteen stories, long out of print and available only
in the rare original magazines and special collections in which they appeared, are assembled in this
extraordinary volume. Accompanying the stories
are the actual illustrations from those original magazines and Damon Knight's candid, insider's commentary on the men, the editors, and the publishers
of SF's first great decade. Included are stories by
such early masters of the genre as: John W. Campbell, Jr., Murray Leinster, L. Sprague de Camp, Eric
Frank Russell, and many more.

SELECTED BY THE SCIENCE FICTION BOOK CLUB

AVON  31708 / $4.95

SFT 9-78